Finding the Lost

"Exerts much the same appeal as Christine Feehan's Carpathian series, what with tortured heroes, the necessity of finding love or facing a fate worse than death, hot lovemaking, and danger-filled adventure." —*Booklist*

"A terrific grim thriller with the romantic subplot playing a strong supporting role. The cast is powerful, as the audience will feel every emotion that Andra feels, from fear for her sister to fear for her falling in love. *Finding the Lost* is a dark tale, as Shannon K. Butcher paints a forbidding, gloomy landscape in which an ancient war between humanity's guardians and their nasty adversaries heats up in Nebraska." —Alternative Worlds

"A very entertaining read ... the ending was a great cliffhanger and I can't wait to read the next book in this series. ... A fast-paced story with great action scenes and lots of hot romance." —The Book Lush

"Butcher's paranormal reality is dark and gritty in this second Sentinel War installment. What makes this story so gripping is the seamlessly delivered hard-hitting action and wrenching emotions. Butcher is a major talent in the making." —*Romantic Times*

Burning Alive

"Starts off with nonstop action. Readers will race through the pages, only to reread the entire novel to capture every little detail ... a promising start for a new voice in urban fantasy/paranormal romance. I look forward to the next installment." —A Romance Review (5 Roses)

continued ...

NOVELS OF THE SENTINEL WARS

LIVING NIGHTMARE

THE SENTINEL WARS

SHANNON K. BUTCHER

A SIGNET BOOK

SIGNET
Published by New American Library, a division of
Penguin Group (USA) Inc., 375 Hudson Street,
New York, New York 10014, USA
Penguin Group (Canada), 90 Eglinton Avenue East, Suite 700, Toronto,
Ontario M4P 2Y3, Canada (a division of Pearson Penguin Canada Inc.)
Penguin Books Ltd., 80 Strand, London WC2R 0RL, England
Penguin Ireland, 25 St. Stephen's Green, Dublin 2,
Ireland (a division of Penguin Books Ltd.)
Penguin Group (Australia), 250 Camberwell Road, Camberwell, Victoria 3124,
Australia (a division of Pearson Australia Group Pty. Ltd.)
Penguin Books India Pvt. Ltd., 11 Community Centre, Panchsheel Park,
New Delhi - 110 017, India
Penguin Group (NZ), 67 Apollo Drive, Rosedale, North Shore 0632,
New Zealand (a division of Pearson New Zealand Ltd.)
Penguin Books (South Africa) (Pty.) Ltd., 24 Sturdee Avenue,
Rosebank, Johannesburg 2196, South Africa

Penguin Books Ltd., Registered Offices:
80 Strand, London WC2R 0RL, England

First published by Signet, an imprint of New American Library,
a division of Penguin Group (USA) Inc.

First Printing, November 2010
10 9 8 7 6 5 4 3 2 1

For Liz Lafferty, whose genuine enthusiasm and keen eye for details have been invaluable to me. Your optimism and love of life are a true joy to those who are lucky enough to call you a friend.

Acknowledgments

As always, I want to thank my beta readers for their continued support. Thanks also to Dawn Shelton for catching all those little mistakes that would otherwise slip by. I don't know what I'd do without you ladies.

Chapter 1

Nika wasn't crazy, and the only way to prove it was to dig up the bones lying inside her sister's frozen grave.

The shovel bit into her palms, rubbing them raw. A cold gust of wind threatened to rip down the hood of her heavy coat and suck the precious heat from her skin. She turned her back to the wind and kept digging. There wasn't time to crawl into the car she'd stolen and warm up. She had to finish this before the Sentinels found her and took her back to Dabyr.

Nika was now much stronger than she had been a few months ago when she'd barely been clinging to life, but with each pitiful half shovelful of dirt, she realized she wasn't yet strong enough to be doing this. Not alone, and certainly not in the dead of night—the only time no one would be around to see her desecrating a grave.

It was dangerous to be here in the dark. She knew that, but she had no choice. No one would listen to the crazy girl without proof, and the bones lying six feet down were the only tangible evidence she could find that Tori was still alive.

Tori was out there. Nika could feel her baby sister's presence inside her splintered mind, amidst all the other sinister, alien beings who shared the space. Tori wasn't like she used to be—she wasn't the sweet, innocent child the Synestryn had taken—but she was still Nika's sister.

She was still loved. She deserved the chance for freedom, no matter the cost to Nika.

Besides, if Nika could bring her home and stop the torture Tori endured, both their lives would be better. They were connected—though not as strongly as they'd once been—and Nika wondered sometimes how her sister had survived this long.

The night the Synestryn stole Tori, Nika had promised her she'd never leave her alone. Now, almost nine years later, she'd kept that promise despite the fact that it had nearly killed her more than once.

Tori was slipping away, and Nika had the feeling that her sister was doing it by choice, that she was pushing them apart for a reason Nika couldn't understand.

Nika refused to give up on her. With or without help, she was going to find Tori and free her from her captors. Or die trying. That was definitely another alternative—perhaps the more likely one, given the way her muscles were already burning with fatigue.

If she couldn't finish the simple job of digging a hole, how could she possibly execute a rescue mission?

After an hour of digging, she'd barely made a dent in the frozen soil. At this rate, she'd still be here come daybreak, when the authorities could see her and drag her to the closest hospital's mental ward. She couldn't go back there. Eight years of being restrained and questioned and tortured by doctors with fake smiles and dead eyes was more than she could stand. If she had to go back to that life, she really *would* be crazy.

And even if that was not where she ended up—if she went back to Dabyr—the chances of escaping the watchful eyes of the Sentinels again were slim. She was going to have only one shot at this—one shot to prove that Tori was still alive and needed to be rescued.

Time to dig faster.

The shovel slipped in her weak grip, scraping off a layer of skin. She should have brought gloves, but hadn't thought that far ahead. Remembering a shovel had been foremost in her mind, consuming the small space she had left for rational thought.

She'd also forgotten money and food. She had no idea how she'd get back home—the gas tank was nearly empty. She had left her cell phone at home so they couldn't use it to track her and find her before she was done. Anything that happened after she'd collected the stranger's bones seemed distant and unimportant.

A tugging pressure pulled at her mind. Nika froze instantly, fighting it. The shovel fell from her frozen fingers. She clutched her head, knowing it would do no good.

She didn't want to go there tonight. She didn't want to be pulled into the mind of a monster to hunt and kill and feed. She had too much work to do.

An eerie howl vibrated the base of her skull, and it was all she could do not to lift her chin and howl along with the creature. Her own vision winked out and was replaced by another's.

Tall, frozen grass parted along her muzzle as she hunted for her prey. The warmth of food glowed bright in the darkness ahead. Hunger roared inside Nika's mind. The remembered taste of blood made her mouth water.

She struggled to pull from the sgath's mind before witnessing its kill, but this one was strong. It liked having her with it. It liked knowing she didn't want to be here, that she suffered.

Nika gritted her teeth and stopped trying to fight its pull. Instead, she focused on the feel of its limbs, the cold earth against the pads of its paws. Wind ruffled its fur, but it was warm, even in the cold.

Not for long.

She took the chill of her own body, the weakness of her own limbs, and forced those feelings into the sgath. The beast stopped moving and a low growl reverberated through it as it fought her. It didn't like what she was doing to it. It didn't like the cold.

A throbbing filled her skull as she fought the sgath. She whispered to it that it was too tired to hunt. Too cold. It needed to sleep.

The sgath roared into the darkness and thrust Nika from its mind, shutting her out.

She landed on her butt, hitting the pitiful mound of

frozen dirt she'd managed to scratch from Tori's false grave. Fatigue kept her glued to the spot as she tried to catch her breath. Her chest burned as the cold air filled her lungs over and over again, coming out in silvery plumes. Her body trembled with cold and weariness.

How could she keep going? How was she going to dig all the way down and open the casket lying below? Why had she thought she could do this alone?

Why had Madoc abandoned her? She hadn't seen him in seven months.

Her older sister, Andra, said the distance was for the best—that he was too angry and dangerous for her to be around him. Everyone seemed to be blind to the truth: He was in pain and he needed her to make it stop. It was glaringly obvious to her, but no one else seemed to see it.

And that, in a nutshell, was the story of her life. She saw things no one else did, and no one believed her when she told them about these things.

All that was going to change as soon as she had the bones. The Sanguinar would be able to tell they weren't Tori's, and if they couldn't, DNA tests would. One way or another, she was going to make the people around her listen.

If she lived through the night.

Already she could feel more sgath clawing for her attention, trying to suck her into their minds. They sensed her weakness. Even though there were fewer of them than there had ever been before—thanks to Madoc's quest to make them extinct—those that were left were stronger and smarter than the rest. They'd evaded Madoc's blade, hidden from him, learned from the mistakes of the others.

Most nights, Nika could resist their pull, but she was weaker tonight, outside the magically enhanced walls of Dabyr, which had apparently helped protect her. Her escape from Dabyr had been nerve-racking. The drive here had been terrifying. All that combined with the effort of physical labor was too much for her.

She wanted to be stronger than this. She wanted to be healthy. She wanted to be *normal*.

Wishing wasn't going to get her or Tori anywhere, so she pushed herself to her feet, brushed the dirt from her hands, and picked up the shovel. It was time to get back to work.

Nika let the cold have her. She let the wind drag her hood from her head, stripped out of her puffy coat, and put the thought of her chilled fingers and aching legs in the front of her mind. Any sgath who wanted to have her along for the ride tonight was going to end up freezing its furry butt off.

"What the fuck do you mean, Nika's gone?" Madoc growled into his cell phone.

Rage was always close to the surface, spurred on by his constant pain, bubbling, waiting to be let loose. His soul was nearly dead, and hiding that fact was getting a lot harder as each day passed. He needed to finish killing all the fuckers that had taken Nika's blood before it was too late, and he no longer cared whether they ate the crazy chick's mind.

Joseph sounded tired. "She stole one of the cars in the garage and left."

Something suspiciously close to fear wriggled inside him, making the pounding pain in his chest swell. He needed some relief. Now. All those fucking hours of meditation he'd just finished hadn't done jack shit.

"Where the hell was her sister?" he demanded.

"Andra and Paul are up north searching for a lost kid. I tried to call her, but couldn't get through. They're probably deep in the bowels of some cave, out of cell phone range."

"If she was gone, then who was supposed to be watching Nika?" He was going to have to find the person responsible and beat the hell out of him. No help for it.

"No one. I keep trying to tell you that she's better now. Stronger. She's an adult and doesn't need a keeper."

"Obviously you are wrong," snarled Madoc. "You should have had someone babysitting her."

"You can have the job anytime you like," said Joseph.

"Not interested." If he got near her, he'd hurt her.

He knew he would. He didn't normally go for scrawny chicks, but there was something about her that turned him on and made him feel violent all at the same time. Not a healthy combination—especially not for Nika.

"So you've said. Too bad you're the closest to her—or at least to where her car stopped. Nicholas tracked the car to Omaha, and since you're nearby, you're volunteering to go check it and see if she's still in it."

"Send someone else. I shouldn't be anywhere near her."

"Why? 'Cause she seems to have a thing for you? Wish I had such problems."

"She doesn't have a *thing* for me. She's crazy. That's why she refuses to stay away. Chick's got issues."

"Don't we all. Listen, just go find her, okay? Nicholas will text you the info so you can find the car. If she's not in it, you'll have to track her down. And hurry the hell up. I don't like having her out there alone at night. Who knows what could happen."

Joseph hung up, leaving Madoc writhing in frustration and fear. For her. The last place on the planet he wanted to be was near Nika, and yet the thought of her alone in the dark, weak and helpless, was more than he could stand.

"Fuck." He flung the curse out into the night, sheathed his sword, and stomped back to his truck. The nest he had been ready to cut into would have to wait. Nika couldn't.

Nika's plan had worked. The sgath hated the cold, and every time they brushed up against her mind, they flinched back in anger.

Of course, the flip side of her brilliant plan was that she was freezing to death. Her body shivered, and she could no longer feel her fingers or toes. The shovel kept slipping, but at least she couldn't feel the blisters forming on her palms anymore.

She worked for another hour without interruption and was smugly pleased with herself. Until she heard the first hungry cry of a sgath hunting nearby. This time, the sound wasn't inside her mind; it was in her ears. It was real, and it was close.

They'd found her.

Panic gripped her by the neck and choked the air from her lungs.

How had they found her? She'd been so careful to drive only during the day, when they were all asleep and couldn't read her thoughts. And tonight none of them had tried to pry from her where she'd gone when she left the safety of Dabyr. They couldn't know where she was.

Tentatively, Nika sent her mind out, searching for any nearby Synestryn. Their alien thoughts and uncontrolled hunger would be easy to find among the humans nearby. Their thoughts were bleak, festering spots of darkness among the bright, clear human thought patterns.

If there was only one Synestryn and it wasn't too strong, she could probably control its mind long enough to kill it with the shovel. If she was lucky.

Her body fell away as she went seeking into the night, searching for the source of that eerie cry of hunger. She found one Synestryn slinking through the darkness less than a quarter mile away. It was small—the size of a large dog—and it was weak with hunger. That hunger gave her the edge.

She could take it.

Nika had just begun to whisper into its mind to come her way when she felt another Synestryn nearby. Then another. There were three, then four, then seven. They were closing in. They smelled blood. Her blood.

Before they could trap her within them, Nika pulled back into her own mind and scanned her body for signs of blood. There was a smear on the leg of her jeans; muddy, but definitely blood.

She looked at her hands. Sure enough, the shovel had scraped off several layers of skin until she bled. The Synestryn smelled it and were moving in to feast.

The car was parked outside the metal fence several hundred yards away. As cold and weak as her legs were, she wasn't sure she was going to make it to the car before they made it to her, but she had to try. She couldn't let them get her blood. Thanks to Madoc's recent killing spree, she was just now regaining the pieces of herself that had been taken the night her family was attacked. She'd spent almost nine years living inside a nightmare, unable to tell what was real and what wasn't, and she refused to go back to that hell.

She'd rather die than let them have her mind again.

Nika grabbed the shovel, knowing it was the only weapon she had to hold them at bay, and sprinted for the fence.

Behind her a loud chorus of rasping howls rose up into the night as the Synestryn closed in.

Madoc found the stolen Volkswagen Bug outside a cemetery, but Nika was not inside the car as he'd hoped. Intense pressure rolled through him in a painful wave, growing until he was sure it would tear him apart. He sucked in huge gulps of frigid air, but it did little good.

He needed to be killing or fucking—bleeding away some of the pressure—not chasing after a girl who was too crazy to not go running off alone in the dark.

Clearly, what he wanted had no bearing on reality.

Madoc fought the pain back with a snarl, slammed his truck to a stop, rammed the gearshift into park, and left the engine running.

One way or another, this wasn't going to take long. If she wasn't nearby, then he'd call Joseph and tell him to send someone else to search for her. If she was, he was going to shove her in the Bug and follow her ass all the way back to Dabyr, where she belonged. No more joyrides. No more scaring the shit out of him. She was grounded.

But first he had to find her.

He leaped the fence and landed with a thud as his heavy boots hit the frozen ground. The wind had picked up, tugging the front of his leather jacket open.

If Nika was out here in this wind, she was going to be freezing her bony ass off. Not that he cared. Served her right for leaving home, where she was safe and warm.

They want to touch me. I don't like it, Madoc. It hurts when other men touch me.

She'd begged him to take her with him last time he was home, to get her away from the male Theronai who came from the four corners of the world to see if she could channel their power and save their lives. That had been seven months ago, when he'd gone home in a moment of weakness, needing to see her again. Unfortunately, watching her flinch away from those men—seeing pain pinch her features—was more than Madoc could stand. He'd hit the road and hadn't been back since.

Best decision he'd ever made. Being on his own was safest for everyone. Besides, he had plenty of hookers to keep him company. That and a pile of nasties to kill was all he needed.

A high-pitched, feminine cry ripped through the cold night air. Fear shimmered inside the noise, and with it came instant recognition. That was Nika's voice. He'd heard her cry out in fear too many times not to recognize it.

Madoc spun around toward the sound, releasing his sword from its sheath with an almost inaudible hiss of steel on steel. He raced over the ground, letting free the rage that was bubbling barely below the surface.

Whatever or whoever had made her afraid was going to die.

He cleared the top of a rise, saw Nika, and nearly came to a dead stop. Half a dozen sgath surrounded her. Her back was against a thick tree. Moonlight shone off her stark white hair, and she wielded a shovel like some kind of war club, batting at the Synestryn that dared to inch closer. Her blue eyes were wide with fear—a familiar sight—but the snarl of rage twisting her mouth was new and completely startling.

She swung the shovel, hitting one of the sgath in the head. There wasn't enough force behind the blow to do any good, and it bounced off, shaking her entire body. She looked unhurt, but that wasn't going to last for long if he didn't step up and take over.

Madoc closed the distance, lifted his blade, and let out a battle cry.

Immediately, six pairs of glowing green eyes turned toward him. A smile stretched his mouth. Playtime had finally come.

Chapter 2

Carmen lifted her sword to block Joseph's swing. Their wooden practice swords clacked together as the hilts locked, and the next thing she knew, a sharp pain radiated from her ribs where he'd poked her with his finger. Hard.

"You can't open yourself up for attack like that," lectured Joseph. His dark hair had been cut short again, showing off more gray at his temples than she remembered. His shoulders seemed to bow as if he was carrying some kind of weight around that no one could see. Maybe he was. As leader of the Theronai, the man probably had a lot on his plate.

Yet he still found the time to train with her nearly every day. No one had ever taken that kind of time with her before. Not the uncle who took her in when her parents died, and sure as hell not her own father. But things were different since the Sentinels had taken her in. The ancient blood running in her veins allowed her to become a Gerai—a human who aided the Sentinels in their war—but that didn't mean they had to put a roof over her head or pay for her education. They could have left her to make her own way, but thanks to Thomas—a Theronai who had sacrificed his life to save another—she now had a home at Dabyr. And a future.

She found herself craving the time she spent with Joseph, soaking up everything he had to teach her. She desperately wanted to make him proud, though she knew she was a long way off from that kind of miracle.

"You were going to chop my head off," she argued. "What did you want me to do?"

"Ducking would have worked. Not being in the way of my sword when it comes at you is always a good option."

Carmen shoved herself away from him in frustration and stepped to the far edge of the practice mat. She was panting, sweating like crazy, and feeling like she was about to fall over. Joseph wasn't even winded.

He'd told her several times that she was going to regret asking him to train her, and now she was beginning to believe him. Not that she could ever let him know. He'd be way too smug and self-satisfied and she'd have to kill him for real then.

She couldn't give up learning to fight. There were too many evil things in the world—things that stole people from their loved ones. Someone needed to kill them, and even though she was only one puny human, she intended to be the deadliest puny human the Synestryn had ever seen.

But the training wasn't going as fast as she'd hoped. She needed to be out there, fighting the good fight. Right now. Frustration weighed down on her, making her anxious and impatient. "This is pointless. It's not like the things I'll be fighting use swords, anyway. Teeth and claws, sure, but not swords."

The worry lines around his mouth deepened with his frown for a second before his expression went back to the neutral, patient mask he always wore while teaching her. "It's good for your reflexes, builds your strength, and even if the things you fight don't use a sword, you need to. It's the best weapon for the job, next to magical firepower. Besides, I'm in charge of what you learn. You don't like it, you can always walk away."

"Nice try. No thanks."

Joseph shrugged. "Your call. Just like it's your call when you let me read Thomas's note."

Thomas. Just the mention of his name made her insides shrivel a little with sadness. He'd been good to her when no one else seemed to care whether she even existed. She'd known him for only a few hours, but those hours had changed her life. Sometimes, she thought she'd fallen in love with him.

"I'm not ready," she told Joseph.

"It's been months since his death."

Months since he'd handed her a note she'd been unable to read. It was his death wish—his dying wish—and she'd promised Thomas she'd let Joseph read it first.

Carmen wasn't ready for that. What if it was full of pity for the slutty teenager who'd come on to a man way too old for her? Way too good for her? She'd thrown herself at Thomas, but he hadn't taken the offer. He'd treated her with respect—something no other man had ever done before him. What if that had all been an act and the note said not to trust the whacko kid who would slide her tits over anything with a penis? What if it said to keep her away from other teens so her trampy ways didn't rub off on the young, impressionable girls?

Not that she'd done anything like that. She'd kept her vow to Thomas and hadn't even thought about a man in a sexual way since coming here. Not one of them could hold a candle to Thomas, anyway. Why bother?

She'd come so close to opening his note several times without letting Joseph read it, but her promise to Thomas kept her from breaking down. Even though he was dead and no one but her would ever know, she felt she owed him enough to respect his wishes.

"I know how long it's been," she said. "I'm not ready." Even as she said the words, she knew she had to stop delaying the inevitable. She needed to grow a backbone.

Joseph sighed and gave her a silent nod. "Are you done for the day? You look like you're about to fall over."

"You'd like that, wouldn't you, Grandpa?" He didn't look that old—maybe mid-thirties—and by his race's standards, he was still in his prime, but even so, he'd been acting like a tired old man lately, and it was time she snapped him out of it.

The faintest hint of a smile pulled at the corner of his mouth. It was good to see. She couldn't remember the last time she'd seen him smile. "Grandpa?"

"You heard me. I know I should go easy on you, seeing as how you're just a walking bag of arthritis, but I need to learn this stuff so I can take over when the heart attack hits."

His smile widened. "Arthritis?"

"Want me to ask Miss Mabel if you can borrow her old walker? I'd hate to see you fall and break a hip."

Joseph shook his head, grinning. "Teenagers," he muttered under his breath. "Get your scrawny butt over here, and I'll show you just what an old man like me can do."

"You sure the Alzheimer's hasn't made you forget?"

"I guess we'll find out."

Nika was going to die. She was going to be slaughtered here tonight and end up breaking her promise to Tori. There was no way she could fight so many Synestryn. They were going to kill her.

Or worse. They'd take her blood and rip the last few hard-won bits of sanity from her mind, sending her back to that dark place where her thoughts were not her own, her body was a wasted shell, and death hovered over her, rubbing its hands in eager anticipation.

The nightmare flashed before her eyes, threatening to make her weak with fear. She didn't want that. She didn't want to go back to that place where she was help-less against the pull of the monsters, where they could rip her from her body and force her to watch the things they did, to revel in the shedding of blood, and the cre-ation of pain and sorrow.

Dying seemed like the better of the two options. Her best chance was to provoke them into a rage so they'd kill her outright.

I'm sorry, Tori. I'm so sorry I couldn't stay with you.

The broken promise cut her deep, slicing at her soul until it bled, but she couldn't let the sgath have her mind again. She couldn't.

Nika swung the shovel, bashing one of the beasts in the head. The shovel bounced off, making her arms sting with the force of her blow, but it did nothing to the Synestryn. It didn't even knock the monster off balance.

And there were six of them, soon to be more, since she still hadn't stopped her hand from bleeding.

A silver arc of light flashed in front of her, and a split second later the head of the closest sgath flew up and away from its body.

A massive man shoved himself between her and the monsters.

Madoc.

He was here. Nika's soul cried out in joy.

She reached out and laid her hand on his broad back, touching him to make sure he was real and not a figment of her imagination.

The warmth of his body radiated out, thawing her chilled fingers. His muscles bunched beneath the battered leather jacket as he moved, fending off the Synestryn, cutting them down with his sword.

Nika closed her eyes and soaked in the feel of him, real and solid after so many months of wishing.

"Get the fuck out of here," he snapped at her. "I'll hold them off."

Nika jerked back to reality. The rabid sound of the sgath fighting him rose until it filled her ears. She couldn't see past him, but she knew fighting off so many of the beasts was going to be difficult if not impossible.

If she ran, he might disappear again. She had to help him, not leave him, so she pressed herself against the cold tree, shed her body, and thrust her mind into the nearest sgath.

It had consumed her blood somehow—likely by eating the flesh of another sgath that had also consumed her blood—and because of that, Nika was connected to it. She could reach inside its mind, take hold, and, if she was strong enough, force it to do her bidding for a short time.

Luckily, a short time was all it would take for Madoc to cut the beast down once she held it still for his blade.

Maneuvering through the thing's mind was like wading through fetid sludge. Every step pulled at her, trying to drag her under. Nika fought it, ignored the rotten filth of its thoughts, and seized control of the sgath's limbs.

It howled in rage, trying to violently thrust her out of its mind, but Nika refused to budge.

Through its eyes she saw Madoc swing his sword. His movements were jerkier than normal—not at all as fluid as they once had been. He was still a glowing powerhouse of strength, but there was something else she could see in him—something the sgath could sense that she could not while inside her own body. It was as if the sgath recognized part of Madoc—a dark, violent part of him that was normally hidden.

Nika was so intrigued by this new vision, she nearly forgot her task.

The sgath she possessed lunged for his throat. Nika grabbed a mental hold of the thing's jaws and clamped them shut before its teeth could make contact. The sgath bounced off, landing awkwardly on its side.

Vertigo twisted Nika's world as the sgath righted itself and moved in for another attack.

This time, Nika was ready. She focused her will, taking control of the sgath's body. She forced it to remain still, to wait patiently while Madoc's blade cut through its side.

Nika felt the sword slice into her. She felt the frantic panic that seized the sgath as it realized death was coming for it.

Madoc lifted his thick arm again and landed a deathblow, severing the sgath's head.

Nika flung herself from the beast's mind before it was too late—before she died right along with the sgath. Her body sucked her back in, like she'd been tethered at the end of a bungee cord. The mental whiplash made her head spin, but she was used to that. The tree at her back held her steady while she regained her balance.

By the time her world had stopped spinning, Madoc had finished slaughtering the last sgath and had turned to face her.

"What the fuck do you think you're doing?" he demanded, his blunt features tightening into a mask of rage. His green eyes were darker than she remembered, or maybe it was simply the lack of light out here in the cemetery.

Nika's mouth opened, but nothing came out. She was

breathing hard, shaking from her efforts tonight, and nearly unable to stand. Words seemed unimportant.

Instead, she pushed herself up, slid her arms inside Madoc's open jacket, and snuggled against his body. Instantly, his heat soaked into her, driving away some of the chill in her bones.

Madoc's body went utterly still. "Don't touch me."

Nika pressed her cheek against his chest, reveling in the steady beat of his heart beneath her ear. Against her breasts, his muscles clenched hard. Her nipples tightened, but she was too lost in his warmth to be embarrassed by her body's reaction to him.

His voice shook, sounding strained, as if it was difficult for him to control his words. "You shouldn't fucking touch me. It's not safe."

Safe or not, she wasn't pulling away from his delicious heat anytime soon. "I'm cold," she told him so he'd leave her be to enjoy herself.

But he didn't. He disengaged her limbs from around his body, stripped off his coat, wrapped it around her, and took a long step back. "Stay away."

His scent clung to the leather, filling her lungs every time she breathed in. His warmth surrounded her, soaking into her chilled skin. Nika slipped her arms into the sleeves and hugged that warmth close.

The dizziness had faded, and although her body was weak from the physical exertion she'd done tonight, her mind felt strong. Solid. Whole.

Whenever Madoc was near, the sgath left her alone. They didn't try to drag her away from her body and show her all the horrible, violent things they could do. They knew better than to try to hurt her when he was around. They were smart enough to fear him.

In fact, everyone seemed to fear him, at least in some small way. Except her.

Maybe they all saw that darkness the sgath had seen in him, and she was the only one blind to that dangerous side of him. Maybe when it came to Madoc, Nika *was* crazy.

She reached for him and he stumbled backward, trying to get away from her.

"I won't hurt you," she told him, letting her hand drop.

"No, but I can't say the same. You need to get in that car you stole and drive your ass back to Dabyr."

"I can't leave. Not until I have the bones."

"What bones?"

"The bones of the stranger lying in my sister's grave."

A frown gripped his blunt features, forcing his brows low over his eyes. "Tori's bones?"

"No. Not Tori's. My sister is alive."

Madoc let out a heavy, long-suffering sigh. "We're back to this, are we?"

"*We* never left *this*. The fact that no one listens to me does not change the truth."

"It's too damn cold out here for you to be playing in the dirt. Go home."

He wasn't going to listen. None of them ever listened to her. Crazy Nika, all soft in the head. Poor, delusional girl.

Nika picked up the shovel and started back toward Tori's grave.

"Where the hell do you think you're going?"

"To dig. I'd appreciate it if you'd stay. I'm bleeding a little, so I'm sure we'll have more company any moment."

Madoc grabbed the back of the leather jacket she wore and pulled her to a halt. "Bleeding?"

"Only a little, but enough that they can smell it."

"Show me."

The way he said it—laced with thinly controlled rage—made Nika hesitate. "Why? It's not as if you care."

"Show. Me."

"Fine. Whatever." She thrust out her hand, and Madoc actually flinched away before he caught himself. He didn't touch her. He leaned over her palm to inspect the damage.

"Fuck," he snarled. "Now we have to get you patched up."

"Not until I'm finished here."

"Oh, you're finished. Those bones can wait."

"Why? Are you afraid to fight the things my blood will draw?"

His green eyes narrowed. "I'm not afraid of anything, little girl."

Just to prove he was wrong, she reached for him. Madoc lurched backward, nearly falling on his butt to avoid her.

"Except me, apparently."

"Don't touch me," he snapped.

Nika ignored him and kept walking toward Tori's grave. "You're going to have a hard time stopping me if you're afraid to touch me," she said over her shoulder.

She heard him mutter a caustic curse before she felt him getting closer.

He stepped into her path, his mouth tight with determination. "We're doing this my way."

Nika lifted a brow. "Not unless you make me."

"You really shouldn't push me. You won't like what happens."

"How do you know?" she asked. "You won't stick around long enough to have any idea about what I like or don't."

"I'm protecting you from yourself."

Nika rolled her eyes. "My hero."

"I'm serious."

"So am I. I'm digging up those bones with or without your help."

Rather than argue, Madoc simply leaned down until his shoulder was level with her stomach, reached behind her to steady her body, and stood up, flipping her over his back.

Her head swam with the sudden movement, and she had to grab onto his shirt to steady herself. "What are you doing?"

"Putting you in my truck. Taking you home where you belong—where you're damn well going to stay."

His pace was steady over the cold ground; each heavy tread of his booted feet pressed his shoulder into her stomach. "You're making me sick."

"Better than dead."

"Put me down." She wanted to pound at his back, but knew it would do nothing but wear her out even more.

"Nope." With a powerful movement, he hefted them both over the low metal fence surrounding the cemetery.

Nika could hear an engine running nearby. She was almost out of time. "Will you at least listen to me?"

"Talk all you want. It won't change anything."

Madoc shifted her weight and set her on the bench seat of the truck. Another moment of dizziness distracted her, but she'd fought through worse. "I need those bones. I need proof that Tori is alive."

"Not my problem."

"If you take me back, I'm just going to leave again."

"Maybe by then it'll be warmer." He climbed up into the truck, crowding her so she had to move over to make room for him.

"You really don't care, do you? You don't care that Tori is out there suffering."

"All I care about is getting you home and getting back to the nest I'd planned on clearing out before I was so rudely interrupted." He reached past her, under the seat, pulled out a first-aid kit, and flung it open.

He tore open a small antiseptic wipe with his teeth, spitting the top of the foil envelope onto the floorboard. "Give me your hand."

At least he was willing to touch her now. Not like she wanted. Not like she'd dreamed about, but it was something. A start, at least. She could work with that.

Nika put her hand out and the sleeve of his black jacket flopped over her fingers. He pushed it up and dabbed at the scrape on her hand. The ugly, matte black ring he wore brushed her thumb, making it go cold, but she refused to complain.

"See. It's not bad," she said.

"Blood is still blood. I'll call Tynan and see if he can meet us."

"No. I don't want him anywhere near me. I'm sick of doctors."

"That leech is hardly a doctor, and you should have thought of that before you left Dabyr."

"Just cover it up. It's not even really bleeding anymore."

Madoc ignored her, pulled out his cell phone, and dialed. "Where are you?" he demanded.

Tinny words she couldn't make out came through the phone.

"Nika's hurt," said Madoc. "Can you meet us?"

Nika grabbed for the phone, but Madoc leaned away, evading her grasp.

"Of course it's serious. She's fucking bleeding."

"It's not serious," yelled Nika, hoping she'd be heard.

Madoc shot her a warning glare. "Yeah. I know the place. We'll be there." He slid the phone back onto his belt, put the truck in gear, and pulled out of the small parking area.

"Buckle up," he told her. "And don't even think about trying anything stupid. I've got a roll of duct tape in back, and I swear to God that if you make me use it, we'll both regret it."

Nika pulled the lap belt around her hips, refusing to move over to the far side of the cab. It was warm next to Madoc, and despite his jacket, she was still shivering from her exposure to the cold.

"Why do you have to act like such a jerk?" she asked.

He turned the heat up full blast and pointed the vents toward her. "It's not an act. If you don't like it, stay the hell away."

The heat began to sink into her, but it only made the shivering worse. Muscles not used to so much physical effort clenched up, rebelling at their abuse. "Where are we going?"

"Tynan is too far away. He's sending Connal to meet us."

"No. I don't know him. I don't want him to touch me."

Madoc shifted in his seat, inching away from her. "Damn it, Nika! You went and hurt yourself. I don't know shit about patching people up. The best I could do would be to slap a strip of duct tape over it. That's not good enough."

"Actually, that would be perfect. Not only would it

stop the bleeding; it would also keep me from getting more blisters."

"You're not going back there to dig up those bones, and that's final."

"I thought you, of all people, would listen to me."

"Why? Because I'm so fucking sensitive?"

"No, because you know I'm not crazy."

"No, I don't. Standing out in the cold in the middle of the night in a cemetery, alone and unarmed, is pretty fucking crazy."

"I need those bones. Please." She put her hand on his arm, and because he was driving, he couldn't flinch away. She felt the thick muscles below her hand twitch as though he wanted to, but she knew he wouldn't risk crashing the car.

A weary sigh filled the silence. "Why, Nika? Why are those bones so important?"

"Because they prove Tori is still alive."

"No. Even if those aren't her bones, all that proves is that we haven't found her body yet. Do you really want to do that to Andra? Do you really want to take away what little bit of peace she found by burying Tori?"

"You don't understand. Tori is still alive. I can feel her. Rescuing her will make Andra feel a lot better than any fake funeral ever could."

"You can't know she's alive."

"I do. We're connected. She's getting weaker, but I can still feel her inside me. I can still feel her suffering."

He shook his head. "This is crazy. You need to let it go or you're going to get yourself killed."

"So what? You've made it clear you don't care about me one way or another."

The truck lurched to the right, screaming to a sudden stop. Madoc slammed the gearshift into park and turned to face her.

"You have no fucking clue what you're talking about. I've spent every spare moment since I met you hunting the sgath for you, trying to free that fucked-up mind of yours. That counts. I may be dead inside, but damn it, that *counts*."

The pain radiating out from him shocked her. She'd always thought of him as invincible. Clearly, even he could hurt.

Nika reached up and pressed her hand against his cheek. Beard stubble tickled her fingers. His jaw clenched, but he didn't pull away.

"You're not dead inside. Why would you think that?" she asked.

His mouth tightened in anger and his eyes closed. A deep breath filled his chest, lifting his shoulders. She could feel him struggling to regain control.

In a carefully modulated tone, he said, "Forget I said anything. I'm fine."

It was a lie. She could feel the taint of it staining his words, which meant he wasn't fine.

Panic exploded inside Nika. She couldn't let anything happen to him. He was too important—not just to her, but to everyone else, too. "What's wrong with you?"

"I'm an incurable asshole. That's all." With that, he turned back to the road, pulling away from her touch, and merged onto the street.

Nika sat back, her mind reeling. He was lying about being fine, which meant something was wrong. Seriously wrong.

Whatever it was, Nika had to figure out what it was and fix it. She needed Madoc too much to lose him. Without him, she was destined to go back to the way she used to be—unable to control the pull of the Synestryn on her mind, unable to resist being sucked into their world of blood and pain and death.

She couldn't let that happen. Not again. One way or another, she was going to figure out what was wrong and find someone who could fix it.

Chapter 3

Connal was already waiting for them when they pulled into the Gerai house. Madoc had been here before—the night they'd taken Nika from the mental hospital. The human doctors had done nothing to help her, and had actually allowed her to fool their minds into thinking she was fine when she was wasting away, unable to eat.

Madoc had known the moment he saw her that she was going to be trouble; he just never suspected how much. He hadn't had a moment's peace since meeting her—not that he really deserved any. Still, he sometimes wondered what his life would have been like if he'd never met her.

He'd be dead already. He knew better than to fool himself into thinking otherwise. He wouldn't have had a reason to live. He would have given in to the pull to remove that frigid black ring, let go of the last sliver of his soul, and be set free. His brothers would have found him and killed him, but not before he'd done some serious damage to them in return.

Who knew how many lives Nika had saved by giving him a reason to hang on? Of course, once he freed her mind and killed the last sgath, that reason would be gone.

Madoc really needed to die before that happened. He needed to give up and let go—dive headfirst into a nest of Synestryn and take out as many as he could before they killed him.

The problem was the timing. If he went to his death too soon, Nika's head would still be fucked-up. If he waited too long, people he was supposed to care about would die.

Better to err on the side of caution while he still had enough control over his actions to do so.

It was time to let go. Hand over to another Theronai his quest to kill every last sgath. It wasn't like he was the only one who could kill the fuckers. There was nothing special about him. He was just one more sword arm, one more warrior.

They didn't need him; they needed him dead before he could hurt anyone. Especially Nika.

"I remember this house," said Nika.

"We brought you here the night we took you from the hospital."

She gave a distracted nod, staring at the modest home set inside an isolated, wooded area outside Omaha. "I tried to run away to get to Tori, but a vampire stopped me. You came in and took care of me."

Madoc snorted. "Hardly. I told you to get your scrawny ass back in bed."

"You fed me. I hadn't eaten in so long."

"You're not still having trouble with that, are you?"

"Not very often. I'm stronger now. I can usually tell the difference between the things that happen to me in my body and the things that happen to my mind while it's in the body of others."

That was some freaky shit Madoc refused to think about too long. Dealing with his own pain was bad enough. Having to also stand the suffering in someone else would be a nightmare.

"Connal's van is here. We should go in."

"I really don't want to do this," said Nika. Her voice trembled, making Madoc feel like the biggest dick on the face of the planet for forcing her.

It was the right thing to do. She was bleeding. The leech would make it stop. It was as simple as that.

"If he hurts you, I'll kill him," he said, meaning every word.

He got out of the truck, and Nika scooted across the seat toward the door. She looked small and fragile inside his leather jacket. The thing swallowed her up, hanging over her hands and nearly down to her knees. Her cheeks were pink from the cold, and the dome light over her head made her white hair glow.

Madoc's heart squeezed, and an odd need flooded him. He'd spent centuries protecting others. It was habit for him at this point, done with no more thought than he gave to breathing. But with Nika it was different. The urge to wrap her in his arms warred with the need to growl and bare his teeth to the world, killing anyone who got close to her. The ferocity of his urges scared the hell out of him and warned him just how close he was to the end.

He could feel the last leaf of his lifemark clinging to his skin, hanging in the middle of its descent. The black ring he wore on his right hand had slowed the leaf's fall, allowing him to cling to the last sliver of his soul and pretend to be normal. At least for a little while. The ring had been given to him by Iain, the leader of the secret group the Band of the Barren. Like all of the men in the Band, he was living on borrowed time. As long as the ring stayed on, he could hold on a while longer, endure the pain racking his body, and free Nika's mind from the sgath that had stolen it.

He'd intended to help her from afar, protecting her from himself, but now she was here, close enough to touch, looking at him with trust shining in her blue eyes.

She had no idea how close he was to becoming a monster.

Nika put her hands on his shoulders to steady herself as she jumped out of the truck. Against his will, Madoc's hands went to her waist, lifting her down. Through the leather and the thick bulk of her sweater, he imagined he could feel the curve of her waist. It was a trick of the mind, since he knew damn well Nika had no curves. She was skin and bones, though her face had seemed to soften a bit since he'd last seen her months ago. There was a fullness to her cheeks that hadn't been there before. With Nika covered by all those layers of clothes, Madoc could almost pretend she was a normal woman instead of a gaunt, frail thing he could break without even trying.

His fingers tightened around her waist and she looked

up at him. "When we're done here, I want to go back and finish what I started."

Madoc watched her mouth move, mesmerized by the curve of her bottom lip. Was it fuller, too, or had he just imagined it? Maybe if he kissed her he'd be able to tell.

"You'll help me, won't you?" she asked.

Finally, the words sank in. There was no way in hell he was letting her go back to that graveyard, but if he told her that, she'd just try to find a way to go back without him. And that was going to happen only over his rotting corpse.

"We'll see," he said. "Let Connal tend to you first; then we'll talk."

"I don't want him to touch me."

"I know. Neither do I, but you know you can't go around bleeding."

A voice rose up from the darkness near the house. "No, she can't," said Connal. "Bring her in before we have a swarm on our hands."

He moved his hands from Nika, but the lack of contact had him squirming. He wanted to reach out and touch her again, but knew better. The less contact he had, the better it would be for her.

Nika let out a discontented sigh and followed Connal inside the house. "Let's get this over with."

Madoc went inside and shut the door. The living room was furnished simply, with a couch and one recliner. Everything was a mix of neutral colors that kind of faded into blah.

Connal motioned to the couch for Nika to sit.

The Sanguinar was shorter than most, and probably weighed only half as much as Madoc. He had a baby face, making him look like he should be in college partying with his frat buddies. His hair fell over his forehead in a stylish swoop, and, like all the Sanguinar, his face was unearthily beautiful.

Nika hardly seemed to notice, unlike most women, who simply stood and stared as soon as one of the Sanguinar walked into a room.

Fortunately, that meant Madoc didn't have to kill him when this was over.

"Take off your coat and sit down," said Connal.

Nika hesitated for a moment, before she relented and shed Madoc's heavy jacket. Beneath that was a bulky sweater that fell partway over her hands, so she pulled that off, too, leaving her wearing only a thin, snug shirt.

Madoc froze in place, staring at her.

Gone was the frail girl he remembered, and in her place was a healthy, curvy woman. She was still thin, but her body had filled out, giving her breasts and hips a fullness that had been absent before. She no longer looked quite so breakable. Sure, he knew he could still hurt her, but it wasn't like before. She wasn't frail.

She was gorgeous. Perfect.

Madoc had stared so long without blinking that his eyes had dried out. Beneath the fly of his jeans he felt his cock swell, and his fingers clenched into fists to keep from reaching for her.

Connal looked from Nika to Madoc and back again. "You look like you're seeing a ghost."

Nika's mouth lifted in a knowing smile. "No, he's used to seeing a ghost and now he's seeing the real person again."

"You're better," said Madoc, his voice a reverent whisper.

"I told you I was. You didn't listen."

Madoc's hands itched to reach out and slide over her body. He wanted to feel the slender curve of her hip, follow it up to the hollow of her waist, and continue on until her breasts filled his palms.

Her nipples beaded up, pressing against the thin cotton of her shirt as if she knew what he'd been thinking. Of course, his stare had probably given him away.

Connal cleared his throat. "I suggest we get moving here. Clearly, you two have things to discuss."

"We do," said Nika. Then she sat down and offered Connal her injured hand, dismissing Madoc.

The leech took her hand in his. Madoc gritted his teeth and planted his feet on the beige carpet, refusing to move. If he did, he'd draw his blade and use it to slice off Connal's head for daring to touch her. It didn't matter that he'd wanted this—that he'd brought Nika here so the Sanguinar could heal her. The only thing that mattered was the fact that another man was touching her.

After poking her skin for a moment, Connal looked up at Madoc with disgust plain on his face. "You pulled me from my work to deal with this? She's not even bleeding anymore."

"Told you," said Nika.

"She was bleeding."

Connal rose from the couch. "It was just a scratch. Next time, don't call me unless someone's lost a limb. Understand?" He didn't wait for an answer, but stormed out of the house, slamming the door behind him.

Leaving Nika and Madoc alone.

The pain inside Madoc's head had been building all night. Killing those sgath had released some of the pressure, but not nearly enough. He needed to be back out there, killing and fucking so the pain wouldn't eat him alive.

"Time to go," he said.

"That depends on whether you're taking me back to the cemetery."

"I'm taking you back to Dabyr."

She crossed her arms over her chest, which pressed her breasts together, pushing them up toward him as if she were offering them to him.

Madoc's mouth watered at the temptation.

"Why?" she asked. "You know I'll just leave again as soon as your back is turned."

"Joseph will keep a better watch over you this time. I'll make sure of it."

"I'm not a child. I don't need a babysitter."

"Apparently, you do."

"Just let me finish digging up those bones and I'll go back quietly."

If he did that, then he'd have to drive her back to the cemetery and spend the rest of the night shoveling dirt when he really needed to be killing something. "You can talk to Andra about that when we get home."

"Andra is never home. She's been chasing missing children in Illinois for the last two weeks. Besides, Andra is not my keeper. I'm an adult. I get to decide what I want to do."

"I think you've shown just how intelligent your independent decisions are."

"I'm doing the right thing."

"Fine. Then do it with someone else. I've got places to be."

"Go, then."

"And leave you here alone?"

"I'll be fine. There's a main road not far—I was paying attention on the way here. I'm sure someone will stop and give me a ride."

"You want to *hitchhike*?"

She lifted a slim shoulder. "Why not? I've never done it before, and after all those years in the hospital, I have a lot of living to catch up on."

"That's it. I'm done with this. I'm having Joseph send someone to come get you." He pulled his cell phone from his belt and dialed Joseph. Before it could ring even once, Nika shot toward him, grabbed the phone, and raced into the kitchen.

Madoc was so shocked it took him a second to react. By the time he chased her into the kitchen, she'd already shoved the phone into the garbage disposal and flipped on the switch.

A horrible whining, grinding sound rattled the sink.

Nika stood there with a smugly pleased look on her face.

Madoc looked from her to the sink and back again. "I can't believe you just did that."

"I'm tired of having people dictate what I can and can't do. I don't need Joseph's approval for anything. Or yours."

She was taunting him. Maybe she didn't mean to, but she was.

Madoc stepped forward, letting the rage that always bubbled below the surface show in his face. He wasn't going to wear his civilized mask with her—not if she was going to taunt the beast.

The garbage disposal stopped, then buzzed angrily for a moment before it fell silent.

Nika stood her ground, but some of the color in her face drained away as she watched him get nearer.

"You're getting dangerously close to pissing me off," he warned.

Her chin went up an inch. "You don't scare me."

"No? Guess that just proves how soft in the head you really are, then."

"You're big and tough and mean, but you won't hurt me."

"You don't know that." Hell, even he didn't know if he would continue to hold on to his control.

"I do. You and I are connected the way Paul and Andra are. I don't understand exactly how to reach you yet, but if you killed me, you'd be killing yourself, too."

Madoc refused to let his eyes move to the luceria ring on his left hand. He knew what he'd see. There wouldn't be any swirl of color showing him that Nika and he were compatible—that she could tap into the vast pool of devastating power he housed within himself. There would be no movement, no subtle hum like a tuning fork after it was struck. His luceria was nearly dead, just like his soul. The colors that had lain within it for centuries, waiting for the time when a female Theronai would awaken them, had faded almost completely. The pale, nearly white band would look as it had for the last year. There was no sense in fooling himself that Nika had changed that.

She couldn't be his. She couldn't save him, no matter how much he wished otherwise.

If he didn't get away from her soon, he was going to forget himself and decide he didn't care that Nika would doubtless belong to another man any day now. Dozens of Theronai had been flying in from overseas, hoping she was their miracle.

So far, the right man hadn't yet shown up, but he would soon. Madoc needed to remember that. Keep his distance. She wasn't a convenient fuck. He had whores for that. Nika was to be protected, even from himself.

"We're leaving," he told her. The sooner he unloaded her onto someone else, the better. "Get in the truck."

"No."

That single word froze Madoc in place. "What?"

"You heard me. I'm not going anywhere with you. Your phone is dead, so you're not calling anyone to come babysit me, which means you're stuck with me. Deal with it."

"Did you seriously just tell me to *deal with it*?"

"I did."

Madoc was done playing. The pain inside him was building, and without an outlet, he'd be crumpled in a sobbing heap by morning. He couldn't let Nika see that.

"Get in the truck. I'll find a phone and call someone to dig up the fucking grave, okay?"

"No. I don't believe you."

"Get in the damn truck, Nika." The warning was clear in his tone. He stepped forward, intending to crowd her personal space and intimidate her, but she didn't back down.

She tipped her chin up and warned him, "You come any closer and I'm going to kiss you."

Hell, no. That was not going to happen. Not even if he lived long enough to watch the sun wink out.

If she kissed him, he'd fuck her. If he did that, he'd hurt her. He wasn't exactly a gentle man when it came to sex. And if he hurt her, then the last, tiny sliver of his soul would shrivel up and die and he'd end up killing the people he was supposed to protect.

Nika eased away from the sink, moving toward him. Her body moved with sinuous grace, and for a moment, he forgot completely about how fragile she'd been only a few months ago. All he saw was the woman she was now—whole, seemingly healthy, and sexy as hell.

"Is that what you want, Madoc?" she asked in a quiet voice. "Do you want me to kiss you? 'Cause it's what I want. I've been thinking about it a lot lately. Especially when I go to bed. I keep wishing you were with me. Touching me. Sometimes I touch myself and pretend it's you."

Madoc's brain sputtered, spinning around the image that created. Nika in bed, naked, with his hands the only thing to cover her. Would she shy away from him or arch into his touch? Would she tell him what she liked, or would he have the fun of figuring it out on his own?

Her hands slid over his chest, up around his neck. The

slide of her fingers over the luceria around his throat
made his body clench. He held his breath, waiting for his
luceria to react to her touch, but nothing happened. She
wasn't meant to be his.

A wave of heat washed through him, and it was all
he could do to keep his hands fisted at his sides and not
pull her against him. As much as he wanted to press his
erection into the softness of her belly, he knew what a
mistake that would be.

It would only make him want more of what he would
never have.

Her lips parted and she went up on tiptoe as if to kiss
him.

Panic flared in his gut and he lurched away from her,
knocking her off balance. She caught herself on the
counter and stared up at him with hurt shining in her
blue eyes.

"You win," he whispered, unable to find enough air
for anything else. "I'll dig up your bones. Anything you
want, just don't . . . touch me again."

Nika nodded her understanding and turned away, but
not before he saw her blinking back tears.

He'd fucking hurt her feelings, but at least he hadn't
done worse. Yet.

Tori Madison heard the footsteps coming down the tunnel
toward the cage where she was kept prisoner. She had no
idea how long she'd been here. In fact, most of the time, it
seemed like her life before the darkness was a dream—
something she made up to keep herself from going crazy.

If it weren't for the touch of her sister inside her mind,
Tori knew she would have died a long time ago. Nika's
gentle presence whispering inside her was the only thing
Tori had to live for.

And now she had to let that go. She had to push Nika
away—block her out.

The Synestryn lord wanted Nika. She'd overheard
him talking about it to the little girl who never grew up.
They were planning on using Tori to lure Nika here.

Part of Tori wanted to let it happen. Her life would

be so much nicer with her sister nearby, close enough to touch and see. But the rest of her remembered that there was a life outside these caves. That life had warmth and sunshine. On the good days, Tori could almost remember what the sun felt like.

Sunshine had been stolen from Tori, and she couldn't let that same thing happen to Nika. She couldn't repay her sister like that, so instead, she worked to distance herself. Instead of wishing for the touch of Nika inside her mind, she focused on something else when she felt that gentle brush of thoughts over hers. She would sing a song she remembered so loud it would echo off the stone walls, blocking out all else.

Slowly, she'd begun to build up barriers that kept Nika out. Tori was lonely and afraid more often than not, but at least her sister was still safe.

The footsteps grew louder. Tori scurried back into the tightest corner of her prison and tried to curl herself into a ball, but that had become impossible. The thing in her stomach had grown too big.

The Synestryn lord Zillah rounded the corner, making the blood in Tori's veins ice over.

She hated him.

The things he'd done to her had been bad enough, but the blood he'd fed her over the years had changed her. She wasn't sure what she was anymore, but whatever it was, it pleased him. Tori knew that meant it had to be bad, just like the thing in her stomach was bad.

Zillah's fingers wrapped around the bars of her cage. They were set into the stone of the cave, trapping her in a dead end with no way to break free. She'd spent hours trying, but nothing had worked.

His fingers were too long, his skin too pale. And he was cold. Whenever he touched her, he sucked the heat from her body, feeding off of it until she shivered.

"How is our child?" he asked.

Tori refused to answer him. Anything she said would only make things worse. Of course, her silence angered him, too. She'd learned a long time ago that everything she did angered him.

His too-long finger crooked, the extra joint curling toward his palm as he motioned for her to come closer.

Tori stayed cowered in her corner. She didn't want him to touch her again.

"Come here," he said, his voice rising in anger.

Tori shook her head.

Zillah sneered and a scary light glowed behind his eyes. Slowly, Tori began to slide over the stone floor. The skin on one leg was scraped away before she could stand. Seconds later, a horde of bugs came skittering into her cell, feeding on the smear of blood left behind.

Tori didn't stop moving until she was pressed hard against the cold bars. Zillah's hand slithered around her leg, wiping away a drop of blood. He licked it from his fingers, his pointy tongue curling around to get every last bit.

Her stomach heaved with nausea, and she had to look away or get sick.

"You should take better care of yourself," he told her, as if it had been her fault that she bled. "You're going to need your strength. It's almost time."

"Time for what?" she asked before she could stop herself.

"Time for our child to be born and for your sister to come into the fold. Maura and I have plans for her."

Nika.

Just the thought of her name made their connection flare to life for a brief instant. She could feel Nika's presence slide inside her mind, warm and comforting.

"That's right," said Zillah, his eyes brightening with anticipation. "Bring her to me."

No. Tori wasn't going to let him have her. She used every bit of control she'd learned and pushed Nika away, shoving her out of her mind. This time it worked. It didn't always, because Nika was strong, but this time, Tori kept her away.

Zillah shook his head, his tongue clicking at her naughtiness. "You'll bring her to me soon."

His too-long fingers slid over her distended belly, sucking away all the heat from her skin. Beneath his hand, the thing inside her leaped as if it knew its father was nearby.

"I won't," vowed Tori.

Zillah just smiled at her. "You will. I promise. When the time comes, you'll do anything to stop the pain. You won't be able to help yourself."

Fear curled around Tori, making her shiver. She knew what he meant. She'd heard some of the others that were kept here talk about it. Their whispers echoed off the cave walls, filling her head with visions of pain and blood. But the screams were the worst. She knew that when the thing inside her came out, it would hurt. It might kill her.

Before that happened, she needed to get rid of her connection to Nika completely. She didn't trust herself not to reach out for Nika when the pain started.

Zillah's hold on her body disappeared, and Tori spilled to the ground.

He turned and walked away, saying, "I'll check on you later. It won't be long now."

Tori sat there, wrapping her arms around her the best she could. The shivers shaking her body would stop in a little while. She just had to hold on until then. Once she was warm enough to think straight, she'd figure out what to do. She'd come up with some kind of plan to keep Nika away.

And if she couldn't, she'd find a way to kill herself before the pain started.

Zillah headed back to his quarters, savoring Tori's warmth as it curled through his bloodstream. It would have been nice to stay longer and soak up more of her delicious heat, but it wasn't safe for the child she carried. His child.

He was close to another success. He could feel it. Another day or two and he'd be able to hold his child in his arms and show him the world he would one day rule.

The only thing that put a damper on his good mood was Tori's lack of cooperation. He sensed she was getting stronger and more able to resist calling out to her sister. Perhaps the child inside her gave her strength. He couldn't be sure. What he did know was that if he didn't bring Nika here, Maura was going to be unhappy.

The only thing that scared him more than death was Maura's wrath.

As if his thoughts had summoned her, she stood waiting for him in front of his desk.

Maura's blond hair was wild today—a snarled nest of tangles around her childish face. The tattered black clothes she wore were better suited to a street whore than the child she appeared to be. Not that Zillah would say a word. He knew better. Maura was no child, despite her appearance. She was older than he was by several lifetimes and had a kind of power he couldn't even begin to understand.

Maura was deadly and Zillah respected it.

"Tell me," she demanded.

Zillah moved around her, giving her a wide berth. If one of her visions hit and she began to flail around, he didn't want to be near enough to her that she could touch him. He'd seen what happened to those she'd touched. Their deaths had been slow and painful.

"What would you like to know?" he asked, pretending ignorance.

"Has she convinced Nika to come to us?"

"No. But she will."

"I want her," said Maura with a pout. "I want Nika."

"I know, and I told you I'd get her for you. Have patience."

"I've been waiting for nine years. That's long enough." Her imperious tone set Zillah's teeth on edge.

"It won't be long now. Only a few days."

Maura stomped her dainty foot. "Now, Zillah. I want her now, before she returns to the safety of Dabyr."

Rather than backhand the brat, Zillah bowed low to cover the anger he knew was twisting his face. "As you wish, my lady. I'll send some of my best warriors to fetch her for you."

Placated, Maura smiled. "There. Was that so hard?"

Zillah did not dare answer that question. "If I may ask, why is she so important to you?"

"She's not. Her mind is. I need to see how it works—how she controls the sgath."

"I doubt she'll ever agree willingly to aid us."

Maura gave a delicate shrug. "She doesn't have to be willing. If she won't play nice, then I'll rip her power from her and take it for my own."

"You can do that?"

An eerie smile gradually stretched her Cupid's-bow mouth. "I can. I've been practicing on your men."

The implications of her statement hit Zillah like a falling tree. "You're the one who's been killing my elite troops."

She took a step closer to him. "You don't mind, do you?"

Shock held his tongue captive for a bit too long. "Of course not. All I have is yours, should you wish it."

"I'm glad you understand that." She turned around in a swish of tattered black lace. "Call me when Nika's here."

Zillah had intended to meet Connal tonight for his monthly feeding, but he was going to have to make other plans. If his minions weren't successful in finding Nika before she returned home, he needed to activate the contingency plan he had recently put in place.

With a thought, he summoned Canaranth to his office. His second-in-command stood silently inside the door, waiting for instructions.

Canaranth was taller than most of Zillah's troops, taking after the human woman who had birthed him. His skin was as pale as the moon, and his hair was midnight black. His eyes had once been equally as dark, but had seemed to lighten over the years, which was odd, but not odd enough for Zillah to take up any precious time concerning himself about it.

"That boy I altered last fall. Is he still alive?"

"Yes. I met him at the mall last week after he sneaked out of Dabyr. He's still rebelling at the confines of that place and the rules of the Sentinels, but our control on him has held."

"Good. I think it's time for him to be of use."

Zillah wrote instructions on a piece of paper and handed it to Canaranth. "Attach this to Beth before you send her out to meet Connal. Send her with three guards. I don't want to leave Tori so close to the birth."

Canaranth bowed his head. "As you wish."

Chapter 4

Madoc didn't bother digging the hole big enough to open the casket; he simply dug a hole wide enough so that he could stand in it, bashed his way through the top of the casket, collected one of the bones, and left the rest alone.

"Is this enough?" he asked, holding up a small femur for Nika to see.

She sat huddled inside his coat at the edge of the grave. She nodded, reaching out for the bone, which she tucked inside the coat, hugging it close, nestled between her breasts.

Lucky fucking bone.

She scanned the woods nearby, keeping watch for unwanted company. "Tynan said he will probably be able to tell if there's any relation between the body this bone came from and our family."

Madoc climbed out of the hole and started filling it back in again. He was covered in dirt from head to toe, sweaty despite the cold wind, and cranky. He hadn't done nearly enough killing or fucking tonight to suit him, making the pain behind his eyes throb and swell until it shoved its way down his throat and made it hard to breathe.

"I'm sure they'll tell you whatever you want to hear if you let them have your blood," he said.

"I need their honesty."

Madoc snorted. "Good luck with that."

Dawn was only an hour or so away, and by the time

it got here, Madoc needed to have them out of the cemetery before the human police came by and started asking questions. If he was lucky, he could drop Nika off at Dabyr and be plowing some whore before lunchtime. The white wig he paid his hookers to wear was in the back of his truck, ready to go.

"You believe me, don't you?" she asked.

"Believe what?"

"That Tori is still alive."

"I believe you believe it. Course, you're fucked in the head, so what do you know?"

"She won't let me in."

Madoc tossed another shovelful of dirt into the grave. "She won't let you in where?"

"Her thoughts. She's keeping me out even though I know she's afraid." Nika looked up at him, her blue eyes bright with concern.

Something deep inside Madoc swelled as he watched her. It made him feel full and whole even as it threatened to make him burst apart. He had no idea what it was about her that did that, but it didn't seem to go away.

He wished like hell he could find a way to make it stop, that he could find a way to fix what was broken inside her so he could stop worrying about her.

He couldn't do either, so he offered the only explanation that came to mind. "Maybe she doesn't want to scare you."

Nika cocked her head to the side and her white hair fell forward, caressing her cheek. The urge to reach out and slide it back behind her ear was nearly overwhelming. Madoc had to grip the shovel tight to keep his dirty hands where they belonged.

"I hadn't thought about that. Maybe you're right. I'm going to talk to her about it."

"How?" asked Madoc, but it was too late.

Nika lay down, and like a switch was flipped, she was gone. Her body went limp, her eyes rolled back into her head, and all the life slipped from her, leaving her looking fake and plastic, like a mannequin.

A surge of panic caught Madoc off guard, slamming into his gut until he couldn't breathe. "Nika?"

She didn't respond. She didn't so much as twitch.

Madoc dropped the shovel and scrambled to get to her. He pressed his fingers to the side of her neck, frantic to feel a pulse. He left smudges of dirt on her pale skin, but beneath his index finger, he felt the beat of her heart, strong and steady.

Her chest lifted, shifting the leather of his jacket. She was breathing.

He pulled her into his arms and held her against his body, rocking her. He flung his thanks out into the universe, letting whoever was in charge hear it. He didn't much believe in God, but if there was one, the fact that Nika was alive after all she'd been through was about as close to proof as he could imagine.

Her slender frame fit against his too well. The rise and fall of her breathing pressed her breasts against his chest. He shouldn't have been able to feel them through the bulk of all her clothing, but he could. Just like he could feel the curve of her hip and the sleek length of her legs dangling over his thighs.

Her eyes fluttered open, so blue they nearly blinded him. So pretty—just like the skies he remembered from his childhood.

"She won't let me in," whispered Nika. "I can't talk to her. I'll have to try again later."

"Don't you ever do that to me again," he demanded. "You scared the hell out of me."

Relief weighed Madoc down, pinning him there on the cold ground. He knew he should get up. He knew he should move away from her and put so much distance between them she wasn't even in his sight.

She reached up and pressed her chilly hand against his cheek. "You're cute when you're scared."

"Cute?" No one had ever dared call him cute. At least, not to his face.

"Your forehead gets all scrunchy like one of those wrinkled puppies."

This conversation was headed to a bad place fast. "Clearly, it's time to get moving."

"I like being out in the dark like this, alone with you. It's peaceful. You always make me feel safe."

Madoc wasn't touching that comment. Not even if his life depended on it. She had no idea just how unsafe she was at the moment—how much he wanted to do things to her. His lust for her mingled too closely with all the violent urges running through him. In some of his dreams, he'd fucked her and made her cry out in pleasure, but in others, he'd pushed her down and forced her. Raped her. She'd begged him to stop and he hadn't.

He had no business being anywhere near her. Already, his hands were tightening on her body like he didn't want to let go. If he didn't put some distance between them fast, he had no idea what he might do.

He asked, "Can you stand?"

"Sure. I'm fine."

"You're not fine. You passed out."

Nika climbed to her feet, holding the bone close to her chest so it wouldn't fall. "No, I didn't. I just slipped out of my body for a minute. I do it all the time."

"I don't like it."

"You didn't complain when I brought Cain back."

"What are you talking about?"

"After he was hurt. I went inside him and helped him find the way back. I helped him wake up."

Madoc had been there after it happened, but he hadn't realized what she'd done. He wasn't sure he wanted to know now. The idea of her being inside the mind of another man was just about more than he could stand. It made him feel territorial, when he knew he should be grateful to her for what she'd done. "We're leaving."

"What about the rest of the dirt?"

"Fuck the dirt."

She flinched as if his words hurt her.

"What?" he demanded.

Nika shook her head, making her hair sway. "Nothing. I have my bone. We can go. I need some money, though."

"What for?"

"Gas. The car's almost empty."

A slow, deep anger simmered inside him as the implication of her words sank in. "Are you telling me that you drove out here all alone with no money to even fill the fucking tank?"

"I forgot."

"Forgot?"

Her chin went up and her stance widened and became defensive. "It's not like I'm used to any of this. I had to learn to drive the hard way before I could leave. I was so worried I wouldn't be able to do it, I forgot to bring money."

"Wait. What do you mean, *the hard way*?" he asked, even though he knew he probably wasn't going to like the answer.

"I mean I had to borrow someone else's mind for a while so I could learn. You know."

"No. I most definitely don't know anything about borrowing someone else's mind."

Nika turned away, striding toward the vehicles. "You're not like me, Madoc. That doesn't mean that I'm wrong, though. I get things done my own way. If you don't like it, don't watch."

Madoc caught up with her and, despite his better judgment, wrapped his fingers around her arm and pulled her to a stop. She was so delicate, all he'd have to do was tighten his fist and crush her bones, so he paid close attention to the pressure he exerted.

"You're not driving back using borrowed knowledge of how to operate a car," he told her.

"Watch me."

She shouldn't push him. He knew how close he was to the edge—how fast he could lose control. But she didn't know. She'd never seen one of his rages. She'd never seen what he could do when provoked. He'd been able to turn all that rage on the Synestryn, but right now, there were none to be found. He was out here alone with Nika with no one to witness a thing.

His fingers tightened around her arm. His blood was

running hot. The dark side of him urged him to show her just how dangerous he could be. Maybe *then* she'd leave him alone.

A sharp jab to his chest startled him. She'd poked him with her finger and was scowling up at him. "Stop being a bully. I don't like it."

"What makes you think I care what you like?"

"I know you. I've felt the thing growing inside you. It's big and it's ugly, but you're stronger than it is. You're a good man."

Madoc let out a humorless bark of laughter. He couldn't help it. "I'm a lot of things, little girl, but there isn't a single part left of me that's good."

Nika grabbed the front of his shirt and pulled him down until he was at eye level with her. He let her do it. He knew better, but the closer she pulled him to her, the more willing he was to let her have her way. He'd let her scream at him all she liked; then he'd put her in his truck and take her home. As long as he didn't give in to his urge to toss her to the cold ground and fuck her, she was relatively safe.

But Nika didn't yell. Instead, before he could figure out what she was going to do, before he could stop her, she pressed her lips to his in a sweet, chaste kiss.

Desire flared to life, eclipsing everything else. He couldn't remember the last time a woman had kissed him—he always took his whores from behind—but even if he could remember, those memories would have faded to meaninglessness inside this moment.

Nika's mouth was soft and warm, her touch so brief and light, it was over before he'd even gotten a real taste of her.

He wanted more. The darkness inside him rose up, demanding more. She was sweetness and light and he wanted to consume her so that that sweetness was all his, forever.

He took her head in his hands, holding her still. He was going to give her a real kiss—one that staked a claim and showed her just what she'd gotten herself into. He'd warned her to stay away. Repeatedly. She hadn't, and this was exactly what she deserved.

Her soft breath feathered out across his cheek. "I always wondered what that would be like. Thank you."

"For what?" he managed to grate out through his clenched jaw.

"My first kiss."

No. Fuck no. He did not just hear that. "First?" It hadn't even been a real kiss, just a peck.

He felt her try to nod, but his grip was too tight to let it happen.

First kiss. Too innocent. Too trusting. He had to let go of her. He couldn't make her cry like he did in his nightmares.

It felt like he was stripping off his own skin, but he managed to move his hands away from the softness of her skin and hair. Smudges of mud from his hands dirtied her wherever they touched.

He stepped back, his chest billowing like he'd been running for days. His heart pounded hard against his ribs, and with every beat, the pressure in his head grew.

Nika reached for him. He took another long step back, evading her touch. If she touched him again, he'd lose control. The darkness would take him and Nika would pay the price.

He reached into his wallet, pulled out several bills, and tossed them on the ground at her feet. "Go," he told her. "Go home and don't try to follow me."

"Where are you going?"

To find as many Synestryn or hookers as fast as he could. "None of your fucking business. Leave. I got the damn bone for you. Don't make me regret it."

She picked up the money, never taking her eyes from him. "You need me. One of these days I'll be able to show you I'm not crazy—at least, not about that."

"Go. Now." Before he stopped her.

"I'll wait for you at home. If you don't come back so we can talk, I *will* come find you."

Her promise fell heavily on his shoulders as she turned and left.

Madoc waited until she was out of sight before he dared to move. The sun was nearly up, making the chances of finding any snarlies slim. He had the number of a whore in Omaha he'd used before. He only hoped he'd get to her before the pain ripped him apart.

Connal rushed to the meeting spot, ten minutes late. He'd already had to change the time, thanks to that paltry scratch on Nika's hand. If he didn't get there soon, he was afraid his food would no longer be waiting for him.

He pulled up to the vacant building and hurried to the door. It swung open easily, and the smell of filth assaulted his nose. He allowed a trickle of power to aid his vision, forcing the darkness to dissipate.

This building was clearly a place where the homeless hid from the cold. Three stained, discarded mattresses lined one wall. A meager pile of belongings filled a rusted shopping cart. A battered metal drum held the remains of a fire left untended for too long.

On two of those three mattresses lay a human corpse. One was missing a leg. Another was still being fed on by small cat-sized Synestryn with barbed heads and spines. The wet sound of their feasting made Connal's stomach turn.

Across the room, handcuffed to a metal pipe jutting from the wall, was the woman he'd been feeding from for months. In front of her was a trio of Synestryn guards.

Each of the guards was tall and spindly—their shape disturbingly humanoid. Their skin was gray and looked slick, almost reptilian. Their mouths had no lips, only sharp rows of teeth left constantly visible. Saliva slid down their chins, adding to the shine of the skin along their too-long necks.

The guard in front blinked with odd, sideways eyelids, then stepped out of Connal's way, indicating he could go to the woman to feed.

Hunger burned inside his belly, clawing at his mind to the point that little other thought was possible. The unwanted distraction Madoc had caused tonight had been nearly more than he could tolerate.

He was allowed to feed only once a month, and Connal had no question that Zillah would withhold the woman's blood if he did anything to displease the Synestryn lord.

"Where's Zillah?" he asked the guard.

The thing's neck twisted around one hundred eighty degrees and hissed in the direction of the woman. Clearly, speech was beyond its capability.

Connal let out a relieved sigh. At least he wouldn't be asked to do any favors for the bastard tonight. Normally, his food didn't come free, and as hungry as Connal was, he was beginning to fear these meetings almost enough to refuse to show. Almost.

As he neared the woman, she cringed away from him, pressing herself back against the wall. She'd been bathed since he'd last fed from her, and he could tell now that her hair was light brown, no longer matted and filthy. Her hazel eyes were just as dead and unresponsive as they had been every other time he'd fed from her.

A pang of sympathy squeezed Connal's heart, but there was nothing he could do for her. Even if he had wanted to set her free, the blood of the Synestryn child she'd once carried—blood he'd consumed when feeding from her last summer—now prevented him from acting against Zillah in any way. He was as much of a slave to Zillah's whims as she was.

At some point over the fall, she'd lost the child. Connal almost asked her what had happened, but thought better of it. She was for food, not conversation.

He gripped her hair and pulled her head back. Her long hair fell back over her shoulder. Only then did he see the note that had been pinned to her shirt.

So much for avoiding Zillah's whims.

Connal ripped the note away to read later and sank his teeth into the woman's neck. A pitiful whimper rose up from her, but he ignored it. The taste of her blood flowing over his tongue was too heady and consuming. All other thoughts vanished as her power filled him up and made him whole.

Strength and warmth flooded his limbs as he continued to drink from her.

He felt her pulse weaken, but didn't care.

"Please," she whispered, speaking to him for the first time. "Kill me."

Shock rocked Connal as he realized he was doing just that. Before it was too late, he willed her flesh closed and ripped his mouth away from her neck.

His hands still held her head still, but her eyes shifted, looking up at him. Tears shimmered there, and the raw look of pleading in her eyes was enough to rip a cry of denial from Connal's chest.

"Please," she said, her voice strained, as if it had been a long time since she'd used it. "I want to die."

Connal let go of her and stumbled back. He knew what Zillah would do to him if he killed her. He'd suffer for a long time before he found any peace in death.

"I can't. I won't," he told her.

She swallowed and suddenly that frozen, dead look came back into her eyes, as if she'd gone somewhere else.

Zillah's note was still crumpled in his fist. He smoothed it flat and read the scrawling text. "Activate Ricky," was all it said, but that was enough. Connal knew what Zillah meant for him to do.

A boy of seventeen was probably going to die because of Connal, and there was nothing he could do to stop it.

Everything had gone so wrong. What had started out as a way to ease his hunger had turned into something far worse than he could have ever imagined. He was Zillah's puppet. His tool. Not only was he aiding the enemy; he was doing something he never would have thought possible.

He was harming innocents.

Connal looked at the woman in front of him. She was dangling by her wrists, not even bothering to support her own weight. Life for her was a series of horrible nightmares. She couldn't even find peace in death—the Synestryn wouldn't allow that. They would keep her alive for her body, her blood, and the power it held over him for as long as possible.

Unless he did something. But what? He knew better

than to think he'd refuse to feed from her again. He knew without a doubt he would. The hunger was too strong to resist—the power of her blood too intoxicating.

The only way he'd stop feeding from her was if she was no longer available. Unless she died or escaped, her hold over him would remain.

A hissing warning came from behind him. The guards were getting agitated.

He spun around and imbued his words with a portion of the power he'd taken from her. "I'm not finished."

The guard cowered, bobbing its head in a sinuous motion.

He couldn't act directly, but maybe he could give the woman the information she needed to help herself. It was worth a try.

He gathered her body up in his arms, bending his head over her as if feeding from her again. He could smell her fear, and for the first time, it sickened him.

"Listen to me," he told her. "Your blood is the key to your escape. Do you hear me?"

The woman remained limp and listless in his arms. He gave her a shake, making her head loll back on her neck. Her blank eyes stared up at him.

He tried to use some of the power he'd gained from her to force her back to reality, but when he reached for it, he hit a wall. Apparently, touching her mind to tell her how to escape was one of the boundaries he could not cross.

"You need to remember what I'm saying, woman. My people can track your blood. They're not all like me. Some of them are . . . good."

The fact that he wasn't one of the good ones was hard to admit, even to himself, but he knew the ring of truth when he heard it.

"One of them may find you," he whispered. "Save you."

And then one of the guards slammed a thick arm into him, knocking him away.

Connal hit the wall and pushed himself back up to his feet. He lifted his hands and said to the guard, "I'm done now. I'll leave."

The guard's head bobbed in acknowledgment, but its claws were bare, ready to rip into Connal if he made a wrong move.

With one last look at the woman dangling from the pipe, he turned and left. There had not been a single sign of recognition in her eyes. They were as dead as the corpses lying across the room.

Grace held her tears back until she was safely outside Torr's suite.

He was getting worse. The paralysis had crept up his body until it was becoming hard for him to hold his own head up. He'd tried to cover his weakness in front of her, but she knew.

Torr was dying.

Grace wanted to do something, but she was powerless to help. Useless. All she could do now was watch him die and give him as much dignity as possible.

Maybe the most compassionate thing she could do was kill him as he'd begged her to do so many times. She could make his death easy. Painless.

The Sentinels would hate her. They'd most likely banish her from Dabyr, but she'd accept that. Even if they executed her, she was willing to let it happen.

Torr had saved her life as well as her brother's. She owed him her life in return.

Grace slipped inside the suite she shared with her younger brother, letting the tears take her. The first sob had gripped her body when she noticed she was not alone.

Gilda, the Gray Lady, the most powerful female Theronai in the compound, sat on Grace's couch. Her long black hair lay perfect and shining against the gray silk of her gown. Every breath she took made the light play over her, caressing her as if it couldn't get close enough.

As always, when Grace saw her, she stopped dead in her tracks, staring, letting the woman's beauty and power sink into her.

Grace wiped her tearstained face and regained as much composure as she could. She knew her eyes were red and her nose was running, but there wasn't much she could do to help that.

She bowed her head, hoping to hide her messy state as well as pay respect to the powerful woman sitting on her couch.

"I've been waiting for you," said Gilda.

"I'm sorry. I didn't know you wanted to see me. If you'd called for me—"

Gilda raised a dainty, elegant hand. "I didn't want anyone to know I spoke to you. What I have to say is between only us."

"Of course, my lady," agreed Grace. It wasn't like she had any other choice. She was at the mercy of these people, as was her brother. They'd been kind, given her brother a home and a future. She'd do whatever they asked of her to make sure he stayed safe.

"Torr is dying."

Hearing the words aloud made it feel more real, made it seem final. Unavoidable. Torr. Dying.

A sob gripped Grace, but she fought it down. "I know."

"I believe I've found a way to save him."

A bolt of hope speared through Grace, making her body tense. Daring to hope was dangerous, but she couldn't stop herself. "How?"

Gilda nodded to a box sitting on the coffee table. It was made of wood, wrapped with bright silver wirework shaped into an intricate vine that scrawled across the entire surface. "With this."

Grace reached for it, but Gilda's harsh command stopped her. "Stop. Do not touch it until I've told you everything." She waved to the empty seat across from her. "Sit."

Grace sat.

"Inside that box is a device created by my ancestors. Their ability to imbue artifacts with power has never been matched. This device was created for the sole purpose of healing."

"Then we should get it to the Sanguinar. Torr is getting worse fast."

"The Sanguinar will not use it."

"Why not?"

"The cost to them would be too great."

"Then who can use it?"

Gilda pinned her with a cold, black stare. The light of Grace's suite seemed to be sucked into the dark depth of her eyes, and for the first time, she saw something bleak and unforgiving inside the woman she'd come to respect. Something frightening.

In a quiet voice, the Gray Lady said, "You are the one who can save him. Perhaps the only one."

"Why me? I'm not special."

"Yes, you are. Not in the way of my people, but among humans, you are special. You can save him, should you wish to."

"I do."

"Not so fast. If you do this, you will pay a price."

"I don't care. Torr saved me. He saved my brother. I'll do anything to save him."

"Anything?"

"Yes."

Gilda nodded. "It is as I suspected, then."

"What is?"

"You love him."

Grace didn't deny it. There was no point. Gilda would know she was a liar if she did. "I love him more every day. It's killing me to watch him suffer."

"If you do this, he'll be healed, but you'll take on that suffering. This device can't create health, only transfer it. From you to him. You'll become weak and paralyzed. You'll be tied to a bed or wheelchair for the rest of your life, if you don't simply die."

Shock left Grace reeling. She swayed in her seat, gripping the soft fabric of the chair for support.

She could save Torr.

If she did, her life would be over.

In the end, there was no real choice. "If I do this, will you protect my brother, care for him as if he were your own son?"

Gilda's beautiful mouth curved in a slow, satisfied smile. "I vow it."

A heavy, comforting weight settled over Grace's shoulders as Gilda offered her promise. Her brother would be safe. Torr would live. It was all she'd ever wanted.

No. That was a lie. She wanted more than that. She wanted a lifetime with Torr. She wanted to have him love her in return, but that was just a girlish fantasy. Regardless of whether Torr got better, he would never be hers. He had bigger, more important things to do with his life than to tie himself to a human woman. She knew that. She'd always known that.

He had a destiny, and Grace was going to see to it that he fulfilled it.

"Tell me what I need to do to save him."

Chapter 5

Nika was greeted by a line of angry faces when she arrived back at Dabyr. They were all waiting for her inside the entrance to the main hall. The glass ceiling high overhead let in the morning sunlight, and several humans sat sipping coffee in the dining area. Other than that, the place was empty, giving the angry mob room to attack.

Andra led the charge.

Her short, dark hair was dusty, and her blue eyes were bloodshot, like they got when she'd been funneling too much of Paul's power. Apparently, they'd just gotten back from a Synestryn killing spree and hadn't even bothered to clean up yet.

If Andra found out that Nika had taken the bone, she'd flip out and take it back to that stranger's grave. Nika couldn't let that happen. "Where have you been?" Andra asked, her voice clipped with thinly controlled anger.

Nika gripped the bone tighter. She still had Madoc's jacket on, which hid her treasure. "I just wanted to get out for a while. Go for a drive."

"A drive?" asked Andra. She stepped forward. She was more than half a foot taller than Nika was, at least in those boots, and she seemed to loom over Nika. "You don't have a license. How do you even know how to drive?"

"TV," said Nika, rather than give Andra the truth. Madoc had seemed freaked-out by her method of learning things, so it was best if she kept that little tidbit to herself.

Andra let out a short, frustrated sigh. "I get that you're feeling better now, and I can't tell you how glad I am that you are, but you cannot go running off like that without telling someone. You scared us."

Nika looked down the line of people. Paul was there, of course—all tall and handsome. He never left Andra's side if he could help it. And Joseph was there, too. He looked more tired than normal, which was saying something. His shoulders sagged under the burden of leadership, and his hazel eyes were rimmed with fatigue.

As the leader of the Theronai, it must have been his job to add to the scolding.

There were also two men there she didn't recognize. One had dark skin and eyes and a quiet stillness about him. He seemed to fade into the shadow of the other paler, thinner man. They both wore the luminescent bands around their throats and matching rings on their fingers that told her they were also Theronai—probably here to paw at her and see if she made their rings turn colors.

Just the thought was enough to make her skin crawl. The blisters from the last group of men who wanted to see if she was "the one" had just finished healing. She wasn't looking forward to another round of torture.

All she wanted to do was get her bone to Tynan and make him tell her what she already knew: It didn't belong to Tori. The fastest way to make that happen was to play along. Nika stared at her dirty shoes, hoping she looked contrite. "I'm sorry, Andra. I didn't mean to worry you."

Andra sighed, releasing all her bluster. "I know you didn't, baby. Let's go get you cleaned up."

Nika cringed at her sister's infantile endearment, but refused to make an issue out of it here in front of all these people. Andra had taken care of her for years. Getting out of the habit wasn't something Nika could expect her to do overnight. Still, she had to make a stand so her sister wouldn't trample all over her wishes with those hard-core boots of hers. "I don't need any help showering or changing clothes."

"You look like you're about to fall over."

"I'm fine. Please just let me be. I am an adult, you know."

Paul stepped up and put his thick arm around Andra's waist. "She looks fine to me—just a bit dirty. We can check on her later, okay?"

"Are you sure?" Andra asked Nika. "I don't mind helping."

"I'm sure. I'll get cleaned up, then meet you wherever you like for blister duty."

Joseph stiffened at that. Behind him, the strange men shared some kind of secret, silent macho-speak.

Joseph scrubbed a hand through his hair. "Look, Nika, if you're not up to meeting the men, I'll make them wait until another day."

Nika shook her head. "I'd rather get it over with. Just give me an hour, okay?" She was sure that would be enough time to wash off the mud, get her bone to one of the Sanguinar, and be back before anyone knew what she was up to.

"Fine," said Andra, "but if you need me, call, okay? We're going to finish up here with Joseph; then I'll be back to the suite to help if you need it before we have to head back out."

Nika nodded. She really needed her own place, but now didn't seem like the best time to bring it up. She'd won one battle, and that was as much as she could hope for in a day. Besides, if Andra was leaving again today, her meddling wouldn't last long.

Joseph, Paul, and Andra turned to go the opposite way, but one of the strangers held back, watching her. He had light hair that had been shaved down to his skin, with only a fraction of an inch of stubble showing. He was taller than his companion and less heavily muscled. There was a hungry look on his face—one she'd seen too many times over the past few months not to recognize it. He was in pain and he thought she could make it stop.

Nika stilled as a familiar fear slid through her. She willed herself to run, but her muscles had clamped down, holding her still like a frozen little bunny. Time slowed.

She tried to breathe through the fear, but it did no good. His hand was stretching out, reaching for her.

A high, pitiful noise spilled out from Nika's mouth.

The man beside him—the second stranger—saw what was happening and grabbed the other man's arm in a tight grip. "Not yet. You heard Joseph."

At the sound of his name, Joseph stopped and turned around, along with Paul and Andra. "Don't!" shouted her sister. "You're scaring her."

Joseph's big body shot through the air and slammed into the pair of men, knocking them both into the wall. They landed in a pile of thick arms and legs.

Nika shoved at her fear hard and fought it down enough to flee. She turned to run, but had forgotten all about the bone. It fell from her coat, clattering onto the hard tile. The small, child-sized leg bone lay there, dull and bleak against the glossy floor.

Andra's eyes zeroed in on the bone, widening in shock and revulsion. "How could you?" she whispered. "How could you desecrate Tori's grave?"

Nika knew that nothing she could say would make her sister forgive her. They'd argued over this too many times to count. Andra knew she'd buried their baby sister. Nika knew she was still alive. There was no room for compromise here. None.

"I'm sorry you had to see that," said Nika. She bent, picked up the bone, hid it from sight, and ran away. No words would fix the pain and grief and guilt lingering in Andra's eyes.

Nothing would except proving Tori was alive.

Andra bit her lip to stave off the tears that burned her eyes. She would not cry in front of strangers.

She'd thought Nika was getting better. She'd started eating again. She'd gained weight. The bouts of dizziness and weakness had grown farther and farther apart. She was even pushing at the boundaries Andra had set—a sure sign she was getting healthier, stronger.

At least, that was what Andra had thought.

The fact that Nika would resort to digging up their

dead sister's bones proved just how wrong Andra had been.

"She really is crazy," said Andra.

Paul's strong arm came around her, and she leaned into him, soaking up the comfort he offered. He pulled her away from the others and shielded her with his body to afford her a bit of privacy. "It's only been a few months. You need to give her some time. Let her pursue this course if she needs to."

A wave of revulsion made Andra shiver. "She's carrying around our dead sister's bones. It's disgusting."

"I know, but if it's the only way she'll give up her delusion, then it's worth it, isn't it? Do you really think Tori would begrudge Nika the proof she needs to heal?"

"No. Tori would have given Nika anything. She was generous and loving to a fault. But that doesn't excuse this. I told her she couldn't do this. I told her it wasn't fair to Tori that after almost nine years of lying in that cave, our sister's remains are no longer safe in the cemetery, next to Mom's."

"We already know Nika's going to take Tori's remains to one of the Sanguinar to see if they can identify them. I'll talk to Tynan and make sure he understands the situation. I'm sure he'll treat this with as much care and reverence as possible."

Andra was sickened by the thought, but what could she do? She knew that if she took the bone back and buried it, Nika would only slip away again later to steal it. And next time, she might not come back in one piece.

She had to let this happen, no matter how much it bothered her. As disgusting as it was, it beat the heck out of burying another sister. "Fine. Talk to Tynan. Tell him to hurry up. I want Tori to rest in peace. She deserves at least that much."

Nika's hair was still wet from her shower when she knocked on Tynan's door. She heard him shuffling around inside his apartment, but it took him a long time to open the door.

Tynan cracked the door open. He was shirtless, wearing only a loose pair of cotton pants. A curl of glossy black hair fell over his forehead, nearly hiding one icy blue eye.

"Can I come in?" she asked him.

Tynan opened the door and let her inside. He looked out into the hall, checking both ways before he shut the door. "You came here alone?"

"Is that a problem?"

Light from the hall spilled into the darkness of his suite. It fell over his chest, shadowing the ridges of muscles and bones in his torso. He was model thin—not at all like Madoc, with his heavy slabs of muscle. Nika had seen the way women looked at Tynan—like he was a long-lost favorite toy—and she'd always wondered what it was about him that drew them in. He was pretty. Inhumanly so, as if he didn't belong here on this planet. He moved with an almost hypnotic grace, and his eyes made her want to stare at him, but he did nothing for her inside. He didn't make her feel whole or safe or warm.

He wasn't Madoc.

Tynan shut the door and flipped on the lights. He had to look around for the switch, as if he rarely used it. "Paul called me and said you'd be coming, but your sister would kill me if she knew you were here with me alone."

"Why? You're not going to hurt me." Nika scanned his suite, taking in the numerous stacks of books and dusty trinkets. The place was done in reds and browns, with little to brighten it up. Heavy curtains hung over the windows, blocking out the sunlight. At least it was warm in here. It had to be eighty degrees, which suited Nika just fine.

"I wish the rest of your kind saw things the same way." He moved a stack of books so she could sit on the couch. "Paul told me why you're here, but I want to hear your side of things."

Nika pulled a thick, white towel out of the gym bag on her shoulder and unwrapped it. "I need to know if this bone could have been my sister's or not. I need proof to show Andra so she'll finally believe me."

"It sounds to me like you already know the answer to your question."

"I do. Andra doesn't. Can you do it? Can you tell me the truth?"

Tynan looked at the bone, then back to Nika. "I can. But not without something in return."

"I'll give you my blood," offered Nika. She hated the thought of letting him bite her, but if that was what she had to do to show Andra the truth, she would.

Tynan shook his head. "That's not going to work. I had a bit of your blood once. It didn't agree with me."

"Then what? What do you want?"

A silvery light flared inside Tynan's eyes for a brief second before it was gone. "Madoc. His blood is powerful. Get him to consent and I'll do as you ask."

Disappointment pushed the air from her lungs. "He won't do it for me. He doesn't like me very much."

"I think you'd be surprised at just how wrong about that you are."

Nika reached for Tynan, wanting to know what he knew. If she touched him, she might get a glimpse into his head, but before her fingers could make contact, he stepped away and was out of reach. "No, you don't," he chided. "I've had enough of you inside me to last a lifetime. I don't know how you live with the chaos in your mind, but after that single drop of blood I took from you, I know without a doubt that I cannot."

"I'm sorry. I didn't realize."

Tynan gave her a weary smile. "Go, now. Talk to Madoc. If he agrees to feed me, you'll have your answer. Until then, I need to rest. The daylight drains me."

Nika wrapped the bone back up and left it sitting on Tynan's couch. It would be safer here than in Nika's room, since Andra was less likely to take it away from Tynan.

She left and walked unerringly through the twisting halls toward Madoc's suite, hoping he'd followed her home, even if it was simply to check up on her. She could have found him blindfolded, surrounded by a thousand other men. There was a dark energy about him—a writhing desperation he fought with every beat of his heart. It was strong, and she had no idea how he fought it day after day, but he did.

His struggle had become harder since she'd last seen him months ago. The pain pulsing inside him was worse. If she concentrated, she could hear the silent screams coming from his soul as it withered away day by day.

She wanted to save him, but she hadn't yet figured out how. If only he'd let her get close enough, spend enough time touching him, she was sure she could solve the puzzle, but, of course, that hadn't happened. He'd been running away from her for months, avoiding her.

No longer. Even if he tried, she wasn't going to let him get away with it this time. Tori needed her to make him give Tynan his blood, and Nika would not fail.

She was nearly to his doorway when she saw Joseph and the two strangers she'd seen earlier round the corner.

"I thought I'd find you here. You said you were going to meet us," said Joseph.

"I had something I had to do first."

"Are you ready now?"

No. She wasn't. She hated letting these men touch her. She hated seeing the looks of pain and horror and disappointment on their faces. Some of them had run away as if scared by what they felt inside her. Some had merely gone pale and walked away calmly, preserving their pride. One of them had actually thrown up at her feet.

Nika didn't know what it was about her that disgusted them—maybe it was the same thing that made a starving Sanguinar refuse an offer of her blood. What she did know was that when these men laid their hopeful hands on her, she was often left with bruises or blisters that took days to heal, and Andra would baby her the whole time.

She didn't have time for that. As soon as Tynan told Andra the truth about Tori, Nika needed to be whole and healthy enough to go find her. She was not going to be left behind this time—seen as too frail and delicate to rescue her baby sister.

Nika looked each man standing in front of her in the eye. "I don't want to do this."

One of the Theronai—the one with skin and eyes the

color of dark chocolate—gave her a reassuring smile. He had a thick accent she couldn't place. "We won't force you, but Joseph has told us of your broken mind. Perhaps we can help."

Nika hated it that they'd talked about her. It made her feel like a child to have her mental health discussed with perfect strangers. "You can't. If you could, I'd know."

"Please let us try."

How many times had she heard that? Too many over the past few months to count. They were always wrong and never learned from the mistakes of those who had gone before.

Nika let out a frustrated sigh and held out her left arm. "Fine. Just hurry. I have things to do."

Joseph moved, putting himself between her and the strangers. "Are you sure, Nika? You look tired. It can wait until after you've slept."

Part of her wanted to put it off, but she knew she wouldn't rest well if she did. She'd be worried about it, thinking about the pain she knew was to come. As much as she didn't want this, getting it over with was better than delaying the inevitable and losing a day's sleep over it.

"I am tired, but it's fine. Let's just do it so I can start to heal."

"We won't hurt you," said the second man in the same thick, broken accent as his companion.

The way he looked at her—so full of hope and yearning—made Nika's stomach tighten. She couldn't be what this man wanted her to be, and as soon as he touched her, all that hope would be crushed. He'd have to go back to his old life of pain and suffering and there wasn't a thing she could do to stop it.

"Just be quick," said Nika. She closed her eyes. She didn't want to see that look cross their faces. This was hard enough without the guilt that came along with her failure.

She felt the heat from one of the men's hands near her arm, close but not touching. He hesitated, as many of them did, as if the wait would somehow change the outcome.

"Do it," she said between clenched teeth, bracing herself for the pain.

Warm, calloused skin met hers. His fingers closed around her in a tight grip. Pain streaked along her skin, setting her arm on fire. She held her breath, waiting for him to let go, but he held on.

The pain grew, multiplying as the seconds passed. Nika tried to pull her arm away, but he didn't relent.

She opened her eyes to see the face of the taller man twisted in a grimace of pain.

"Let go!" she shouted.

Joseph grabbed the man's arm and tried to pull it away, but his grip was too tight.

The skin around his hand turned bright red, searing as if she'd laid it against a hot coal. She struggled harder and another cry of pain ripped through her.

Rational thought scattered under the strain as her thoughts tried to flee the agony of his touch. She felt her mind crack and fling out pieces of itself into the world, seeking shelter.

Nika tried to control it, but she hadn't been prepared for this. She was tired from too much effort last night and not strong enough to stop this involuntary reaction.

Her body grew weaker and it became difficult to stay standing. She locked her knees, praying Joseph would force the man to release her. If she could just hold on a few more seconds . . .

She felt her body jerk as both men pulled on the other. Then, from the corner of her eye, she saw a huge fist fly past her head and slam into the jaw of the man burning her.

The man let go and stumbled backward, knocking both him and his companion over.

A wave of dizziness whirled through Nika and she grabbed for the wall to steady herself, but it was too far away.

A pair of strong hands caught her and kept her from falling, but these hands didn't hurt.

Madoc. She'd know his touch anywhere.

"What the fuck were you doing to her?" He shot the harsh question at Joseph.

Joseph looked at the angry, blistered spot on her arm, then back to the man on the floor who was bleeding from his split lip. Guilt tightened his mouth, making the lines around it deepen. "Get her out of here. I'll deal with him."

"No. I'll deal with him," said Madoc. "You take the girl."

"You're the only one who can touch her. Besides, from the look on your face, you'd just kill him."

"So?"

"So, that's not the way we do things. He lost his head. You know how it is—how desperate the pain can make us. I'm not going to kill a man for doing something I've thought about doing way too many times for my own comfort."

A low, warning rumble rose up from Madoc's chest. "Don't you dare."

The man who'd hurt her pushed himself to his feet. Nika backed away from him, tripping on her own feet in her haste.

"Go, Madoc. Get out of here," said Joseph.

Nika regained her balance and tugged on Madoc's arm. She really didn't want to be the cause of any more bloodshed, and if she didn't get him to leave, there was definitely going to be more.

"Take me home, Madoc. I'm tired."

He looked down at her, and his blunt features relaxed. His green eyes slid to her arm and he let out a violent curse before picking her up and heading down the hall.

The part of her that needed to prove she was independent warred against the part of her that loved being close to him like this. In the end, the practical side won. She hadn't spent the last several months getting stronger only to be treated like she'd break if the wind blew too hard. "I can walk," she told him.

"Nope."

"Where are we going?"

"To see the fucking bloodsucking leech, Tynan."

Nika flinched at his harsh words, and the slight hesitation in Madoc's gait told her he'd noticed.

"He won't heal me," she said. "My blood hurts him."

"Good. Serves the bastard right."

"Stop, Madoc. There's no point in waking him up again today."

Madoc stopped dead in his tracks and looked down at her. He wasn't a traditionally handsome man, but the rough planes of his face drew her in and made her wish she had the nerve to stroke her fingertips over his skin.

"Again?" he asked. "You've seen him today? Are you hurt somewhere I don't know about?"

"No, I had to take the bone to him, and he was really tired when I stopped by. Let him sleep. My arm will be fine."

"Did he try to take your blood?"

"No. I just told you it hurts him."

Madoc's chest lifted with a sigh, which pressed her shoulder against hard muscles she wished he'd let her feel with her fingers. Every time she reached for him, he'd back away.

And then it struck her that he was a bit too busy holding her to back away now. She could do whatever she wanted, and he'd have to drop her to stop her.

Before she lost the opportunity, she slid her uninjured arm around his neck and nestled her nose just beneath his ear. His scent went to her head, making it spin. There was nothing flowery about him, not even the smell of soap, just the scent of his skin and the warm peace it brought her to breathe him in.

She felt his muscles clench around her, holding her tighter as he began walking again—quicker and in the opposite direction. She didn't really care where he took her. After so many months of wishing for him to come home, she was simply glad he was here, close enough to touch.

"Tynan told me he would only help me learn the truth about that bone if you gave him blood. Will you help?"

"Tynan's had plenty of my blood. Tell him to use that."

"So you won't help?"

"Sorry. He'll have to find another sucker."

Great. Now what was she going to do? Maybe Paul would help.

They came to a stop in front of the door to the suite she shared with Paul and Andra. He pounded on the door with the toe of his boot. No one came.

The light on the electronic lock turned from red to green and the door popped open.

"Knew he was watching," said Madoc under his breath.

"What?" asked Nika.

"Nicholas. He's the man behind all the security cameras. He has remote access to all the doors and let us in."

Madoc took her inside and set her on the couch. Nika tried to hold on to him, but he managed to pry her arm free and back away. "Paul? Andra? You home?"

No one answered.

"Afraid to be alone with me?" she asked.

"Fuck, yes. And you would be, too, if you weren't crazy. You need to listen to your sister and keep your distance from me."

It stung that he called her crazy, but it hurt even more knowing he didn't want to be around her. "You won't hurt me. I don't know why Andra can't see that the way I do."

He ignored her comment and scrubbed a hand over his face, then looked around like he was hoping for a means of escape.

"Why do you hate me?" she asked. "Are you afraid crazy is contagious?"

He frowned at her in confused shock, like she'd sprouted horns. "I don't hate you. I've never hated you."

"You can't stand to be near me. It amounts to the same thing."

"No. It really doesn't."

"Then why? Why do you run away? Do I hurt you in some way?"

He went into the small, open kitchen, grabbed a few ice cubes, and wrapped them in a thin towel. "Here. This might help."

Nika took the towel and pressed it against the blisters, hiding the flinch of pain the pressure caused. "You didn't answer my questions."

He paced between the couch and the TV, back and forth, every movement jerky and agitated.

"Are you not even going to talk to me now?" she asked.

"Damn it, Nika, you need to stop pushing. I'm doing the best I can here, trying to keep myself under control."

"What do you mean? Why do you have to control yourself?"

"You really don't get it, do you?"

Nika shook her head. Her hair was nearly dry now, but still cool against her skin. "I would if you'd explain it to me."

He kept pacing, ignoring her. Nika was sick to death of being ignored. She'd spent years being talked about rather than being talked to. She'd wasted years trying to get the people around her to listen. She refused to sit quietly while she asked perfectly reasonable questions and was ignored.

Nika stood and put herself in front of him, barring his path. "Stop pacing and answer me. Why do you keep avoiding me?"

His mouth tightened like he was trying not to say anything, but in the end, the words won. "I avoid you because I want things from you that you can't give me. Because when I'm with you, I forget why I shouldn't just take them."

"What things? You've never asked me for anything."

"And I never will. It's just not right."

"What's not right?"

His jaw bunched and he looked away, deliberately ignoring her.

Something snapped inside Nika and let free a wave of anger so strong, it nearly made her sway with the force of it. She grabbed the front of his knit shirt, shoved her fist into his hard chest, and yelled, "I won't let you ignore me. I won't let you treat me like I'm not here. I matter, damn it. I may be crazy, but I *matter*."

He blinked in shock at her outrage. "Of course you matter. What the hell made you think you don't? You're one of the most important people on the face of the fucking planet. I'd do anything for you."

That last part doused her anger, stopping it cold. "You think I'm important?"

"Why the hell do you think I try so hard to stay away? There's some man out there somewhere who is going to find you and give you a kind of power you can only dream about—he's going to give you the power to take back what the Synestryn have stolen from you. I can't be the person who gets in the way of that, and if you don't get away from me, you're going to die before you can find him."

"What if *you're* that man? You're the only Theronai who I can stand to touch me. When you're around, I feel like myself—sane and safe. No one else makes me feel that way. Why can't it be you?"

Madoc's eyes closed in regret. She saw his throat move as if he was having trouble swallowing. He held out his hand, showing her the luminescent ring he wore. Gently, he wrapped his fingers around the fist she had tight around his shirt. The other ring—the cold black one—irritated her skin, but she ignored it.

"See?" he asked.

Nika looked at the ring. It was pale, almost white, and the few strands of color within it moved so slowly she had to stare hard to tell they were moving at all. "What am I looking for?"

"A change. Color. A feeling. Something. Anything. I've been looking for it since the day I met you and haven't seen a thing."

"So?"

"So, that means we're not compatible. I can't help you."

"Are you sure?"

He gave her a solemn nod.

She didn't want to believe him. She didn't want to imagine her life with another man—any man. She wanted Madoc.

"Maybe Gilda or one of the Sanguinar can fix it."

"There's nothing to be fixed. It's just the way things are. You have to accept it and move on."

"That's what Andra said about Tori. Sometimes, the way things look is not real. If I accepted that Tori was dead, then I'd be giving up on her, dooming her to die alone in the dark."

"Sometimes that's the way things are."

Nika shook her head. "Not with me, they aren't. I'm not giving up on Tori, and I'm not giving up on you."

"If you don't, I'm going to hurt you. I don't want to, but I will."

Nika shrugged. "Then I get hurt. It won't be the first time."

"And that is why I can't stay here. I can't stick around and make it easy for you to destroy yourself."

"If you leave again, I'll follow you. There's something wrong with you. I can see it. Something dark is growing inside you. Hurting you. You need me to protect you from it."

Madoc's green eyes widened and he took a long step back, wrenching her hand from his shirt. "You don't know what you're talking about. You don't see anything."

"I do. You can lie to yourself all you like, but I see the truth. You need me, and I'm not going to let you go."

He held up his hands and continued to back up. "Stay away from me. I mean it."

"If you leave, I'll find you."

"I go places way too dangerous for you."

"I'll still follow."

"I don't believe you."

Nika stood her ground. This was too important to let go. "Try me."

Chapter 6

Madoc didn't dare risk that Nika would follow through on her threat. He was still going to leave, but not until Andra knew the score. He'd make sure Andra kept her locked up nice and tight, where nothing could hurt her.

Something dark is growing inside you.

How could she know that? How could she see it?

Maybe the better question was, how could everyone else *not* see it?

Madoc reached for his cell phone, only to realize it was lying in pieces at the bottom of a garbage disposal in Nebraska. Fortunately, his freakish memory allowed him to have memorized every phone number he ever saw.

He went to the phone hanging on the wall in the kitchen and dialed Paul's cell phone. No answer. He dialed Andra with the same results, refusing to leave a message.

"They're gone," said Nika. She'd curled up on the couch, tucking her legs under her. Her pale hair fell just to her shoulders, sliding along the slim column of her throat.

She was heavier now than she had been months ago, her skin less pale. The distance he'd put between them had clearly been good for her. She'd filled out, was no longer a walking skeleton, and seemed lucid and healthy.

If he didn't get away from her soon, he'd do something to fuck that up and she'd be stark raving mad again before he could stop himself from making the mistake.

"Where did they go?" he asked.

"Check on the fridge. Andra always leaves me a note."

Madoc hadn't noticed the note before, but he found it, read it, and wanted to pound his fist into the stainless steel. "A little girl went missing last night in Ohio. Andra had to leave immediately to find her."

Nika nodded. "This happens all the time. I doubt we'll see her or Paul for a day or two."

Too long. That was way too long to stick around. He was going to have to find her another babysitter. "Who watches you when they're away?"

Her body stiffened in indignation. "No one. I am an adult."

"What about Grace?"

"She hasn't needed to take care of me for months. I'm better now, Madoc. Certainly well enough to take care of myself."

"So I keep hearing."

"Maybe you should listen."

Not likely. He'd seen what happened when Andra wasn't around—what that Theronai had done to her. The ice pack he'd made her covered the angry red blisters that fucker had left on her arm, but he still knew they were there.

He started forward, intending to lift the towel and check the damage, when he caught himself and stopped in his tracks. He was the last person on the face of the planet who should play nursemaid.

"I'm going to go talk to Joseph."

"Talk to him all you like. It won't change a thing. He can't make me stay here any more than you can. I'll go where I want, when I want. I have a lot of living to catch up on after all those years in the mental hospital."

"You're not going to catch up on anything if you get yourself killed."

"Then I die, but I'll do it living life my way. I deserve to make my own choices." She rose from the couch, yawning and stretching. The top of her shirt pulled up, exposing a narrow band of skin above her jeans.

Madoc's eyes were riveted to the sight. A faint shadow slid down the center of her stomach, deepening as it reached her navel. Her pants were loose on her hips, and he was sure that if he gave them the slightest tug, they'd go down without a fight, baring her so he could touch and taste. His mouth started to water and his hands lifted toward her before he realized what he was doing. He knew without a doubt that if he touched her, he'd lose control. He'd strip her naked, lay her out, and take her before anyone even had time to respond to her screams for help. For all he knew, people were used to her screaming delusions and wouldn't even bother to respond. He'd have all the time he needed to slake his lust and ease some of the pressure throbbing inside him.

The idea had way too much appeal, and part of him began calculating his odds of getting away with it. To hell with his honor. What good was it, anyway? It sure wasn't going to ease his pain, save his life, or keep his soul from dying.

A line of sweat broke out along his brow as he fought to remember what Iain had told him when he joined the Band of the Barren. *Pretend to be noble. Pretend you give a shit. It's the only way to keep from being sent to the Slayers.*

Would someone who was noble be figuring out how long it would take to get her naked? Would he be thinking about whether her screams for help would be answered before he could get off inside her?

The cold, dead spot where the last leaf of his lifemark hung on his skin seemed to buzz in irritation.

Maybe he should just rip the black ring Iain had given him—the one that slowed his soul's death—from his finger, and let the end come. He was so sick of fighting it, sick of keeping up with all the lies.

Iain had told him it wouldn't be easy, but he'd been pretending to be one of the good guys for years, and no one knew except those he'd recruited into the Band. He'd fooled everyone.

Maybe Madoc just wasn't cut out for this playacting shit. He was a walking menace to everyone around him.

Her voice barely filtered through the lust and anger pounding in his system. "Talk to Joseph if you want. Hunt down Andra. Do whatever it is you think you need to do. I'm too tired to stop you and not interested in wasting my energy. I need to rest up."

"For what?"

"For when I leave my body to find Tori. I'm going to try to talk to her again after I've slept."

Leave her body? Hell, no. "You're *not* going to do that thing again—that thing you did in the graveyard."

"It's cute you think you can stop me. Feel free to stay if you like and watch over my body."

Yeah, right. He knew exactly what he'd do to her if that happened. His dick was hard already, just thinking about it. "Not a smart idea," was all he could manage to choke out.

Nika gave him a sad smile. "Then go. I need to sleep."

Sleep. That was a good thing for her to do. Safe. So much better than leaving her body—however the hell that happened.

She moved toward him. Madoc moved out of her way. She shook her head in irritation as she passed him to throw the wet towel into the sink. "You really are afraid of me."

"I'm afraid *for* you. There's a difference." One he'd have to go into graphic detail to explain to her, so he really hoped she didn't start asking questions.

He should have fucked a whore before coming back here, like he'd planned, but the notion of Nika on the road alone had nagged at him, forcing him to follow in her wake in case her car ran out of gas or she got arrested for driving without a license.

Besides, no matter how many times he used a hooker, the pain would always come back. Relief was fleeting and tainted by the knowledge that the pain would return for him at any moment. Fearing that pain was sometimes worse than suffering through it. The best he could hope for was a distraction, and Nika certainly provided that.

"Go, Madoc. I'm tired of making you squirm. Just leave."

He'd hurt her feelings. He could hear it in her voice. He wanted to be sorry, and maybe part of him was, but the smarter part knew that if she hated him, she'd be a lot safer, so he walked out without bothering to offer an apology.

The farther away from her he got, the better off they'd both be.

Then why the hell wasn't he walking to his truck? Why was he headed back to his suite, where he planned to stay until he knew she was well guarded?

Leaving her body? Was she nuts?

A grim laugh rumbled in his chest. Of course she was nuts. That was the whole problem. She wasn't sane enough to leave alone, and she wasn't sane enough to stay away from him.

Clearly, he was crazy, too, because somewhere deep down, a part of him thought he could actually help her rather than just make things worse. If that didn't make him certifiable, he didn't know what would.

As exhausted as Nika was, she couldn't sleep. The pull of the monsters on her mind was weaker during the day, but there were a few Synestryn presences inside her that were strong enough to make themselves known even while the sun burned overhead. Usually, they didn't bother her, but she could feel one rousing from its sleep, poking at her, tentatively looking for weaknesses.

She tried to shut it out, put up her barriers, and sleep, but every time she closed her eyes, she saw the twisting, malignant darkness growing inside Madoc.

It hadn't been there the last time she saw him—at least not like this. Something was wrong and he was hiding it, even from her.

It was killing him.

She wasn't going to get any rest until she figured out what it was, and she really needed her rest if she was going to find Tori. The farther away she was from someone, the harder it became to find them as well as find her way back to her body. She didn't want to locate her sister only to find that she couldn't get back into her body and do anything with the information.

Besides, she worried that if she didn't make it back, her body would slip away and she'd be left to roam around, unseen and insubstantial, for eternity. The thought scared her almost as much as having her mind ripped apart by demons again.

Nika's grasp on reality was stronger now than it had been since the attack. She wasn't going to do anything to mess that up. Sleep was mandatory, and she knew the one person who could hold the Synestryn at bay long enough for her to get it.

She pulled her weary body from the bed, went to Madoc's quarters, and knocked on the door.

"Go away," came his gruff reply.

"Let me in."

"Not gonna happen. Go home."

Nika tried the door. It was locked, but she guessed that Nick or someone else was watching through the security cameras that covered every inch of the hallways. She went to the nearest one, looked into it, and said, "Open Madoc's door."

She had no idea if anyone heard or saw her, but when she got back to the door and saw the light turn green, she knew someone up there was watching.

The door opened two inches before Madoc's hand slammed against it and pushed it closed again. The light turned red.

"I'm going to kill Nicholas," growled Madoc.

"I need to see you."

Silence greeted her.

"Fine," she yelled through the door. "I'll just sit out here until you decide to let me in."

She heard something heavy being moved across the floor, then thud against the door. No more unlocked doors for her.

The rejection stung, but that was just too bad. Time to get over it already. She'd wait as long as it took. He had to come out sometime.

Nika put her back to the door and slid down to sit against it. The chilly air surrounded her, sliding easily through her thin cotton nightgown. She wished she'd thought to throw some clothes on before she came here, or at least a robe. Chances were that if she left now, Madoc would escape, jump in his truck, and it would be another seven months before she saw him again.

She feared that by that time, whatever it was that was growing inside him would consume him and there'd be nothing left of her Madoc.

Her Madoc. Nika snorted at that. He was no more hers than the moon was. She could enjoy being in its presence, but it was too far away to touch, always distant and cold.

At least when she was this close to him, she felt safe.

Fatigue pulled at her until she gave in and lay down, curled up in front of his door. If he left, she'd wake, and in the meantime, his presence nearby would guard her dreams and fight any Synestryn that dared to invade her mind while she slept.

Nika haunted him.

Madoc could not get her out of his mind. Part of him wanted to cradle her and hold her close, protecting her from the world's evils, but the rest of him wanted her writhing on his cock, screaming out her pleasure while he pounded into her.

He had no idea why he couldn't get her out of his mind—why one crazy woman had the ability to tie him up so completely, knotting his insides until the space between taking her and protecting her seemed too small a thing to care about.

Madoc lay on his bed, his erection rising from his naked body, throbbing in time with his pulse. He wrapped his fingers around himself as he imagined Nika sliding down his body, taking his cock in her mouth. Her white hair slid forward, tickling his thighs, while her big blue eyes stared up at him as she sucked him.

His phone rang, jerking him from his fantasy.

"What?" he snarled into the receiver.

"Nika's asleep outside your door," said Nicholas.

"Don't care." It was a huge lie, but one he was going to stand by.

"You need to let her in or take her back to her suite. You can't leave her lying out there with strangers who want to paw at her roaming the halls."

"Not interested. Do it yourself."

Nicholas's voice rose in irritation. "Anyone could come by."

"You can keep an eye out for her. It's not my job."

"You need to deal with her. Clearly, she has some reason to be hanging outside your door."

"She's crazy. No help for it."

"Damn it, Madoc! She's not even dressed. She's wearing a nightgown, all curled up like she's freezing."

"Get her a blanket."

"Don't you think that if I could touch her, I'd be out there already, taking care of her?"

The picture Nicholas painted made a protective rage swell up inside him, but he knew that if he opened that door, Nika was going to be the one to regret it. No one seemed to understand that like he did.

Of course, his cock thought opening the door was a great idea. She was all sleepy and vulnerable. He could lay her down on his bed and bury himself inside her before she even had time to wake up. If he covered her mouth, he could muffle the screams.

She might even like it. She sure as hell kept throwing herself at him enough to make him think she was asking for it.

Something in that logic was flawed, but with Nicholas's voice buzzing in his ear and Nika right outside his door, he didn't have enough mental space to figure out what it was.

Silence filled the line, like Nicholas was waiting for a response.

Pretend you have honor. The reminder rang inside Madoc's head.

A man with honor would not be thinking about fucking a crazy chick's brains out. He'd open the door, take Nika home, and tuck her safely into her own bed.

She'll just come back, a dark voice whispered inside him. *Why bother?*

Impatience rang in Nicholas's tone. "One of those foreigners is going to pass by and think he can touch her. Don't you think she's already blistered enough?"

"Call Joseph." If Madoc opened that door, he was going to bring her inside and hurt her a hell of a lot more than a few blisters could.

"Screw it. I'll do it myself."

"Good choice."

"You know, you're probably right. It's been a long time since I've seen any action. My cameras are pretty good, and I'd bet my favorite gaming PC that she's not wearing panties. I'll check and give you the juicy details later." The line went dead.

Rage poured into his system, making his head pound. Nika was his, damn it. No fucking way was Madoc going to let Nicholas get anywhere near her.

He dropped the phone and was off his bed before it hit the ground. He jerked the sheet from the bed, wrapped it around his hips, and shoved the kitchen table away from the door. It toppled over, hitting a wall hard enough to leave a dent in the drywall.

Madoc opened the door and saw Nika curled up in a tight ball. The racket he'd made getting to her hadn't even made her stir.

Something in the general vicinity of his chest broke open and bled as he looked at her. It was torture being so close to her, knowing it was wrong, knowing what he wanted to do.

But who else was there to take care of her? Her sister was gone. None of the other Theronai could touch her but him, and none of the humans here was strong enough to be entrusted with her care.

He was her only option, and as shitty as that was for her, they were stuck with each other. At least until the right Theronai came along. And he would. Madoc had to believe that as much as he dreaded it.

He picked her up, enjoying the weight of her in his arms, the feel of her against his bare chest. He would have liked it better if she'd been naked, but even with the barrier of cloth between them, the contact seemed to calm something raging inside him even as it tempted him to let his lust take the wheel.

Madoc kicked the front door shut behind him, laid her in his bed, covered her up to her chin, and left the room, shutting the door behind him. He knew that if he looked back, he'd climb right in that bed with her and find out firsthand whether she was wearing panties.

Pain hammered at his bones, and he knew that if he didn't do something to stop it, his body would fly apart. Mere flesh could not house so much pain. Every step he took away from her made it worse, so he didn't go far— just outside the bedroom door.

He unsheathed his sword, set it on the floor, and knelt beside it. Years of meditation allowed him to slide into that space where time became nothing and his body faded, along with the pain and lust that threatened to drive him mad. It would all be there, waiting for him when he was done, but until then, he would occupy this gray, meaningless place to keep Nika safe from himself.

Grace plastered a bright smile on her face and walked into Torr's suite. "How are you doing today?" she asked, trying to sound like her usual cheerful self.

"Better now that you're here," said Torr. The words were more slurred today than before, though whether that was because she was later than normal or because he was worse, she couldn't be sure.

He lay on a hospital bed in his living room. The standard furniture that had been shoved to the walls rather than removed was now gone. Grace had no idea who'd done it, but it made Torr's condition seem somehow worse. Instead of hoping that they'd find a cure and the bed would no longer be necessary, it seemed that now people were giving up on him, accepting that this was going to be the way things were for the rest of his long, long life. He'd given up on himself months ago. Maybe he didn't like the hopeful reminder.

His dark hair had grown out since the night of the

attack so that it was now long enough to cover his
ears. She secretly liked the new look and the way the
silky strands felt sliding between her fingers when she
groomed him. She'd kept his beard shaved for him,
though, relishing every moment she was allowed to
spend touching him.

His long body made him look thinner than he really
was, though he had lost a lot of weight. Muscles that had
grown hard with centuries of use had wasted away inhumanly fast, making him appear shriveled.

Grace still thought he was beautiful, especially his
pale amber eyes that followed her wherever she went.
Moving his head had become increasingly difficult for
him, but his eyes rarely left her, making her feel self-
conscious and alluring all at the same time.

She sat on the edge of the bed, taking his hand in hers,
even though she knew he couldn't feel it. "I wanted to
talk to you."

"Sounds serious."

She shook her head, feeling her curls bounce around
her shoulders. "Not really. I just . . . need to leave for a
little while."

"Where?"

"I need to take a little time for myself, maybe take
a trip to see the ocean. I've always wanted to see the
ocean." She'd probably never get to now, but the best
lies were those bathed in the truth.

"That's good. You should go."

Even as his words encouraged her, his eyes told another story. After so many months of seeing each other
every day, he'd probably grown as used to her visits as
she had. She was going to miss being able to touch him.

"I don't want to leave you," she told him. At least that
part was true.

"I can't go."

"I know. I'll miss you."

A faint smile lifted one side of his mouth. "Too fun
to miss me."

"I could never have that much fun."

His eyes slid over her features and she wondered if

he'd lose his ability to see, too, if this thing she was going to do didn't work.

"What?" he asked. "Something bothering you." His speech was more broken today. More halting.

"It's nothing," she lied. "I'm just worried about my brother. He's having some issues in his classes. It's no big deal. I'm sure he'll work through it."

"Wish I could help."

She stroked his hair away from his forehead, committing the feel of it to memory. She'd always have the memories of touching him to keep her company.

"You're going to get better," she told him, meaning every word. "You're going to help so many people, you won't even be able to remember all their names."

"Grace," he started. She knew where he was going and refused to let him. "Chances—"

"No. I don't want to hear about the chances you'll never get better. I believe in miracles. I have to. You *were* mine."

"Hero worship. Useless."

She did smile then. A real smile. "My case of hero worship has kept you shaved and fed. Don't knock it."

His eyes slid over her cheek and centered on her mouth. "Never."

Grace knew if she let herself, she'd stay here and put off what she knew she had to do. It was time.

Time to say good-bye.

"I'm going to change your sheets before I go to work my shift in the kitchen; then I'm going to hop in a car and drive until I see the ocean."

"Bring me a shell?"

"Two, if you're good."

She had mastered changing the sheets with someone lying in the bed while caring for her comatose mother. Torr was a lot heavier, but Grace had gotten stronger and managed it without trouble.

She was going to miss that strength.

While he was lying on his side, she slipped the palm-sized, pronged disk from her pocket and pressed it into his skin, right over the scar left by the creature that had paralyzed him. A drop of blood slid over his back, but she wiped it away on the dirty sheets.

On anyone else, the sharp, barbed prongs on the disk would have hurt going in, but Torr never felt a thing.

She finished her work and got Torr looking comfortable again. "Want to watch some TV?"

"No. Tired."

"I'll close the curtains, then, so you can sleep."

She pulled them shut over the sliders, dousing the room's only source of light. A thin strip of sunlight slipped under the curtains, guiding her feet.

Grace went back to Torr's side, and before she lost her nerve, she leaned down and kissed him, telling him without words how much she loved him. How much she was going to miss him.

His lips were cool, and she could feel him struggling to move them against hers—trying to deepen the kiss.

She didn't let him keep struggling. The wound to his pride would be too painful, and she didn't want that for him.

"Soft," he whispered, slurring the word.

Grace smiled down at him, committing his handsome face to memory. It was the one image she wanted to take with her and hold close.

"I love you," she said. She hadn't meant to admit it, but the words spilled out, the feeling too big and powerful to be denied a voice.

His pale eyes widened and his mouth moved as he started to say something.

Grace turned and ran. She didn't want to hear him tell her not to love him, that he could never love her back. She didn't want to hear him tell her that they had no future together. She *knew* that. She knew that he was an ancient warrior from a strong, magical race and she was a mere human. She knew she was a fleeting moment in his long life when he was the center of her short one.

She knew all these things and still couldn't stop herself from loving him.

Grace raced all the way back to the empty suite she'd prepared. The key card she'd stolen opened the lock without incident. It would have been nicer to do this in her own bed, surrounded by familiar things, but she didn't want her brother to find her. That wasn't fair to do to him after the difficult life he'd already had.

A swelling wave of fear broke inside her, making her hands shake. For a brief moment, she let herself consider turning back from her course.

But where would that leave Torr? At the rate he was going, he wouldn't even be able to swallow soon, wouldn't be able to talk. What kind of life was that? He had so much to offer the world—so many people who needed to be saved the way he'd saved her and her brother.

She owed him this. Even if she hadn't loved him, she had a responsibility to repay him for saving her and her brother's lives. She had a responsibility to the countless others he would save when he was whole and healthy.

Hesitating was the most selfish thing she'd ever done and she knew it.

Before she could lose her nerve again, Grace positioned the matching disk, sticking it to the wall with a glob of putty so it lined up just right. She stripped off her shirt and bra, moved so the prongs of the disk aligned against her spine, and shoved back with all her weight.

The metal teeth sank into her skin, stealing her breath with the pain. It streaked through her, consuming her world. Then, after a few moments, there was nothing. No pain, no feeling at all.

That nothingness began to spread down her spine, into her legs. Fast. Much faster than she'd expected.

She stumbled toward the mattress lying on the floor, where she had food and water stacked within reach. She'd hidden so no one could reverse the process until it was too late, but because of that, she didn't know how many days it would be until someone found her. It wouldn't do Torr any good if she died of dehydration before this magical device had finished its work.

She pulled a sheet up, covering her bare breasts, but even that small effort had left her panting. So much for her plans to drink and eat. She knew now that the pro-

cess was happening way too fast. Hopefully, it would finish before she died of thirst.

An odd, vibrating cold slid through her in the wake
of the numbness. It climbed up her body, inching higher
with every passing second. Soon, her ribs were gone, then
her shoulders. Her arms were next, then her fingers.

Fear and satisfaction mingled together, causing Grace
to panic even as she smiled.

It was working. Whatever had happened to Torr was
being transferred to her through the device Gilda had
given her. She was taking on his paralysis, freeing him.

She imagined the look of surprise on his face as the
feeling came back to his limbs. He'd be weak at first, but
he'd get strong fast. She knew he would. He'd be back to
his old life, wielding a sword against the demons before
her next birthday.

Tears slid from her eyes, wetting the hair at her temples. She was going to miss their time together so much.
She'd never again touch him or hold his hand or stroke
his hair.

And then she closed her eyes and saw his face and
felt the silky texture of his hair sliding through her fingers when she washed it, the rough stubble of his beard
when she shaved him. A hundred little memories were
right there, waiting for her to call on them and calm the
panic that weighed her down.

She might never walk again, never feel again, but
she'd always have the time they'd spent together to keep
her company.

Chapter 7

Carmen had never quite gotten used to sleeping during the day, but she did her best to keep the same schedule as the Theronai did—waking at night in order to fight the Synestryn. Of course, they didn't need nearly the same amount of sleep she and the humans did, and Joseph seemed to sleep even less than the rest of his kind. Whether it was because he didn't need it, or because there was simply no time, she wasn't sure.

It was late afternoon when she finally got the courage to seek Joseph out in his office. She knew he'd be awake and busy, but this was important.

It was time to suck it up, be brave, and let him read the note that Thomas had written nine months ago on the night he died. If it said horrible things about her, so be it. Carmen needed to move on with her plans, and this was the last thing holding her back.

She knocked on the open door. Joseph's head came up, and when he saw her, he smiled.

"Is it time for our training session already?" he asked, frowning at his watch.

"No, I came to give you this." She held the letter out to him. It was a small bit of paper, folded and smudged with a drop of dried blood. It was wrinkled and worn from the hours she'd spent holding it, trying to find some connection to the man who had changed her life. He was dead now, but she liked to think that part of him lived on in her.

She was determined to make Thomas proud, wherever he was, which was why she'd spent hours every

week training to become a warrior. She'd never be as
strong as the Sentinels, or have any kind of magic power,
but she'd worked her ass off to learn to do the best job
she could. After nearly a year of training, she felt it was
time to move into the field and start hunting.

Joseph took the note. His long fingers slid over the
drop of dried blood reverently, as if he were remembering his fallen brother. "Are you sure?"

Carmen nodded. "It's time."

He unfolded the paper easily. She almost laughed, considering how many times she'd tried to do that very thing,
only to have her hands go still and start shaking. She'd
told Thomas she'd let Joseph read it first, and no matter
how hard she tried, she couldn't break that promise.

Joseph's hazel eyes scanned the page. There was no sign
of emotion on his face. No revulsion, no disappointment.
Nothing but a carefully controlled blank expression.

"Well?" she asked, twisting in anticipation.

Joseph's throat worked as he swallowed before speaking. "He was a good man. I forget sometimes how good."

"Tell me."

Joseph read from the paper: "'Claim this woman as your
kin. Protect her as you would your own flesh and blood. All
I possess is now hers to do with as she sees fit.'"

Shock and outrage slammed over Carmen, knocking
her into a chair. "How could he?"

Joseph's brows drew together in confusion. "How
could he what?"

She gripped the arms of the chair, trying to push herself up, but all her strength was gone. "Claim me? Like
I'm some kind of prize? What the hell was he thinking?"

"That you needed protection. That I would be able
to provide it."

"You didn't even know me. You hardly know me
now." He sure as hell didn't know about what a slut she'd
been all her life. Shame had forced her to hide that from
him. "How could he think to ask you to do something
like this?"

Joseph moved around his desk toward her. "It's no
big deal. I've been treating you like a daughter since you

walked through our door. It won't change anything between us other than to make our relationship official."

"No. I don't need another father. The one I had was bad enough. And I already experienced the joy of being given to an uncle who didn't want the burden of raising another kid. I'm nineteen, perfectly capable of taking care of myself, and don't need anyone pitying me."

"This isn't about pity. Thomas cared about you enough to see to your safety as well as your future."

Anger erupted inside her, making her shake. She pushed herself up, getting in Joseph's face. "Of course it's about pity. Thomas saw me as some sort of charity case. Poor, slutty little girl with no one to love her. Screw that!"

Joseph's frown deepened. "Slutty? What are you talking about?"

She wasn't going to tell him how she'd thrown herself at Thomas. How he'd known she was so desperate that he'd felt the need to guilt her into keeping her legs closed.

Carmen shook her head. "You don't know me at all. I suppose it's best that way."

"I know you better than you think. We've spent hours together. I've seen your strength and courage and so much stubbornness you could easily be my daughter. I've been known to have a bit of a hard head myself."

"No. This isn't going to happen." She was not going to be anyone's charity case, tied to someone out of guilt and some stupid tradition. She was not going to be handed off to yet another man who didn't want to have anything to do with her.

"Too late. It already has. This is Thomas's death wish, and I'm honor-bound to uphold it. From now on, you're my daughter, and I plan to make sure everyone knows it."

Nika woke up suddenly, as if someone had shouted her name. It wasn't the first time this had happened. She'd felt this before when someone was in need.

She opened herself up, reaching out with her mind to find the source of that need. Maybe Tori had called for her and was ready to let her in again.

Nika lay quiet and still in a bed not her own. Madoc's

scent clung to the sheets, comforting her, making her feel stronger, braver.

Nika! The call came again. It was a ragged cry of pain, tight with fear and so powerful it left her mind reeling.

It wasn't Tori. For a moment, Nika suffered a stab of disappointment until she realized the masculine nature of that cry for help. It was Madoc.

She flung the covers off and hurried toward him, desperate to get to him before it was too late. Whatever was wrong was killing him, sapping his strength and his will to live.

Sunlight filtered in through heavy curtains covering the windows, allowing her to see where she went.

Nika didn't have to go far—just into the next room. He was lying on his side on the living room floor right outside the bedroom door. His body curled in on itself, shaking with pain. His sword lay within arm's reach, unsheathed, as if he'd been intending to use it. A sheet was twisted about his hips, but the rest of him was beautifully bare, displaying powerful muscles that tightened and bunched as they clenched in his sleep.

Suddenly, the urge to touch him was irresistible. Her hands began to shake against the need to slide over his naked skin. Her body warmed until she was sure her nightgown would lift off of her body from the waves of heat radiating out from her. Not that she'd mind if it did. The idea of pressing herself against him while naked made her nipples tingle and tighten. She'd never felt this way about anyone before in her life, and it was as unsettling as it was exciting.

She knelt beside him and splayed her trembling hand on his shoulder.

The warmth of his skin always shocked her, and for a moment, she closed her eyes and let that delicious heat sink into her. She spread her hands flat and let them slide over the masculine contours of his body, touching him as he'd never allowed her to do while he was awake.

She didn't know why he avoided her touch, but right now, that hardly seemed to matter in the face of so much sensation. Her body was rejoicing, every cell singing in praise as it soaked in his heat. She could get lost in the sensation of flesh on flesh, though something in the back of her mind warned her that wasn't why she was here. She had a job to do, but couldn't quite remember what it was.

The curve of his shoulder was hard and smooth. It led to his thick neck, where the luminescent band of his luceria lay against his skin. The necklace shimmered in time with the beat of his heart, drawing her eye, making her ache for something she couldn't name.

Andra wore Paul's luceria now, and everyone here had told her that when she found the right man, she'd wear his, too.

She wanted Madoc to be that man, despite his abrasive nature. Despite the fact that he didn't want her.

Nika slid her finger over the band, enjoying the slippery feel of it, wishing it was hers and that she could keep it against her skin forever.

Surely that feeling wasn't normal. She'd never felt that way toward any of the other Theronai who'd come to her over the past few months. She'd never been drawn to them, wishing for things that had no names, feeling the loss of their presence when they left her side. Only Madoc made her feel that way.

Maybe he was wrong about their not being right for each other. Maybe if she tried, she could prove to him they were compatible. Maybe then he wouldn't mind being near her.

She gave the luceria an experimental tug. Andra had told her all about how she'd done the same and Paul's luceria had fallen off easily.

Madoc's didn't budge.

She pulled harder, but all she seemed to do was make the section where her fingers touched fade even more, losing the color Madoc seemed to think was so important.

Defeat made Nika's body slump, driving the air from her lungs. She wanted so much to feel like she belonged in this world—that she was more than just the crazy girl no one could touch. She'd come so far, fighting every day to regain another slice of herself. She'd forced herself to eat and get stronger, to get out of bed and explore her new home. But she'd never truly fit in here. She wasn't human, and yet she wasn't a Theronai, either. At least, not one who was able to fight the war that raged on in secret outside these walls.

She'd spent most of her life as a useless drain on her sister. The only person who'd ever truly needed her was Tori, and now she was pulling away, too.

After so many years of being with Tori through all the horrible things she'd endured, Nika wasn't sure she even knew how to be alone. If Tori abandoned her, what would she do?

Nika wasn't going to let it happen. She was going to bring Tori home, where they could be together all the time. She'd take care of her the way Andra had taken care of Nika. They'd be a family again.

As the image appeared in her mind, Madoc was part of it. In her fantasy world, he would become part of their family, too, the way Paul had.

Of course, fantasy and reality were two different things, and after the years she'd spent learning to separate the two, Nika knew the chances of that happening were slim. His luceria didn't respond to her, and if he didn't find the woman who could make it respond soon, he was going to die. *That* was reality.

His lifemark was nearly bare and completely still. She'd seen the other men's trees sway with the breeze outside, but not Madoc's. Almost all the leaves had fallen, and those that were left seemed . . . wrong. They were flat. Dead.

She knew that losing all the leaves on his lifemark was a bad thing. It meant his time was nearly up. Once the last leaf fell, his soul would begin to die and he would go to his death—one way or another.

The thought of no more Madoc in her life scared Nika more than any Synestryn she'd ever encountered. She needed him, and her hope was that one day he'd need her, too—that she'd be more to him than just some crazy woman he had to protect.

Her tactile journey led her down his right arm to his wide, calloused palm and thick, blunt fingers. Small scars dotted the backs of his hands and forearms—a testament to his years in battle. Strength radiated out from his hand, even in sleep. She'd often envied the strength of the men around her, but with Madoc, envy was never a problem. With him, she felt something different, deeper. It wasn't so much that she wanted to have his strength as it was that she wanted that strength to touch her, surround her, and keep her safe.

But now, holding his hand in hers, all she could think about was what it would feel like for him to touch her. Like a woman. Like Paul touched Andra when he thought Nika wasn't looking.

A slow, needy kind of heat built up inside her at the thought. She'd never been with a man before. Her curiosity had driven her to watch other couples—to slide inside their minds to see what it was they hid from her behind closed doors. She'd learned so many secret things that way, but never before had she thought she might like having someone do those things to her. Until now.

An image of Madoc's hands moving over her naked body filled her mind. She could almost feel him cup her breasts, feel him grip her hips as his powerful body moved against her. Inside her.

Desire swelled inside her until she wasn't sure her body could hold it. An odd fluttering tickled her lower abdomen, and her grip on Madoc's hand tightened.

One way or another, before Madoc ran away again, she was going to seduce him. She had no idea how she would manage it, but she'd find a way. He was going to be hers, even if she could keep him for only one night.

Nika lifted his hand and pressed it against her cheek. His fingers felt good, but the ugly matte black ring he wore seemed to dig into her skin. That ring was cold, despite his body heat, and it irritated her skin. Surely the thing was uncomfortable for him to wear.

Nika hated touching it, but she grabbed the ring and started to pull it off when he moaned in his sleep, reminding her why she was here. It certainly wasn't so she could fondle him.

He needed her. He'd called out to her, and she'd been so distracted by his body she'd nearly forgotten.

She guessed that calling for help was something he'd do only while asleep, when his sense of pride was dampened, and there was no way Nika could deny him. She knew their fates were tied together, even if he and everyone else refused to believe her. Even if that blasted luceria didn't believe her. She *knew*.

The fact that he needed her even a little made her feel stronger than she had in years. She wasn't going to let him down.

Nika released her mental guards, abandoned caution, and flung herself from her body into his.

Pain slammed into her, nearly knocking her back out of his mind. Screaming agony writhed inside him, scraping at his mind with sharp claws, shredding his soul until it bled.

She had no idea how he could stand it. Clearly, this was why he'd called for her. The Synestryn were doing something to him, torturing him.

The fact that she'd taken time to touch him when he was suffering like this made her want to shrivel in self-disgust. How could she have been so selfish?

She had to help, but she couldn't possibly fight pain this intense, so instead, she tried to accept it and let it slide over her.

It didn't work. The pain pounded into her, battering at her as it tried to drive her back. A part of her huddled against the pain, weeping in despair of ever escaping it. If her body were here, it would have been ripped to shreds, torn into pieces too small to ever be put back together. How Madoc could survive it, she had no idea, but she knew she had to help him. She couldn't let him endure this on his own.

She forced herself to relax more, to let the pain slide past her like water, leaving her unaffected. She imagined herself as a tiny pinpoint of nothingness—too small to be a threat, with no surface for the pain to push against.

Slowly, the agony began to fade. The dark talons scraped by her, missing the tiny little bit of nothing she had become. The power of that pain still pushed against her, forcing her to go along with it, but she could concentrate now and find the source.

It was like swimming against a current, and each bit

of progress she made was hard-won and exhausting. Slowly, she inched toward the source of his pain, determined to slay it. After what seemed like days, she eventually made her way to the source.

Before her loomed something she'd never seen before in any of the people she'd visited. It was huge. Powerful. Hundreds of tentacles had sprouted from a pulsing, black mass to weave through Madoc like acidic vines. Everywhere they were, there was pain—waves of it radiating out so that no part of him went without agony.

As she neared, the tendrils seemed to reach for her as if drawn to her presence inside him. Whatever these things were, they *knew* her. She could feel it—sense their hunger to touch and possess her.

How was she going to fight something like that?

She had no clue, but the only hope she had was to follow one of the tendrils back to the center of the mass and slaughter it.

Moving along, evading the twitching movements of the tendril, she watched as it grew thicker and stronger the farther she went. It lunged toward her, but she flinched away, dodging it. She didn't know what would happen if one of these things got hold of her, but she wasn't willing to risk it to find out.

Slowly, she fought her way against the current of pain until she saw the center mass of this . . . thing. There was one small spot that was different from the rest—one bright, glowing patch the color of summer sunshine.

Nika was drawn toward that spot, unable to stop herself from moving nearer, from reaching out to brush against it and bathe in that light.

The tiny speck that was now her consciousness slid into that light, and instantly, she felt a sense of utter contentment. Complete and perfect peace. This warm, glowing light engulfed her, cradled her, and held her close. It whispered to her of hope, love, and joy, and she believed every word it spoke into her. She could stay here for the rest of her life and be happy. Here, she needed nothing. Time meant nothing. All the trials of the world fell away. Here, she was literally in love.

It was at that moment that she realized where she was. This black mass of wicked tentacles with its one single, perfect spot was Madoc's soul.

Shock rippled through her, but it was distant enough that she wasn't bothered like she knew she should be. There was something wrong here—something she wasn't seeing, but the urge to ignore that and simply bask in the light was nearly impossible to fight.

Nika spun around, feeling like a child with no worries in the world. The edges of this glowing spot drew inward, shrinking around to hold her close.

That was when the realization hit her. This perfect shiny spot in Madoc's soul was shrinking. The festering black agony was eating away at it, consuming the light, snuffing it out.

His soul was dying despite the fact that there were still leaves on his lifemark.

Horror exploded within her, sending her reeling. It yanked her out of that bright, perfect place, through the hideous, writhing tentacles, and back into her own body.

". . . hell do you think you're doing?" Madoc's angry voice filled her ears, too loud and grating.

She flinched away from the noise, wishing she could go back into the blissful silence.

"You were inside my head, weren't you?"

Her throat was too tight to speak, so Nika shook her head.

"Don't lie to me. I felt you in there. Were you trying to read my mind?" His green eyes were bright with rage and his chest rose and fell with every angry breath.

Nika struggled to rejoin reality. She couldn't tell how long she'd been out of her body, but the effort of sustained contact had left her drained and confused. It seemed odd and slightly wrong to feel things through her senses again. Everything was harsher and more intense. Even the feel of her nightgown against her skin seemed too much to bear. The dim light in the room could not compare to that of Madoc's soul, and yet it was too bright, burning her eyes.

She felt his hand grip her shoulders and wanted to

lean into his embrace and let him hold her until the world righted itself again.

"Answer me," he demanded.

"No. Not your mind," she tried to explain, but how could she? If he was angry because he thought she'd read his mind, he'd be furious to know she'd been inside his very soul. "You called for me."

"I did not." Indignation clipped his words, making them come out short and hard.

"You did. I was asleep, but I heard you. You called my name and I came."

"You dreamed it."

Fatigue pulled at her, weighing her down. Explaining was too much work. Besides, he wouldn't believe her. People never believed her. It was easier not to say anything and let them think she was crazy. "Maybe I did. There was too much pain for it to have been real."

"Pain?" The word seemed to choke him. "Are you hurt?" His green eyes were bright with concern as they roamed over her body, checking for injury.

"Not me. You."

He let out a sigh of relief and pulled her close, hugging her against his bare chest. His palm cradled her head, holding it close to his heart. She could sense the branches of his lifemark struggling to reach for her, but they remained frozen in place beneath her cheek.

Nika snuggled closer, crawling into his lap, holding on to him in case he spazzed again and tried to push her away. His scent calmed her nerves. His heat eased her skin until her nightgown was no longer grating against it. Even her fatigue seemed to fade as she soaked in his body's heat.

"You're making me crazy," he said in a quiet voice.

"It's not so bad. You might even like it."

"Don't joke. This is no time for jokes."

She pulled away enough to look up at him. His expression was tight. Closed. She stroked the side of his face, enjoying the feel of his beard stubble beneath her fingertips. "You're too serious. Life is short. You should enjoy it."

"Enjoying things my way would be a really bad idea for you." He was staring at her mouth now, making Nika nervous enough that she felt the compulsion to lick her lips.

His eyes followed the movement. His body clenched, and as close as she was to him, she could feel the strength of that motion as it shook her. Against her hip, she felt his penis harden.

"You like me," she said, hearing her awe shine through in her voice.

"That isn't about like, little girl."

The *little girl* comment stung, but maybe that had been a childish way of putting it. She wasn't exactly used to talking to a man about sex, so she tried again. "You want me."

"I *want* you to get off of my lap." He tried to shift her away from him, but she held on, clinging to his neck. She liked feeling the proof that he wanted her, and she hadn't felt it quite long enough to believe it yet. What she really wanted to do was touch his erection with her fingers, but she didn't think he was ready for that yet. It seemed a little forward.

"Why can't you admit it?" she asked. "We're both adults. We're allowed to want each other, right?"

His lips flattened out. "Time to get you back home."

"I'm staying here until I'm ready to go. We have important things to discuss."

"The hell you are."

"Why? Are you afraid I'll invade your brain and turn you into my mindless zombie slave?"

"Hardly." He got up and set her away from him, then fled across the room. He kept the sheet bunched around his hips with one hand while scrubbing the other over his face. The whole time, he refused to look at her.

"I guess I was mistaken about the fact that you like me. You might want me, but you don't like wanting me. I get that. But it's not like I'm going to attack you. Give me one good reason why I can't stay. You keep saying you're going to hurt me, but you've never even come close, despite all your bluster and that potty mouth of yours." Nika sat on the floor, watching him, waiting for an answer.

"Keep pushing and you'll find out the hard way."

"Please," she scoffed. "I've been *inside* monsters scarier than you on your best day."

"I doubt that."

She got up off the floor and walked over to where he was standing. Maybe getting into his face wasn't the smartest thing she could do, but she was tired of his running away.

She pushed him until he stumbled back onto the couch, and leaned down until she was at eye level with him. "I'm sure you do. I'm sure you think that you're big and tough and mean and the world will come crashing to an end if you have to be stuck with me for one more minute."

"Not the world, Nika. *Your* world."

"Why? What do you think you're going to do to me that's so bad?"

He didn't answer, and his silence pissed her off. Self-control had never been her strong suit, and right now, it was nowhere to be found.

She reached down, grabbed him by his luceria, and gave him a shake. "Answer me! What do you think you're going to do that's so horrible?"

He wrapped his fingers around her wrist. Beneath his grip, her skin tingled, but she was too busy reeling from the ferocity he displayed to pay much attention. He bared his teeth and said, "I'm going to fuck you."

Shock rattled her for a moment, and she found her mind reeling to make sense of his words.

That wasn't the way Nika would have worded it, but she found his harsh language didn't put her off. In fact, that slow, simmering heat inside her that had started when she'd fondled him in his sleep was bubbling up again suddenly, making her feel warm and tingly.

He'd thought about making love to her, and that idea thrilled her to her toes.

"Okay," said Nika, sounding breathless.

Madoc blinked. "Okay? I say I'm going to rape you and that's all you have to say?"

"It wouldn't be rape."

"The hell it wouldn't."

Nika had never seduced a man before, but she had a few ideas about what might work.

She let go of his luceria, slid her hands over his shoulders, and straddled his lap. The hem of her nightgown slid up, revealing her thighs. Madoc looked at them, then shut his eyes tight.

He grabbed the couch cushions on either side of her, gripping the fabric as if it were the only thing keeping him from flying out into orbit.

"I've thought about being with you," she admitted. "Not at first, when I was sick, but lately, I'd hear Paul and Andra going at it, or see another couple looking at each other in a certain way. It always made me think of you."

"You're just saying that so I won't take you home, though God only knows why you want to be around me."

"I'm saying that so you'll get over yourself and realize that I have opinions of my own. I'm not that fragile shell of a woman you left behind last year."

"This isn't funny, Nika."

"No, it's not. It's sad, because you've been afraid of something that wasn't a problem."

"The hell it's not a problem. You have no idea what you're talking about. I bet you're still a virgin."

"Yeah. So?"

He lurched up from the couch, set her down, and moved away from her so fast, she lost her grip on him. His gait was awkward, and he kept that sheet held in his fist so tight his knuckles turned white.

With his eyes wide and his jaw clenched, he said, "You need to leave."

"I thought we'd just decided I didn't need to. You don't have to be afraid to hurt me anymore. I want to have sex with you."

His whole body clenched like she'd hit him, and he spun around, giving her his back. "Leave. Before it's too late."

Instead, Nika walked up to him and wrapped her arms around him, pressing her chest against his wide back. Beneath her cheek, his whole body vibrated with tension. "I want to stay."

"I'm not going to take any virgins."

"If that's really such a big problem for you, then I'll go find one of the teenage boys downstairs, take care of the problem, and be back in ten minutes. I understand from gossip that they don't take long to finish."

He turned around, but she didn't let him go. He spun inside her embrace until she could feel his erection pressing against her belly. Those tinglies started to expand into something more. Something needy and hard to ignore.

"You do that, and Joseph will have to execute me for murdering a kid."

He wasn't lying. She could see the fury in his face, feel it shimmering in his body. She remembered the black mass of his soul—saw it reflected in the ferocity in his eyes, and knew that she had to do something to fix it.

Unfortunately, she had no clue what that something might be.

"So what you're saying is that you don't want me, but I can't be with anyone else? Should I stay a virgin forever?"

"Works for me."

"Are you really that selfish?"

"I won't be alive much longer. Just wait until I'm dead. That's all I ask."

"No. I'm not making you any stupid promises. I've wasted enough of my life locked in a hospital. I won't let you or anyone else get in the way of me living."

"What I'd do to you would not be something you'd remember fondly."

"How do you know? What if you're the only man who can ever touch me?"

His eyes squeezed shut as if he needed to block out the sight of her. "Please. Don't let me hurt you. I don't want to hurt you."

"You won't. This feeling we have for each other, it

proves I'm right. You and I belong together. You were looking for some kind of feeling when we touched. I'd say this counts."

"Then why didn't my luceria come off when you pulled on it?"

"I don't know, but I have an idea."

Madoc groaned and stared at her mouth. "Please, Nika. You're killing me."

She pushed him down to the couch, and like a fool, he let her.

"Maybe if you kiss me, it will come off."

"That's not the way it works."

"Maybe you should kiss me anyway."

If Madoc kissed her, he knew how it would end. He'd rip that flimsy bit of fabric from her body and take her right here on his living room floor. Despite her innocent protestations to the contrary, that was not what she wanted.

She deserved to be cherished and treated with care. Loved. He couldn't give that to her. There wasn't enough left of the man he used to be to give her anything that even approached love. The best he could even hope for was to fuck her fast enough that she wouldn't suffer long.

Nika stared into his eyes, looking like she meant what she said. He knew better, but he couldn't blame her for her ignorance.

She was a virgin, and she was squirming on his lap like she didn't even know what came next.

Holy hell. She was going to blow his mind if she didn't stop moving. He'd just explode into a bloody mess and they'd be mopping what was left of him off the ceiling for a week.

He needed to get out of there. Put some distance between them. Go kill shit. Something.

Pretend you have honor.

It had never been harder to follow Iain's teachings than it was now, with this willing woman so close and eager for him to kiss her.

An honorable man would have known that her kisses

belonged to another and respected that. So that was what he was going to do. He was going to move away, walk out the door, and leave. Only this time, he wasn't coming back. If he did, he knew what he'd do. He knew Nika would be the one to pay.

His time was up. He'd had a good run. Killed lots of snarlies. He'd even managed to kill enough sgath that Nika was no longer quite so fucked in the head. Sure, she wanted to screw him—which meant she was still crazy—and had a tendency to leave her body, but at least she didn't spend all her time afraid anymore.

He'd done that for her. He could die knowing he'd accomplished at least that much.

He'd also die without knowing what it was like to kiss her—really kiss her. He'd die never getting to hear her cries of release, or feel her slick heat around him. But he'd also die never having caused her to scream in pain he caused. That was worth suffering through this non-stop erection he was sporting.

Madoc ignored the pain pounding in his body and slid out from under Nika, knocking her sideways onto the couch.

The look of hurt shining in her pale blue eyes made his stomach clench, but there was nothing he could do about that. He hoped that one day, when she finally found her Theronai, she'd look back on this and thank him for walking away.

Madoc grabbed the clothes he'd tossed onto the floor and left, shutting the door behind him. A few seconds later, he'd dressed in the hall and was headed for Tynan. He'd give the bloodsucker the blood Nika needed for her quest so she wouldn't be forced to beg for help, then leave behind his death wish—a wish the Theronai would be honor-bound to carry out. Whatever the hell that might be.

The only thing he really wanted he couldn't have.

Time to get over it already. Once he was dead, he wasn't going to miss a single fucking thing.

He felt naked and off balance without his sword. It had been strapped around his hips for centuries, ready and willing to shed Synestryn blood. Without it, he hardly even felt like a Theronai at all.

Madoc had knocked on Tynan's door three times before the leech finally answered. He shoved his way into the Sanguinar's suite, held out his arm, and said, "Take what you need to help Nika."

Tynan's ice blue eyes flared with hunger, but he didn't move. "This is becoming a habit with you—bleeding for that woman."

"You complaining? I can find someone else to bleed me."

"No. Not at all. Just an observation." He waved to the couch. "Sit."

Madoc sat and stared off into space. He didn't want to see what the leech did to him. The idea of a guy sucking on his wrist was about more than he could stand. He wouldn't have done it for anyone but Nika.

Nika.

He could have had her. She wanted him. Or at least she thought she did.

Maybe she did. Maybe she was one of those chicks who got off on the darker side of him. Wouldn't be the first time he'd seen it. Now that he was away from her, he was more in control of himself. Maybe if he went back, he could find a way to be gentle. Sweet.

And then what? He'd fuck her, then go kill himself? Nika was already crazy. He wasn't sure how that kind of thing would set her off. For all he knew, she'd blame herself—think she was so awful she had to commit suicide to fix it.

Best to leave well enough alone. He'd found the strength to walk away. He didn't know if he could do it a second time.

Walking away was his last gift to her and he was determined to make it stick.

Chapter 8

Tynan willed Madoc to sleep with a single, powerful thought as he fed from the Theronai's vein. Madoc drifted off easily, not even bothering to fight him, as Tynan had expected.

Something here was definitely not right.

Part of Tynan didn't care. Power coursed through his body, making him feel strong and solid. He knew this heady rush wouldn't last—that he had to share this power with others of his kind—but that didn't mean he couldn't enjoy it now, for the brief time it lasted.

Madoc's blood was nearly as powerful as that of Lucien, one of the full-blooded princes of Athanasia—a distant world that was the source of the Sentinels' magic. Lucien had come here last summer to see his daughters. Tynan had been weak then—too weak to keep going. He was ready to seek his rest in the chambers below Dabyr when Lucien had offered to feed him.

For those few, brief moments, Tynan had understood what his life would have been like had his kind not been banished, cursed, and cut off from the source of their power. Had his grandfather the Solarc not been a greedy, megalomaniacal bastard, none of Tynan's kin would be starving or weak. They'd have more than enough blood to ensure their survival as well as that of their children.

But the Solarc was not kind. He was not forgiving. He'd decreed the gate between their worlds closed, and now, millennia later, all the Sanguinar suffered for a mistake their fathers made before they were even born.

There was no sense in dwelling on that which could not be altered. The best he could hope for now was to help his people survive long enough to see Project Lullaby to its completion. Once the strongest of the human bloodlines was restored, there would be enough power to feed the Sanguinar. They'd never be the powerful creatures they'd been created to be, but at least they'd live without constant hunger.

At least then there'd be enough food to go around for some of them to have children of their own.

After so many centuries of experiencing nearly everything life had to offer, the only thing Tynan truly wanted was a child of his own. Until he could be sure that child would not suffer from starvation, he'd vowed not to bring a life into this world.

The temporary high of consuming Madoc's blood made breaking his vow tempting, but he'd fought temptation often enough that he did so now with hardly a conscious thought. It was better to focus on the immediate things surrounding him and leave his dreams for the times when he needed something to distract him from the hunger.

As a matter of habit, Tynan used a small amount of the power flowing into him to read Madoc's mind. What he found left him deeply concerned.

Madoc was going to kill himself. Tonight.

Tynan couldn't let that happen. Madoc's blood was too rich, its power too recently tapped to let him waste it in death. He knew the leaves on the Theronai's lifemark were fake—painted there by someone Tynan could not quite see—but there was something else about him that Tynan had sensed last year, when Madoc had shared his blood for the first time in order to save Nika's life.

There was a dark energy hovering about Madoc, close to his skin. He couldn't tell exactly what it was or where it came from, but he knew what it did. It kept Madoc's last leaf suspended on his skin, unable to completely fall.

If any of the other Theronai found out about this, they'd have Madoc killed.

Tynan wasn't going to let that happen, either.

The only solution was to save the man's life, and the only way to do that was to find his female counterpart.

Nika, perhaps? Tynan wasn't sure. The two hadn't spent much time together, from what he could tell, and even if they had, the manifestation of signs of compatibility could very well be obscured, not only by the fact that his lifemark was bare, but also by whatever energy it was that kept that last leaf frozen in stasis.

Without experimentation, Tynan couldn't be sure what to think. The only thing he knew for sure was that Madoc needed to live. If he had to experiment to make that happen, then he would, even if it meant suffering through the horror of drinking Nika's blood.

The single drop he'd consumed last year had nearly driven him mad in the space of a few brief seconds.

Just the thought of having his mind shattered like that again was enough to make Tynan shake. If it hadn't been for years of mental control, he would still be screaming from that one drop, locked inside that nightmare she endured. Unless, of course, it had simply killed him.

He'd warned all his brethren that her blood was tainted and that they should avoid taking it unless the circumstances were dire.

Madoc's death qualified as dire. His blood could feed Tynan's kind for years. That alone was worth Tynan's risking his life.

He dialed Logan. It was still daylight outside, so he had to let the phone ring, then dial again before Logan was able to rouse himself from the grip of sleep.

"I need you to come home," he told Logan.

"Why? I thought you wanted me to follow Iain to see if I could retrieve one of the Synestryn offspring."

"Something more important has come up. I'll send someone to take your place. How far away are you?"

"Three hours." Logan's voice was thick with sleep.

Tynan looked at Madoc sprawled on his couch. "Try to hurry."

"What's going on, Tynan?"

He didn't want to say too much over the phone. He

didn't trust that Nicholas or one of the other Theronai wouldn't be listening in on his call. They had all kinds of technological gadgets Tynan didn't understand. "I need you here in case things go wrong. In case I need my second-in-command to perform his duties."

When Logan spoke again, all signs of sleepiness were gone from his voice. "What are you planning?"

"Something necessary."

"I'm leaving now," said Logan.

"It's still light out."

It had been several years since sunlight had touched a Sanguinar's skin, causing one of the Solarc's Wardens to come hunting for blood and retribution. Everyone wanted to keep it that way.

"I'll be careful. Wait for me, okay?"

Tynan hung up the phone without answering him. He'd wait as long as he could without risking Madoc.

In the meantime, he had plenty of uses for Madoc's power. First, he was going to tweak the cure he'd been working on to reverse the Theronai's infertility so the next batch of serum was ready to test on Angus. Next, he was going to muck around inside Madoc's thick skull and do his best to remove the Theronai's plan to kill himself. Then he was going to figure out whether the femur Nika had brought him could have belonged to her sister. He hoped not, because it could mean another female Theronai was out there somewhere.

If he could get the Theronai breeding again and help pair up another two couples, that would go a long way toward saving his people from starvation. Of course, he had about three hours to do whatever he was going to do before risking his life by taking Nika's blood.

He truly hoped Madoc stayed asleep long enough for him to finish his work. He'd seen the way the man looked at Nika, and he did not want to be on the receiving end of Madoc's fury.

Nika stayed in Madoc's suite after he left. She liked it here. Even if he couldn't stand to be near her, she liked being surrounded by his things. His presence filled the space, cradling her body while she went seeking her sister with her mind.

If Tori was out there, she was unreachable. Nika didn't know if her sister had completely pulled away, or if the magic that had been embedded into the very walls of Dabyr somehow prevented her from making contact.

Nika could still feel that Tori was alive, but that faint pulse of life was so weak that unless she was touching it, it was easy to think she'd imagined it was still there.

If Nika didn't get to her soon, she was afraid her sister truly would be dead. It was time to make Tynan give her that proof one way or another.

Nika made a quick stop by her suite to put on clothes before she went to see the Sanguinar. The sun had just begun to set when she knocked on his door. It took him too long to answer, so she knocked again.

The door cracked open a couple of inches. Tynan's icy blue eye peered out at her. "I'm not ready for you yet. Come back in an hour."

"I don't have that kind of time. I need to know now."

A low, familiar groan sounded from inside Tynan's suite. A flare of panic brightened his eyes for a moment before he covered the slip.

He was hiding something.

"Who is that?" she asked.

"An hour, Nika. Leave me to my work."

Nika thrust her hand into the doorway, knowing Tynan would not dare risk hurting her. Every Theronai in the compound would come swooping down upon him if he did.

"What are you doing?" he demanded.

"Finding out what you're hiding."

"This is none of your affair. Leave."

Another deep groan filtered through the opening, and this time, Nika recognized Madoc's voice.

Anger flared inside her, giving her a moment of strength. She shoved the door open, making Tynan stumble back, and raced into the room.

Madoc lay sprawled on the couch, looking limp and boneless, like he'd passed out. She knelt on the couch by his side and touched him, letting him know she was here.

Her head whipped around so she could glare at Tynan. "What did you do to him?"

"You really shouldn't be here yet. We have to wait for Logan."

Nika had no idea what he meant, but all she cared about was Madoc. "Answer me, or I swear to God I'll find a way to force-feed you a gallon of my blood."

Tynan's pale skin went papery white at her threat. "He's fine. I put him to sleep for his own good."

"I doubt he'll see it that way." Nika slid her fingers over his forehead, smoothing his hair back, and noticed that some of the blisters on her arm were mostly gone. There was a patch of skin that had healed in the shape of a man's hand. That was what had happened when Madoc grabbed her and she felt that odd tingling. He'd healed her and probably hadn't even known he'd done it.

"He gave me the power I needed to study the bone. I have your answer."

She immediately forgot about her arm. "And?"

"I compared the bone's marrow to Andra's blood and they don't match. The child was blooded, but only mildly so. She had only a trace of Athanasian blood—perhaps not even enough for her to qualify as a Gerai."

Relief welled up inside Nika, spilling out in tears. She squeezed Madoc's hand. "I need to call Andra. Wake Madoc up. We have to go find her."

Tynan moved closer, gliding across the floor. The lights in the room seemed to dim as his eyes flared with a bright, eerie light. "We'll call her in a minute. First, I need to know something."

Nika felt heavy, unable to move. A skittering panic crawled up her spine as Tynan neared. She hadn't feared him for a long time, but now all the reasons she had were coming back to her.

He was a predator. He wanted her blood.

No, her blood hurt him. Didn't it?

Nika wanted to scream, but her throat seemed to shrink until there was no room for sound. All she managed to get out was one pathetic squeak of fear, and even that was cut short.

"Hold still, little one," he crooned as he neared. "This won't hurt a bit."

Nika wanted to close her eyes, but they were locked on Tynan's, and she was unable to move. She felt trapped by his gaze, held prisoner.

Tynan leaned down, tipping her head back. He bared his fangs and a moment later, Nika was falling.

Madoc felt Nika's hand tighten around his. He knew it was hers even though his eyes were closed. No other woman had skin as soft and bones as delicate as his Nika.

No. Not his. He had to remember that, though right now, he couldn't seem to figure out why. His head was foggy, his body heavy, like he'd been drugged.

He heard her voice twisting with a soft cry of terror before it was cut short.

He opened his eyes to see what was wrong and saw a man's dark head bowed over her, kissing her neck.

Rage slammed into Madoc, burning off the haze that filled him. He shot to his feet, reaching for his sword, only to find that it wasn't there. That confused him, but not enough to stop him from killing this man.

He grabbed the fucker's hair and ripped him away from Nika.

Blood spilled down her neck and confusion glazed her eyes.

Tynan landed across the room, sprawled on the floor. He scrambled backward, sending stacks of books tumbling. "You don't want to do this," said the leech.

Oh, yes, he did. The need for violence was clawing at him, spurring him on, cheering louder with every step he took.

"Madoc, stop." Nika's voice was soft and weak, but the plea was still clear.

Madoc didn't give a fuck. He was past caring. This bloodsucker had gone too far this time. Too fucking far.

He reached down and pulled Tynan up by his hair until his legs dangled over the ground.

Power flowed like icy water through Tynan's voice. "Put me down."

The compulsion to obey made Madoc grit his teeth in an effort to resist. He stood frozen in place. An itchy buzz filled his head, but it was a mere nuisance compared to the fury driving him now. His blood burned in his veins, pounding in his temples as the power within him seethed and boiled, looking for a means of escape.

It took several rapid beats of his heart before Madoc finally regained control of his body enough to speak. "So you can hurt her again? Not a fucking chance. No one will ever hurt her again."

Madoc grabbed Tynan's head in his hands and twisted until he heard bones break. Tynan's body went limp and crumpled to the ground. The silvery light in his eyes winked out as he stared sightlessly at the ceiling.

Nika's voice seemed loud in the deathly quiet of the room. "You killed him."

Madoc turned to her. Blood stained the collar of her shirt. Her hand was pressed against the wound, but a slow trickle still leaked out. The look of horror on her face burned into Madoc's brain, making his head pound. He'd never be able to get that image out of his mind.

She looked from Madoc to Tynan's body and back again.

Madoc reached for her. She backed away. "I can't believe you killed him."

Neither could Madoc—at least, that one remaining sliver of the real him that was left. The rest of him roared in victory, thirsty for more blood and ready for the next fight. Bring on the world. He'd tear it in two with his bare hands if that was what it took to keep Nika safe.

He needed to stop her bleeding. He reached for her, but she shrank away, staring at him like she'd seen a monster.

Madoc let his hand fall and retreated toward the door. She'd just seen him kill a man who was supposed to be his ally—a man who was helping her find out the truth about her sister.

Tynan wasn't going to be helping anyone ever again.

Madoc had taken his life, and there wasn't even enough of a soul left in him to feel sorry for what he'd done.

He had to get out of here. He had to get away from Nika before he hurt her, too.

Madoc raced out of the suite, bumping into Logan hard enough to knock the man into a wall. He didn't stop. He started to run and kept running to the armory, where he found a clean blade that had never before been used in battle. He buckled it around his hips, got in his truck, and left Dabyr knowing he'd never again go back.

The sun was down and there were plenty of Synestryn within a few hours' drive. All he had to do was find a group big enough to take him down.

Iain awoke from his semiconscious meditative state as soon as full dark had fallen. He did not allow himself the luxury of easing back into his pain the way he used to when he was younger. Better to dive in headfirst and get it over with.

Agony ripped through his body, making him grit his teeth to keep from crying out against it. After so many years of his carrying this burden around with him, it still startled him every night just how much pain one man could stand without dying.

Slowly, his breathing and pulse slowed and the sweat that had broken out across his naked body began to evaporate. As soon as he was settled back within the familiar confines of his endless torment, he rose from where he knelt, picked up his sword, and slid it back into its sheath.

The Gerai house where he'd chosen to spend the day was dark and quiet and near the cave he intended to clean out tonight. It took him only a few minutes to shower, dress, and grab a couple of apples from a bowl in the kitchen on his way out the door.

Out here in rural northern Missouri, it smelled like winter—cold and dead. His guess was that a storm was coming in soon, which meant it was time to get moving. He didn't want to be on the roads if things turned bad.

He wanted to be in that cave, slaying the Synestryn and the evil they had created.

Children. The Synestryn had begun creating offspring that had the faces of human children.

Bile rose up in Iain's throat as the memories of last night's hunt came back to him, unbidden. He didn't know what to call the beast he'd slain, but it sure as hell hadn't been human. No human child had six arms that ended in wicked claws dripping with poison. Based on the dead human woman he'd found with a distended belly, it was possible that some part of that abomination had been human, but not enough that he was going to let it claw his face off.

It might hurt to live—to keep going every day—but that didn't mean he was going to die easily, as some of his brethren had done. He was not a quitter. He refused to end his life like some kind of coward. It didn't matter whether his soul was dead. As long as he kept breathing, he'd keep fighting.

He'd promised he would.

His hand strayed to the locket worked into the hilt of his sword and the lock of flaming red hair that lay within it.

Serena.

She'd been gone a long time, but his promise to her still held power over him. It still gave him a reason to live, which was much more than many of his brothers had.

They'd never been able to have the life together they'd been meant to have, but he was grateful for the promise he'd made.

Iain slid his big body behind the wheel of his SUV and headed for the cave. He pulled up close to the entrance, donned his armored leather coat, gloves, and face mask, drew his sword, and moved in for some prime-time killing.

Chapter 9

Meghan Clark flipped her windshield wipers to high, hoping they would clear away enough snow to allow her to see the road. Less than thirty feet in front of her, the snowplow's taillights were barely visible through the blizzard. Fine granules spewed out of its back end, allowing her to stay safely on the road, even if they were creeping along slower than she could walk.

She had to be crazy. That was the only explanation for why she was this far north at this time of year. March in Phoenix was beautiful. Warm. Sunny. She could have waited a couple more months to leave home and fulfill her promise to the strange man who had cured her father's cancer last year.

But no. She had to come now—was compelled to come. Dad was doing well, getting around on his own again, and the need to fulfill her end of the bargain that saved his life had become too much to resist. She could barely sleep anymore, and was consumed with this restless, itchy need to get going. So she had. She'd thrown some clothes in a suitcase and headed out from sunny Phoenix two days ago.

It was just her luck that whatever was driving her had sent her into the far reaches of Minnesota during a blizzard. When that strange man had made her agree to take a trip north, he really meant it.

Most of her time with him was hazy, but she knew two things for sure. First, that man had saved her father's life;

and second, there was nothing she could have done to stop herself from coming here, blizzard or not.

The plow truck in front of her abruptly stopped and made a three-point turn in the middle of the road, leaving a solid white path ahead of her. The snowplow's headlights shone on a sign that was only partially visible beneath the layer of snow clinging to it. Something county line.

Apparently, this county's road-plowing service ended here. Perfect.

Meghan sat behind her steering wheel on the road, watching the red glow of the truck's taillights slowly disappear in her rearview mirror. If she was smart, she'd turn around and follow him—wait for the weather to clear.

The restless, itchy feeling inside her intensified at the thought, becoming almost unbearable.

Meghan let out a long sigh, eased her foot off the brake, and moved forward onto the pristine surface covering the road ahead.

Nika watched Madoc leave, not daring to stop him. Things were much worse than she'd suspected. Tynan's limp body was proof of that.

Madoc had killed him. Nika still couldn't believe it.

She stood there, shaking, her body frozen in shock.

How could this have happened? How could things have gone so wrong so fast? She'd thought Madoc was all bark and no bite. Clearly, she'd been dead wrong.

Nika knelt beside Tynan's body, reaching out a bloody hand to close his eyes. As her fingers got close, he blinked.

She jerked back, letting out a yelp of surprise.

"Nika. You're hurt."

She turned toward the deep, cultured voice to see Logan standing in the doorway. His eyes zeroed in on her neck. His nostrils flared and, without looking away, he shut and locked the door behind him.

"Madoc killed him," she whispered, still not sure it had really happened. Maybe this was some sort of trick of her mind—something the Synestryn had done to confuse her. If so, it was working.

"Back away from him, child. He's not yet dead. I can hear his heart beating."

Nika stared down at Tynan. He sure looked dead.

"Come to me, Nika. Let me close your wounds." Logan held out his hand, keeping a careful eye on Tynan.

She tried to stand but shock had robbed her of her agility, and she stumbled into a bookcase. Logan darted across the space, faster than she thought was possible. He grabbed her arm and eased her away from Tynan, into a nearby chair.

"Hold still," he said, then pressed his fingertips over the two puncture wounds for a brief second and closed his eyes.

Tingles bubbled over her skin until she felt the need to pull away. She didn't, though, not knowing what that might do.

"That feels like what Madoc did when he healed my blisters." She held out her wrist, checking to make sure she hadn't imagined that, too.

The handprint of healed skin was still there, outlined by angry red blisters.

Logan used the collar of her shirt to wipe away the blood. "Madoc healed you?"

She felt off balance and uncertain. Everything seemed so far off it was as if nothing could touch her.

Madoc had killed, and deep down, she knew it was somehow her fault. He'd tried to warn her he was dangerous, but she didn't listen.

She nodded. "One of the Theronai grabbed me."

"Where was Madoc going?"

"I don't know."

There was a horrible crunch, followed by a sickening sucking sound from where Tynan lay. He flopped onto his back and lay there, panting. "I know."

Logan went to him, leaned down, and they spoke too low for her to hear. When Logan looked at her again, his face was grim. "If you don't find him, he's going to kill himself."

Slowly, Tynan pushed himself to a sitting position. He looked gray and gaunt, but he was alive. Logan had been right.

"We can't let that happen," said Tynan. "We need him. *You* need him."

She'd always felt that need, but it hardly mattered now. "He doesn't want me."

Logan laid a hand on Tynan's shoulder as if to quiet him. "Madoc doesn't know what he wants right now. He's not himself. He's . . . sick."

"Not sick. Dying. His soul is dying," she whispered.

Logan nodded slowly. "I know you weren't raised as one of us, but surely you know what that means—what will happen if Joseph finds out."

"He'll kill him."

Tynan rubbed the back of his neck. His voice was still quiet, like breathing was difficult. "You have to find him. Stop him."

"How?"

"You have to take his luceria."

"I tried. It didn't work."

"I felt the power of your blood combining with his inside me. It was . . . incredible. That's why I'm not dead right now. I was able to heal myself because of that power."

"You took her blood again?" asked Logan in confusion. "You said it was dangerous."

"There was no other way. I had to know."

"Know what?" asked Nika.

"If the two of you were compatible."

"Madoc says we're not. He says we'd know if we were."

"He's wrong. His blood mixed with yours, keeping it from hurting me. I also have fed from enough bonded Theronai pairs to know what I felt. He's using some kind of magic to slow the normal aging process of his lifemark. That magic must be getting in the way of your bonding."

Realization hit her as all the pieces fell into place. "The black ring," she whispered.

"What ring?" asked Logan.

"He wears this ugly black ring. It's unnaturally cold."

The two Sanguinar shared a look that seemed to communicate something she didn't understand.

Logan rose to his feet, stripping off his shirt. "Go in the bathroom. Clean the blood off and change into this shirt. Then you need to leave. Immediately. Find Madoc; take off that black ring, even if you have to cut off his hand to do it. Once you do that, you should be able to take his luceria."

"And if I can't?" she asked.

"Then he's going to die."

"What about Tori? She's still alive. I have to find her."

"How?"

"I don't know. She won't talk to me anymore. She's keeping me out."

"Then you truly do need Madoc," said Logan. "His power could help you find her, okay? He'll make you stronger."

Nika wasn't sure about anything anymore. It all seemed too surreal and distant. She wanted to save Madoc, but she couldn't forget about Tori, either. And she couldn't forget the sight of him twisting Tynan's neck.

"Nika," snapped Logan, his voice impatient. "You need to go now. He doesn't have much time left and there's nothing Tynan or I can do for him. You're the only one who can save him."

"I should bring help. There's no way I can overpower him."

"Anyone you would ask to go with you would be honor-bound to bring him back for execution. Is that what you want?"

"No. Of course not."

"Then no one else can know. Tynan and I know how to keep a secret, but it can't go beyond us. Do you understand?"

She did now. "If I tell anyone, Madoc dies."

"Correct."

Madoc was sick. He needed her.

In the end, Nika knew there was no real choice to make. She cleaned away the blood, put on the borrowed shirt, and went to get the keys to Andra's new truck.

She wasn't sure what she'd find—the man who took care of her or the monster who killed without remorse— but she knew she had to look.

Meghan had been driving on the unplowed road long enough that she could feel her shoulders moving up toward her ears. Her back ached with tension, as did her knuckles. Driving in this white mess was maddening, but she couldn't seem to make herself stop. Whatever was compelling her had only grown stronger with each mile that passed.

Wind blew a wall of snowflakes at her windshield, blinding her for a moment. When they cleared, a man was standing in the middle of the road.

Meghan panicked for a brief second, but it was long enough for her to make the mistake of trying to stop. She braked and swerved, sending her car into a spin. The world whirled around her in a blindingly white display before the side of her car slammed into something hard. Her head hit the window and everything winked out of existence.

Alexander rushed over the snow to check on Meghan. He hadn't intended her accident to be quite so spectacular, but it was necessary to his plan.

John Hawthorne could not suspect any manipulation. He was the kind of man who would ask too many questions—questions that could cause Alexander and the rest of the Sanguinar problems. John's meeting with Meghan had to look accidental, and it had taken almost a year of planning to make that happen.

Meghan's car was slanted in a shallow ditch against the tree she'd hit. The passenger's side of her car was crumpled, but the engine was still running, keeping her warm.

Alexander shivered in the cold even as he tried to ignore it. John's mind was too strong to make him do anything against his nature, and leaving town to seek out a woman nearly two thousand miles away was definitely not in the man's nature.

So Alexander had devised a plan that would allow John's impressive protective instincts to come into play. With the lovely Meghan as a victim, John would be helpless to resist her.

Alexander made sure no snow blocked the car's exhaust system; then he went to Meghan's side. His hands were frigid as they moved over her face, seeking out any serious injury she might have. He wanted her rattled, not incapacitated.

Her warmth called to him, urging him to draw her closer, but Alexander resisted. John would be driving past here in only a few moments. There wasn't much time.

Alexander needed to be sure there was no internal damage, so he lifted her wrist to his mouth and slid his fangs into the delicate vein throbbing there. Her blood flowed over his tongue, and for a moment, he was lost in the taste of her. Her blood was more powerful than most humans', and the urge to drink his fill and sate his hunger pounded through him.

He needed to have enough of that delicious power to erase his footprints in the snow, without making her too weak to do what he needed her to do.

Before it was too late, he let a small amount of power spill from him, seeking out any injuries she might have. There was a bruise on her head, but it was nothing serious. She was already sliding back toward consciousness and would awake in the next few minutes. He needed to be gone before that happened.

With a force of will, he healed her skin and pulled her wrist from his mouth.

Alexander positioned her so the bruise on her head was visible through the window, opened her coat, and unbuttoned her shirt enough to display her ample bosom. If he was going to set a trap for a human man, he might as well use all the bait at his disposal.

*   *   *

Nika had been on the road for only twenty minutes when she felt the first tug of a sgath on her mind.

Panic slithered through her, making her hands sweat as they clenched on the steering wheel.

This couldn't be happening now—not while she was on the road and snow was coming down faster and faster, and Madoc was getting farther away from her with every passing second. It was the worst possible time.

She gripped the steering wheel tighter and tried to lock every mental barrier she had into place.

The next pull was stronger, more forceful. It made her head spin until she had to pull Andra's new truck to the side of the road before she slid off.

"Madoc!" She called out for him, wishing now that she hadn't killed his cell phone.

A low, hungry growl reverberated inside her skull. She caught a flash of huge paws sinking silently into a thin layer of snow, felt a chill invade her hands and feet, smelled the cold air. Her stomach twisted with hunger.

Hunt, kill, eat.

The sgath wanted her to come with it. She made it smarter, stronger.

"No," Nika growled into the cab of the truck as she fought the monster's pull.

Then there were two. They tugged at her mind, trying to pull it in different directions.

Outside the walls of Dabyr it was easier for them to reach her.

"Madoc." Her cry was weaker this time, and she knew she was losing this battle.

Nika scrambled for her cell phone and dialed Andra. No answer. She tried Grace, with the same useless result. Tynan was the only other one she could think to call.

He answered immediately: "Did you find him?"

"No. I need help. The sgath want me. I need Madoc."

"Hold on."

He was gone for too long. Nika had begun to shake from the effort to resist them. Before, the cold had helped, so she rolled down the windows and let the winter air flood the truck.

The sgath jerked away from the cold, giving her a moment to catch her breath.

Tynan came back on the line. "Nicholas has a tracking device on all the cars. The one Madoc took is not far from you. Hang up so he can call you and talk you through it, okay?"

Nika nodded, forgetting he couldn't see her for a moment before she answered, "Thanks."

She hung up and her phone rang again immediately.

Nicholas's voice sounded weary, but gentle. "Heya, Nika. I hear you're in a bit of a bind. Can you drive?"

Her teeth were chattering, but at least the cold kept the sgath at bay. "Yeah. Think so."

"Okay, then. Let's go find Madoc."

He guided her to a highway, then had her exit in only a few miles.

"I put his phone in the garbage disposal," she admitted.

"Don't worry. Knowing him, he deserved it. I'll get him a new one."

If he lived long enough.

"How much farther?" Beneath the snow was a gravel road, but it seemed less slick than the paved roads had been.

"You should be able to see his truck any minute. On your right."

The truck lurched as it passed over a deep pothole. She cleared the top of a hill, and down in the next valley she saw the gleam of chrome.

"I see it."

"Great. Need anything else?"

As she got closer, she could see that the truck sat empty. She slowed, and through the open windows, she heard a metallic hiss followed by an enraged roar.

She knew that voice. Madoc.

Nika turned toward the sound and saw Madoc with his back to a blunt rock outcropping. In front of him were half a dozen sgath, only they were bigger than any of the ones she'd seen before. Their sharklike teeth were bared, and glowing yellow saliva dripped from their jaws.

"God, no," she breathed.

"What?" asked Nicholas, the word tight with panic.

Nika had forgotten she held the phone until she heard his voice. "He's going to get himself killed."

She dropped the phone, dug under the seat for Andra's shotgun, grabbed a handful of extra shells, and ran toward Madoc, screaming to get the monsters' attention.

Madoc heard Nika's war cry and saw her racing across the snowy ground. Her white hair flew out behind her as she leaped over a fallen tree.

Fuck. The woman was going to get herself killed before he could do a thing to stop it. He had to get between her and them before she got too close.

Rage poured through him, giving him strength and speed. Three of the sgath had turned to look at her. He plunged his sword into the back of the skull of the closest one, pushed himself over its body, and jerked the sword from its twitching carcass from the far side.

Two of the beasts abandoned him and lunged toward her. She stopped, skidding over the ground, leveled the shotgun, and fired.

Her eyes squeezed shut and her body jerked with the force of the weapon, but her shot had hit one of the sgath, knocking it into the next.

They went down in a pile of claws and teeth, fighting each other for a few precious seconds.

Madoc jumped toward them, slicing through the air as he landed. This sword's balance was different from the one he'd used for centuries, and because of that, his aim was off by a fraction. Rather than lopping off the head, he missed and his sword lodged in one of the sgath's shoulders.

The thing turned on him, baring its teeth. Madoc kicked it in the head with his boot, stunning it.

He heard Nika scream his name in terror. His gaze went toward her, unable to go anywhere else in the face of a scream like that. He saw her point at something behind him; then her body crumpled to the ground like a puppeteer had cut her strings.

Madoc bellowed and headed for her, needing to catch her before she hit the ground even though he knew it was a futile attempt before he'd even started moving. He felt something tug on the back of his leather jacket; then a cold blast of wind hit his back as claws barely missed his skin.

Madoc turned toward the sgath, his sword lifted to defend against another attack.

The sgath that had slashed his jacket to pieces was in the process of clawing at him again, only now that the blade was in the way, it ended up severing its own paw.

Behind that one, there were still four more coming for him. Only one of them was injured. Those weren't good odds on the best of nights, but tonight, with Nika lying helpless only a few feet away and Madoc fighting with an unfamiliar sword, the odds were fucking grim.

Instincts embedded in his DNA demanded that he protect her. He'd come here tonight to die, knowing that the sgath left alive were strong, smart, and fast. A six-on-one fight was a lost cause waiting to happen. If he took out half of them before he died, he'd be lucky. But the rules of the game had changed. Nika was at stake now, and that changed everything.

Madoc bellowed, rushing the closest sgath, forcing it back with a series of fast, short jabs from his sword. None of the strikes hit, but they moved the fucker back enough that he wasn't going to be trampling Nika with his booted feet.

The injured sgath was busy licking up a puddle of its own blood, which would heal it, but there was nothing Madoc could do about that. He'd kill it when he could. There were four more to deal with right now.

Two of them moved out to his sides to flank him while the one in his face kept his attention. He saw them moving, knew what they were doing, but there wasn't a thing he could do to stop them until the odds were more in his favor.

Madoc swiped at the one nearest, angling to his left.

The one on his right let out a deep hissing kind of growl, and the others' ears twitched as if listening.

Then, as if they'd choreographed it, all four of them charged at once.

Madoc fell back. One of them got in a hit on his arm. Its claws cut through his leather jacket and raked over his skin. He could feel the sting of poison as it entered his system and knew he was totally fucked now. First, his reaction speed would slow; then he'd simply collapse, leaving Nika defenseless.

Like hell. He'd just have to take them all out before that could happen.

The sgath snarled and snapped as they fought to get closer. He kept his sword moving to fend them off, unable to get in a clean blow. With each beat of his heart, his movements became slower, his mind foggier.

He was failing Nika, letting her die. These things were going to kill him; then they'd tear her delicate flesh apart and feed on her blood.

Rage exploded inside Madoc, driving back some of the effects of the poison. He kicked one of the sgath away with his boot, giving himself a little room to maneuver.

Of course, that gave them room, too, and the one that had already gotten in a blow came back for seconds. Only this time, it wanted a bite.

Sharp yellow teeth closed in on Madoc's thigh. He saw the bite coming, but was too busy with the other sgath to stop it. He braced himself for the blow, hoping it wouldn't take his leg clean off and fuck up his balance.

Then suddenly, there was a streak of oily fur where the thing had been a second ago as one of the other sgath attacked it. It turned on its own kind and sank its teeth into its fellow sgath's neck.

Madoc didn't question his luck. There wasn't time. With those two distracted, he had a fighting chance.

He shoved his blade through the bottom jaw of the sgath on his left, pinning its mouth shut. Then he levered its heavy body at the tip of his sword, flinging it at the one left standing. They toppled over. Madoc didn't wait for them to regain their balance. He followed, hacked the head off one, and leaped over the pulsing arc of black blood that spewed out of its neck.

A hard boot to the side of the next sgath's head kept its teeth away, but its back claws caught Madoc's leg. Pain and fury collided in his chest, coming out as a ragged bellow.

Madoc sliced off the offending paw and shoved his sword into the thing's gut. It wriggled and howled as he cut it open. It took only seconds to kill, but each one of those seconds left him slower and groggier than before.

The two that were fighting continued to do so while Madoc sneaked up behind the one trying to heal itself with its own blood. His blade dived down in a deadly arc, but his strength was fading and the cut wasn't clean. His sword lodged in the thing's spine. It bucked, knocking Madoc to the ground. The motion shoved the sword in deeper, which must have cut through something vital. The thing collapsed, twitched twice, then went still.

By the time he managed to push his shaking body up, only one sgath remained. Its jaws were shining black with the blood of its kin and its glowing eyes fixed on Madoc.

He was too weak to defeat it. He could barely lift his blade.

The thing stalked toward him, its body shaking as if something was wrong. Madoc braced his feet apart and blinked in an effort to clear his fading vision. As he neared it, it lifted its head as if offering itself up as a sacrifice.

He didn't trust what he was seeing. It had to be the poison fucking up his vision.

Or maybe this was some kind of trick.

Madoc lifted his sword. He'd use every last scrap of strength he had defending Nika. It probably wouldn't be enough, but he had to try.

The thing came closer. A deep growl slid from between its teeth, but they stayed clamped shut as if held that way by an invisible muzzle.

It got to within sword range and stopped.

He had no idea why it would do such a thing, but he didn't question his luck. He lifted his sword and lopped off the thing's head in one clean stroke.

The motion knocked Madoc down. He could smell the blood of the sgath mixed with the scent of his own.

It wouldn't be long before they had company.

He reached for his phone, hoping to call for help, but it was gone. He hadn't replaced it.

Fuck.

Madoc peered over the cold ground to where Nika lay. Her hair was the color of the snow surrounding her. Her breath came out in white plumes, proving she was still alive.

He ached to go to her, to curl himself around her body and hold her close. He wanted her to be the last thing he felt before he died.

But he was bleeding, drawing nasties from their dank hidey-holes. He needed to get as far away from Nika as possible.

Madoc pushed himself to his feet, only to fall down again. He was too weak to stand, so he pulled himself over the frozen ground, crawling away. The poison was raging through his system now, making him cold, slowing his limbs, and stealing his thoughts.

But he remembered Nika. Her soft skin only he could touch, her pretty eyes so full of trust, her boundless faith in him. He'd take his memories of her with him. No fucking poison on earth could steal those from him.

Chapter 10

Nika almost got trapped inside the dying sgath's mind. She knew she had to stay until the last second and hold it still while Madoc killed it. He was weak and bleeding. Without her help, he would have died.

But the sgath was strong and it fought her hard, nearly winning several times. In staying inside its mind while it died, she'd nearly died, too.

She came back into her frigid body and immediately began to shake. A groggy kind of light-headedness settled over her, and she idly wondered if the effect was from her mental wandering or possible hypothermia.

As soon as she was able to move, she surveyed the area, looking for Madoc. The headlights cast enough of a glow for her to see a trail of red in the snow.

Madoc's blood.

Her world spun in panic, making her dizzy and breathless. Beside her, the truck's engine hummed. Below that was the tinny, distant sound of voices.

Her cell phone. Help.

Nika found the phone in the snow and grabbed it up with clumsy hands. She pressed it to her cheek as she struggled to stand. "Help," she said. "Madoc's hurt."

"Nika?" It was Nicholas's voice. "Are you okay? Are you hurt?"

"No. But Madoc is."

She was still wobbly, but she had to find him. Her legs shook with every step, but she forced them to move and take her to Madoc.

"Help's on the way, Nika. I've called in everyone nearby. The chopper's in the air. Just stay on the line with me, okay?"

Movement caught her eye. She saw Madoc crawling over the ground, pulling himself along on his belly.

She raced to him, slipping in the snow as she went. From here, she could see the wet shine of blood covering his arm.

She fell to her knees at his side, feeling like her guts were being squeezed. He wasn't supposed to get hurt. He was too strong for that. He was supposed to be invincible.

"Madoc." His name came out as a whisper of fear.

"Get away. Blood."

"I don't care. I'm not leaving you alone."

She grabbed his hand. He tried to pull away but was too weak.

"Go. Please. Can't fight."

"Help is coming." She only hoped it would get here in time.

She started to ask Nicholas how much longer it would be when she realized that she'd dropped the phone somewhere along the way. She didn't want to leave Madoc, but she needed to know what to do to save him.

"I'll be right back," she told him.

She hurried back along the path she'd taken until she found the cell phone. Lying only a few feet away was Madoc's sword.

She very well might need that if the Synestryn came, so she grabbed it up.

The metal was freezing. The weight of it startled her. The way he whipped this thing around, she half expected it to be light.

She didn't know how she was going to swing it if things got bad, but she knew she'd find a way.

By the time she got back to Madoc, he'd crawled another few feet.

"You can't get away from me," she told him. "Stop trying." And to make sure he did, she rolled his heavy body over onto his back.

His face was ashen. His eyes had dilated until only a

thin ring of green remained. His body trembled and his breathing was way too fast.

Nika righted the phone and said, "Something's wrong with Madoc."

Nicholas was still there, sounding relieved to have heard from her again. "Tell me what happened."

"He was attacked by sgath."

"They hit him?"

"Yeah."

"It's poison. The Sanguinar can fix it. Just hold on. Help should be there any minute."

"What do I do?"

"Is he bleeding badly?" asked Nicholas.

He'd lost a lot of blood, but none was gushing out. "Bad enough."

"You need to leave him, Nika. Get as far away as you can."

"No."

"It's the middle of the night. His blood will bring Synestryn down on you."

"That's why I need to be here. To fight them off."

"You can't fight them off. You need to run."

From somewhere to her left, Nika heard a long, hungry howl. The Synestryn had caught the scent of Madoc's blood.

"Run," whispered Madoc, his eyes pleading with her.

Nika set the cell phone down where he could hear reassurances that help was on the way; then she stood and picked up Madoc's sword.

She didn't dare try to lift it up before the last second for fear her arms would give out too early.

"Run," he panted.

Nika spared him a quick glance. His skin seemed grayer, and a panicked sense of desperation made her body tense.

"I'm not leaving you. Not now. Not ever. Get used to it."

Behind her, she heard an engine roaring and tires screaming. In front of her, she heard more howls join the first.

Her body shivered against the cold. She couldn't feel her toes anymore, and her fingers were aching from the frigid metal hilt.

A shimmering light glowed as bright as daylight on her left. She wasn't sure what it was, so she turned toward it, splitting her attention between the howls and whatever threat that light posed.

"Nika! Nika Madison!" a distant voice shouted from the direction of her truck. Help.

"Here!" she yelled, standing her ground over Madoc.

The shadowy shapes of two men were running toward her. She couldn't see who they were, but they had all the right parts to be human.

They got close enough to see. She didn't recognize either of the young men, but they were definitely human and both armed with shotguns.

They positioned themselves so one was on each side. "See anything?" the older one asked. She guessed he was a few years older than her, but not much.

"No. Heard them howling, though."

"Looks like the cavalry's coming," said the younger man in front of her. He nodded toward the light.

"What's that?"

"Portal. They'll be here any second."

As the last word left his mouth, the light solidified, then ripped open in a perfect line as if someone had split the air with a blade. The line widened and Helen stepped through, followed closely by her husband, Drake. Seconds later, Angus and Gilda spilled through as well.

Relief made Nika sway, and if it weren't for the sword poking against the frozen ground, she might have fallen.

Angus gave her a reassuring smile, which made the lines on his craggy face deepen. "You did well. We'll take it from here." He lifted his hand, silently asking for the sword.

Nika's arm didn't move, so he came to her and lifted the blade away from her numb fingers. One of the young men wrapped his coat over her shoulders and the warmth made her moan in thanks.

Helen flipped one of her twin braids over her shoulder, waved a hand, and a long line of flames erupted from the ground several yards away. Drake drew his sword and stood by her side, scanning the area.

Gilda lifted the hem of her gray gown and knelt beside Madoc in the snow. She pressed her dainty hands on either side of his face, and bent her head as if in prayer.

A series of short yelps rose up from the trees nearby. They were closer now.

"The two of you need to get Nika away from here," said Angus to the humans. "We'll follow shortly."

"I'm not leaving him," said Nika.

"You'll just be in the way. We'll bring you to him when it's safe."

She was not going to be pushed around like a child. This was too important for her to bend. "No. He's mine and I'm staying."

Drake peered over his broad shoulder, sharing a questioning look with Angus.

"Yours?" asked Angus.

"Yes."

"You know what you're saying, don't you?"

"I do," she said, making her statement ring out loud and clear.

"I thought he said you weren't compatible."

"He was wrong."

"Then why haven't you—"

Irritation and fear made her cut him off before he could ask any dangerous questions. "We're working on it."

"Incoming," said Helen. She lifted her arms away from her body and her hands erupted in flames.

Angus pointed to a spot next to Madoc. "Stay there next to Gilda. Don't move unless I tell you. Got it?"

Nika nodded. As long as he didn't ask her to leave Madoc, she'd do whatever he wanted.

Gilda's eyes were closed and her forehead was creased in a frown of concentration. A fine tremor passed through her every few seconds.

Nika didn't dare interrupt her to ask what she was

doing. She wanted to touch Madoc—to hold his hand—but she feared even that might mess Gilda up. So, Nika hugged the borrowed coat around her body to keep her hands busy and bit her lip to stay silent.

An explosion went off a few yards away, shaking the ground.

Nika's head jerked up to see a ball of flame consume a trio of furry Synestryn the size of large dogs. Now that the flames lit the area, she could see there were at least a dozen more coming out of the trees.

Helen's arm moved like she was pitching a baseball and another group of demons exploded into flames.

"We've got more in the east," shouted one of the young men.

Angus glanced at Gilda. "She's not done yet. We're going to have to do this the hard way."

The men nodded and took up positions on either side of Angus. "You two guard our flank. I'll cut down the middle."

"I might be able to help," said Nika. "If they have any of my blood in them."

"No," said Angus. "It's too dangerous. If you want to help, keep watch and let us know if anything gets through."

She could do that. It wasn't enough, but it was something.

Gilda lifted her head, letting out a long, slow breath that turned silver in the cold air. "I've slowed the poison. That should give us time for a Sanguinar to show up."

"Are they coming?"

She gave a weary nod. "Logan's on the helicopter. He'll be here soon."

Gilda struggled to stand, so Nika helped her up. Nika wasn't exactly a bounty of strength, but the desire to help burned bright inside her, unable to resist.

Gilda frowned at her as if startled by the offer of assistance, but she took Nika's hand. "Thank you."

She rose to her feet, took position at Angus's left side, and waited for the Synestryn to come.

*   *   *

For the first time in Gilda's long, long life, she felt old. Worn-out.

There had been a time when she could have opened a portal, healed Madoc, and still fought off a horde of Synestryn without breaking a sweat. But now, before she'd even risen to her feet to fight by Angus's side, she was exhausted.

Helen had slain all the demons on her side of combat and was now coming to clean up the mess Gilda had left behind.

The younger woman smiled as she fought, the fire flowing freely from her hands as if she'd been born to it. There was a kind of freedom in Helen now that hadn't been there only a few months ago. She was growing into her power even as Gilda was drawing away from hers.

The distance between her and Angus was getting wider, making it harder and harder for her to tap into his power. Since he'd agreed to allow Tynan to try to restore his fertility, they'd hardly spoken.

She'd kept her word and refused to allow him to share her bed. That refusal had grown into a chasm between them that seemed to widen every day.

She was losing him.

Gilda flung out a short burst of wind, hoping to knock a pair of demons off their feet for the men to slay with their swords. Instead, she barely ruffled their fur, and the effort left her weaving on her feet.

Helen stepped forward, lifted her hands, and a wall of fire spewed forth, tossing the flaming beasts into a rocky outcropping, where they hit hard and then stopped moving.

While Gilda panted, trying to catch her breath, Helen finished her job.

Shame burned bright inside Gilda—shame for her weakness and shame for all the things she'd done to the people around her.

She'd alienated everyone she loved and betrayed those she loved most.

The fighting had died off, and she knew Angus would

come to her as he always did. Despite her treatment of him, he still performed his duties and upheld his vows.

His wide hand came into her field of vision, reaching for her. "You're tired. Come and rest in the warmth of one of the vehicles while we get ready to move."

Gilda ached to take his hand and feel the loving warmth of his skin against hers. She hated the rift that had grown between them. She wanted things to be like they used to be before all her lies had come between them—before she'd betrayed him and all the other male Theronai by sterilizing them without their knowledge or consent. None of them knew that she was the cause. Her lies had hid her betrayal well.

And yet, if she took Angus's hand, that would simply be one more lie. As much as she wanted his touch, she knew she wouldn't allow it. She couldn't lose another child, and if Angus touched her, her resolve would crumble. And if Tynan's cure had worked, she'd conceive.

That could not happen. Never again.

So, rather than lie to him and offer him any sliver of hope that things could be as they once had been, she turned her back on him and walked away.

The stab of rejection he felt leaked through their connection before it was hastily controlled. Gilda pretended she hadn't felt it. Her warrior had his pride and it was the least she could do not to take that from him, too.

Chapter 11

John Hawthorne knew better than to be out in weather like this, but the dreams he'd been having for the past week had pushed him out the door.

Just like in his dreams, it was dark and snow was falling at the rate of an inch an hour. And just like in his dreams, there was this nagging itch in his gut telling him that someone out here needed his help.

His windshield wipers slapped across the glass, packing a frozen layer of snow around the edges of their reach. His Jeep managed pretty well on the roads, but he had to crawl along at a frustratingly slow pace to make sure he didn't slide off.

The farther he went, the more that feeling in his gut nagged at him.

He scanned the road ahead, but couldn't see far. Someone had come this way recently, judging by the tracks in the snow that had only started to fill up again. Then, suddenly, the tracks he was following swerved into a full circle and ended as they left the road.

John brought his Jeep to a slow stop a few feet in front of the crashed vehicle. The headlights of the other car were still on, the windshield wipers still keeping their frantic pace. He flipped on his hazard lights, grabbed a flashlight, zipped up his coat, and got out to see if the driver needed help.

A gust of wind sucked the air from his lungs as he hurried back down the road. Now that he was close enough, he could see that the car was angled in a shallow ditch. A layer of snow had already begun to build up on the car's roof and the driver's-side window.

He used the sleeve of his coat to wipe away the snow and shone his flashlight inside. The beam landed on the curve of a woman's cheek and John had the oddest sense of recognition flow through him. It was as if he should know her, though he had no idea from where.

Rather than waste time worrying about it, he opened the car door, praying she was still alive.

Her eyes were closed and a dark bruise had formed along the left side of her forehead. Her lips were parted, but it was too warm in the car to see her breath. As John stripped off his glove to feel for a pulse, his eyes traveled down to see if her chest was moving.

It was, and all he could do was stare. She had fantastic breasts, and he was sure he could see just the barest hint of lace peeking out from the edge of her shirt.

John scolded himself for being a pig and pressed his fingers against the side of her neck. Her pulse seemed strong and steady.

Her eyes fluttered open, likely from the chill contact of his touch, and she sucked in a pained breath.

"Easy," he said in a quiet voice. "You've had an accident."

A deep frown creased her brow and she lifted her hand to her head, looking at her fingers as if she expected to see blood.

"What happened?"

"You slid off the road."

"There was a man in the road," she said in a confused tone; then fear widened her brown eyes. "Did I hit him?"

She tried to push herself upright, but John held her still, pressing her shoulders back against the seat. "Hold on and stay put. I'll check."

John couldn't imagine anyone walking around outside on a night like this. Chances were she saw a deer, but better safe than sorry. The idea of someone lying in a snowy ditch was too scary to ignore.

He shut her door to help her stay warm, then went

to the road, looking for signs of deer or man. It took longer than he would have liked, since visibility was so low, but he trudged over at least a hundred yards in both directions, just to be sure. There had been nothing but pristine snow.

When he went back to her, she was standing outside, weaving unsteadily on her feet as she brushed snow off the front of her car.

"I didn't see anything," he told her.

Relief made her voice faint. "I don't see any blood or dents on the car, either."

"It was probably just a deer."

She shook her head as if to clear it. "I was sure it was a man."

"Could you have fallen asleep at the wheel?"

"Maybe," she said, though she sounded uncertain. "Maybe I'm not remembering right from that bump on my head."

John's breath curled out in a silvery plume. "Whatever happened, we need to get you checked out. I'll drive you to the hospital. It'll be faster than waiting for an ambulance."

"No. I'm fine. I don't need to go to the hospital."

"You could have internal injuries. A concussion."

"It wasn't that bad. I just need to report the accident."

John wasn't convinced that skipping a hospital was a very smart idea, but she seemed okay and was getting steadier by the second. Besides, she was a grown woman, capable of making up her own mind. "I'll stay with you until the police show. Just in case."

"My cell phone won't work out here. I already tried. Can I use yours?"

John had intentionally left his at the office, knowing that his vacation would be useless if his employees knew they could reach him. Without it, they had to solve their own problems, since none of them knew the number of his cabin. "Sorry. Don't have one. You can use my landline. I don't live far from here."

"I appreciate the offer, but I should probably stay with my car."

"Not in this storm. It's too dangerous. We'll report the accident from in front of a fire." John took her arm and gently pulled her back onto the road. The fact that she leaned on a stranger for support showed just how unsteady she was. Her sneakers were caked with snow and the legs of her jeans were wet up to her knees. "We need to get you warmed up and make sure you're okay."

"Are you sure there's no one lying out here in the snow?"

"I didn't see any footprints, and you hadn't been here long enough for your car to be covered, so if you'd hit someone, I think I would have seen them."

She nodded, looking so weary and confused it made John want to hug her. Instead, he pulled her up against his side to support her over the slick ground, feeling the slim curve of her waist beneath her jacket. His fingers tightened slightly and itched to slide down onto her hip.

Instead, he kept his hand firmly off her body as they made their way to his Jeep.

"I'm John Hawthorne," he told her as he opened the Jeep's door for her to get in.

"I'm Meghan Clark. Thank you so much for stopping to help me."

She looked up at him from the passenger's seat. Her dark eyes were shadowed with worry, and the need to erase that worry was so intense, all he could do for a long moment was gawk at her, speechless.

Something deep inside John flipped over and stretched as if waking from a long sleep. He had no idea who this woman was or why she was out here, but the need to take her home and get her warm and dry seemed more important than any of those details.

John had never allowed anyone to visit his vacation cabin before. He preferred to leave it sacred in its isolation—just for him and him alone. But now, he couldn't think of anything he wanted more than to get Meghan tucked away, safe and sound. Isolation be damned.

Meghan could not get warm. She tried to hide her shivering body and chattering teeth from her rescuer. He'd turned the heat up as high as it would go on the drive here, and was now crouched in front of the stone hearth, working to light a fire.

The small cabin was clearly some kind of masculine retreat. Fishing gear was stacked in one corner. A fully stocked gun rack hung on the wall by the door. The couch was big and worn, obviously chosen for comfort rather than style. A sturdy wooden coffee table was scuffed and scratched.

Meghan looked to John's booted feet, figuring he'd likely propped them up there more often than not.

A small kitchen filled the other side of the open space. The counters were mostly bare. There were a couple of dishes drying in a rack. Through an open door, she could see a bed with the covers rumpled on one side.

She wondered how it was that a man like John slept alone. She'd met him less than an hour ago and had already considered asking him if he was married.

She hadn't. Her unusual lapse in judgment—getting into the car with a stranger and letting him take her home—was likely a result of her head injury. Not that she could turn back now. She was stuck here until the police came to get her.

John stood and turned to her. "There. That'll warm the place up soon."

Firelight flickered behind him, outlining his legs. Meghan's eyes traveled up his body, and oddly, she wished he'd take off his coat so she could get a better look.

Drawn by the warmth, Meghan stepped forward, extending her hands to the fire to warm them. A sigh of satisfaction rose up from her, and John's jaw clenched.

He cleared his throat. "How are you feeling? I can still take you to the hospital."

"No. I'm better. Fine. Really."

"You sure?"

"Yeah."

He nodded. "Let me know if you change your mind."

"I will."

"I'll go make us some hot cocoa. You should probably get out of those wet jeans. I have some sweats you could wear while they dry."

Meghan opened her mouth to refuse his offer, but instead said, "That would be nice."

John went through the open door, leaving Meghan to sort out what the hell she thought she was doing.

Getting into a car with a stranger was bad enough. Letting him drive her to his home was worse. Getting undressed in his house crossed the line.

It had to be the head injury. That was the only explanation she could find.

He came back out. "I laid some clothes on the bed. Feel free to get a shower if you think it will help you warm up."

"I shouldn't—" she started to say, when John reached for her. His fingers brushed featherlight over her forehead, outlining the bruise.

"You're safe here. I promise," he said, and Meghan believed him.

She knew she didn't know this man, but she felt like she did. She felt like she'd always known him. "Thanks."

He nodded. "I'll call the sheriff. We'll get you back on your way as soon as possible."

"Okay," she said, but at that moment she realized that the urge to go, to move, had left her. Whatever it was that had been driving her was gone now, as if she'd reached her destination.

Looking at John's face, at the gentle care shining in his hazel eyes, Meghan wondered if perhaps she'd found whatever it was she'd been sent to find.

Before she could dwell on that bizarre idea too long, she went into his bedroom, grabbed the clothes, and locked herself in the bathroom.

When she came out fifteen minutes later, rosy and warm from her hot shower, and saw John's face, she knew the news wasn't good.

"The sheriff said his men are busy dealing with accidents all over the county and that if you're safe, you should just stay put. Looks like we'll be spending the night together."

Joseph didn't think his night could get any worse.

Grace hadn't shown up for work and was apparently missing. Some of the human teens had gotten into a fight and several of them had needed stitches. The Indonesian Theronai wanted to know where Nika was. Two more Theronai from Australia were due in tomorrow. Nika had left and gotten herself into a mess with Madoc that was taking valuable resources away from their objectives. Iain hadn't reported in for weeks, so Joseph had no idea how Iain's hunt for the Synestryn offspring was progressing. They still hadn't caught the saboteur he knew in his gut still lived among them. And to make matters worse, Carmen was refusing to speak to him. She'd skipped practice, which was the one bright spot in his day.

He didn't see what the big deal was. What the hell was so wrong with him that she didn't want to claim him as her adoptive father? She'd been taking his advice and learning from him for months. He'd taken care of her basic needs—given her a place to live, food. He'd even convinced her to take a couple of online classes from a nearby community college.

Wasn't that what fathers did?

Joseph let out a long sigh. He was so tired. Weary down to his bones. Maybe it was time to step down and let someone else take over leadership of the Theronai for a while. He didn't think he was going to last the remaining years of his term.

Not that there was anyone else clamoring for the job. Like him, they all preferred being out in the field rather than behind a desk.

His phone rang and he almost let it go to voice mail. But as shitty as his day had been, he figured it couldn't get any worse.

"Yeah," he answered.

Nicholas was on the line, his voice tight. "We've got another problem."

The pounding behind Joseph's eyes grew heavier. "Is someone else hurt?"

"It's Thea. She was raped."

Rage poured through Joseph at the thought of someone hurting one of the humans under his protection. He shot up from his desk and headed down the hall, gripping his cell phone hard. "Where is she?"

"Briant is tending to her. She refuses to talk to anyone. The only reason Briant knew was because he saw what had happened to her when he took her blood to heal her. He called me."

"Who did this? I swear I'll kill them myself."

"It was Chris. He's turned."

Joseph came to a dead stop. He could hear voices flowing out of the main hall, sliding around him but not quite sinking in. He felt cold. Dead inside.

He knew what he had to do and the thought nearly killed him.

"Where is he?" asked Joseph. "I need to confirm that it's true."

"You can't go alone. I'll get Liam and meet you in the training yard."

"Where is he, Nicholas? Tell me."

"No. If he's turned, he could kill you. I can't let that happen. We need you too much. We're doing this together."

"I'll find him myself, then." He couldn't stand the idea of sentencing Chris to death, but even worse would be forcing the rest of the Theronai to watch it happen, knowing that they could be next.

His feet felt heavy as he headed toward Chris's suite. The sword at his side was a cold reassurance and he prayed he wouldn't need to draw steel on the man who had been his friend for more than a century.

Joseph rounded a corner and saw that Nicholas and Liam had already beaten him to the door and were barring his path.

"Step out of the way," he ordered his men.

Nicholas's scarred face darkened and his mouth went flat. "We go in together."

"I need to do this alone."

"You can't," said Nicholas. "You've been away from the battlefield too long. You're out of practice and more likely to get yourself killed than not."

Outraged resentment made Joseph's spine straighten. "I am not weak," he snapped.

"I didn't say you were. I said you were out of practice. Big difference."

"Out of my way."

Joseph had always thought of Liam as a gentle giant. He rarely spoke and spent as much time playing with the human children as he did killing Synestryn. But there was nothing gentle about the fury blazing in his eyes right now. "He hurt Thea. I'm not going to let him hurt anyone else. Including you."

With that, Joseph rapped on Chris's door.

All three men's hands went to their swords, though both Liam and Nicholas prevented Joseph from getting within reach of the door.

A bleary-eyed Chris swung the door open, glaring at them. A trio of nasty scratches burned along his cheek, and the neckline of his T-shirt was ripped.

Thea had fought him. The fact that she'd had to made Joseph want to roar in pain. He should have protected her. He should have known something like this could happen.

"That slut sent you, didn't she?" spat Chris. "I didn't do anything to her she wasn't begging for and you all know it."

He spun around in disgust, leaving his door open for them to enter.

"Show me your lifemark," said Joseph.

Chris stopped in his tracks and slowly turned around. His nostrils were flared in anger and his hand moved to his sword. "What?" he asked in a chillingly quiet tone.

"You heard me. Take off your shirt."

"No. Get the hell out."

"That's not going to happen. You've been accused of a serious crime—one I know you never would have done unless your lifemark was barren."

"I'm leaving," said Chris. "I don't have to take this kind of shit from any of you."

"I'm your leader. You'll do what I tell you to do."

"Oh, yeah? You're too weak to order me to do a damn thing. You have to bring backup with you like some kind of human."

Joseph refused to let that remark bother him now. Later, he knew he'd spend a lot of time going over things in his head—wondering if his men weren't right to question him. But not right now. Right now, he was going to pretend he was still strong enough to enforce his leadership upon a man whom he would likely have to sentence to death.

"Take the shirt off or I'll do it for you."

"Fuck off."

Joseph drew his blade and slashed it between Nicholas and Liam, slicing a cut along Chris's chest.

Chris drew his blade, but Nicholas and Liam were ready for trouble and charged him. Nicholas took control of his sword arm while Liam drove him to the floor. Chris's head hit hard enough to stun him.

Joseph bent down and ripped the shirt open the rest of the way.

Chris's bloody lifemark was barren.

A wave of grief threatened to drive Joseph to his knees. He swiped the edge of the shirt over the cut, just to make sure that the blood wasn't obscuring a leaf or two. It wasn't.

"How long?" asked Joseph. His voice sounded thick and shaky.

Rather than answer, Chris roared in defiance and fought against the men's hold.

"Answer me or I'll bring in a Sanguinar to rip it from your mind."

"Fuck you."

Joseph's hand moved slowly, his limbs heavy with resignation as he dialed Briant. "How's Thea?"

"Sleeping. I repaired the physical damage and removed the memory at her request. She'll be fine in a few days."

"Thank you."

"If you need me to, I can serve as her witness. Her memory is mine now."

"That won't be necessary. I have all the proof I need. Come to Chris's quarters. I need you to question him."

"I'm sorry. I'm too weak after tending Thea."

"You can have all the blood from him you need. He's no longer one of ours."

"His lifemark is bare," guessed Briant.

Joseph didn't answer him. The burden of what he had to do now was already bleak enough. He didn't want to talk about it. "As soon as you're done with Chris, I'm taking him to the Slayers."

Chapter 12

Madoc woke to the feeling of Nika's touch on his face. He recognized it before even opening his eyes.

She was safe. He hadn't gotten her killed. For a moment, he let himself revel in that, letting the feeling ease some of the pressure pounding inside him. His precious Nika was safe.

Her featherlight fingers slid along his brow, over his eyelids, along his cheek until she was stroking his mouth. He couldn't resist the urge to flick his tongue out a tiny bit so he could taste her skin.

"You're awake," she whispered.

He opened his eyes and stared up at her. She was lying next to him on a bed, leaning over him. Any anger he felt at having his plans to die tonight interrupted vanished. If he'd died, he wouldn't have been able to feel her touching him right now. He knew it was wrong, but he didn't care. "Surprised me, too. I thought for sure I was a goner. What happened?"

"Nicholas sent backup. Helen, Drake, Angus, and Gilda. They fought off the Synestryn, and we met Logan at the nearest Gerai house so he could cure the poison."

"Logan? He's here?" Madoc tried to push himself up to find the leech before he could take Nika's blood the way Tynan had. Nika pressed her hands to his bare chest, straddled him, and leaned her weight into him. She wasn't heavy enough to keep him on the bed, but the feel of her palms on his skin did the trick. If he moved away, she'd stop touching him. He didn't want that.

"Don't worry. Drake paid the blood debt since I couldn't."

Anger flooded him at the thought of her offering to bleed for him, making his voice rough and curt. "Don't you ever offer to feed one of those leeches. Understand?"

She didn't answer his question. Instead, she pressed a kiss against his forehead.

Madoc's gaze went to her breasts, which were just the right size to fill his palms. A wave of lust crashed into him, making him grit his teeth to keep from bringing her to his mouth so he could suckle her through her shirt.

She straddled his stomach, and he could feel the heat of her sinking through the layers of cloth between them. Behind her, his dick grew hard, tenting the sheet that covered him.

Apparently, his bloody clothes had been stripped away, leaving him naked. All he had to do was get her out of her pants and slide her down a few inches. He'd finally be inside her, filling her, fucking her.

The small part of him that was still good screamed at him, reminding him she was a virgin. Off-limits.

Madoc fisted his hands in the sheet, forcing himself to keep them at his side.

Nika's lips moved over his brow, tracing the same path her fingers had. He could smell the sweet scent of her skin, see her rapid pulse beating in the hollow of her throat.

His luceria would look so pretty there. So right.

If only.

Madoc refused to go there. Wishful thinking hurt like hell, and he didn't need any more pain in his life.

He'd been so close to escaping it all. So close to peaceful, painless oblivion.

"Why are you doing this to me?" he asked. His voice was a harsh, angry whisper.

"You need me. Just relax and let me do what I need to do."

"Oh, no, you don't." He started to push her up and her sharp little nails dug into his chest.

She actually bared her teeth at him. "I really don't

want to make you bleed again. We've had enough Synestryn for one night, don't you think?"

"Get off of me, Nika. I mean it."

She ignored him, pressing delicate kisses over his temple, down his cheek. Everywhere she touched him tingled, as if the cells were standing up and rejoicing at the contact.

Madoc tried to think about something else—cutting the heads off sgath, sharpening his sword, all those boring meetings with Joseph—but nothing seemed to take his mind away from the soft heat of Nika's lips as they moved unerringly toward his mouth.

"Why are you doing this?" he asked.

"Because you need me. Because we need each other. I can't let you keep running away, and seducing you is the only way to get you over your fear of hurting me."

"I'm not going to fuck you," he said.

"I like the term *making love* better. We'll do that instead."

Girly names changed nothing. Fucking was still fucking. "Not going to happen. I'd really rather not hurt you, but if you don't move away, I'm afraid I'll do just that."

"No, you won't," she said with complete confidence.

Her mouth nibbled at the corner of his, coaxing him to join in and kiss her back. Her breath filled his lungs, making his head spin. He couldn't think straight when she was kissing him. He needed backup.

"Drake," he yelled, a little more breathlessly than he'd intended.

"He's outside with Helen. They're guarding the house, letting you rest and recover."

"You're sure as hell not letting me rest."

"You'll rest better after."

After he'd made her scream his name in climax. After he'd come inside her.

It sounded way too good, too right.

He knew it wasn't, though. He knew how wrong it would be to claim her like that when he knew the next chance he got, he'd go to his death. Only this time, he'd do it right. He'd go too far away for anyone to find. He'd make sure there was no chance of getting out of it.

He'd lock Nika away, drug her, tie her up—something—anything to keep her from following him.

Her mouth settled over his and the ability to think about anything else vanished. The tip of her tongue slid along the seam of his lips, tempting him to open up and let her inside.

If he did, he wouldn't stop. He knew that. He wasn't strong enough to come back from an openmouthed, all-out kiss with Nika.

Madoc turned his head, feeling a line of sweat breaking out along his brow.

"I'm too weak for this. I've just been poisoned, woman. Have a heart."

He could feel her smile against his lips. "Don't worry. I'll do all the work."

She was going to kill him. Madoc wasn't going to need to find a nest of Synestryn. Nika was right here, twisting his insides, making his brain overheat until he knew it would explode.

He locked his lips together tight, refusing her entrance.

Nika sat back, sliding her hands over his chest, down his arm. Her fingers kneaded his muscles, as if enjoying the feel of them. She lifted his right hand and placed it over her breast. "It's okay if you touch me," she said.

Madoc let out an involuntary groan of need.

Her nipple beaded up against his palm. His fingers curled in against his will, cupping her. "No. It's really not." And yet he couldn't pull his hand away. He was going to have to cut his arm off to get himself to stop touching her.

Nika smiled down at him. It was a knowing, purely feminine smile filled with the promise of heaven and hell combined.

He stared at her, wondering what she was going to do next. Would she slide his hand under her shirt, or maybe strip out of it so he could see his hand moving over her naked skin?

Oh, yeah. That was definitely what he wanted to do. Naked Nika.

Instead, she started kneading his hand, pressing on all the small muscles he used to grip his sword.

A moan of pure bliss erupted from his lips and his eyes closed as he enjoyed the feel of her fingers massaging him.

A second later, he felt the ring Iain had given him slide from his finger and his world came crashing to an end.

He jackknifed up in the bed, grabbing at the ring, but Nika had flung it across the room, out of sight. "No!" he shouted, but it was too late.

He felt the last leaf of his lifemark complete its fall, felt the last part of his soul's light wink out, and then a calm sort of numbness descended upon him.

He looked at Nika's face, saw a flash of worry shine in her blue eyes, but it didn't matter. She'd done this to him, and now she was going to face the consequences.

Whatever reason he'd had a moment ago to hold back had gone—vanished into oblivion. All that was left was his hard, aching cock and the woman straddling him.

A smile gradually stretched his mouth. "Playtime."

John had to shove his hands in his pockets to keep himself from reaching for Meghan. She'd laid her clothes near the fire to dry them, and though she'd tried to be discreet and hide them under her damp shirt, he'd seen her lay her panties out, too. Which meant she was bare beneath the loose flannel pants he'd given her.

He'd picked them because they'd shrunk when he'd washed them and were the smallest thing he had. He hadn't imagined that the green and tan plaid would turn him on nearly as much as it had.

John handed her a mug of hot cocoa and grabbed the blanket off his bed. Maybe if he covered her up, he'd be able to keep his thoughts where they belonged and off her body.

Her blond hair was short and damp along the tips where it had gotten wet in the shower. It clung to her neck, baring her throat. The neckline of his sweatshirt gaped, showing off the delicate line of her collarbones. For one insane moment, he wanted to lean forward and press an openmouthed kiss along the smooth skin between her neck and shoulder.

He wondered if she had a bra on under that sweat-shirt, or if every time he wore it from now on, he'd think about the fact that her bare nipples had grazed the fabric sliding against his chest.

Meghan curled her legs under her and accepted the blanket with a thankful smile. "So, what brought you out in the snow tonight?" she asked.

John wasn't going to tell her about his odd dreams. He didn't want her thinking he was some kind of lunatic. Instead, he lied. "I'd gone into town for supplies to ride out the storm. Guess I should have gone earlier."

"How long do the snows up here normally last?"

"The forecast said it would stop by morning."

"That's good. I have no idea how you can live with this cold."

It hit him then that she clearly wasn't from around here. The idea that she would soon be on her way back to her life bothered him, though he had no idea why it should.

"Where are you from?" he asked.

"Phoenix."

"Wow. That's a long way to come. Do you have family in the area?"

"No."

"Here for work?"

"No. I just thought it would be nice to visit a place I'd never been to before. Guess I should have checked the weather first, huh?"

Something in the way she said it made him think she was lying, but he couldn't put his finger on what it was. "Guess so."

She lowered her eyes, staring at his chest. "I'm sorry to have put you out like this."

"It's fine. Really. I'm only here for a few more days, anyway."

"You don't live here?"

"I vacation here, but my time is almost up. Got to get back to the grind."

"What do you do?"

"I'm a builder. I have a new development we're

breaking ground on as soon as the last of the permits are in. Lake homes, mostly."

Her eyes lit up. "Sounds fabulous. I've always thought it would be fun to be an architect and design homes."

"So, why not do it?"

She sipped her cocoa. A bit of foam clung to her upper lip and John had to grit his teeth to keep from licking it away so he could taste the sweetness of melted marshmallows against her skin.

"I was thinking about it. Then Dad got sick."

"I'm sorry."

"It's fine. He's better now. It was bad for a while, but he's back to his old self now. I think he's got himself a girlfriend." She said that last part with a smile that made her eyes light up.

In that moment, she was the prettiest woman he'd ever seen, and that sense of recognition he'd had when he first saw her came rushing back. He knew her. Somehow. He had to. How else could it be that he would look at her and everything inside him would feel . . . right?

He reached out and slid his finger over hers as they cupped the mug. Her skin was incredibly soft and warm, and it was all he could do to keep his touch innocent, when what he really wanted was to strip her bare and glide his hands over every naked inch of her.

She went still, staring at him with wide eyes. He watched her pupils dilate and her lips part as she pulled in a deep breath.

John took the cocoa from her hands and set it aside.

"What are you doing?" she asked in a breathless whisper.

He leaned forward and cupped her face in his hands. She didn't fight him; in fact, if anything, she leaned toward him.

He stared at her mouth. She licked her lips and that small movement made him feel like someone had applied an electric current to his spine.

"I have no idea," he replied, and settled his mouth on hers.

At first, her kiss was hesitant, but as soon as his tongue

swept out over her lip, tasting the sweetness left behind, that changed.

Meghan's mouth opened and she went up on her knees, grabbing his head in a fierce grip. Her tongue played with his, stroking him in a way that made him think of hot bodies sliding against each other. A low, needy sound purred in her chest, and her fingernails dug into his scalp.

She pulled away, panting, staring at him with a mixture of lust and accusation. "What did you do to me?" she demanded. "Did you drug me?"

"Never. I swear I'd never do that to a woman." But he knew what she meant. Even after a few brief seconds of her kiss, John was ready to lay himself out and let her do as she willed with him. Normally, it took him weeks before he decided to sleep with a woman—sex simply wasn't worth the headache that came after a breakup, and at thirty-two he sure as hell wasn't some young, punky kid who let his dick lead the way.

But none of his normal commonsense morals were anywhere to be found right now. His head was spinning like he was drunk and his entire body was shaking with the effort of resisting the need to sink inside her sweet body over and over until he could no longer lift his head. Whatever was going on here wasn't normal.

He just couldn't bring himself to care.

John slid his hands down her neck and splayed his fingers out over the skin his loose sweatshirt left bare. She was so slender and delicate. So soft. If he didn't kiss her again, he wasn't sure he'd survive. Still, he couldn't do this if she didn't want him.

"Do you want me to stop?" he asked, tensing as he waited for her response.

Her shoulders lifted and fell with each rapid breath. Her cheeks were flushed, as was her mouth. Her hands still had a tight hold on his head and he could feel her fingers moving over his scalp in indecision.

"No. I should but I don't," she finally said, and John's world began to spin again.

A smile slowly filled his soul as he lowered his head to kiss her. She tasted of chocolate and the promise of hidden pleasure, and he knew in that moment that he'd never get enough of her.

Meghan never slept with strangers. Never. Until now.

John's clever fingers had them both stripped naked before she even knew it had happened. The worn fabric of the couch was rough against her back, but she didn't mind. Her body was singing and warm and the taste of John filled her head until there was no room for anything else.

His hands slid down her flank in a caress so soft it made her shiver. His mouth left hers, trailing a line of hot kisses along her jaw and down her throat. He nipped at her collarbone, then kept sliding down until his mouth covered her nipple.

Pleasure shot though Meghan, making her back arch off the couch. It was too good. Nothing real ever felt this good.

For one brief moment, she thought she must be dreaming, but then John parted her legs and pressed his erection against her hot center. She could feel the throb of his pulse against her clit as he rubbed back and forth, sliding against her.

Meghan sank her fingers into his thick hair and widened her legs, trying to get him to give her what she needed.

"Please," she heard herself say in the silence of the cabin.

John looked up at her, his hazel eyes dark with desire. He pushed himself up over her, making the delicious muscles over his chest and arms bunch with strength.

She grabbed his tight butt and forced him forward. She was slick, hot, and ready, and he slid in easily, his aim just right. And he kept on sliding, sinking deep, inch by inch, until there was no room left for him to go.

Meghan forgot how to breathe as the pleasure of being filled consumed her. It had been so long she'd almost forgotten what it was like to feel the heady weight of a man atop her, to feel the steely length of him stretching her. Her whole body tingled and she knew it wouldn't be long before her orgasm claimed her.

"So good," he growled against her hair.

She was beyond words, so she simply clung to him as he moved inside her, stroking her higher with each gliding thrust.

His pace sped up and Meghan's toes dug into the cushions. He slid his arms around her, holding her close as she felt the first wave of her climax break deep inside her.

She let out a gasping cry of pleasure and felt John's arms tighten around her as his own body clenched in orgasm. They crashed together, their bodies locked inside the glorious intensity of their release. A deep, pulsing pressure let loose inside her, over and over as the last glowing remnants of pleasure began to fade.

Distantly, she realized that this was different from any other sex she'd ever had. What they'd shared here tonight had somehow changed her life. She was simply too spent to care.

As she let fatigue take over, she felt John lift her and tuck her into his bed. He slid in behind her, wrapped his arms around her, and pressed a soft kiss against her temple.

Alexander slipped into John's cabin unnoticed. The strain of using his power to shield his presence left a grinding hunger deep in his belly, but there was no help for it.

He moved to the bedroom and slid his hand under the blankets until he found the naked skin of Meghan's abdomen. With a mere whisper of power, he sped the course of time within her womb by a few days—just until he felt a tiny soul spark to life inside her.

His plan to unite John and Meghan had worked. Soon, another strongly blooded child would be born, adding to the dozen other successes he'd had this year.

As tired as he was, the urge to rest was nearly overwhelming, but there wasn't time. He had three more couples to unite, somehow.

He had to keep the faith, keep working, and believe that Project Lullaby was going to save his people from starvation.

Chapter 13

Nika wasn't sure what exactly had just happened, but part of her was beginning to think taking that ring off had been a mistake.

Something about Madoc had changed. The way he looked at her now was darker somehow, more dangerous.

It made her body heat and sent a shiver coursing along the inside of her skin.

She splayed her hand against his bare chest, reveling in the feel of his muscles, tight beneath her palm. The branches of his lifemark swayed toward her touch as if reaching for her.

A spike of victory went through her. It was working. Finally, after all this time of knowing they were meant to be together, she had proof.

"That's supposed to happen, right?" she asked him.

Madoc looked down, saw the motion for only a brief second; then his green gaze went back to her, sliding over her face until it settled on her mouth. "Don't fucking care. Lie down."

His deep, rough voice sank into her and she had to stifle another shiver. She had to focus. She had a job to do. She couldn't simply do as he asked, no matter how nice it sounded.

Nika didn't move. She wasn't sure what to do now, but she knew she was supposed to take his luceria.

She reached for it, but Madoc was faster. He gripped her wrist and rolled them over so she was lying under him. He held her there, staring down at her with a look so hungry, she almost wanted to run.

Almost.

Running was no longer an option. Then again, it never really had been. She'd known this moment would come. She'd lain in bed at night thinking about it, dreaming about it, touching herself. After months of waiting for him, she was glad he was finally right here with her.

The feel of his weight on top of her made her body sing. She widened her thighs to make more room for his big body to settle between them. Madoc shifted his hips, rubbing his erection against her in a way that sent zingers of sensation rioting through her.

Nika sucked in a breath and let it out in a soft moan. "Do that again."

Madoc blinked several times, as if trying to clear his head. His body was still, his face contorted into a mask of painful restraint.

"Madoc?"

"This isn't the way it's supposed to be," he said.

"What?"

He didn't answer her. He gave his head a hard shake and gritted his teeth.

"Let go of my wrists."

"Mine," he growled, tightening his grip.

She looked him right in the eye. "I'm not going to leave you."

He didn't release her. His mouth came down onto hers in a fierce kiss.

Nika's toes curled and she opened her mouth against his so she could taste him. As the tip of her tongue met his, his body tightened like he'd taken an electric shock. A noise too rough to be a moan rumbled through his chest, vibrating against her nipples. She felt them bead up tighter, and rubbing against him was too good to resist. The only thing better would be if she could feel his bare skin against hers.

"Need my shirt off," she whispered into his mouth.

Rather than pulling away from their kiss, he reached

between them and shoved the fabric of her shirt and bra up over her breasts, baring them.

The first contact of her nipples against his chest sent a shocking, sparking sensation into her skin. It didn't hurt, but it was too intense to be called pleasure. She'd never felt anything like it before, but she knew she wanted to feel it again.

Madoc had gone still above her. He'd felt it, too.

She took his head in her hands, forcing him to look at her. "Don't you dare stop," she warned him. "I need this."

A slow, dark smile curved his lips. "There is no stopping now." He lifted his left hand, showing her the ring of the Theronai. It was nearly white, but the faint colors left were moving, swirling frenetically within the band. "See. You were right. You *are* mine."

He reached between them and pressed the ring against one nipple. It was vibrating, and the feel of that humming against her sensitive flesh made her cry out.

"Like that?" he asked as if he already knew the answer. "Then you're going to love this."

He slid his hand down over her stomach and unbuttoned her loose jeans. The ring left a trail of tingling skin in its wake. Nika's breathing sped up and her body heated, going liquid. Despite the cool air, sweat broke out along her hairline.

Madoc's fingers found their way inside her panties and he cupped her mound, his big hand covering her completely. The ring settled right over her clit—near but not touching, not nearly close enough. The shimmering sensation humming from the ring set her nerves on fire and made her writhe beneath him.

She spread her legs wider, opening herself up so he could make direct contact. Her hips moved, seeking what she needed. And then suddenly, his hand was gone.

She looked up, trying to figure out what had gone wrong. Madoc knelt between her knees, his body beautifully naked, his penis thick and stiff, jutting out from his body.

Nika's mouth went dry and the need to touch him overwhelmed her. She reached out and wrapped her hands around him. He was smooth. Soft skin stretched over rock hardness. The contrast was completely surprising and totally intriguing.

A drop of liquid leaked from the tip of his erection. She touched it with her finger, sliding the slickness over his skin.

Madoc let out a sound so low she could barely hear it. But she felt it vibrate through her arms and settle in her chest.

She looked up at him, opening her mouth to ask if he was okay, but the words got stuck in her throat. He was staring down at her, his jaw tight, his muscles clenched. The look of need darkening his eyes was so intense it made Nika's insides melt. She wanted to give him whatever he needed, whatever he wanted. Forever.

She scrambled to her knees and jerked the shirt and bra over her head, tossing them to the floor. They were going to get in the way of feeling his skin against hers.

He watched her with those hungry eyes roaming over every section of skin she revealed. Nika knew she was no great beauty. Years of suffering and starvation had left her flat-chested, too skinny and bony, but Madoc didn't seem to mind. He looked at her like she was everything he'd ever wanted, like the rest of the world had ceased to exist.

She slid her arms around his neck, feeling the hum of his luceria as she grazed it. Her nipples pressed into his chest, his erection throbbed against her stomach, and the intense warmth of his body everywhere it touched hers made her groan in delight.

"Take off your pants," he told her.

Nika ignored him and kissed him instead. His wide hands gripped her hips, then moved up to her waist and over her back. He pulled her hard against him, nearly driving the breath from her body, but she didn't mind. Who needed oxygen when she had Madoc's mouth on hers, his tongue licking along her lips and gliding against her own?

Her head spun and she was breathless when he finally pulled away from her. His cheeks were dark and his powerful chest rose and fell with his uneven breathing.

His mouth moved like he was trying to say something, but no words came out.

He wrapped his arms around her and eased her body down to the bed. Instead of coming over her as she'd hoped he'd do, he moved to her feet, gripped the open waistband of her jeans, and pulled them down her legs. He gave a rough jerk, and socks, underwear, and shoes all went flying.

He surveyed her naked body and pulled in a deep breath, making his nostrils flare. "All mine."

And she was. She always had been. "You're mine, too."

He gave her a dark smile, then prowled up her body on his hands and knees. He braced himself over her, shoving her legs apart with his knee, and leaned down to flick his tongue over her nipple. Nika sucked in a breath and arched her back, pulling his head down for more.

He drew her into his mouth, creating a suction so good she dug her nails into his scalp so he wouldn't pull away. His hand stroked down her side, over her stomach, and his fingers slid between her labia. She was slick, and as hot as his skin was, his fingers felt cool against her heated flesh.

She felt the blunt tip of one finger pressing into her, stretching her.

Madoc groaned. "So fucking tight," he said against her breast. "But not for long."

Madoc couldn't think straight. He stared down at Nika's naked body and all he could think about was getting inside her. He knew there was something he was supposed to do—something he was forgetting—but compared to taking her, everything else was unimportant.

Her blue eyes were darker than usual, more like twilight than a bright winter sky. Her mouth was swollen and red, her lips parted. A rosy flush spread down her neck and across her chest. Her nipple tightened against his tongue and she let out a soft groan.

She grabbed his head as if she actually had a chance at controlling him.

Something dark and powerful rose up inside him,

balking at the challenge. No one was ever going to control him. He'd do what he damn well pleased, when he pleased.

And right now, what he pleased was getting his cock as deep inside Nika as possible. He wanted to feel her virgin-tight body yielding to him as he drove deep and hard.

He shifted his body so they were lined up just right and lifted her head so she could see. "You watch while I take you," he ordered her.

Her blue eyes fixated on the space between them as the tip of his cock pressed hard, stretching her open. She was slick enough that he could slide in just a bit, but her muscles resisted the invasion.

"Relax," he growled at her. "Don't you dare fucking fight me."

"I'm not," she whispered.

She was lying. She had to be. She was trying to stop him.

A seething darkness seemed to swirl through him, demanding that he take her hard and fast. She was tempting him on purpose. Testing him.

Madoc wasn't going to let that challenge go unanswered.

He surged forward, sinking deeper. Nika's eyes fell shut and a gasp whispered out of her mouth. Her hands clenched around his arms as if she was trying to pull him closer.

He was definitely going to get a hell of a lot closer before they were done.

Madoc ripped his arms out of her grasp and pushed her thighs higher. His hands looked huge against her legs, almost brutal.

A faint flicker of worry made him hesitate for a brief moment before it was washed away by a surge of need.

Her head fell back to the bed. Her tight pussy was quivering around him, so slick and hot he knew he wasn't going to last much longer before he came. And when he did, he wanted her to feel it—to be so deep inside her she'd never again be able to forget she belonged to him.

Madoc pulled back just enough that he could see her

wetness shining on his cock before he slid back in and kept sliding. He felt some resistance, but he wasn't going to let it stop him. He pushed past, wringing a gasping cry from Nika, and finally, after several rocking thrusts, he was where he belonged.

Her breathing was fast and her heartbeat was so frantic he could see her breast trembling in time with her pulse. The flush of color and the sheen of perspiration covering her chest were proof she was enjoying what he had to give.

Not that it mattered. All he cared about now was finishing what he'd started.

Madoc pulled away and surged back, shaking her body with the power of his stroke. Her fingers reached blindly for him, landing on his chest.

He felt the bare branches of his lifemark reach for her, arching toward her touch as if starved for it.

Too late. It was too late for her to save him, but he didn't fucking care. Right now, with her supple body beneath him, her tight pussy hugging his cock, and her fingers on his skin, nothing else seemed to matter.

Madoc began to move, setting a hard, fast pace. He wasn't going to last long the first time he took her, but he wanted to wring as much pleasure as he could from it before he gave in.

Sweat cooled his back. The bed rocked, making the floorboards squeak. From somewhere outside the room, he heard voices, but they meant nothing. The only sound that mattered was the faint sighs lifting from Nika that were growing louder with every move he made.

His body tightened as his climax neared. His movements became more frantic, his pace faster. A brilliant tingling swept over his skin, sinking into the base of his spine. He pushed Nika's hips higher, buried himself deep enough that she let out a grunt; then he let go.

Mind-numbing pleasure gripped him hard as he spent himself within Nika's slick body, spurting inside her over and over again. He went weak, collapsing over her, panting.

He felt her squirm beneath him. "I can't breathe," she

said. She didn't sound like a satisfied woman, replete with pleasure. In fact, she sounded upset.

Whatever.

Madoc flipped onto his back to give her room, and that was when he saw the stain of blood smearing his cock.

That flicker of worry that had nagged him before came back with a vengeance. He pushed himself up and saw the red spot on the sheets just as the bedroom door burst open.

Logan stood there, staring at them, almost in a panic. "I smell blood."

"Get out!" yelled Nika, covering her nakedness with her arms.

The Sanguinar's eyes moved over her body and a killing rage consumed Madoc. He let out a feral growl and leaped from the bed. Logan's eyes went to his dick and a look of understanding fell over the bloodsucker.

"Madoc, no." Nika was behind him, wrapping her arms around his waist as if she could actually stop him from killing the leech. "Don't do this. He was only worried about me. He knows about the ring—about how you're out of time."

It was the feel of her hard little nipples against his naked back that stopped him. He wanted to fuck her again more than he wanted to kill Logan, but only by a little.

"Get out," he ordered Logan.

"You can't let the others see you like this," Logan told him. "They sent Chris to the Slayers only a few hours ago. You'll be next."

"Like hell."

Logan looked over his shoulder as if someone was coming. "Now, Nika. There's no more time." And then he shut the door.

Madoc spun around to face her. "What the hell was he talking about?" he asked.

"This," she said as she reached up and grabbed his luceria in her fist.

The band that had been with him his entire life broke open and slithered away from his neck. Nika lifted her arms to fasten it around her slender throat and pointed to the floor. "On your knees, Madoc," she said as she handed him his sword.

Instincts embedded in him for centuries drove him to his knees as he scored a cut over his heart and uttered the vow, "My life for yours." He dipped his finger in the blood flowing down his ribs and pressed it against the luceria, grazing her breasts with his forearm.

The pale band shrank to fit close to her throat. It looked so fucking beautiful there, all he could do was stare.

Nika's shoulders slumped in relief. "About freakin' time," she muttered, then in a louder voice said, "You're mine, Madoc. If you go out to kill yourself again, you're taking me with you."

The weight of her vow—such as it was—crashed down on top of him, crushing the air from his lungs. That seething darkness that had woven its way through his soul seemed to freeze in place, cowering at the power in her words.

In that instant, the little sliver of the man he'd been born to be sparked back to life and he realized what he'd done. Her blood was smeared over her inner thighs. He'd taken her hard, ripping her virginity from her as if it were of no more worth than a discarded tissue.

Shame burned hot in his chest. Every selfish moment seared itself in his mind, ripping a low cry of grief from his lungs.

"I'm sorry," he breathed out, knowing the words would never be enough to make up for what he'd done. He'd ruined something beautiful. Destroyed it. She'd given herself to him and he'd ground that gift beneath his heel.

Madoc reached for her, ready to beg for her forgiveness, but it was too late. His world faded and the vision the luceria wanted him to see descended upon him.

Madoc was flung into Nika's mind. He saw her life through her eyes, felt it through her skin.

He felt the claws of the sgath that had hurt her the night her family was attacked. They raked over her skin, making her bleed as the burn of poison entered her

bloodstream. He felt the sgath's slimy tongue trail along
her flesh, lapping up her blood.

Around her, he sensed a buzzing movement too
fast to see. He tried to slow down the passage of time
so he could make out what that movement was, but all
he could see was the vague shape of a man pressing his
hands against her. It wasn't one of the Sanguinar, but
the feel of what he did had that same kind of tingling
quality that healing did.

Someone had saved her life that night. That was why
she hadn't died from the sgath poison.

Madoc wished like hell he could see who it was so
he could thank the man for giving him a chance to keep
Nika safe.

Time resumed its normal flow. Nika was weak and
dizzy. She couldn't move. A lethargic daze had settled
over her, but her eyes remained fixed on her baby sister.

Madoc heard the vow she'd given Tori never to leave
her—the vow she'd kept to this day.

Nika's world winked out and when she came to, she
was in a hospital. Fever burned inside her as she fought
off the remains of the sgath poison. One of the hospital staff hovered around her, poking and prodding her,
injecting her with medicine that did no good. Nika's
sole focus was on Tori, and that was what gave her the
strength to keep fighting.

It was days after Nika had been sent home that the
first attack on her mind came.

Madoc reached for his sword, only to find he had no
sword, no body. He was huddled in a corner of Nika's
memories, unable to do more than witness what happened to her.

Rage made him flail at the boundaries of this vision,
but in the end, he was helpless. All he could do was suffer through as Nika had, experiencing whatever it was
the luceria demanded of him.

Nika was ripped from her body, flung through space,
and forced to inhabit the alien mind of the sgath that
had taken her blood. Panic exploded inside her. She
knew this was no nightmare. It was real.

She tried to stop it—to pull back into her body—but the creature's hold on her was too strong and her mental defenses too weak to fight it.

That night, Nika was along for the ride, trapped inside a monster, forced to hunt and kill a teenage boy. She felt like it was her fault—that she should have been able to stop the thing from killing. The stain that failure left on her soul still haunted her to this day.

Madoc wanted to reassure her that it wasn't her fault. The death of that boy wasn't her sin. She had still been a child herself, only twelve. She wasn't responsible for the acts of an evil monster.

Even as Madoc reached for her to gather her in his arms and convince her to forgive herself of a crime she did not commit, he knew it was futile in this bodyless existence.

As the Synestryn fed on the boy, one of its fellow sgath attacked it, fighting for the kill. A feeding frenzy started, and the sgath that had taken Nika's blood was attacked, its flesh eaten by its hungry brothers.

Even as Nika's mind rebelled at such an appalling display, she had the instinctive knowledge that being inside the sgath when it died could kill her as well.

She fought as the thing's blood soaked into the ground, struggling to get free. The monster didn't want to let go of her. She made it stronger, somehow. Faster and smarter.

It didn't want to die alone.

Frantic, Nika forced all her fear into the sgath, using that emotion to propel her out of its weakened mind before it died. She was sucked back into her own body, but by then it was too late. Her blood—the blood that sgath had used to take over her mind—now flowed through a dozen more of its kind.

They all wanted her inside them, making them faster and stronger, too. She felt them pull at her, tugging at her mind as if they were trying to rip it from her. She hardened herself, fighting back, refusing to give up for Tori's sake.

But she was too weak. She didn't know how to fight

off one, much less a dozen. Her mind cracked and splintered. Glittering shards of what made Nika who she was were cast into the night. Each of the sgath claimed its own piece, ripping her sanity from her.

That was the night Nika went crazy.

Madoc had no idea how she'd survived it—how she'd lived long enough for him to hunt and kill the things that haunted her, so she could reclaim all the fractured pieces of herself. He wasn't even sure if what he'd done had been enough.

Tori had been the one who'd really saved Nika's life.

The tenuous connection between the two sisters shimmered like a braid of spider silk. Over the years, it had thinned until only a single strand remained. Nika refused to let that strand break. He felt her determination to hang on to that connection even as Tori worked to sever it.

Why she would do such a thing, Madoc had no idea, but part of him hoped she'd succeed. Nothing could ever harm Nika. Not even her own sister. He refused to even consider letting it happen.

Nika was his lady now and he was honor-bound to protect her with his life, if need be. He could no longer allow her to run around at night, risking yet another attack by a Synestryn who would rip away bits of her mind. He'd managed to slay most of the sgath, but what if one of the stronger Synestryn got some of her blood? What if she couldn't fight it? What if his sweet Nika was left damaged beyond repair, living in a nightmare, forced to remain forever locked inside the monsters while they killed?

It was her worst fear. He could see the malignant pulsing of that terror echoing through her mind, shaping her every move.

She'd rather die than go back to that world of blood and death and insanity.

Madoc was going to make sure it never happened, even if she ended up hating him for what he now knew he had to do.

Chapter 14

Nika knew that the luceria would give her some kind of vision once she put it on—some peek into Madoc's life. She wasn't sure what it could show her that she didn't already know. She'd been inside him, seen the darkness that plagued him, and bathed in the light of his soul. How could a view of what his life had been like, or what made him the person he was, top that?

But what she saw was no flash from the past, as she'd heard described. What she saw was something she'd never even considered.

The future.

It swirled around her, more a concept than a series of events. Comprised more of emotion than anything, the flow of possibilities was endless, pattering against her like hot rain. With each drop that fell, she saw another possible future.

Some were horrible, tainted with blood and death. Others were so sweet, she could almost feel the tears of joy sliding over her cheeks. She smelled a baby's skin in one moment; then in the next, she felt the chill of Madoc's lifeblood leaking through her fingers. The thrill of a battle won surged inside her, only to be cut short by the debilitating grief of both her sisters' deaths.

Nika was laughing and crying, raging at the world and celebrating miracles. The barrage of emotions kept coming at her, swarming over her until a single one remained.

She felt trapped. Useless. Desperate. Defeated.

Those emotions coalesced into a vision so real, she knew without a doubt that the luceria was showing her more than simply a possibility. It was showing her her future.

She was locked inside Dabyr, a virtual prisoner. She recognized the space as Madoc's suite, but it wasn't the walls that kept her here. It was a vow she'd made in haste.

She'd promised him she wouldn't get hurt and that vow had allowed him to imprison her inside Dabyr, where he thought no harm could come to her. It had allowed him to keep her there while the last connection she had to Tori winked out of existence.

At that moment, Nika knew that her sister was dead, and it had been her vow that killed Tori. Nika also knew that her failure would be the thing that killed her. The guilt would eat her whole, leaving her an angry, wasted shell of a woman.

Madoc would suffer watching it happen, being unable to do anything to stop it. The two of them would drift apart. The darkness that lurked inside him would grow.

Andra would blame herself, and Paul's inability to fix it would gnaw at him, making him angry and afraid. Their relationship would suffer, too.

As their connections weakened, so did their magic. Battles became harder to win. More human children were stolen from their parents. Countless people died.

Nika couldn't let any of that happen. She was meant to fight by Madoc's side—to take the same risks he did. She wasn't meant to be protected from her birthright.

Whatever she did—whatever promises he tried to force from her—she had to stay strong and refuse to give him that vow that would destroy the lives of so many.

"Promise me," she heard him say outside the confines of the vision.

Nika opened her eyes and looked down at Madoc. Blood ran down his chest. His naked body was shining with perspiration, his muscles knotted with fear.

He gave her a little shake. "Promise me you'll do whatever it takes to stay safe."

That was the trap the luceria had warned her about. Her vow given to him now would ruin her life and the lives of so many others.

"No," she whispered, even as the desire to give him anything he wanted burned inside her. "I can't promise you that. I won't."

Madoc rose to his feet to loom over her. His face was dark with rage, and she could feel the subtle vibrations running through his muscles as if he were holding himself back. "Why the hell not?"

Before she could answer, a hard pounding rocked the bedroom door.

"Nika, are you okay?" asked Helen, her voice tight with worry.

"Out of the way," came Drake's deep voice; then he barged into the room, his sword drawn. He came to a dead stop, staring at the naked couple in front of him.

Madoc let out a warning growl and ripped a sheet from the bed, draping it around Nika's body. She clutched at it, capturing his arm as well to hold him back.

"I tried to tell them you were busy," said Logan.

Drake averted his eyes but did not put his sword away. "Logan, you know I don't trust you any farther than I can toss you off the end of my blade."

Helen put a staying hand on her husband's shoulder. "We need to get back outside. Their blood will be drawing company here."

Drake nodded and looked at Madoc. "Get yourselves cleaned up; then get outside and lend a hand. We've already saved your ass once tonight. Helen's tired."

"I'm fine," she said, tossing her twin braids back over her shoulders.

Drake's eyes followed the motion before sliding over her breasts. "Yes, you are. Let's go."

The pair of them left, but Logan remained in the doorway, his pale eyes cautious. He looked at Madoc. "Did it work? Did she get to you in time?"

Madoc's hold on Nika's body tightened. "Guess we'll see. If my lifemark buds again, we're safe. If not . . ."

"It will," said Nika, letting every bit of her faith flow through her tone.

Madoc cupped her cheek, his touch so gentle she had to blink back tears. "You and I have a lot of things to talk about."

She knew what he meant. He wanted to wrap her up and tuck her away somewhere where her life would have no meaning. That wasn't going to happen.

But now was not the time to argue about it. Right now they needed to wash off the blood before they were all trapped inside this house, sitting ducks for every Synestryn within miles.

"Later," she told him. "After we've showered."

Something inside Madoc had definitely changed since Nika had put on his luceria; he just wasn't sure it was enough to turn him back into the man he used to be. All the violent feelings he thought would go away were still there, pounding inside him, demanding release. He wanted to kill Drake and Logan for looking at Nika's body. The only difference was that now he also felt bad about it.

Drake was his friend. He shouldn't have wanted to kill the man for taking the time to see if Nika was okay. He should have thanked him for caring enough to look in on her.

He *knew* that; it simply didn't change the fact that if the man did it again, it might be the last thing he did.

That wasn't right. That wasn't the way Madoc wanted to feel for his brothers. And it sure as hell wasn't the way he wanted to feel toward Nika.

He wanted to be gentle with her. Loving. Or at least not scare her and hurt her like he had.

Madoc started the shower, testing the temperature so it wouldn't burn her skin. Once it was right, he stepped away so there was room for her to get in.

She shed the sheet, letting it fall to the floor. Her back was to him, but the feminine lines of her back drew his eyes down to the prettiest ass he'd ever seen. She was pale and smooth and so mouthwatering he had to grip the counter to keep himself from shoving her against the wall so he could take her from behind.

She peered over her naked shoulder. "Are you coming in with me?"

Hell, no. If he got in that shower, he was going to fuck her again. It didn't matter that he'd made her bleed a few minutes ago, or that he was sure she had to be sore. All that would matter was the slide of hot water over her skin and finding a position where he could take her deep and hard without slipping and bashing both their skulls in.

"I'll wash up in the sink. I need to get out and help Drake."

Her blue eyes narrowed. "You're still afraid of me."

"Hardly. Afraid of what I might do *to* you? Absolutely. You should be, too."

"You still don't get it, do you? I've known from the first moment I saw you that you would never hurt me."

"I'd say the proof of how stupid that idea was is smeared all over the insides of your thighs. I made you bleed."

"Only a little. And it's not like it could have been helped. Any man would have done the same thing."

The idea of another man taking her made his vision go red around the edges. That killing rage was back, blasting inside him, making him wish for something he could beat into a slurry. He had to take several deep breaths to calm down enough to unclench his jaw.

Nika held her hand out to him. Her slender fingers were wet. Water sluiced over her breasts and down her belly, making her skin turn pink from the heat of the shower.

"Come here," she said. "You don't have to be afraid of me anymore."

Against his better judgment, Madoc took a step forward. Then another. He couldn't seem to resist the pull of her hand reaching for him.

Her wet fingers closed over his, tugging him toward her.

"This is a mistake," he muttered.

"Maybe. Maybe not. Don't you want to find out?"

He did. More than he wanted his next breath.

He stepped into the tub and Nika pulled the curtain closed behind him. A feminine smile filled with victory curled her mouth. "See? That wasn't so hard, was it?"

Oh, he was hard all right. Throbbing with the need to take her again, but he managed to clamp his lips shut and nod.

She soaped up her hands and slid them over his chest, washing the blood away from the shallow cut that had already healed shut. The branches of his lifemark swayed, reaching for her slippery fingers wherever they went.

It had been so long since Madoc had felt his lifemark move like it was meant to, he had almost forgotten what the sensation felt like. The gentle rippling just under his skin was comforting. Normal. No buds had formed along the branches yet, but that could take time. He wasn't going to worry about it.

For now, all he was going to worry about was making sure that every drop of blood was washed from her skin.

That, and keeping his dick to himself.

He spun her around so the water sprayed over her, keeping her warm, then took the soap from her hands.

"We need to be quick," he said. "We can't leave all the fun to Drake and Helen."

"I'm looking forward to seeing what I can do. All that power inside you is calling to me, begging me to let it out."

Madoc's hands moved over her shoulders, sliding along the luceria. It was still paler than it should have been, but as he looked, he could see silvery white swirls sliding inside the band. They were the same color as Nika's hair had been under the winter moon as she stood in the graveyard.

The luceria tingled at his touch, giving off a happy buzz.

His soapy hands moved down her body, sliding over her tight little nipples, down her flat belly, and through the pale curls between her thighs. He wanted to wash away every trace of blood—every scrap of pain he'd given her tonight. He knew the memories would always remain, but there was nothing he could do about that but try to replace them with better ones.

His fingers parted her folds, slipping gently over her skin as he washed her. The urge to slide his fingers inside her was nearly overwhelming, but he held back, worried he'd cause her more pain.

His ring was still vibrating in time with her necklace, and as it grazed over her clit, she sucked in a sharp breath.

Nika's head fell back in pleasure as she enjoyed the sensation. Madoc only wished that he'd been able to make her feel that way when he'd had her in bed.

He had a lot of making up to do. She hadn't gotten off even once.

Normally, he wouldn't have cared, but with Nika, nothing was normal. It was a point of pride, and he was going to make her come, even if he had to get creative to make it happen.

A bounty of ideas filled his head, making his mouth stretch in a grin.

"Can two people really do that?" she asked.

Madoc stilled as surprise settled over him. "You can already read my thoughts? That usually takes a while."

"It's what I do."

A wicked spurt of lust shot through him. "Then tell me what you think about this."

He formed an image in his head of her splayed out, naked and writhing in his bed, while he took her with his mouth.

Her nipples hardened against his chest and she let out a soft moan. "Can we do that now?"

Madoc wanted nothing more, but duty called. They'd already lingered longer than they should have. As powerful as Drake and Helen were, it wasn't smart to leave Nika's protection up to only one couple. "It'll have to wait until we get back to Dabyr."

She went stiff in his arms and looked up with a defiant tilt of her chin. "We're not going back there. We're going to find Tori."

Madoc felt Nika slam a wall up between them. Her posture changed. The languid softness in her gaze went hard and cold. The feminine welcome that had been flowing through her only a moment ago dried up, leaving a cold, bleak space between them.

"If you think I'm going to sit back while those monsters continue to hurt my sister now that I have access to your power, you're the one who's crazy."

"I hate to interrupt again," said Logan through the bathroom door, "but we have a substantial number of Synestryn approaching."

Madoc took that news as an offering from heaven. Rather than shake sense into Nika, or do something he'd regret, he was going to get to vent his frustration on some snarlies.

"Come on," he told her. "I want you where I can keep an eye on you."

Keep an eye on her. Like a child.

Like hell.

Nika tucked her fury away as she slid on the sweats Logan had found for her.

A section of bedding had been cut away, along with the smear of blood she'd left behind. That, along with all of the other bloodied linens, was gone, and a fire was burning in the living room hearth.

She hurried through the room and peered out the window. Sure enough, a pile of demons was out there, corralled by a sinuous line of fire Helen had created.

"I want you to stay in here," said Madoc. "Logan, you make sure she does."

"I thought I was supposed to help you fight," said Nika.

"Not you, honey. Even if you did know what you were doing—which you don't yet—you're too fragile for a fight. You stay here. Stay safe." He kissed her forehead and darted out the door, sword in hand.

Nika turned to glare at Logan. "You try to stop me

and I'll find a dozen new and interesting ways to make you regret it."

Logan lifted his elegant hands, a small smile playing at the corners of his luscious mouth. "I would never dare to stand between a woman and the man whom she plans to teach a lesson. I prefer to watch the show."

Nika nodded and slid on a coat. Her hair was wet, making her shiver as soon as she hit the cold night air. She hung back near the house, safely inside the protective ring of fire, watching and listening for a chance to help.

Despite what Madoc thought, she was not fragile. She was not useless. And she was going to prove it.

"What's the situation?" she heard Madoc ask Drake.

"We have several groups sectioned off by fire. We're taking them on one at a time. West to east. Stay to Helen's right, out of her line of fire."

"Right. Got it."

Nika watched as Helen's body erupted in flame. It seemed to flow up through her, as if she were sucking heat from the earth. Consumed by a wavering red-orange glow, she lifted her finger and pointed at a ring of fire about ten feet across. Inside that ring were a dozen demons of various types.

Fear crawled along Nika's skin, but she refused to flee. This was her calling, too. Just like Helen. She belonged on a battlefield and she wasn't going to let anyone get in her way.

Once she learned the trick to killing these things, she would use that knowledge to free Tori.

Nika let only a small section of her mind free so she could remain standing, and sent it into Helen's. The woman was so busy, she hadn't even noticed the slight intrusion.

Helen's body seethed with power. It flowed into her through her luceria, filling her up and making her whole in a way Nika had never realized existed. Seeing that— feeling it—was like pulling in her first breath of air. Now that she'd had it, she didn't want to give it up.

There were so many things going on inside Helen's head, it was hard to keep track. Foremost was the barely leashed power of the flames she commanded. Secondary to that was a string of ideas moving back and forth between the couple.

As Helen began to snuff out a section of flames so the demons could come at them only one at a time, Drake predicted her intentions and stepped forward, his blade ready to cut the first demon down before it had time to move.

He ducked to the left as a spear of flame shot from Helen's hand into the head of a scaly Synestryn. Drake was so close to the shot, the tips of his hair had to be singed, and yet the motion hadn't slowed his fight.

The concert of thought and action vibrated between the couple, allowing them to work as a seamless unit. It was humbling and beautiful to watch.

Nika was so distracted by that connection—so full of yearning for what the couple shared—she nearly forgot why she was here, hovering silently in Helen's mind.

She needed to learn to use her power the way Helen did.

Nika focused on the mechanics of magic, on how Helen controlled the flow of energy into her depending on what she intended to do with it—taking into herself only what she needed to perform each task. There was a conduit between them invisible to the naked eye, but inside Helen's mind, the connection glowed bright, pulsing with life and power.

Fiery energy roared through that conduit, was focused and shaped by Helen, then shot out into the night, burning demons, or flinging them back, or heating the air around them until they choked from lack of oxygen.

After a few moments of study, Nika thought she could emulate Helen's actions, but once she left the woman's mind, the knowledge seemed to dribble out of her memory, fading as the seconds passed.

Before it was all gone, she reached for Madoc's power the way Helen had with Drake, but rather than a wide pipeline of seething power, she found only a minuscule strand of energy flowing into her.

Disappointment fell over her and she leaned back against the door to steady herself.

Nika wasn't anything like Helen. She was weak and inexperienced. Maybe with time she could become more like the other woman, but Nika didn't have time. Tori needed her now.

Madoc shouted something Nika didn't hear clearly over the roar of fire and snarls of demons, and another section of the fiery wall winked out, letting a new group of Synestryn escape their ring of flames. He was waiting for them, and each powerful shift of his body left another corpse littering the ground.

Firelight glistened off the black blood pooling at his feet and cast his face in stark relief. His big body was outlined by flame, leaving him a dark patch of deadly motion against the brightness.

Nika watched him and craved things she couldn't name. Parts of her that had lain dormant began to wake and the need to join him and fight by his side was nearly overwhelming.

Once again, she put the image of what Helen could do into her head, using that as an example, and pulled on the delicate strand of power hovering between them.

It leaped into her, streaking through her, filling her. The skin under the luceria hummed and warmed, helping to drive away some of the chill sinking into her bones. As Nika pulled more power into herself, it ricocheted inside her, bouncing off her bones, making them ache.

She let it build inside her, accumulating until there was enough to strike out at one of the demons. Using Helen's example, she let the energy streak through her, exiting from her fingertips in a gush of flames.

At least, that was what was supposed to have happened. Instead, a sorry spray of sparks dribbled from her hand, burning her fingertips.

She yelped and shook her hand, trying to rid it of the painful flames.

Madoc spun toward the sound, roaring in defiance. A demon saw the opening and lunged for his throat. Nika froze in panic, staring at its serrated teeth, glossy with saliva as it went for the kill.

She tried to scream a warning, but her lungs had closed up and she couldn't make a sound.

A split second before the thing hit, a ball of flames knocked it back away from Madoc. It rolled aside, yelping in pain. A wall of fire shot up from the ground, separating him from the monsters, protecting him.

Madoc raced over the ground, not even bothering to look behind him. He was at her side in the space of three seconds, and in that short time, Nika realized what she had done.

She'd nearly killed him. If Helen hadn't been here to save him, that thing would have ripped his throat out when he'd reacted to the sound of her pain.

That could never happen again.

His eyes darted over her. "Where are you hurt?"

"I'm okay."

"What the hell are you doing out here?"

"Trying to help."

"Go inside and stay there until this is over. You're going to get yourself killed."

Or someone else.

There was no sense in fighting him. He was right. She had no idea what she was doing.

Nika turned around and went back into the house. Logan was there, waiting for her inside the door.

"Would you like me to heal those burns?" he asked.

She shook her head. They weren't bad. Just painful. "No. I think I'm going to need them to remind me of what's real and what isn't."

Chapter 15

For the first time in nearly a year, Torr's feet were cold. He'd gone to sleep feeling nothing and woken up feeling cold.

A thrill of excitement rippled through him. Maybe whatever the Sanguinar had done was finally working, or maybe the venom that had paralyzed him had begun to wear off. Either way, he felt something, and that alone was worthy of rejoicing.

He tried to wiggle his toes and felt the slide of a sheet gliding across his skin. Or maybe he'd imagined it.

He did it again, and this time, his whole foot twitched.

Tears of joy slid out of the corners of his eyes and his first thought was that he wanted to share this good news with Grace.

Then he remembered she'd taken a trip—a vacation of sorts.

Disappointment rose up for a brief second before he realized what this meant. He had a few days to regain his strength. Maybe he could even be sitting up by himself by the time she came back.

Maybe when she came home, he could even greet her on his feet and hug her as he'd wanted to do so many times.

Of course, there were more things he wanted to do to her than just hug, but all of that could wait until he was strong enough to be a real man for her—the kind of man she needed.

He felt a stirring in his groin, saw the sheet draped over him twitch with the beginnings of an erection.

Relief made his head spin. He hadn't thought he'd ever feel that again. No matter how much Grace had turned him on, he'd never once been able to get hard. And now just thinking about her, he was getting aroused.

There was no way he'd ever be able to thank her for all she'd done. She hadn't once given up hope that he would recover. She'd stayed by his side, keeping his body moving so it wouldn't waste away. Maybe it was all that effort that drove the venom out of his system. Maybe *she* had cured him.

Torr owed her his life, and as soon as she got home, he was going to devote his to making her the happiest woman on the face of the planet.

He could hardly wait.

Dawn drove away the last of the Synestryn.

Madoc was shaking by the time the fight ended, though whether from exhaustion or fear for Nika, he wasn't sure.

She could have gotten herself killed. That thought pounded around inside his head, threatening to drive him crazy with an uncomfortable combination of terror and rage.

She was so precious. He couldn't let her risk herself like that again.

Madoc found her in the living room. She had her legs tucked against her body and was hugging them close, staring at nothing. Her eyes were red, as if she'd been crying, but dry.

He breathed out a sigh of relief. He really didn't think he could have handled the sight of her tears.

She hadn't noticed him yet, though he was only a few feet away. Whatever she was thinking about consumed her complete attention.

Madoc stared at her, soaking in the sight of her safe and whole. Her white hair was damp and a total mess. Soot stained her cheek and both hands. The clothes she wore hung on her, droopy and bedraggled. And yet, despite all of that, she was still the most beautiful, precious woman he'd ever seen.

She deserved better than him. He knew that. He knew that he was too rough and harsh for someone so delicate. He also knew that he would do whatever it took to make her happy and to find a way to be the kind of man she deserved. He wasn't ever going to let her go, and because of that, he had to step up, be a better man. Kinder. Gentler.

Maybe a soulless man like him could never love, but Madoc was determined to give her everything else she could ever need or want.

His heart clenched hard, then opened up, bleeding something into him that took his breath away with its power. He went light-headed and braced his feet to keep from spiraling to the floor. His skin fizzed along the surface as if a million tiny bubbles were popping all at once.

A shivering warmth spread over his chest, almost too much to bear. That warmth grew and spread out over the branches of his lifemark.

Madoc lifted his shirt to see what was wrong.

A thousand tiny buds had formed along the branches of his lifemark. They sprang forth before his eyes, swelling with life.

He pulled in a sharp breath. Shock radiated through him, making him sway on his feet.

From the corner of his eye, he saw Nika rise from the couch. She came to him and pressed her hand against his skin.

Joy sang through his body as his lifemark reached for her touch, swaying and shivering with her nearness.

"I don't know how this happened," he told her. "I thought it was too late for me—that my soul had died when you took off that ring."

She looked up at him, her blue eyes shimmering. A smile as bright as sunlight tipped the corners of her full mouth up and he knew he would always have this image of her inside him for as long as he lived. "Apparently not," she said. "I'm sorry I scared you, though."

Madoc covered her hand, pressing it flat against his chest. He liked the feel of her fingers on his skin too much to resist. He closed his eyes, letting her touch flow through him, calming him.

So much had happened tonight. Both good and bad. He was still reeling from it all, trying to figure out what to do next.

Helen and Drake were in one of the bedrooms cleaning up and getting some sleep. Logan had left to rest underground. Madoc had thought he'd crash here, too, but with Nika's touch, he was no longer too exhausted to drive home and get her to the safety of Dabyr.

As he looked down at her, staring into her pale blue eyes, all his past sins came flooding back to him. He'd hurt people. He'd even killed. Tynan. He knew what that meant—what he had to do. He had to answer for that crime, and the punishment was death.

He'd beg Joseph for a stay of execution—just long enough to find another Theronai compatible with Nika. She needed someone to take care of her and give her the power she needed to fight off the Synestryn who wanted to invade her mind. He was afraid that without the power he or one of his brothers could offer, it would be too easy for her to go back to the way she had been before—trapped in a living nightmare.

He couldn't let that happen to her again.

Joseph would respect Madoc's death wish and let him find Nika another Theronai. He was sure of it. He'd send out the word to each Sentinel stronghold for Theronai to come to her, even though she was currently taken. She wouldn't want to let the men touch her, but he'd find a way to convince her to see reason. He'd pay Logan the blood debt to heal her blisters.

As much as he hated the idea of her suffering, he knew that a few blisters were nothing compared to the mental torture she'd endured. She was strong. He'd make sure she stayed that way.

And then, when they found a compatible man, Madoc would find a way to let her go into the arms of a man who deserved her—one who hadn't murdered an ally.

One who would be gentle with her and treat her like the precious treasure she was.

Regret tightened his throat. He could almost imagine the kind of life they could have had together, but it was better if he blocked those images out. It was going to be hard enough letting her go without thinking about what could have been.

Madoc cleared his throat. "We should probably get moving."

"Where?"

"To Dabyr."

Nika went stiff and stepped back. Her hand slipped away from him and his shirt fell back over his chest.

Something was wrong. He could see it in her face. "What is it?" he asked, ready to solve or kill whatever was bothering her.

"I can't go back there."

Madoc frowned. "Why not?"

"You'll imprison me. Everyone will suffer."

The pain radiating out from her was so thick he could almost see it. "What are you talking about?"

"The luceria warned me. I can't go back there with you."

"It's not safe anywhere else."

"Exactly." Her voice broke on the word and he saw her swallowing as if trying to fight off tears.

Madoc stepped forward, but Nika backed away, keeping distance between them. Instinctively, he reached for the new link between them, searching for the reason behind her odd reaction.

Their connection was new, but even with only a minuscule conduit between them, he could feel the panic shrieking inside her. It was so sharp, he pulled back, shocked at the intensity of her emotions.

"What the hell is going on, Nika? Talk to me."

"The luceria warned me that you'd lock me away at Dabyr. Tori will die. So will a lot of other people."

"That's ridiculous."

"The luceria didn't think so."

"The luceria doesn't think. It's just a thing."

Nika shook her head, making the tangled white strands slide over her jawline. Her eyes were wide and her stance was defensive—almost protective. "You're wrong."

"Nika, please." Madoc reached out for her, wanting to comfort her, but she backed away, bumping into the couch.

"Stay away from me. I mean it."

"We really need to go home. I won't imprison you." How could he when he would live only long enough to see her unite with another man?

"Promise me," she demanded. "Promise me we'll find Tori."

Madoc couldn't do that. Any promise he made her would stick. He'd be forced to uphold his end no matter what. If he promised her they'd find Tori, then they'd spend their time running around instead of finding her a suitable Theronai. With a death sentence looming over him, Joseph would never allow him that kind of freedom.

Plus, what if they looked and never found her? He couldn't trap them both in a promise like that—he couldn't have Nika roaming the world looking for a sister she might never find, unable to stop even if she wanted to.

"No," he told her in a low voice. "I can't do that."

"See. I knew it. The luceria was right. You *do* want to cage me."

"It's not that. We don't even know if Tori is alive."

"I do. I know it."

Nika had known a lot of things that seemed impossible for her to know before, and generally, Madoc was willing to take a risk on his own behalf, believing her. But not if Nika was at stake, too. He refused to risk her in any way.

"I believe that *you* believe she's alive," he said carefully, not wanting to insult her by calling her a liar. "But I also know that your mind is not your own. What if that thought was planted in you somehow by the Synestryn that took your blood? What if it's a trick to get you to come to them the way they tried to do with Andra?"

"She's alive," stated Nika, confidence ringing in her tone. "And I'm going to prove it to you."

With that, she stepped forward, grabbed Madoc's hand, and lifted it to her throat until the magnetic pull of both halves of the luceria locked them together.

That contact strengthened the flow of power from him into her, allowing her to use more than he'd thought possible.

As energy sparked through their link, Madoc felt the pressure he'd been living with for centuries begin to ease.

A long, slow breath hissed out from between his clenched teeth and his vision began to fail. Bright spots of glowing white formed in his eyes until he was completely blinded by them.

His body hummed, vibrating with the rush of energy Nika took from him.

"Look," she ordered him. "See what I see."

With that, Madoc felt his body fall away and his mind raced through space at a dizzying speed.

Joseph stood on the hilltop as the sun rose. Beside him, bound, gagged, and seething with anger, stood Chris.

A deep sense of grief threatened to swallow Joseph whole, but he knew he couldn't let it sway him from this path.

Chris had to die before he could kill the people Joseph and the others were sworn to protect. The vow Chris had made to protect humans and guard the gateway had bound him for as long as his soul lived, but now that it was dead, no promise could hold him.

Chris had to die.

Joseph waited, knowing the Slayers would come. They always did, despite the stagnant war that separated their races. Duty came first. Always.

A man Joseph had never met before strode up the hill. In his jeans and T-shirt, he looked like any other man in America. Except for his slightly pointed ears, which one had to be looking for to even notice. The brown leather jacket he wore hung open, as if the chill didn't bother him.

Usually, the Slayers came in a pack, but this man's confident stride said he didn't seem to need strength in numbers.

"I'm Andreas Phelan," he announced, thrusting his hand out to Joseph.

Shocked by the man's greeting, Joseph shook his hand, feeling the unnatural warmth of his skin. "Joseph Rayd."

"I've heard about you. My grandfather says you're a man of honor."

"Is that so?"

Andreas nodded, his tawny eyes going to Chris's lifemark, barren of leaves. "I'm in charge of the Slayers now."

"What happened to the previous leader?" asked Joseph.

His eyes went to Joseph's, and the impact of that steady gaze hit Joseph hard. "I ripped his throat out with my teeth."

Clearly, this was not a man to fuck with.

"Things are changing, Joseph Rayd," said the Slayer. "Many of my kind can smell it coming. Things are getting worse."

Joseph looked at the man who had once been his friend. Chris's face was bright red with rage, and if it hadn't been for the magically enhanced bonds that held him, Joseph knew the man would have tried to kill him by now.

"At least we can agree on that much," said Joseph.

"I've heard rumors that you've found blooded women roaming the country."

Joseph wasn't sure how much to share with a man who, despite how he appeared, was his enemy. "I'm sure they were exaggerated. You know how rumors are."

Andreas smiled slowly. "I can smell a lie, you know. But I understand. You and I aren't friends. Yet."

With that enigmatic remark, he grabbed Chris's arm

and hauled him down the hill. Over his shoulder, he said, "I'll deliver his body to you when it's done."

Joseph stood there for a long time, watching the two men for as long as he could. The next time he saw Chris, he'd be dead. He wanted to remember the man for who he had been rather than what he'd become.

But even more than that, he wanted this to be the very last time he ever had to stand at the top of this hill and sentence another one of his men to death.

They had to find more women. Fast. And it was his responsibility to see that it happened.

Joseph walked back down the hill, feeling a century older than he had on the way up.

Nika was desperate to find Tori and prove to Madoc she was still alive. The man was so stubborn, she knew that unless he saw her with his own eyes, he'd never believe.

Not that he actually had eyes in this state. Neither of them did, but they'd be able to use Tori's.

If Nika could reach her.

Dragging Madoc's mind along with hers slowed her down. She felt like she was trying to swim while carrying a fifty-pound weight, but there was no other way. He had to be with her.

Nika concentrated on the fragile connection she had with Tori. It was even harder to sense now than it had been only a few hours before.

At one point, Nika would have been able to slide along that pathway with ease, landing inside Tori's mind, able to comfort her and ease her pain. But not anymore. Tori had grown stronger since they'd started feeding her Synestryn blood. Her defenses were more formidable.

Why Tori didn't want Nika to be with her, she had no idea, but whatever her reasons, Tori was winning the battle.

Madoc's power slid into her, giving her new strength. Maybe she could use that strength to force Tori to let her in.

With no more than a thought, power flowed into Nika. That single delicate strand that stretched between them seemed to glow bright for a split second before it sputtered back to near invisibility.

Nika funneled energy into that strand, imagining it was an electrical wire spanning between them. The strand pulsed once, then twice, then continued to throb faster and faster until it shimmered.

Victory made Nika feel light, easing the burden of carrying Madoc with her.

Before it was too late, Nika hauled both of them along that strand, barreling through space until they landed solidly inside Tori's mind.

As always, their mental meeting place resembled the bedroom they once had shared—the place from which Tori had been taken.

It was darker than Nika had remembered. It was night outside the windows. The bedside lamps had been broken. Festering, oily patches coated the walls, rather than purple-striped wallpaper.

Tori sat on the bed, her back to Nika, as she stared out the window. Her hair was long now, pooling on the mattress beneath her. She was bigger, too.

It had been so long since she'd last seen Tori, sometimes it was easy to forget she was seventeen now.

"How did you get in?" asked Tori without turning around. "I thought I was stronger than you now."

"I had help."

"A man," she said, shuddering as if disgusted. "I don't like having him here."

"He needed to see you were still alive."

"He's seen. Now send him away."

Nika turned to where Madoc's mind hovered inside Tori's. Here, he appeared as solid and real as if they were back in that Gerai house in Nebraska. Confusion tightened his features as he looked from Tori to Nika and back again.

"Are you hurt?" he asked her, his voice gentle with concern.

A dead laugh came out of Nika's sister as she turned and rose from the bed. Her skin was a sickly white, almost translucent. Beneath, her veins were visible, pulsing with blood too dark to be human. Her blue eyes had once shone with childlike innocence, but now were bleak and desolate. Her hands stretched over her pregnant belly, curling into claws as if she wanted to rip the child from her body.

"I wish they'd only hurt me," said Tori.

Shock made Nika go cold. She reached for Madoc, fighting the urge to fling herself away from this place and cuddle inside the warmth of his embrace.

"What have they done to you?" he asked in horror.

"I'd say that's a bit obvious. And if you don't want it to happen to Nika, then get her out of here before they find her."

"Time to go, Nika," said Madoc.

It was a good thing he was not in control here.

Nika turned to him, glowering. "I'll go when I'm ready. Until then, you just zip your mouth and stay put." To Tori, she said, "We're going to rescue you. All I need to know is where to find you."

"Even if I did know, I wouldn't tell you. I can't be saved. It's best if you go before they get you, too."

"Maybe you should listen to her, Nika," said Madoc. "I want to save her, but not at the risk of your life."

Nika ignored him. "It's not too late. It can't be too late." She'd only just now regained enough sanity and strength to come for Tori. She hadn't fought through all those years of nightmares only to fail now.

"It is." Tori's words were hard and cold—not at all like the child Nika had once known. "Go."

"I made you a promise."

"You won't have to worry about that for long. This thing inside me will be born soon. Most of the girls don't live through that."

"How many of you are there?" asked Madoc, his voice a low growl of menace.

Tori shrugged. "I don't see them. I just hear their screams stop suddenly and know."

"We've got to get you out before that happens to you," said Nika.

"It's too late for me."

Nika sensed that trying to change Tori's mind about that was a losing battle. But maybe another angle would work. "What about the other girls there? Maybe we could save them."

Tori's eyes fell shut and she seemed to be fighting herself. "If he finds you, he'll hurt you like he's hurt me. I don't want that."

"Who hurt you?" demanded Madoc.

"Zillah. He runs this place, along with a girl who never grows."

"Maura," whispered Madoc.

"You know her," said Tori, as if offering condolences.

"I know of her."

"Then you know you can't let Nika come here."

"Stop it, both of you," ordered Nika before their conversation got carried away. "I *am* coming, and there's not a thing either of you can do to stop me. The only question is whether you're going to tell me where you are, or if you're going to make me rip it from your mind."

"I already told you I don't know. They've never let me out. I've been in these caves so long, I can't even remember what sunshine looks like."

Grief for her sister and her lost childhood welled up inside Nika. She was fighting not to cry, battling for control over her emotions when the room grew bright.

Outside the dirty bedroom window, the sun rose in a brilliant display of orange and pink. The movement was faster than was natural, but every other detail down to the last trailing wisp of clouds and the swaying of the trees in the distance was perfect, as if it had been videotaped.

"There," said Madoc. "That was my favorite sunrise of all time. Summer 1803."

Tori reached out until her fingers were bathed in light. Dirt clogged her ragged fingernails and the black blood seemed to flow out of her hand as if hiding from the light. "Thank you," she whispered. "It's even more beautiful than I imagined."

"How did you remember it that perfectly?" asked Nika, trying to focus on something so she didn't cry.

"I remember everything I see."

Tori lifted her face to the sun, closing her eyes as she basked in the light. "Do you really think you can save the others?" she asked. "Give them back the sunlight?"

"If we know where you are, we'll do whatever it takes to get everyone out alive. Even you," said Madoc.

"I don't know how to help you, then. I don't even know what country I'm in."

"Then stop fighting me. Let me be with you like you used to do. Let that connection between us grow back to what it used to be and I'll be able to find you."

"No. I don't want you with me when this thing comes. I don't want you with me when I die."

Fury blazed through Nika, making her grow inside the ethereal context of Tori's mind. Her head hit the ceiling and she loomed over her sister, her voice a deep boom. "You're not going to die."

Tori let out a humorless laugh. "You're going to have to be a lot bigger than that to scare me. I live with demons, remember."

Nika deflated, returning to her normal size. "I didn't mean to scare you. I just want you to listen to reason. I'm not alone. Madoc is with me. He has dozens of powerful friends who will help us rescue you. You can't give up yet."

"What happens to you if I die while you're in my mind?" asked Tori.

"That's not going to happen."

Tori looked at Madoc. "She knows she'll die, too. I've sensed the knowledge inside her. When things were bad—when the blood they fed me nearly killed me—I sensed her fear of death."

"Is it true?" Madoc asked Nika. "Will you die if you're with Tori when she dies?"

"*If* she dies. She doesn't know that will happen."

"You're evading my question. Will you die, too?"

Nika bowed her head. "Yes. I think so."

Madoc pulled her against his side, holding her close. Even within this nonphysical space, she still felt comforted by his touch. That comfort allowed her the strength to keep fighting for her sister.

"What if I were to promise to leave your mind before the baby comes?"

"It's not a baby," snarled Tori, whirling around and baring her teeth. "It's a thing. A monster."

Nika held up her hands and kept her voice calm. "I'm sorry. I didn't understand."

Madoc's grip had tightened and his stance had shifted so that he was between Tori and Nika. "I agree with Tori that you can't risk your life, but what if there's another way?"

"What way?"

"Did you see anything the night they took you? Street signs, buildings, landmarks of any kind?"

"A few, maybe."

He looked to Nika. "If I can see those memories, I might be able to figure out where she went."

"How?"

"I've roamed this country for years. I remember everything I see. I might be able to recognize something in her memories."

"It's worth a shot," said Nika. "What do you think, Tori? Will you let him try?"

Tori stepped closer. Madoc pushed Nika behind him as if he needed to protect her from her own sister.

Nika moved out of his reach and saw Tori's dirty hand press over Madoc's brow.

A second later, the room exploded in a million shards of light, and Nika and Madoc were flung out of Tori's mind.

Tori shivered in the cold dark. She kept her eyes closed for as long as possible, holding on to the memory of that sunrise. She could almost feel the heat of it on her skin, the way it had driven back the tainted blood they'd shoved into her.

For a moment, Tori had almost felt like a real person again, rather than a thing to be used.

Tears leaked out from behind her closed lids, their

warmth startling against her chilled skin. She missed Nika so much. Having her in her mind had been so nice. So comforting.

She couldn't let it happen again. If birthing the thing inside her didn't kill her, she knew what would happen. She didn't want Nika there when Zillah hurt her again—put another thing inside her.

Before, wishing for death had been easy. She'd had nothing to live for but more pain and loneliness. But now, thanks to Madoc, she found herself craving the sun and its warmth.

She wanted to live long enough to feel sunlight on her skin for real, just one more time.

If Zillah ever found out, he'd see that desire as a weakness to use against her. He'd taunt her with it, dangle it in front of her in an effort to gain her cooperation, then take away all hope of her ever having it.

Tori wasn't going to let him have this, too. She was going to bury Madoc's gift deep, locking it away where Zillah would never sense it. And then, when she felt death coming for her, she'd pull the memory out and wrap it around her so she wouldn't have to die alone in the darkness.

Chapter 16

Madoc felt like someone had snapped a giant rubber band against his brain.

He was back inside his real body, crumpled in a heap on the floor with Nika. His stomach heaved dangerously. He tried to extract himself from her so he wouldn't throw up on her, but before he could, his stomach settled and his head's spinning began to slow.

Madoc let out a low moan, unable to stop the unmanly noise from escaping.

Nika was panting. "Sorry. It's not usually that rough."

Madoc helped Nika sit up until her back was propped against the couch. "I would really prefer it if we never did that again."

"I'll try to warn you next time," she said.

At least then he could brace himself.

"Do you know where Tori is?" she asked.

Tori had sent a barrage of images into his head a split second before shoving him and Nika away. Those images were there, in his mind, but were too much of a jumbled mess to make sense of. "I'm going to have to sort out the images first. It may take a while."

"You know we don't have much time."

"I know. But I also know that we're not going to rescue her and the others alone. We need to gather the men—go in with everyone we can find. We'll go back to Dabyr and talk to Joseph so we can plan our attack." He wasn't sure if Joseph would let him come along or not.

He might simply lock him in a cell beneath Dabyr until Nika's new Theronai was found.

The idea of being imprisoned like that made something dark and dangerous rise up in him. His soul might not have completely died, but he clearly wasn't rid of the blackness that had nearly consumed him. He was going to have to fight it back and struggle to do what he knew was right.

Maybe he could convince Joseph to let him go on this one last mission. They would need all the help they could get, and there weren't many men alive who were better with a blade than he was.

"I told you I'm not going back there," said Nika.

"I'm not going to imprison you. I really wish you'd stop worrying about it."

"I have to worry. There's too much at stake."

She was right about that. She just didn't know how right yet. "We're just going back to gather the men."

"You won't try to make me stay there while you go after her?" Her voice sounded uncertain, untrusting.

"If we need you, you'll be right by my side."

"Exactly. *If* you need me. You won't. You don't think you need anyone."

"I need you," he said. "Without you I die. Isn't that enough?"

"No. Not even close. I want what Helen and Drake have. What Paul and Andra have."

"We can have that, too," he lied, unwilling to crush her dreams just yet. She'd have them—just not with him. "It's going to take some time. I can't risk your life now, while you still have so much to learn. You don't even know how to protect yourself."

"I'll learn."

"Before Tori's baby is born?"

"Yes. I'll go into Gilda's mind. Learn from her."

Madoc lifted her hand, pointing to her burned fingers. "Looks like you tried that with Helen and it didn't exactly work out, did it?"

"I need to do this, Madoc. She's my sister. I promise I won't take any unnecessary risks."

As she uttered the words, Madoc felt them settle over his shoulders, their weight reassuring.

Maybe this was one of those times when he needed to give in. Compromise. She'd promised to be careful and was now bound to abide by that promise. Maybe this partnership thing meant he needed to give her something in return. It might be the last thing he ever gave her.

Playing nice wasn't his strong suit, but a lot had changed in the past few hours. For Nika, he had to try to be a better man.

"I promise that we're only going back to Dabyr long enough to gather our forces and to figure out where Tori is. If I leave to fight, you can come with me. Okay?" It still gave him an out. If Joseph locked him up, Nika would have to stay at Dabyr, where she'd be safe.

Nika nodded. "That wasn't exactly a promise never to imprison me, but I'll take what I can get for now. Tori has to come first."

"Good. Then it's settled. Let's grab Drake and Helen and head home."

John woke to an empty bed.

It wasn't the first time it had happened, but it had never before hurt like it did now. He and Meghan spent yesterday together talking, laughing and getting to know each other while road crews worked to clear the highways. Her rental car had been towed so it could be repaired. John had thought she'd stay with him at least until it was done. Especially after last night, after making love so many times he swore he'd be able to tell the difference between her and a thousand other women simply by the way she breathed, by the feel of her skin.

Apparently, he'd been wrong.

The note she'd left on her pillow said she'd taken a cab to the airport. She had to get home, back to her life.

What about his life?

It seemed so empty and bleak without her in it. She'd brought music to his world, and now that she was gone, everything was gray silence.

John wasn't about to let it end like this. John had met countless women, but Meghan was the first one who made him consider what his future could be like if he shared it with someone else. For the first time, the idea of forever with the same person was not an alien concept he couldn't wrap his head around.

The only problem was, John had to find her.

She hadn't left her phone number, and a quick search online for her name turned up no listed number. He did, however, remember her mentioning the name of the place where she worked.

Phoenix was a hell of a long way away, but not nearly as far as he was willing to go for a woman like Meghan. Besides, it was too damn cold here, anyway.

John showered, packed a bag, and was on his way to the airport less than fifteen minutes later.

Madoc struggled with the images Tori had put in his head while Helen drove the four of them back to Dabyr. Drake was on the phone, speaking to Nicholas about rallying the Theronai. Apparently, Joseph was gone and unable to issue the order to have those who were out return.

It also meant that he couldn't sentence Madoc yet.

Whatever. Madoc couldn't do anything about that, and if he didn't unscramble the thoughts Tori had put in his brain, it wouldn't matter whether the men were ready to go into battle. They wouldn't know where to go.

Nika sat in silence beside him in the back of the car, staring out the window at the sun as it rose overhead.

"I can't imagine what it would be like to live without the sun, can you?" she asked him.

"The Sanguinar seem to be okay with it," said Madoc, hoping to distract Nika from worrying about her sister. Seeing the pain on her face broke his heart, and he wanted to do whatever it took to wipe it away.

Nika shifted in her seat, turning toward him. Her eyes matched the color of the sky behind her, and for a moment, Madoc forgot all about their job.

She was so pretty. So delicate. He had no idea how he'd gotten lucky enough to have her for his own, but he knew for certain that he would do whatever it took to keep her safe and make her happy for as long as she was his.

Once they found Tori, he'd convince Nika to stay at Dabyr with him. They'd keep each other company, make up for lost time, and find comfort in each other.

He only wished that he'd be free to go out and hunt down the creature who'd raped Tori and who knew how many other girls, and choke him to death on his own dick.

As he allowed the notion of what she must have endured to enter his thoughts, rage pounded through him, making the confines of the car seem too small.

Nika's hand fluttered to her throat, trembling as she touched the luceria. "I don't know what you're thinking over there," she said, "but I don't like it."

Immediately Madoc squelched the thought and focused instead on the scenery passing by them. "Sorry. I'll be more careful."

He was going to have to learn to control himself better. He couldn't allow the link he now had with Nika to upset her.

Madoc pulled in a deep breath, forcing himself to calm down. One thing at a time. First, he had to untangle the mess Tori had given him and make sense of it. That was step number one. After that would come finding Tori and facing his sentence.

Nika touched his hand. "You're frustrated. Angry. Afraid. I've never seen you afraid before."

"I'll get over it."

"Have you figured out where we're going yet?" asked Drake from the front seat.

"I'm working on it."

"Work faster. Nicholas is calling everyone in, but they won't stay long. You know how it is."

Madoc did. In addition to hunting and killing every Synestryn they could get their hands on, the men were also all searching for the women they knew were out there. Besides Tori—who was thought to be dead—there was at least one more female Theronai roaming the world. Jackie, daughter of Lucien, who'd fathered both Helen and Lexi.

It was a race to see who could find her first, and the only thing giving hope to his fellow Theronai.

"I know," said Madoc. "I'm doing what I can."

"Let me help," offered Nika.

"I don't know how you could. Tori didn't put these images in your head. She put them in mine, and they're so scrambled together I can't make sense of them."

"Maybe I can. I know the way Tori thinks. I've been in her mind for years."

Madoc shrugged. "It's worth a shot."

Nika unfastened her seat belt and crawled into his lap, straddling him. The heat between her thighs burned through his jeans, and he set the land speed record for fastest erection ever.

Madoc shifted, trying to unpinch his manhood. The motion made Nika bounce on top of him, which of course, made her breasts jiggle beneath her cotton shirt.

He knew he was staring, but he couldn't stop himself. All he could think about was how good her hard little nipples had tasted against his tongue, how they'd tightened even more when he'd sucked them.

As if she were reading his thoughts, her nipples puckered, pressing against her shirt.

She wasn't wearing a bra. As small as she was, she didn't really need one, but that meant all he had to do was lift up her shirt and he could kiss and lick and suck her nipples until she begged for more.

That thought stopped him cold. Nika wasn't likely to beg for more of what he'd given her last night. He'd hurt her. Made her bleed.

"None of that," she chided. "It was perfectly normal and I'm not going to let you make me feel bad about it."

"You're reading my thoughts?" he asked, ripping his eyes away from her tits, just in case.

"You asked for my help. Besides, I think I like some

of those thoughts you're having. We'll try that whole sex thing again later."

When they weren't in a moving car. With an audience.

Helen was driving. She glanced in the rearview mirror and met Madoc's gaze. "I think a bit of privacy might be in order here," she said; then his ears popped as she put up a soundproof barrier of air around him and Nika.

"They can't hear us now, can they?"

"Nope."

A slow, languid smile lifted Nika's mouth and Madoc could do nothing but stare. He still hadn't forgotten a single one of his fantasies involving her mouth. Only now that it was the worst possible time for him to be thinking about them, each one of them came back in rapid succession.

"We'll try all that, too. Soon," she promised. "But you've got to stop thinking those naughty things and focus on what Tori gave you."

Right. Tori. They had a very young, very scared, very pregnant girl to save. The fact that she also happened to be Nika's sister was just added motivation.

Madoc valiantly ignored his boner and closed his eyes so he wouldn't be distracted by Nika's mouth again. He focused on the tangled snarl of images Tori had forced into him and let them all flicker through his mind. They went by so fast, he couldn't make sense of them. They were just a blur of light and color, too insubstantial to actually understand.

"We need to slow them down," whispered Nika.

Madoc heard her with his ears, but he also felt her voice inside his head, too. It was odd having her this close, but not uncomfortable. She seemed to be able to invade his thoughts without taking up any space, without crowding him.

He felt a stream of power flowing out of his body, heating the luceria around his finger as it passed into Nika. He had no idea what she was doing with the energy, but whatever it was, it felt nice. Pressure inside him eased. He pulled in a deep breath, feeling her breasts press against his chest.

It was going be so nice to get her naked again, just once more. This time, he'd be gentle. Careful. He'd take her slow and easy. There'd be no more blood. No pain. Only pleasure—so much of it he'd be able to wash away all memories of how he'd ripped her virginity from her and left her bleeding.

"Stop it. I'm tired of you beating yourself up over that. I enjoyed myself quite a bit."

"Not nearly as much as you should have."

"How do you know?"

"I know. Next time, so will you."

"We'll see about that."

There was a buzzing feeling in his skull; then suddenly, something about the images zooming through his head changed. They slowed down until they were flipping through his mind at a rate he could actually see.

Like a bizarre slide show, each flash of events passed through him. Most were of dark cave walls. In some, he could see the chubby arms and legs of the girl Tori had once been as she looked down at herself. In others, her limbs were longer and thinner. In the next moment, she was chubby again.

"The order is jumbled," said Nika. "We need to sort it out and get back to the night she was taken."

"Do you know how to do that?"

"I think so. Hold on."

Again, Madoc felt a flow of power falling out of him. The tiny connection between them flared, allowing her to take on more of the energy stretching his insides.

As she did whatever it was she was doing, the strain he'd been carrying around for years began to ease. For the first time in decades, he felt like he could pull in a full breath.

He was so thrilled by this victory that he hadn't been paying attention to the images.

They stopped, and he felt Nika's body tighten even as he sensed her fear invading his thoughts, like a dank little tendril of smoke.

Madoc put his attention back where it belonged and saw what had scared Nika so much.

It was the face of a man who wasn't quite a man at all. The top of his skull was a bit too wide, his black eyes too deeply set. His bloodred lips were peeled back in a hideous smile, displaying two rows of pointed teeth.

Zillah.

The name echoed in his mind like a shotgun blast. This was the thing that had stolen Tori. The creature who had hurt her. Raped her.

"Don't look at him," he told Nika. "Change the image to something else."

Her voice shook with fury. "I want to watch him die."

"So do I, but that will have to wait until we can find him. Show me something I can use."

Nika was trembling, though whether with fear or rage, he couldn't tell. He swept his hands up and down her back, hoping to calm her. The feel of her slender back under his palms managed to soothe something inside him, too. She was here, in his arms, safe and sound, and nothing and no one was going to change that.

The image shifted; this time, it was a close-up of the open, salivating jaws of a sgath. Nika swiftly went through several blurry images as if wanting to get away from that one. The next one she stopped on was of their childhood bedroom.

"That's before the attack," she said. "The window isn't broken yet. I'll move forward a bit."

The next time she stopped, he saw what it had looked like for Tori the night she'd been taken. As a sgath pulled her out of her window, she stared back at a much younger Nika.

She was just a girl. Her hair had been dark then, not the fear-bleached white it was now. Blood leaked from a wound on her leg, but she ignored it. She was reaching out toward Tori, her lips parted as if speaking.

"Okay. This is it," she whispered. "You need to find where she went. I'll move through the thoughts one by one."

What Tori had seen that night flowed past Madoc like a movie. He scoured each image, searching for landmarks, signs, or anything else that might lead him to where Tori was.

He saw nothing familiar. There was still some kind of distortion happening. So much of what he saw was simply . . . wrong.

Failure bore down on him, crushing the breath from his lungs. How was he going to admit his inadequacy to Nika? He didn't want her to see his failures. He wanted to be her hero.

"You're not a failure," she said. "We'll just have to try again."

Already he could feel her shaking with fatigue. She was new to his power, and no matter how badly he wanted to find Tori, Nika had to be his first priority.

"We need to stop."

"We can't," said Nika. "We're too close."

"We have time to figure this out. It will take at least a day to get everyone home and ready to move."

"I want to go tonight."

"I realize that, but if we move too soon, we won't have enough manpower to save her. I know you don't want that."

Her gaze hardened and her mouth tightened. "He's just one man—one creature. I could kill him myself if I got close enough. All I need is a weapon."

"I'm not going to let you risk yourself like that. We're going to do this right. No one is going in alone. Period."

"You're not going to hold me back from Tori. No one is."

"I'm not trying to. I'm trying to help you see reason. I can't seem to control the images without you, and you're too tired right now to be much help. The best thing you can do for Tori is to get a nap on the way home; then we'll try again."

"I won't be able to sleep. Not now that I know what they've done to her. I should have known before now."

"Why? You said she'd been pulling away for a while."

Nika nodded. "That's why. She didn't want me with her when he raped her. I should have been there."

"No," said Madoc, his voice too loud and angry. He reminded himself to be gentle. "She protected you out of love. Don't cheapen her gift by regretting it. Besides, how do you know that it wouldn't have been worse for her had you been there to witness it, to suffer with her?"

"She's just a girl."

Madoc drew in a calming breath and smoothed his hand over her hair. "We'll bring her home soon."

"Tori doesn't have much time."

"I know."

"If that baby—or whatever it is—comes before we find her, she might not make it."

Madoc couldn't let Nika's imagination go there—not when there was still a chance. "She'll make it. We'll get the Sanguinar working on a way to get her through the birth and make it safe for her."

"And the baby?" asked Nika, shuddering.

Madoc had no answers. "We'll deal with that when the time comes."

"I can't even imagine what she's been through—how she was strong enough to endure it and still try to protect me. Who was protecting her?"

"As of now, we are. All of us. She's one of our own and we'll find a way to bring her home."

"Maybe I shouldn't have told Andra she's alive. Maybe it would be kinder for her to never know what really happened to Tori."

"Andra's strong. And Tori's not dead yet. There's still a chance."

"You think so?"

"You found a way to save me when I was sure I was a lost cause. I'm sure we'll do the same for her."

Nika snuggled against his chest, tucking her head under his chin. "You keep telling me that, okay? I have a feeling I'm going to need to hear it more than once."

Madoc tightened his arms around the most precious woman to have ever existed. She hadn't given up on him when there was no reason to hope. The least he could do was keep her hope alive long enough to help her get through this.

Whatever happened, she wasn't going to be alone. He was going to be right here with her, giving her hope, holding her close, and, if need be, drying her tears.

Nika was his now, and for as long as she was, he would not fail her.

She'd stayed up last night, watching over him while he was injured. She needed her rest. He still wasn't convinced she was completely healthy.

"Sleep for a while," he whispered. He gathered up minute sparks of power floating in the air and used them to put the faintest hint of compulsion in the words. "We'll be home soon."

Nika's body relaxed against his and her breathing evened out as she fell asleep.

Madoc leaned back in the seat, closed his eyes, and forced himself to go through those horrible images again, one by one. He needed to learn how to control them, remove whatever was distorting them, and make sense of them so Nika never had to see them again.

He knew that if anything happened to Tori, these images would be the things that haunted Nika most.

Chapter 17

Dabyr was buzzing with activity when they arrived. The underground parking lot was nearly full. Curious teens tried to appear nonchalant as they eavesdropped for a clue as to what was going on.

Madoc ignored all of it and carried the still-sleeping Nika straight to his suite. He wasn't sure if he did it because he was worried she'd park herself in the hall again, or if it was because he liked the idea of getting her in his bed. Maybe a little of both.

He tucked her in, safe and sound, and simply stared down at her.

So pretty. So perfect. His chest ached just looking at her.

He wished there was more time to linger, but there was too much work to be done. It was time to face Joseph.

Madoc strapped his old, familiar sword around his hips and had just left his suite when he nearly ran into Nicholas.

The man's face was hard to read behind the network of fine scars, but his eyes said plenty. He stared at the space where Madoc's necklace had once been, his hand idly sliding over his own luceria.

"I had to see for myself," he whispered. "It's true."

Madoc nodded, fighting down the odd mixture of pride, joy, and grief swelling inside him. "Yeah, it's true."

Nicholas clapped him on the shoulder. "You're one

hell of a lucky bastard. And I expect you to buy me a beer for playing matchmaker."

"Matchmaker?"

"Sure. I'm the one who kept opening up doors so the two of you could be together. And don't think I've forgotten what you did to my camera last year. You owe me."

Something warm opened up inside Madoc, but it wasn't entirely comfortable. He swallowed a couple of times to free his vocal cords of whatever had locked them up. "Thanks," he finally managed to get out. "You're a real friend."

"'Bout time you finally realized that. Asshole." Nicholas's face cracked around a smile. "Come on. Joseph just got in. He's going to need a briefing. Better it comes from the horse's mouth."

By the time they got to Joseph's office, it was already crowded with people. Drake and Helen sat quietly to one side. Gilda was huddled in the corner, crying. Angus stood near her, but hadn't offered her any sort of comfort, which was odd. He'd known those two for centuries and they could hardly keep their hands off of each other.

Angus's jaw was clenched so tight, Madoc wondered if the man's muscles wouldn't pop out of his jawline.

Joseph sat at his desk, rubbing his temples. His eyes were sunken, his shoulders slumped.

He looked up at Madoc. "What's the emergency?"

Madoc looked at Drake. "Didn't you tell him?"

"He just got back from delivering Chris to the Slayers. We thought we'd give him a minute," said Drake.

"Just tell me and get it over with," said Joseph. "I've already had to take a friend to his death. This day can't get any worse."

Joseph looked so tired, Madoc decided to take pity on the man and keep it short and sweet. He straightened his shoulders. "I'm sorry, but you're going to have to kill me, too. I killed Tynan. I realize this means my life is forfeit, but I ask that you let me help Nika find another Theronai to take my place before you carry out my sentence."

"Tynan's not dead," said Nicholas, frowning. "I just saw him a while ago."

"As did I," said Angus.

Confused, Madoc said, "But I broke his neck. I felt it."

Joseph's face had darkened. "I will deal with this and you privately," he told Madoc. "The rest of you, out."

"Wait," said Drake to Joseph. "Madoc hasn't told you the rest. About Tori."

Madoc really wanted his sentencing to be over, but what he wanted now wasn't the issue. "Nika's younger sister, Tori, is alive. And pregnant."

The room fell into shocked silence.

"How do you know this?" asked Joseph. "Andra thinks she found her remains in that cave last year."

"Andra was wrong," said Madoc.

"How can you be sure?"

Madoc looked right into Joseph's eyes and said, "I saw her."

"Where? When?"

Madoc didn't like this part. Nika had a reputation of being crazy. She believed Tori was alive, which made the idea tainted. "Nika took me to see her. We, ah, visited her mind."

Everyone in the room stared at him like they were expecting a punch line. When it didn't come, they all started talking at once.

Crazy. Madoc heard the word several times, though he didn't know who had said it.

"Stop it!" he shouted.

From the direction of his suite, he felt Nika wake up. His agitation had caused it and he wanted to lash out at everyone in the room for daring to disturb her rest.

Nika's soothing presence cooled his anger, allowing him to pause before he did something he'd regret. She was getting closer, and by the time she got here, he wanted to be in full control.

"You've got to admit," said Joseph, "it sounds a little far-fetched."

"And killing things with magic isn't?" he demanded.

"What about Tynan living after I nearly snapped his head off his neck?"

Joseph shook his head. "Tori was taken most of a decade ago by demons known for killing and eating children. The chances of her still being alive are next to zero. Couple that with the fact that Andra and Paul found a corpse wearing the same clothes as Tori when she was abducted, and it gets even harder to believe, even without the mind-visiting stuff."

"Nika does it all the time. Hell, she was in Helen's mind last night, learning how to channel magic."

Helen frowned. "I don't think so."

"Well, she was."

"Do you have any kind of proof?" asked Joseph. "If we're going to gear up for an assault, we need to be using good information, not the daydreams of a mentally challenged woman."

Madoc felt a flash of anger explode below the surface of his skin. He forced himself to keep his hand away from his sword, though he had no idea where he'd found that kind of control. The need to make Joseph pay for the insult in blood was pounding through him. Only the cooling presence of Nika in his mind stayed his hand. "You need to stop right there before you say something I can't ignore."

From the doorway, Madoc heard a faint intake of breath. He was compelled to turn toward the sound and saw Nika standing there.

"No, Madoc. Let him go on. It would be nice to know what he really thinks." She was breathing fast. Her cheeks were flushed, as if she'd run there. Her white hair was tousled from bed, and the imprint of a fold in the pillowcase creased her cheek. She came in and stood next to Madoc, and put her hands on her hips.

He could feel the hurt radiating out from her, making her tremble slightly—not enough to see, but enough that he could feel the stirring of air between them.

"I didn't mean to hurt your feelings, Nika," said Joseph, as if talking to a child. "Really. I just need to know what's real here, and what isn't."

"I'll be happy to show you, but you're not going to enjoy it."

She glanced at Madoc, and he knew from that mischievous look in her eyes that he was not going to like what happened next. "Catch me?" she asked before she did that thing where she collapsed to the ground like someone had yanked the life from her body.

Madoc scooped her up before she hit the ground. She was limp, lifeless. Only the trickle of power being tugged out of him let him know she was safe and sound. That trickle grew, making him wonder whether Tori was fighting Nika's connection again.

"I really hate it when she does this," he muttered as he settled into a chair, cradling her in his lap.

"Does what?" asked Joseph. Then he went still. His face went blank. His eyes flared wide. Small, almost strangled sounds came out of his throat.

Angus stepped forward.

"Don't," said Madoc. "She's not going to hurt him."

"He looks like she is doing just that."

"If you'd seen Tori, you'd look like that, too. She's completely fucked-up."

Suddenly, Joseph sucked in a long breath and bent double, as if trying not to throw up.

Nika's eyes opened, tears clinging at the corners.

The room was utterly silent. They looked at Nika with a newfound respect—one bordering on fear. If it was that easy for her to slide inside Joseph's mind, he guessed they were each wondering who was next, and what Nika might see if she went poking around.

Madoc was certain that he was not the only man here with secrets to hide.

Which meant he was going to have to keep a close eye on her here, too. If one of the other men was hiding a barren lifemark—or worse—he was not going to want Nika to find out. Not only would she be in danger outside Dabyr, but she would be in danger here, too. And there was no way Iain was going to give up the names of the men in the Band. He was the only one who knew who they were. Madoc wasn't going to be able to trust any of the unbound men.

Madoc's grip on her tightened. What the hell was he going to do with her? He had no business guarding such a precious gift. He was going to fuck up and get her killed. And the damage he would wreak once she was gone was not something he liked to think about.

Everyone was still too quiet. The silence was growing eerier by the second.

Madoc had to clear his throat before he could speak. "Do you believe her now, or do you need another display?"

"One was plenty." Joseph pushed himself upright, but he was still a little paler than normal. "What you showed me was real, right? Not some mind trick?"

"It was real," said Nika. "If I wasn't so tired, I could have kept us there long enough for you to talk to her. She doesn't want me near her anymore."

"We're going in after Tori. It's just a question of how we're going to get her out alive. How far away is she?"

"We're not sure. Nika and I are working on finding her. She put some pictures in my head that might show us where she is, but they're scrambled."

"We'll have them unscrambled today," said Nika, completely confident.

He loved that about her—her absolute faith that he would come through. It never failed to awe him.

"Do you know anything else?" asked Joseph. "Any other clues that might tell us where she is, how many other humans there are with her, or how many of the Synestryn we'll need to take down to reach her?"

"All I know for sure is that some fuckhead named Zillah has her."

Gilda's black eyes landed on Madoc, making him squirm.

She pushed herself to her feet. "Did you say Zillah?"

"Yeah. Know him?"

Gilda and Angus shared a look. He reached for her as if wanting to give or receive comfort, but Gilda ignored his outstretched hand.

"He's the one who convinced Maura to switch sides and work for him. He's a powerful Synestryn. All I really know is that he commands thousands."

"Tori has seen Maura. She might still be with him. Tori included him in that jumble of images she gave me. He looks almost human. When the fuck did they start looking like us?" asked Madoc.

Angus pulled in a deep breath. "We thought he was an anomaly."

"Angus, don't," said Gilda.

"No. It's time. They need to know," he told his wife.

"Know what?" demanded Joseph.

Angus turned back to the group. "We didn't tell anyone that the Synestryn were starting to look more human because we worried what the men close to the end of their time might do. How many humans would die because of mistaken identity?"

Joseph stood, pressing his hands flat on the desk as he leaned toward Angus, his face red with barely controlled rage. "You told me their attempt to look more human had failed the night you killed that abomination—that demon with a child's face. You should have told me about Zillah. As your leader, *I* should have known."

"We chose not to tell you what we learned. There was nothing you could have done with the knowledge," said Angus.

"How do you know? You never let me try."

Gilda's face twisted with rage. "We almost died trying to get Maura away from him. If he's strong enough to nearly kill a bonded pair of Theronai, there was no way you or any of the unbound men here could have stopped him with swords alone. You would have tried and you would have died. I couldn't let that happen."

Joseph's hands bunched into fists. "It was my decision to make. Not yours. Who knows what I might have been able to do. Maybe Tori would never have been taken at all. We'll never know now."

"It was my decision," said Gilda. "Don't punish Angus for something I did."

"He went along with it," stated Joseph, his voice as cold and final as a grave.

"And I'd do it again, too. We were upholding our vow to protect humans, Joseph. If that means keeping secrets, so be it."

This was going to get out of hand fast. Madoc couldn't let that happen. Too much was at stake. "Tori doesn't have time for us to argue about this right now. She's due any day and says that a lot of the girls there don't make it through labor."

"There's more than one girl there?" asked Helen, horrified.

Drake laid a hand on her knee.

Angus shook his head in regret. "Last year we found a demon that looked like a human child. It wasn't. It was venomous, fanged. It attacked us and tried to kill us, but I think it's clear now where it came from."

Joseph nodded. "That's why Andra has been so busy. Why so many blooded children have gone missing. They've been stealing them, using them for more than just food."

"How is that even possible?" asked Gilda. "Human and Synestryn can't interbreed—they're too different."

That sparked Madoc's memory. "Last year, when we took Nika from the mental hospital, she was freaked-out because they were feeding Tori blood, because they were changing her. When we saw Tori in her mind, she looked odd. I'm not sure if what she looked like in her head is what she really looks like in person, but her blood was too dark under her skin. Maybe whatever it is they do to these kids allows them to grow up and bear children that are part human, part Synestryn."

"I didn't imagine what they did to my sister," stated Nika. "I was there. I saw it. I felt it. I know she's hidden some things from me, but I remember the way the blood burned her mouth and throat. I remember how many times she threw up, only to have them do it again. They changed her."

The room fell silent as the implications sank in.

"It seems to fit," said Joseph, "but I don't want to

jump to any conclusions. The Synestryn have been able to reproduce without any problems. Why would they go to all this trouble?"

"It doesn't make sense," said Nicholas. "If they looked more human, they'd be less scary. Part of their mojo would be gone."

"Not to mention the fact that they're diluting the power of their own bloodlines," said Gilda. "They're weakening themselves by doing this."

"No," said Helen. Her face had gone ashen and she was trembling badly enough that Madoc could see it across the room. Drake's arm circled her shoulders and she leaned into him. "They're trying to become more human."

"Why?" asked Gilda, incredulous. "What possible reason could they have to do that? They'd be weaker, live shorter lives. That's what happened to the Slayers."

"If they look human, who among you would be able to hunt them down and kill them? If their offspring *are* part human, where do you draw the line? Who dies? Half humans? Quarter humans? How do your vows to protect humans deal with this?"

Madoc had no idea. All he knew was that Iain was the only one he knew who had volunteered to hunt down these abominations. And his soul was long dead.

"What better way to protect their young than to turn them into the one thing you're sworn to protect? They're counting on your honor, using it as a weakness."

"Helen's right," said Madoc.

"We are so screwed," whispered Joseph. "We've got to stop this. Now. Before it's too late."

"Assuming it isn't already," said Drake.

Joseph put on his game face. "We need to rescue these kids, have the Sanguinar study them to see if what's been done to them can be undone. And whether we can stop it from happening again." He turned to Nicholas. "How long before everyone is back?"

Nicholas checked his phone, pressed a few buttons. "We'll have a dozen more men here before nightfall; the rest will take longer. I don't know when Paul and Andra will be back. Zach and Lexi are still helping rebuild the African stronghold. Unless someone's got a portal up their sleeve, it will take them more than a day to get back."

Everyone looked at Gilda. She shook her head, making her long, dark hair sway. "I'm too weak to open a portal right now."

Angus's deeply creased face darkened with rage, his mouth tightening into a pale, flat line.

"We can't wait for them to get here," said Nika.

"We need all the help we can get," said Joseph. "If we go in unprepared for whatever numbers they may have, we're going to be massacred. No one will get out, including Tori."

"We need to go in during daylight, when we know they'll all be confined to the dark, contained," said Madoc. "If this Zillah prick gets away to do this again, we'll be right back where we started from."

Joseph turned to Madoc and Nika. "Do you have any idea how many we'll be up against?"

Madoc shook his head. "Sorry."

"I can ask Tori," offered Nika.

"Is that safe?" asked Madoc.

"Safer than not knowing how many bad guys there are, I imagine."

"Do it," ordered Joseph. "But don't take any risks. Gilda, how many people can you port at once?"

"After I rest, maybe four."

Madoc frowned. He knew he'd seen her transport more fighters than that before. From the grim look of frustration on Angus's face, he had, too.

"Rest, then. You, too, Helen. We're going to need your firepower if Andra's not back in time. Maybe even if she is. We'll regroup in the dining hall at sunset and see where we stand and plan our attack."

The room began to empty out. Joseph said, "Madoc, Nika, hold on a sec."

Nicholas was last to leave and he pulled the door shut behind him.

"Congratulations to both of you."

"Thank you," said Nika.

Joseph looked at Madoc. "I need to know how strong the two of you are, where Nika's strengths lie, and if there are any problems that are going to sneak up and bite us in the ass."

Madoc took Nika's hand, hoping she'd understand what he had to do and eventually forgive him. "Our bond is still new, weak. Nika seems to have great skills when it comes to mental manipulation, but that's all. She's not a fighter. She doesn't belong in combat."

"Like hell I don't," said Nika, ripping her hand from his. Betrayal shone in her blue eyes. Fury tightened her mouth. "You told me you wouldn't make me stay here."

"You don't belong on the front lines."

"I saved your life last night. I held those sgath still while you killed them. That's nothing to sneeze at."

"Yes, you did. But you could only control them one at a time, and that was only because they had your blood running in their veins."

"I can fight."

"How?" asked Joseph. "Like Andra? Can you blow things apart? What about fire? Tell me what you can do and I'll listen."

Nika looked at her singed fingertips. "I tried fire. It didn't work so well. I just need practice. Once Andra gets back, I'll learn what she can do and try that, too."

Joseph shook his head. "We don't have a lot of time. I think it's best if we use the skills you already have, rather than you exhausting yourself trying to learn new ones."

"I am not useless," she growled, the feral sound surprising Madoc.

"Of course you're not," said Madoc. "We just need to play to your strengths. You're the only one who can talk to Tori and gather intel for us."

"Assuming Tori lets me. She keeps pushing me away, like she did with us. She doesn't want me near her."

Madoc wanted so much to comfort her, but he didn't know how. Even worse, he wasn't sure she'd let him now.

"She let you in," he said. "I'm sure she wants to be out of that place as much as we want her out."

Nika looked up at Joseph. "When you go, I'm coming with you."

"We'll see how things play out," said Joseph.

"No. We won't. I'm going—Madoc promised—and anyone who tries to stop me will regret it." She looked pointedly at each man before turning on her heel and leaving.

Joseph let out a weary sigh and sank into his chair. "What do you think?"

"I think I'd like nothing more than to lock her up here in a room with no sharp corners where I know she'll be safe. I also think that if I tried it, she could find ten kinds of hell to bring down on me."

"Is she ready for battle?"

"No, but she's also not stupid. And we need her. I'll protect her. We'll stay well behind the fighting."

"I think that's best, at least until you two are ready for action."

"That may take a while. I won't let her push herself and suffer a setback. I can't let her go back to that screaming nightmare she suffered before we found her. Which means I can't let her spill her blood."

"Hard not to in combat."

Which was why Madoc planned to never let her get close to one. "I think her strengths are going to lie more in what happens before a fight. If she can learn to use her ability to control one of the Synestryn to gather intelligence or sabotage a nest, she's going to be one hell of a weapon."

"If she lets you live that long. I saw murder in her eyes when she left here."

"Yeah. We're still working out the kinks in our relationship."

"I suggest you work faster."

"What about my sentence?"

Joseph turned on his speakerphone and dialed. It took several rings, but a groggy Tynan picked up. "Yes?"

"You alive?" he asked the Sanguinar.

"Obviously."

"Thanks." Joseph hung up, looking at Madoc. "You didn't kill him."

"I meant to. I wanted to. I was glad when I thought I had. That alone is worthy of punishment. That's the law."

"Fuck the law," said Joseph. "The rules are changing under our feet. I can't keep up and I'm sure as hell not going to sentence you to death for something I've fantasized about doing myself a time or two. If he accuses you, I'll deal with it then."

"He will. He deserves justice."

Joseph leaned forward over his desk, anger clipping his words. "And I deserve never having to take another friend to his death. Everyone's just shit out of luck on the justice front. Now get the hell out of my office and do your damn job. Chances are you won't live through the battle, anyway."

Madoc didn't allow himself to feel relieved. He knew better. Tynan now held his life in his hands, and after all he'd done to him, Madoc was certain this was far from over.

Chapter 18

Nika had rarely felt more alone than she did now. Even among her own kind she felt like an outcast. She saw the way the others were looking at her—as if she'd committed some kind of crime by going into Joseph's mind. Even though he'd asked her to.

She hadn't done anything wrong. She hadn't pried into his secrets or made him dance on his desk as she'd briefly considered doing. All she'd done was give him the proof he needed to know that Tori was still alive. Just as he'd asked.

And yet, somehow, that had shoved a wedge between her and the others, as if they feared what she might do to them.

Nika flopped back on her bed, trying to let the frustration leak out of her. She needed to focus right now, and worrying about what other people thought was not going to help her concentration.

Andra, she called out with her mind. *Please come home. I need you.*

Nika listened, but felt nothing—not a stir of emotion or a flicker of awareness. Wherever Andra was, she was too far away to reach.

Nika was on her own. It was up to her to do what was best for Tori. Anyone who didn't like it could go screw themselves.

For once, it was going to be Nika leaving Andra the note on the fridge, rather than the other way around.

She packed a small suitcase with a few clothes and toiletries, then wheeled it to Madoc's suite.

She knocked on the door. He opened it partway.

"I'm moving in. If you try to keep me out again, I'm going to grab hold of a body part you like and start twisting."

A hint of a smile played at his mouth. "And just which part would that be? I can think of a couple you could twist that I might actually enjoy."

She shoved at the door and he stepped back, letting her in. "Stop playing around. We have work to do."

"I've never had a woman boss me around before. I'm not sure if I like it. Maybe you should do it some more so I can figure it out."

"I've had about enough of all the macho crap around here. I'm tired of being treated like some kind of wilting flower. You don't treat Andra like that."

"That's because she could blow my head off with a single thought."

"And you don't think I can?"

"Not twice, anyway. You'd need my power." He was being too light—almost like he was hiding something.

Nika let out a short shriek of fury. "Stop it. This is serious. We need to find Tori."

"And we will. It's just nice to not hurt anymore. It's making me all giddy."

She lifted a brow, staring at him. "You haven't been giddy a day in your life."

"How do you know? I was a little boy once."

As big and manly as he was now, she had a hard time believing that, even though she knew it was true.

She pulled in a long breath, hoping it would ease some of this tension burning inside her. Knowing Tori was still out there scraped her insides, making her temper shorter than normal.

"We need to find her, Madoc. We need to bring my baby sister home."

He took the suitcase handle from her fingers and wrapped her arms around his waist, pulling her close. "We will."

"You said yourself I'm not strong enough."

"But you're not alone. We'll have a small army with us when we go. Those fuckers don't stand a chance."

Nika buried her nose against his chest, pulling in the scent of his skin. The fabric of his shirt was in her way, so she shoved it up until she could press her cheek against the hard contours of his chest. Beneath her ear, she could almost hear the creak of living wood as his lifemark swayed at her touch.

Madoc cupped the back of her head in his big palm, holding her close, like he actually wanted her there. She was so used to him pushing her away, she didn't know what to make of it.

She tried to look up and read his expression, but he held her still, so she sent a tiny tendril of her mind through their link, hoping to figure out what was going on inside his head.

Lust slammed into her, ruthless and clawing, hungry and desperate. She reeled back from it, shocked at the intensity.

"Sorry," he muttered. "You weren't supposed to see that."

"What was that?"

"I think it's kind of obvious. I want you."

"That was more than want."

He shrugged, and she felt the powerful bunching of muscles against her cheek. "I'm used to it, I guess. Don't worry. It's under control. We should get to work."

He let her go and she pulled away, shaking. Her nerve endings were sparking, tingling from just that brief contact. She had no idea how he could stand it—how he could be so nonchalant about something like that.

"Work?"

He tapped his temple. "You know. We need to puzzle out those images Tori gave me."

Right. She knew that. "O-okay."

Nika was still shaking, but he was right. If he could ignore that writhing lust while it was inside him, she could ignore the tiny little brush she'd had with it.

"You should sit down," he said. "You look a little shaky."

"I'm fine. Let's just do this."

Madoc pulled his shirt down and sprawled on the couch. He patted his knee. "Want to sit on my lap again?"

She did, but only if he was naked, which wasn't going to get them very far at all. "I think I'll sit beside you."

"Suit yourself."

Nika sat and took several deep, calming breaths. "Close your eyes and try to keep your thoughts on the job, okay?"

"Yes, my lady. Anything you like." He closed his eyes and sat there, all relaxed.

Now he was compliant. Why hadn't he been like this seven months ago?

Maybe because his soul was no longer dying. That could have something to do with it.

Nika lifted his hand to her throat until the two parts of the luceria connected. They locked together and power seemed to pour into her. She shivered at the sensation, loving the feeling of so much strength after years of weakness.

"Here I come," she warned him before she slipped out of her body and into his.

He let out a deep moan of satisfaction. "That's nice. We should do this more often."

Nika ignored the compliment and went right to work. "Show me."

Madoc felt like he was sunbathing. On the inside.

Everywhere Nika touched him, he was warm. He'd managed to tuck his lust for her away in a dark corner, but he felt it seething inside him, wanting to be set free.

Later. Much later, after Nika had healed from before.

The thought of her blood was enough to reinforce the barricade and ensure he behaved like the gentleman she deserved for as long as he was allowed to stay with her.

And there were other, more important barricades he had to put in place now that she was inside his mind— things he didn't want her to know.

Tynan held their future in his elegant hands. As ruthless as the Sanguinar were, Madoc had no doubt that Tynan would take the first chance he got to crush him. He was going to stay away from the leech for as long as possible, delaying the inevitable. And until then, he would not allow what might happen to taint his time with her.

"Show me what Tori gave you." Nika's voice reverberated in his mind, a soft caress of sound and light.

Madoc recalled Tori's memories, playing them in what he thought was the right order. Most of them were dark and distorted by her childlike perspective. Many of them were blurry with tears. "Everything's too big," he said to Nika. "It's hard to match anything up to the way I see things."

"Hold on," she said; then a moment later, he felt Nika's presence weave sinuously inside his mind, as if searching for something. He had no idea what she was doing, but the feel of her there, a part of him, was both disturbing and erotic. He felt smarter, more aware of his surroundings.

The graze of his clothes against his skin was amplified. The hum of the ceiling fan overhead tickled. The scent of the leather sofa seemed sharper, while the womanly scent of Nika's skin made him break out in a sweat. He swore he could almost taste her skin on his tongue.

"I can see why the sgath like this," he said. "You're nice to have around."

"Don't you dare distract me. I'm working here."

"Right. Working."

Something inside Madoc's head shifted and the images Tori had given him all changed. Everything shrank to normal size. The giant images of Tori's childlike perspective righted themselves. The trees no longer loomed overhead. Even the stars looked closer.

Stars.

"That's it," he said, excitement rolling through him. "They let her see the sky."

"Will that help?"

"We know the date and time she was taken, right?"

"Yes."

"Show me the rest of the images."

Nika did. Several times during her abduction Tori had looked up. The sky had been clear that night. She'd gone southeast. He was almost certain they could use star maps to figure out her general vicinity. Once he got that close, the slope of the ground and the surrounding landscape—even most of a decade later—would likely be recognizable enough to lead them right to her.

"How close can you get?" asked Nika, her voice excited.

"I'm not sure. Why?"

"Because the closer I am to her, the stronger our connection will be. If we're close enough, and if I use your power, she won't be able to keep me out."

"How close do we need to get?"

"I don't know. It depends on whether she blocks me. We can head southeast and track her down while we wait for everyone else to gather."

"It might be safer to go as a group. They might know we're coming and set a trap."

"We won't go in after her alone. I don't want to fail to save her. But don't you think the chances of the two of us being noticed are slimmer than the chances of an entire group? We don't want to give them time to prepare for our attack."

"You can't let Tori know we're coming. If she's been . . . compromised, she might give our intentions away."

"She'd never do that."

"She'd never *willingly* do that. You know as well as I do that they could force her to tell them. They could torture her or go into her mind the way you do."

Nika's throat moved as she swallowed. "You're right. I don't want to do anything that has even a remote chance of hurting her more. It's probably best if I don't even know what our plans are, in case she can somehow see inside me the way I can her."

Madoc nodded. "I'll talk to Joseph. We'll keep you out of the loop."

"But you won't leave me here. Promise me."

He didn't want to do that. If he promised her, he'd be bound to that promise. And yet, she was reaching out to him, asking for his trust.

It had been a long time since Madoc had felt trustworthy. Nika had given that back to him and he wanted to do something for her in return. "I promise I won't make you stay here when we go."

The weight of his vow and what it meant wove around him, chaining him to his word.

He wasn't sure if he'd made a good decision or a terrible mistake, but there was no turning back now.

Angus couldn't let this go on any longer. Seven months was long enough. He had to find a way to get through to Gilda.

Through the closed bathroom door, he heard the bathwater run, then stop. He didn't bother to knock, knowing she'd tell him to go away—that she wanted to be alone or some nonsense. Instead, he simply opened the door and walked in.

She jerked, covering her naked breasts with her arms. She'd never done that before, and it was just more proof of how far apart they'd drifted.

He let her see his displeasure in his face as well as shoving it through their link. The mental push was harder than it should have been; their link had shrunk more even since yesterday. "I've seen you naked a few thousand times."

Her chin went up as she let her arms fall back into the water. "You startled me. That's all."

Angus ignored the lie, sat on the edge of the tub, and began unlacing his boots.

"What are you doing?" she asked.

"Getting undressed."

"Why?" There was a hint of fear in her tone, and Angus wanted to pound his fists into a wall to vent some of his frustration.

"Seven months, Gilda. It's been seven months since you let me touch you. Our bond is growing weaker by the day, and now the lives of several young women are in the balance. At least one of them is one of our own, and I'm damn well not going to be the cause of her death."

Angus shed his clothes and stepped into the tub.

Gilda shrank back from him, pressing herself as far away as the giant soaking tub would allow. "Are you still letting Tynan experiment on you?" she asked.

"Yes. Nothing has worked. I'm just as infertile now as I was last year."

"How can you be sure?"

Anger was getting harder and harder to fight with each day that passed. He couldn't stop it from coming through in his words now. "Because I jerked off into a cup. Tynan checked under a microscope, and nothing has changed."

"I told you that if you agreed to these experiments, I wasn't going to let you bed me. I haven't changed my mind."

"Fine. You know I won't force you, but I'm damn well not going to sit by while our bond fails. I'm going to touch you, and it has nothing to do with sex."

"No," she said, standing. Water sluiced down her curves. Her glorious body was just as beautiful to him now as it had been centuries ago. Age and the birth of their children had done nothing to take away from her perfection.

Angus swallowed, trying to ease the grinding sexual frustration he'd lived with for way too long. "No?" he asked, his voice deceptively gentle. The last thing he felt right now was gentle, and if she bothered to reach out for him through their link, she'd know it.

Her chin quivered a moment before she pulled herself together. "If you touch me, I'll forget my intentions. You'll seduce me, and I'll never be able to forgive myself for giving in."

"You make it sound like letting me make love to you would be a bad thing."

"I won't have another child. I won't watch another

child die, or worse, be lured by the Synestryn to kill and destroy everything I hold sacred."

"I'm not asking you for another child. I respect your wishes. I even bought condoms and learned how to use them. But what I'm not willing to do is throw away everything we've worked for—everything we've spent our lives creating."

"It's too late," said Gilda. She was shivering now, her flesh rough from the chill.

Instincts embedded in him deeper than his own bones forced him to stand and warm her with his body heat. When his arms came around her, she went stiff, but there was nowhere for her to run away fast enough to escape him.

He felt her body convulse on a silent sob. For years his sweet wife had suffered. Grieved. He hadn't been able to do anything to fix it, so he'd learned to live with her constant sadness and silent rage until he accepted it as normal.

It wasn't normal. Gilda used to laugh. She used to tease him and smile and play.

She hadn't been normal since Maura had run away and joined forces with the Synestryn.

"It's not too late," he assured her, forcing his conviction through their shrinking link.

"I've done things, Angus. Unforgivable things."

His grip on her tightened. She was still cold, so he eased her down into the hot water, settling her against his chest. His lifemark still loved her touch, and it shivered toward her as if it had been starved of that touch for way too long.

"What you did to Sibyl and Maura was understandable. Our son had died. You were grieving. Distraught." And because of what Gilda had done, his girls would never grow up. As much as that hurt, he'd forgiven her, hoping his daughters would follow his example.

They hadn't.

"That's not what I'm talking about," she said. "There are things about me you don't know. Terrible things. I'm not sure how much longer I can live with these secrets. They're eating me from the inside, gnawing at me."

Angus was careful to hide his shock. He thought he knew everything about his wife, but perhaps he'd been wrong. "Whatever it is, it can't be that bad."

"It is. I've taken so much from you. From all of you."

"What are you talking about, love? The only thing you've taken from me is your touch. We're past that now, aren't we?" He hoped so. He hoped that her letting him hold her now was a sign her stubbornness was at an end. Finally.

"Once I tell you, you won't want to touch me ever again."

Angus tilted her body, hooked his thumb under her chin, and turned her head so she would look at him. "There is nothing you can do that I wouldn't love you enough to forgive."

Her dark eyes glittered with tears. "You're wrong, Angus."

"Tell me. Tell me what you've done that's so bad, because I think *you're* wrong."

A single tear spilled over, and the sadness he saw in her face nearly made him weep. "I've tried to live without you these last seven months. I thought the distance between us would make my betrayal easier to bear."

"What betrayal?"

Angus tried to reach through their link and see what was going on in her head, but he couldn't get through. All he could feel was her barely constrained panic and a sense of grief so thick he didn't know how she could stand it.

She looked down in shame. "It was the night Isaac died."

Isaac. Their youngest son. He'd died in battle, along with three other Theronai. But that had been so long ago. Two centuries. As much as he still ached for his lost son, he also felt a huge swelling of pride for what he'd done that night—for the man he'd grown to become and the countless lives he'd saved. He'd sacrificed his life, but it hadn't been in vain. The descendants of the humans he'd saved that night still lived on, making the world a better place.

Angus caressed her arm, hoping to comfort her. "Love, anything you did that long ago I already know. Whatever it is you think you did, I've already forgiven you."

"No. You're wrong. I've hidden it. So carefully, so deep, I know you've never seen my shame."

"Then tell me now so I can forgive you and you can heal. Let's get past this. The lives of our people depend on our strength, our example."

"Yours, maybe. I'm afraid my example has been lacking."

"Tell me, Gilda. I can't imagine a thing you could do so bad I would stop loving you."

She fell silent. Pulled in a breath. Her body shuddered, as if uttering the words after holding them in so long was a struggle. "The night Isaac died, I was destroyed. I knew the moment I heard the news that my heart would never be whole again. I couldn't bear the pain, and knew I couldn't allow it to happen again. I couldn't lose another child."

Angus remembered that night, despite his desire to forget. Their link had intensified their pain, as they each not only suffered their own grief, but the other's as well. Rather than cling to him for support, as he'd ached for her to do, she'd fled—run into the hills and shut down. When she came back, she was colder. Harder.

"I went into the woods," she said. "I gathered as much power into me as I could hold, hoping it would kill me and take away the pain. I raged at the unfairness of our son's death. Why hadn't it been me that had died instead of him? Why hadn't it been one of the other men? I'd already given so much to this war. How could God take our last living son, too?"

Angus had no answers. He sat in silence, giving her time to work up her courage to say whatever it was she had to say.

"The power in me kept growing and yet I didn't die. That made me angrier. I knew I couldn't ever again allow another child of mine to die, so I vowed never again to conceive. I would not give any more of my heart's blood to this war."

Her voice quieted, vibrating with shame. "I hadn't intended for my magic to do what it did. I hadn't planned any of this, or had a single conscious thought as to what it might mean, but there was so much power, so much grief and rage that it went out of control. The power ripped from my body, doing my unconscious will, shimmering out from the top of that hill in waves so strong I could see the trees shake as it passed."

"What magic?" asked Angus. "What had you done?"

"For years our people have believed that our men are infertile because of something the Synestryn did to us. I've let them believe it, but it's a lie." She pulled in a deep breath. "I did it, not our enemy. It was me. My magic spread out over the face of the planet, rendering every male Theronai sterile, because only then could I be sure I'd never conceive."

Shock choked the breath from Angus's body. "*You* did that to us? To me?"

She didn't answer. She didn't have to.

How could she have done that? How could she have destroyed their entire race so utterly? He couldn't fathom why she would have done something like that, even in her grief. He knew she hadn't consciously planned to sterilize them, but that intent had come from her—from somewhere inside her he didn't recognize. A dark, selfish place.

Angus needed some time to digest this news, to process it and make sense of it. His entire perspective shifted. Not only did he now know that his ability to have children had been stolen—not by his enemy, but by his wife—he also realized something he never thought possible.

Gilda could lie to him. She'd been lying for years. Centuries.

That was the betrayal that hurt most. He'd given her everything he had, everything he was. He *breathed* for her. She was his very blood. He could no more keep a secret from her than he could stop the Earth from spinning. Lying to her seemed inconceivable.

And yet she'd lied so easily to him, which made him wonder what else she'd lied about.

Angus hated seeing her in this light. He hated looking at her, wondering what other secrets she held from him.

He felt her reaching for him through their link, and for the first time in memory, he blocked her out. Not because he didn't want her to feel his pain, but because he couldn't stand the thought of having her inside him right now.

Angus settled her body against the wall of the tub and got out. He needed some time to think. To be alone. Or at least away from Gilda.

He didn't even bother drying off, just dragged his clothes over his wet skin and left. As he shut the door behind him, he caught a glimpse of the luceria ring on his finger.

The deep storm-cloud gray swirls that had been frozen in place for centuries—the patterns that had been with him so long he'd memorized their every curve—began to move.

The bond he had with Gilda, his Gray Lady, was coming undone. He knew that if it was broken, it would mean his death. The fact that the notion didn't bother him overmuch told him just how deeply Gilda's betrayal had cut him.

Gilda's tears dripped into the water. It had grown cold, making her shiver, but she didn't get out. The small punishment the cold gave her was nothing compared to what she deserved.

She should have known that the weight of her secret would not be relieved by telling Angus. Instead, the hurt she'd caused him weighed her down even more.

He was too good a man for her. He didn't deserve the pain she'd heaped on him.

He didn't deserve her—being chained to her for eternity.

Gilda knew what she had to do. She had to pull herself together, use every bit of waning strength she had to rescue Tori, and pray to God that the girl would be compatible with Angus so she could set him free.

Of course, there was only one way she could do that. She'd promised him she'd stay by his side as long as she lived, which meant she'd have to die.

The idea didn't scare her. She was tired of living with all this grief, tired of fighting, and watching the people she loved die. As hard as it would be to let Angus go, especially into the arms of another woman, she knew it was the right thing to do.

The Sentinels needed Angus. He was too strong a warrior to let go. He would live on and keep fighting for as long as it took to defeat the Synestryn.

Gilda couldn't.

Now that the decision was made, everything else seemed so simple. So clear.

She got out of the tub, put on her favorite silk gown, and went to say good-bye to her daughter. Sibyl wouldn't speak to her—she hadn't in decades—but by God, she would listen.

Chapter 19

Ricky answered his cool new cell phone—the one the guy with the creepy eyes gave him. Their meetings were fuzzy, but he remembered the guy saying someone would call.

"Hello?"

"It's time," rasped a whispering voice over the line. "Do you understand?"

"Who?" asked Ricky automatically.

"Nika Madison."

Even though the voice didn't tell him what it was time for, deep down Ricky knew. He had a vague memory of a suitcase of supplies someone he knew had given him. He couldn't remember who it was, but he had hidden that box in the back of his closet. He hadn't even remembered it was there until now.

Instructions flooded his mind, compelling his feet to move. He abandoned the video game he'd been playing and went to his room, ignoring the angry voices of his buddies behind him.

It was only a short walk from his room to where he knew he'd find her.

Ricky suffered a moment of fear that the giant, angry Theronai Madoc might be there, but that fear seemed to evaporate as soon as it came, leaving him numb.

All he had to do was what he was told and everything would be fine. He'd be free to live his life, no longer a prisoner of Dabyr and all its stupid rules.

*　　*　　*

Madoc left to talk to Joseph. Nika had lain down to reach out for Tori when someone knocked at the door.

She opened it, and a young man, about sixteen years old, stood there.

"Can I help you?"

"Is Madoc here?" he asked, looking past her almost nervously.

"No. He's—" She didn't have time to finish the sentence. He barreled through the doorway, grabbing her throat in one strong hand. He kicked the door shut behind him and shoved a rag over her nose and mouth.

A sharp, medicinal scent burned her nose and throat. She clawed at his arm, but it did no good. Her fingers had gone weak, boneless.

The world began to fade away, and with one last panicked thought, she shouted Madoc's name.

Ricky had done it. He'd knocked the crazy chick out. Now all he had to do was get her outside the walls and he was free. No more Sentinel prison. No more boring school all year round. No more rules.

The guy with the creepy eyes was going to give him more money than he could spend in one lifetime. They'd already gotten him an apartment and a sweet ride. And they'd promised not to kill the girl—he'd made sure of that.

Ricky was no murderer.

He peeked out into the hall and saw no one coming. He grabbed the big suitcase, rolled it into the suite, shoved the crazy chick's body in it, and zipped it closed.

She was so skinny, she fit easily. No sweat.

He'd pop her in the trunk, then drive out the gates. He was allowed outside the walls during daylight one day a month. Today was that day, and it was going to be the last time he ever had to ask for permission again.

Madoc!

Nika's shout slammed into his brain, propelled by pure, raw panic. Fear exploded inside him as he realized she was in trouble. Big trouble.

He was halfway to Joseph's office, but he spun on his heel and sprinted back the way he came. He reached out for her through their link, feeling nothing.

If she was dead . . .

His feet pounded hard. He accidentally shouldered a kid out of his way as he passed, slamming him into a wall. The kid tripped and fell, but Madoc didn't give a fuck.

He ripped his cell from his belt and dialed Nicholas. "Something's happened to Nika. Can you see her?"

"I'm looking now. Hold on."

Madoc kept the phone pressed to his ear and fumbled for his key card as he ran, dropping it. He didn't stop to pick it up. "Unlock my door or I'm breaking it down."

He rounded the corner, saw the light on his lock turn green, and slammed through the opening like a battering ram.

"Nika!"

She didn't answer. A frantic, ten-second search of the place showed no sign of her.

Nicholas's voice buzzed in his ear. "There was a boy at your door. He pushed his way into the suite. Came out thirty seconds ago towing a big suitcase."

Madoc had passed him. "If he hurt her, the little pissant fucker's going to die."

He charged back out into the hall, chasing down the kid. As he cleared the corner, he saw the boy look over his shoulder, panic, and sprint away, leaving the suitcase behind.

"I see him," said Nicholas. "Let him go. Take care of Nika."

Like he had to be told that. He'd find and kill the fucker later. Right now he needed to get to Nika.

It seemed to take forever to reach the end of the hall. It stretched out into eternity, growing longer with every step he took.

What if she wasn't in the suitcase? Even worse, what if she was, but it was too late?

A million different thoughts flooded Madoc's mind, clogging it with terror. He felt streaks of wetness drying on his cheeks, but paid them no attention.

Finally, he reached the bag and ripped the zipper open.

Nika lay curled inside, her head bent at an awkward angle. She didn't make a sound. He couldn't see her chest move.

A wounded sound poured out of him with every breath. His hands shook as he reached for her.

Her skin was warm. So soft.

He pressed his fingers against the side of her neck, but he was shaking so hard, he couldn't tell if what he felt was her pulse or his own trembling.

His fingers brushed the luceria and the faintest hint of color danced within the band. It wouldn't do that if she was dead, would it?

Madoc lifted her out, shoved the black nylon away, and cradled her in his arms as he hurried to Tynan's suite. He was the best healer they had. Even if he hated Madoc, he had to help Nika.

Liam appeared beside him. "Nicholas said you might need some help. What can I do?"

Madoc felt her chest rise, pressing against his. She was alive.

Relief threatened to buckle his knees, but he held it together and kept moving forward.

"Wake up Tynan. He needs to fix her."

Liam said nothing, but he sprinted ahead.

Tynan's door was hanging open when Madoc got there. He rushed inside, through the living area, and down the stairs to where Tynan slept.

Liam had already woken him, though he didn't look alert. His voice was thick and groggy as he said, "Lay her down."

Madoc didn't. He didn't want to let go of her.

Tynan rubbed his eyes and gave himself a shake. "What happened?"

"I don't know. Some kid knocked her out and stuffed her in a suitcase."

Tynan leaned over her, making Madoc go tense. He didn't want the fucker touching her blood. Not ever. But how else was he going to figure out what had happened to her?

The Sanguinar straightened, picked up Nika's delicate wrist, and felt for her pulse. "She's been drugged. I can smell it. Give her a few minutes to wake up on her own."

"Can't you do something?"

Tynan stared at Madoc with more than a hint of anger glowing in his ice blue eyes. "I'm weak. Some asshole broke my neck yesterday."

"I'll give you blood. Whatever you need. Just make her better."

"It's not enough. Not after what you did to me."

Madoc swallowed hard, trying to dislodge his pride from his throat. "I'm sorry," he told Tynan, staring right into his eyes. It was a dangerous thing to do with a Sanguinar in the best of circumstances, and these were far from that. "I lost control. Joseph already knows. You'll have your justice. There's no excuse for what I did."

"None," agreed Tynan, his gaze cold. "Though we both know the reason."

Madoc shot a worried glance toward Liam. He wasn't sure if he could still be sent to the Slayers now that his lifemark was no longer bare, but he didn't want to risk being forced apart from Nika. No one could ever know he'd once been a candidate for death.

"My blood oath," offered Madoc. "I offer you my blood oath to save Nika's life and make up for the harm I caused you. I freely give you as much blood as you need, as often as you need, so long as it doesn't impede my ability to protect Nika."

"That's a good start, but it's not enough."

"What more can I give you?"

"Children. I want your vow that you'll let me try to cure your sterility."

Madoc didn't even need to think twice, though he knew that whatever Tynan intended to do to him would probably hurt like hell. "Fine. Whatever you need to do. Just save her. Please."

A flare of white light spilled from Tynan's gaze. A slow, victorious smile stretched his mouth. "Done."

*   *   *

Tynan counted Madoc's vow as a great victory. The man had no way of knowing that Tynan never would have asked for his death. He needed him too much to throw away perfectly good blood for the sake of justice.

Madoc also didn't need to know that Nika was perfectly fine, and that the drug she'd breathed in would dissipate within a few minutes, leaving her nauseated, but with no lasting damage.

Madoc's panic was a lever Tynan could not refuse to use. And now he had another candidate for his fertility experiments. Not a bad day's work.

Tynan took Madoc's offered arm and drank deep, sending the man to sleep to avoid any more unfortunate accidents. Tynan's neck was still stiff from yesterday.

Liam stood over them, watching, so Tynan finished feeding on Madoc's powerful blood and made a show of healing Nika.

It took little effort to speed the effects of the anesthetic in her system and wake her up. While he was at it, he healed the few small burns on her fingertips and the bit of bruising he'd sensed along the walls of her vagina.

Little Nika was no longer a virgin, a fact that Tynan found promising, considering Madoc was now his personal guinea pig.

"She'll be fine," Tynan told Liam. "She just needs to rest a while. I'll keep Madoc here for a bit longer."

"He stays, I stay," said Nika, her voice groggy.

"Then I'm staying, too," said Liam, clearly mistrustful of Tynan's intentions.

Tynan shrugged. "Suit yourself. I'm not going to do anything to him he didn't give me the right to do."

Let them watch. He didn't care. Madoc was his now, and he intended to make the most of his new subject. He'd give Madoc the fertility serum he'd been working on, and then implant him with an insatiable appetite for sex. Between those two things, he'd know in a month or two if his latest cure had worked.

*   *   *

Tori's pains had been getting worse all day.

She knew what it meant. She knew that the dull ache in her back meant it was time. The thing inside her was ready to be born.

Darkness seemed to close in around her, forcing the chill of the cave walls against her skin. It sucked the heat from her blood, and along with it, all hope that Nika and that man would find her before it was too late.

No one had come for her, and until now, she hadn't realized just how much hope she'd put in the stupid idea that they might find her. She would have been better off not hoping at all, because now the loss of hope seemed almost too much to stand.

Beneath the skin stretched too tight over her belly, the thing shifted, causing a bulge to slide under the surface.

Tori wished she didn't hate it. She wished that some kind of maternal instinct had kicked in, helping her get through these last few long months. As hard as she tried, she couldn't imagine it as a real baby with soft pink skin that smelled sweet. All she could see was Zillah's fangs, the way sweat beaded up on his pale gray skin, and his too-long fingers as he held her down.

Tori shoved the memory away and focused on keeping her emotions in check. Whenever she was afraid, the need to reach out for Nika was harder to resist.

Unfortunately, Tori was scared to death. The thing inside her was going to come in the next few hours, and it could easily kill her. And if it didn't, she knew what her future would hold. Once the thing was born, Zillah would come for her again. He'd hurt her again and put another thing inside her.

Somehow, death seemed better.

Another painful spasm gripped her back. She sucked in a breath and forced it out between her teeth.

She would not call out for Nika. She would not repay years of her sister's companionship and kindness by letting her suffer through the birth of this thing along with Tori.

Nika deserved better.

"It's time, isn't it?" she heard Zillah say from deep within the shadows outside her cell.

"No," lied Tori.

"Have you called her yet?"

"Who?" she asked, just to make him mad.

He stepped out from his hiding place to where she could see him. Excitement made his black eyes sparkle. He smiled as he unlocked the door and stepped inside. "Don't worry. I can be patient."

"Wait as long as you want. I'm not calling her."

"You will." His words rang with complete confidence. "Before our child is born, you will."

Chapter 20

Madoc woke up in his own bed. Sunlight filtered through the closed blinds, giving a soft glow to the room. Nika was tucked beside him, curled into his body. Her slender fingers splayed over his waist and her cheek rested over his heart.

He was a bit fuzzy on how he got here. The last thing he remembered was being in Tynan's room.

He turned to look at the bedside clock to see how much time had passed. Sitting in front of it, obscuring the red numbers, were four bottles of sports drink. A note was taped to the top of one.

Rehydrate. You're going to need it. T.

Tynan.

So, the attack on Nika and the blood oath hadn't been a bad dream.

In the space of a heartbeat, he relived the entire event. The panic of knowing something had happened to her, the fear of losing her, the need to make it better and never let anything ever happen to her again. It all slammed into him, robbing him of breath.

Madoc rolled over and wrapped his arm around her, thanking whatever god was listening for her safety.

Nika squirmed in his too-tight embrace, so he relaxed the pressure. Her breasts slid over his bare chest, and he could feel the velvet drag of her nipples against his skin.

She was naked. He could feel it now, all that soft, warm skin sliding against his.

They were both naked.

Madoc couldn't remember how that happened, but before he had time to ponder it, a wall of lust crashed down on him, making him hard. He gritted his teeth against it, struggling not to crush Nika in his embrace.

Her eyes fluttered open and she gave him a smile so sweet it nearly broke his heart. "You're awake," she whispered. "How are you feeling?"

Like shoving his cock into her. He didn't say that, though. He kept his lips pressed together, knowing that if he opened them, he'd kiss her. And if he kissed her, he wouldn't stop until he was driving hard and deep inside her.

Nika frowned and rose to her knees, pressing her hand against his head as if checking for fever. "Are you okay? Tynan said you needed to drink a lot."

He understood her words, but he couldn't seem to care about responding. Her breasts were beautifully bare, hovering near his head. She reached over him for a plastic bottle, and Madoc couldn't stop himself from shifting just enough to capture her nipple in his mouth.

Nika gasped and moved closer, flowing over him, lining herself up so he didn't have to stretch his neck to reach her.

He grabbed her shoulders, holding her steady while he kissed his way to her other breast so he could taste it, too.

"I'm not sure we should be doing this," she said, breathless. "You're dehydrated."

He didn't give a fuck about that right now. All he cared about was whether she was wet enough to take him.

She pulled away, and he let her go only because he really wanted to get her under him. Before he could manage to move her there, she slipped away and rolled over his body until she was standing on the floor beside the bed. She grabbed one of the bottles and thrust it at him. "Drink. Sanguinar's orders."

If that was what it would take to get her to comply, he'd do it. He sat up, ripped the cap off, and guzzled the bottle down, staring at her the whole time. A trickle escaped the corner of his mouth and Nika's eyes followed it down his chest.

She licked her lips as Madoc tossed the empty bottle to the floor.

Nika knelt on the edge of the bed and leaned forward. Her tongue met his skin, following the path the liquid had taken down his torso.

Madoc's body clenched. He felt her sliding inside his head, poking around. He didn't want her to see how raw his need for her was, how consuming and demanding. He wanted to be gentle with her. Go slow. Make up for what he'd done before.

He gripped her arms and pulled her up until he could kiss her. Her mouth was soft and sweet against his. Her lips parted to let his tongue slide in and taste her.

He groaned, knowing no other woman would ever taste half as good or go to his head quite like Nika did. No matter how hard he tried, he couldn't resist her. She was his weakness, and, at the same time, everything he'd ever wanted.

This time, he wasn't going to lose control. This time he was going to treasure her, go slow and give her the kind of pleasure she deserved. Even if it killed him.

Her hands roamed over his chest, making his lifemark shiver in delight. Her fingers were warm and supple as they kneaded him, tugging him closer as her breathing sped up against his mouth.

She pulled her lips away and stared at him with eyes a much darker blue than normal. Her pupils swelled, her irises thinned out, and her eyelids were low and heavy, as if she was having trouble keeping her eyes open. A bright pink flush was spreading out over her neck and chest, so pretty he couldn't stop himself from kissing it.

He worked his way down her neck, nipping and kissing as he moved down. Nika's pulse pounded in her neck. He flicked his tongue against the luceria, and it sent a shock of power winging through his body.

Her sharp intake of breath told him she'd felt it, too.

"Like that?" he asked.

An incoherent moan was her only response, but she tilted her head to the side, inviting him to do it again.

He did, and this time, that shock went straight to his groin, making him hiss in a breath against the acute pleasure of it.

The link between them throbbed, and he could feel a frantic kind of need spilling out of her. He recognized it as sexual frustration and wanted nothing more than to ease her, but not until he knew she was ready. He couldn't stand the thought of hurting her again.

She straddled his stomach, reaching under the sheets behind her to grip his cock in her delicate hand. He knew she intended to shove him inside herself, but it wasn't time for that. "Not yet. Soon."

A feral snarl shaped her mouth, making her look like a woman who wasn't going to take no for an answer. Her white teeth glowed bright, her lips were swollen and red from his kisses, and right now, Madoc couldn't think of a single thing beyond getting her mouth around his cock.

He knew that wasn't what he was supposed to be thinking about, but he couldn't seem to help it.

"Is that what you want?" she asked, staring down at him.

Hell, yes. There was no way he was keeping his rampant thoughts to himself. He didn't even try. He let her see what he wanted. He let her see her white hair spilling over his thighs as she sucked him into her sweet mouth. He let her see her thighs spread wide as he returned the favor, licking and sucking her until she came against his mouth.

Her body vibrated with fine tremors as she inched her way toward his groin. The sheets covered his erection, but didn't hide it. She pulled the fabric down, sliding it over his cock in a sensual caress.

Madoc shuddered, clenching his fists to keep from shoving her down where he wanted her. He needed to be gentle. Careful. He couldn't hurt her again like he did last time.

In fact, he shouldn't even be doing this at all.

"You're not going to hurt my mouth," she told him. Before he could answer her, she flowed down between his thighs with a natural grace that made it look like she'd been doing this for years.

Wet heat closed around his cock as she slid her lips over him. Her tongue swirled over the head, licking away the drops he couldn't keep from spilling in his excitement. With voracious enthusiasm, she sucked and licked, learned what he liked, dragging a string of searing curses from his lips. He felt her in his head, sliding through his thoughts, and the intimacy served only to make him hotter.

He wasn't going to last much longer at this rate. All her innocence and excitement were going to kill him, and he'd be damned if he got off again without making her come first. It was a point of pride. His woman would never again go without the screaming kind of pleasure she deserved. And then some.

Before he forgot his good intentions, he pulled her sweet mouth away and pushed her back until her head was hanging off the end of the bed. He lifted her feet, hooked them over his shoulders, and moved up until her thighs were draped over his arms.

Like this, the contrast between his strength and her fragility was startling. His arms were as thick as her legs, reminding him of just how fragile she was.

"I can take whatever you have to give," she assured him. "You won't break me."

Her trust in him was humbling. It tore down walls he didn't even know he'd built, baring him in ways he'd never been with any other woman.

As big and tough as he was, she could still make him tremble.

Madoc turned his head and kissed the inside of her thigh, right above her knee. His tongue flicked over her skin, leaving a hot, wet trail of feather-soft touches. As he moved up her body, her legs spread wider.

"I'm going to kiss you," he told her. "Make you wet enough to take all of me."

She shivered and Madoc felt a spike of lust spear through their link into him. Her lust.

A smile of victory stretched his mouth as he bent to kiss and lick and feast on her.

Nika was dying. She had to be. Nothing but death could feel this intense.

She knew what was happening to her. She'd been inside the minds of other women when they climaxed, but it was nothing like this. She wasn't sure if it was the mental connection or the physical distance that had muted those feelings, or if she somehow felt things differently from other women, and right now, she couldn't concentrate enough to figure it out.

Madoc's mouth and fingers were driving her higher, forcing her toward something blinding and beautiful. She gripped his hair, not sure whether she wanted to push him away or pull him closer. These feelings were almost too bright to bear. Only the knowledge that he wouldn't hurt her drove her worry away.

She felt the connection between them flare; then his hulking presence was inside her mind, fitting there as if he'd been a part of her all her life. He was warm, strong, demanding. He found her lust and magnified it with his own, letting her see just how much he wanted her.

Images of them together tangled in sensual poses fluttered through her as he showed her all the things he intended to do to her.

Nika's nerve endings were already on fire as pleasure streaked through her. Those images and the feel of Madoc seated deep in her mind sent her flying, disintegrated her as her body began to spasm. The intensity of it was shocking, almost painful. Only the victorious surge of satisfaction she felt coming from Madoc told her that it was safe to let go.

She flung herself into the pleasure and trusted Madoc to keep her safe as the next wave hit her.

Slowly, her body relaxed as a vibrating kind of warmth settled over her.

Her body shifted on the bed as Madoc moved her. Until then, she hadn't realized she'd nearly fallen off.

He hovered over her, giving her the sexiest smile she'd ever seen. "I feel so much better now," he told her.

"*You* feel better?"

"Much. I love watching you come."

He was still in need. She could feel that easily enough, in both his mind and his body, and yet he wasn't rushing her as he had before. She wanted to ease that need and give him the kind of pleasure he'd just given her.

Nika felt slow and languid, but she had a seemingly endless source of power at her command, so she pulled some into herself and used a burst of magically enhanced strength to push Madoc to the bed.

"My turn," she said, straddling him as she'd wanted to do earlier.

His mouth was drawn tight with lust, so she bent forward to kiss it. He gave her what she wanted, meeting each thrust of her tongue with one of his own. The slippery motion caused heat to pool in her belly. The hunger inside her that he'd so recently quenched began to grow again.

Nika needed to be filled with him. She needed to feel him inside her, stroking deep. It was the only thing that could sate her need.

She was a bit clumsy as she maneuvered them together, but Madoc was patient, letting her take her time. He was big, and even though she was slick, she still felt the wicked stretch as her body made room for him. Zingers of sensation raked along her spine, making her shake. She wanted to just slam down and take all of him, but his hands on her hips held her up, rocking her, making her go slowly.

"You're killing me," she told him.

"I refuse to hurt you again."

"Then let me move."

"Soon." Sweat beaded up along his hairline, and the tendons in his neck stood out, telling her she wasn't the only one suffering.

Rather than argue with him any further, she simply

focused on the link between them and let everything she was feeling flood into him.

Madoc sucked in a breath. His fingers clenched on her hips and he pulled her down, seating her all the way.

Nika had never felt so full. She struggled to breathe, feeling her muscles clenching around him. It was an odd kind of completion, having him in her body and in her mind at the same time. She could feel everything he did, from the throbbing pressure in his erection to the faint shifting of his hair from the ceiling fan overhead.

He needed her to move. She could feel that now. So Nika moved.

The groan of pleasure Madoc let out was the sweetest thing she'd ever heard. He pulled her down against his chest, rolled her beneath him, and began a slow slide and retreat.

The first time had been nothing like this. There was no pain, no tension, only the slick glide of skin on skin and his hungry mouth on hers.

The pressure inside her built. She could feel it growing in both of them, too sharp and demanding to resist. His thoughts whispered inside hers, knitting them together in a way she hadn't known existed.

His powerful body surged as their need increased. She felt that pleasure building inside him as he opened himself up to her. The connection between them swelled and pulsed with power.

Madoc lifted her hips with one hand, grinding her against him in a way that brought tears to her eyes and stole the air from her lungs. And then everything came crashing down. Madoc's body tensed as he drove deep. He swelled inside her and the first hot jet of his release pulsed in her core, setting off her climax.

She cried out, holding him tight as his release filled her. The waves crashing over her throbbed in time with his, melding the sensations together into one continuous blur of perfect sensation. It seemed to go on forever, but once it was over, it was gone too soon.

They were both still breathing hard when Madoc flipped them and draped her over his chest. He was still hard inside her, still throbbing in time with their rapid heartbeats. Sweat cooled across her back, but her front was blissfully warm.

Madoc hadn't shoved her away this time. He was still inside her mind as deeply as he was inside her body.

Which was why she could hear his thoughts. Not only had he been planning to give her away to another man; he was also still planning to keep her here when everyone else went to rescue Tori.

"I don't care how good in bed you are," she said, pushing herself up on his chest to look down at him. "There's no way you're convincing me to stay behind."

He opened his mouth and said something, but Nika couldn't understand a single word. All she heard was the sound of her name in a scream of pain that echoed inside her skull.

Tori. Tori was trying to reach her.

Nika opened herself up and pulled some of Madoc's power into her so she could find where that contact had come from. As soon as she did, a wrenching pain shot through her body, making her jerk against Madoc. She'd never felt anything like it before. It cut off her breath and shrank her world down to a pinpoint of light. Everything else went gray.

She heard herself scream, felt Madoc's hands on her body and his thoughts in her mind.

"Tori!"

I'm sorry, she heard her sister sob. *I'm so sorry.*

Chapter 21

Gilda had lifted her hand to knock when her daughter's door opened. Sibyl looked up at her, her eyes the same pale blue as her father's.

Angus. Gilda already missed him.

Sibyl's blond ringlets were tangled, her dress wrinkled, which was not at all like her. Dark crescents hung below her eyes, dulling their normal sheen.

"I guess it's that time," said Sibyl.

Gilda was shocked at being spoken to after suffering her daughter's silence for so long. "What time?"

"For you to die."

"You've seen that?" Gilda hated it that her daughter was plagued by visions of the future, but she'd never considered she'd have to endure seeing her own mother's death.

"I've seen many things. Too many." Sibyl stepped back, allowing Gilda to step inside her suite. The frilly furnishings seemed wilted today, their normally bright pink dull and dingy.

Gilda settled on the dainty couch. "I won't stay long. I know things are strained between us, but I felt compelled to see you again."

"Nothing between us has changed," said Sibyl. "I can't suddenly forgive you because you've decided to kill yourself, can I?"

"I'm not asking for your forgiveness. I was just hoping that you'd . . . let me hold you one more time."

"I'm not a child. You've trapped me inside this child's body, but I'm not a child."

"You'll always be my child. Just as Maura is."

"Maura won't talk to me about you. She refuses."

"You speak to Maura?"

"Sometimes. When she's afraid."

Gilda hated the idea of her little girl being afraid, but Maura had made her own decisions. She had to live with the consequences, just as Gilda did.

"Will you tell her I still love her?" asked Gilda.

"She won't believe me. She doesn't believe you can love someone who has no soul."

"Of course she has a soul."

"Maura doesn't believe that. She says you ripped it from her when you tore us in half while still in your womb."

"What I did to you was foolish. We needed more women to fill our ranks. I thought having twin girls would help us win the war."

"Maura and I weren't meant to be twins. You took the defenseless child growing inside your body and *cut it in half*. How could you have done something like that? How could you have ripped a tiny soul in two when you were the one charged with keeping it safe?"

"I didn't mean for it to be like that. Twins are born all the time. I didn't realize I was doing anything unnatural."

"You didn't realize. Just like you didn't realize what you were doing the night Isaac died?"

Gilda shook her head. Grief for her son stormed inside her still, even after all these years. "It was another mistake. One of many. I'm so sorry that you and Maura were left to suffer because of my choices. I only meant to protect you."

"You make it sound so reasonable, as though any mother would have done the same thing."

"I didn't know what would happen to you. I swear it."

"How could you not have known? You came to us that night, woke us from a dead sleep for that sole purpose."

"No. It wasn't like that. I needed to hold you—to grasp onto my two living children and reassure myself you were okay."

"That's not the way I remember it. I remember you lurching into our room. I remember you were crying. The front of your dress was wet with tears. Maura and I were scared. We didn't know what had happened and you were crying too hard to tell us. We hugged you, trying in our childish way to comfort you. We would have done anything to make you feel better, and you used that to wring from us a promise we didn't understand."

"I didn't know what it would do."

"How could you not have known? You looked us each in the eye and said, 'Promise Mommy you'll never grow up.' You knew the power that promise would hold over us."

"They were just words. I didn't want you to grow up and join the fight. I didn't want you to die like your brother had earlier that night."

"We were eight years old. We didn't understand what that promise would cost us. I remember giving it to you and feeling the breath being crushed from our lungs. I remember the panic that gripped us as that promise bored into our souls, caging us in these tiny bodies."

"I'm so sorry, Sibyl. I never meant to hurt you."

A hollow laugh rose up, too old for the body from which it came. "You did a fine job of it without even trying."

"One day you'll understand."

"How?" demanded Sibyl. "When I grow up and have a child of my own? You've stolen that from me. You've taken from me everything I should have had, including driving Maura—the other half of myself—away."

"No. I didn't do that."

"You did. She left because she couldn't stand the sight of you. She couldn't stand the reminder of what we should have had, what we should have become."

"She chose to change sides."

"No. She chose to run away, and the only place where she would be safe was with our enemy. It's not as if she could have lived on her own."

"She betrayed us," said Gilda, knowing Maura had learned to do so from her.

"*You* betrayed us. Your actions set all of this in motion. I'm sure the damage you've done hasn't even finished playing out yet—at least, not for me and Maura."

"If I could take back what I've done, I would."

"It's too late for that. Your time is nearly up."

"So you can see that—see my future."

Sibyl nodded.

"And your father's?"

"You'd have to ask Maura. It's her turn."

"I wish I could see her again before I die," said Gilda.

"Don't worry," said Sibyl. "You will."

Madoc's heart was going to explode from his body. First he had the most powerful orgasm of his life, and now Nika was screaming in pain, writhing in his arms.

"Tori!" she yelled, reaching out as if she could actually see her sister.

"Nika, come back to me." He didn't know what was happening to Tori, but he knew for sure he didn't want Nika anywhere near it, whether in body or mind.

She went still, then opened her eyes and looked up at him. Tears leaked from the corners, wetting the pale hair at her temples. "She was here. For just a minute. They're hurting her."

Nika still clutched her stomach. Her legs were curled up tight against her body, and Madoc was certain he knew why. "She's in labor. There's nothing you can do."

Nika shoved herself away from him, stumbling from the bed. Her clothes were draped over a chair, and she hurried to put them on. "I have to find her."

"How? All we know is that she went southeast."

"She called out for me once. She will again."

Madoc started to dress, because he knew she'd be tearing out of here at any minute, and he didn't want to follow her bare-ass naked down the hall and scare all the human children. "And you'll be incapacitated by the pain again."

She pulled a shirt over her head. "I don't care. I'll be ready for it next time."

Madoc wanted to force her to stay here. She was too precious to risk. He knew she'd give her life for her sister in a heartbeat and he couldn't let that happen. He didn't want Tori to die, but if she did, he didn't want her to take Nika down with her.

"Just what do you think you'll have to gain by running off in a panic? We need to go to Joseph and do this the right way."

"How long do you think that will take? How long do you think Tori has? I can't wait."

Madoc grabbed her arm, being careful not to grip her too hard. "What good will it do you to find her if we can't get her out alive? We have to gather the men."

"Fine. You talk to Joseph. Gather whoever you like, but we're leaving now."

Meghan was on her way out of the office when she came to a rocking halt.

John Hawthorne leaned against the trunk of her car, his thick arms crossed over his chest.

Just the sight of him made something deep inside her loosen up. A familiar pang of arousal shot to her womb and made her knees go weak. She wondered if he'd always have the power to do that to her.

She hadn't expected to see him ever again. He was just one bright, secret spot in her life she'd hold close and never forget. Seeing him here, in her town, at her work, was completely shocking and completely unacceptable.

"What are you doing here?" she asked, checking over her shoulder to see if any of her coworkers were nearby. Luckily, they weren't, but that wouldn't last for long.

"You left. I wasn't ready for that, so I came to find you." He said it as if it was the most reasonable thing to travel nearly two thousand miles to finish a conversation.

"You can't be here."

"Why not? It's a free country."

"If someone sees, they'll tell my father."

John lifted a brow. "You're twenty-eight. I'm pretty sure you're allowed to date by now."

"It's not that."

"Then what is it?"

Meghan didn't know how to explain it. Her father had his pride. If he thought caring for him was robbing her of anything, he'd push her away. She wasn't convinced he was strong enough to live on his own yet. Sure, he was better, but what if he had a relapse?

"We had a great time, John. But you just can't be here. Please go."

"Are you married?" he asked, his face darkening with rage.

"Heavens, no. Nothing like that. I just can't be involved right now. I have too many responsibilities."

"So do I, but here I am anyway. I thought the two of us had something special."

"It was special. Can't we just leave it at that?"

"That's not enough for me. I have feelings for you, Meghan. I want you to come back with me so we can see where things take us."

Meghan's heart squeezed in longing. She wanted so much to give in and throw caution to the wind. Maybe they'd last a week and be at each other's throats, but maybe there was something real there. She'd certainly never felt like this about another man before.

But what she wanted wasn't as important as taking care of her father. He had to come first.

"I'm sorry, John. I really am. But this is as far as we go."

John's mouth tightened in anger and he swallowed as if shoving it down. "I don't believe that. And I don't think you do, either."

Before she realized what he was doing, he moved in and kissed her.

Meghan's body responded as it had the countless other times he'd kissed her. Her skin heated, her limbs went liquid, and she flowed into him as if she'd been made to do just that.

He coaxed her lips open, feathering his tongue against

her mouth. He tasted like secret dreams—so heady he made her dizzy.

His hand cupped the back of her neck while the other one slid down her spine to her bottom. Streamers of sensation rioted through her bloodstream until she was left breathless, wet, and longing for things she knew could never be hers.

John ended the kiss but didn't pull away. "Invite me home."

She wanted to. She wanted to fall into bed with him and never get out. "I can't. My father—"

"Take me to meet him. Maybe we'll hit it off. You won't know until you try."

Her resistance was crumbling, no match for the pleasure she knew John could give her. "If he meets you, he'll know how I feel."

"That's a good thing, right?"

"No. He needs me right now. I can't abandon him."

"I'm not asking you to."

"You don't understand. He'll push me away. He'll think he's robbing me of my future."

"He is."

"It's my choice."

John pulled away, regret lining his face. "I understand," he said, then turned and walked away.

Meghan watched him go, feeling like he was taking something vital with him—something she'd never be able to survive without.

Torr couldn't believe how fast he was recovering. It was like a switch had been flipped, and the feeling in his limbs was coming back to him all at once.

Only two hours ago, he hadn't been able to lift his own head, and now he was sitting on the edge of his bed. Granted, he was still wobbly, but even that seemed to be fading fast.

There was some kind of commotion going on inside Dabyr. He could hear tense voices and hurried footsteps outside his door. The woman who had brought him food earlier hadn't known what was going on.

Torr had hid from her how much he'd improved. He didn't want anyone spoiling the surprise for Grace. He wanted to see the look on her face when she saw him.

There was no longer any question in his mind that he could greet her on his feet. In fact, if all went well, he was going to be able to do more than just greet her. He'd be able to make love to her the way he hadn't allowed himself to think about except in the deepest reaches of his dreams.

He was sure as hell thinking about it now. If she didn't come back soon, he was going to have to do something about his nearly constant erection. Clearly, his body was making up for lost time.

Using the bed for support, Torr pushed himself to his feet.

He almost crumpled under the weight of his own body, but managed to stay standing. After a few seconds, he'd gained his balance and reached out for a nearby chair to steady himself. He took a step, then two, before his legs could take no more and he had to slide down into the chair.

Elation made him feel light and his jaw ached from grinning so much.

Grace was going to be so surprised. Finally, her tears would be ones of joy.

He thought about calling her and asking her to come home, but she deserved her break. She'd spent way too much time keeping his sorry ass clean and fed. She needed a little time to herself.

Instead, he dialed her seventeen-year-old half brother, hoping he'd know when she was getting back.

Blake Norman answered the phone with a distracted, "Hello." In the background, Torr could hear the sound of laser guns being fired and the excited shouts of other boys in the room.

"You have company?" asked Torr.

"Yep. Playin' games. Whatcha need?"

"Do you know when Grace is coming back?"

"What do you mean? She's with you, isn't she?"

"She couldn't travel dragging me around with her."

"Travel? She'd never leave this place, not after what happened to us."

Torr was struck silent for a moment. "She didn't go on a trip?"

Blake made a bunch of shushing sounds until the room he was in went quiet. "She said you were getting worse and that she was going to be staying in your suite for a few days. She's not with you?"

A bad feeling began creeping up Torr's spine. "She's not with me."

"Then where the hell is she?"

"I don't know, but I'm going to find out."

Torr dialed security, hoping to get Nicholas, but instead he got one of the Gerai who helped when Nicholas wasn't available.

"Hey, Nate," said Torr. "I was wondering if you could help me with something."

"Sure."

"Can you find out if Grace has left the compound recently?"

"Hold on a sec." There was some clicking of keys; then Nate said, "She didn't check out a car and her security card hasn't been used at the gate. She could have gone with someone else, I suppose."

"Do you keep track of when she uses her key card?"

"Yeah, all that stuff is logged."

"Can you see when the last time she used hers was?"

"Around noon yesterday."

"Who has left since then?"

Nate read off a list of names. It was short.

"Can you check to see if the cameras showed her in any of their cars?"

"What's going on here, Torr? Is she in some kind of trouble?"

"I don't know. She told me she left town. She told her brother she was staying with me. I have no idea where she is."

"Okay. Give me a few minutes and I'll go through the security footage. Our face-recognition software will find her and tell me the last place she was seen. Call you in a few. Will you have someone there who can pick up the phone?"

"Yeah," he said, feeling cold and more afraid than he had in a long, long time.

Now that he thought about it, she had been acting a little odd the last time he saw her. He'd chalked it up to stress, but maybe she'd been trying to tell him she was in some kind of trouble. Maybe the toll of taking care of him had worn her out and she'd had some kind of breakdown.

Ten million things went through his head, each one worse than the last.

His phone rang, and he scooped it up, his weak fingers clumsy on the plastic. "Did you find her?"

"It's kinda weird, but she went into a vacant suite and hasn't come out again. I can't leave, but I'm sending someone to check it out."

"What room number?"

Nate told him, then said, "I'll call you back as soon as I know what's going on."

Torr didn't tell him not to bother. He was going to go there himself and find her and then give her hell for sneaking off like that and scaring him. She didn't have to lie and tell him she was leaving town to get a break from him. All she had to do was tell him she needed some time off. He would have understood.

He grabbed his sheathed sword, knowing he was going to need some kind of cane to keep from falling on his face. The suite was only one hall away, but as wobbly as he was, it was going to feel a hell of a lot farther.

John refused to give up on Meghan. He couldn't imagine that any man capable of raising a daughter like her would also be capable of keeping her from living her own life.

There was only one way to find out.

Like some kind of creepy stalker, John followed her back to her home. As soon as she pulled into the garage, he hurried to the front door, hoping her father would be the one to answer so she wouldn't have the chance to slam it in John's face.

The man who answered the door came up only to John's nose. He was thin, but not sickly, and peered up at John with a clear, questioning gaze. "Yes?"

"My name's John Hawthorne. I'm a friend of Meghan's from Minnesota. Mind if I come in?"

The man's eyes lit up with interest and he smiled. "Of course. She doesn't have many people stop by these days. Not like she used to when she was a kid. That girl had people parading through this house back then."

"Dad, I'm home," she called from somewhere off to the left.

"Just in time. Your friend's here."

Meghan stepped through a doorway and stopped cold. "You followed me home?" she asked in shock.

"I figured you wouldn't invite me over, so I had to be rude and show up on my own."

Her father took a protective step toward his daughter. "Is this man causing you trouble?"

"No, Dad. He just doesn't know when to give up."

"Can we talk?" asked John.

Sadness tinged her voice. "I've already said all there is to say."

"Please. We can't let it end like this."

"Just go, John. This is already hard enough."

Her father was listening to every word, watching each of them carefully. John hated that there was an audience for this, but that was her choice. Not his. He would have rather discussed this with her in private.

He knew before he said the words that she wasn't going to like him discussing this in front of her father. "I can't go until I know whether you might be carrying my baby. We didn't use a damn thing, and you never said whether you were on birth control."

Meghan's eyes went wide with shock, as if she'd just realized what he had realized on the way over here: She might be pregnant. Why he hadn't even thought about it before, he had no idea. He'd always been responsible.

Hell, he had a condom in his wallet. He simply hadn't thought about using it.

Her hand moved to her stomach in an unconscious gesture.

That was all the answer John needed. He found himself praying to God she was pregnant, because at this point, he was willing to resort to whatever slimy tactics he could find to keep her in his life. A baby would tie her to him and give him the time he needed to convince her she could love him for real—the way he knew he loved her.

The realization was a bit stunning, but it warmed him from the inside out and made his path forward as clear as day.

Meghan's father crossed his arms over his chest and said, "Obviously, the two of you have things to discuss. I'll be in the kitchen making dinner. For three." He directed that last part at Meghan. "You go kicking out the father of my possible future grandkid before dinner and we'll have words."

He walked away, leaving the two of them alone in the foyer.

Meghan had gone pale and had pressed her hand to the wall as if to steady herself. "I hadn't even considered ... I'm sure I'm not ..."

"Pregnant," he offered, bothered that she couldn't even say the word. "You look like you're going to fall over. Can we sit down?"

She nodded numbly and led him into the next room. She sank onto the couch, but rather than sitting across the room, as she'd probably intended, he sat down next to her.

John wasn't a man to mince words, so he just blurted out, "I want to try to make things work with you. Come live with me."

"I can't. My dad."

"Bring him, too. I have plenty of room. That cabin is just a spot I go to get away. I have a real house, too—big enough for all of us."

"It's too cold for Dad. His arthritis—"

"Will be greatly improved with all the exercise a grandchild will give me," shouted her father from the kitchen. The man peeked around the corner, grinning like he was already planning what to do with a child they didn't know existed yet.

In that moment, John decided he liked the man. He wouldn't mind having him as a father-in-law at all.

"My work is here," she said.

"I know lots of people up there. I can help you find a good job. Or I can give you one at my company."

"That's a horrible idea and you know it."

"As bad an idea as never seeing each other?" he asked.

Her face crumpled in pain, and he knew then and there that he wasn't alone in his feelings for her. She felt something, too. Their time together had been more than just great sex, though it had definitely also been that.

"We hardly know each other," she said.

John cupped her face in his hands. The bruise from her accident was still there, reminding him just how precious she was—how easily she could be taken away from him. Every second counted, and he wanted to spend as many of them as he could with her.

"I know enough to want to know more."

She covered her hands with his and pulled them away. "I can't uproot myself and my dad just to see if we can make a go of it."

John nodded slowly. "Okay. Fair enough. It'll take me a few weeks to get things settled on my end. I was just getting set to break ground on a new development, so I'll have to take care of finding someone to take over for me—transfer the contracts to them, or maybe sell the business. I'll talk with my lawyer and see what makes the most sense. I'll need to put my house on the market, but I think we should keep the cabin, don't you? It'll be nice for family vacations."

Meghan blinked at him. "You're going to give up your life—your business, your home, your career?"

"I can have those anywhere. I can only have you here. I'll have to learn the ropes again—new building codes and whatnot—but I'm good at what I do. I'm sure I can find someone willing to take me on for a while. I can work my way up to the top again."

"Why? Why would you do that?"

He frowned at her, confused. "Why wouldn't I? Jobs come and go. There's only one of you in the whole world. And if we're lucky, one special little boy or girl who will be coming into our lives in a few months. I'd give up just about anything for the two of you."

"What if there's not a baby?"

"Then there's not. At least, not yet. We'll have more time alone to get to know each other. But either way, I've made up my mind. I want to be with you."

"Why?"

"Because I love you." As he said the words aloud, everything fell into place with a happy little click. The thought of giving up what he'd spent years creating didn't even bother him.

"You do?" she asked. Her chin started to wobble.

"Don't sound so surprised. I'm sure I'm not the first man to have fallen for you. I hope to God I'm the last, though."

Tears shimmered in her eyes. "It's not possible to love someone so fast."

"Why not?"

"That's just not how it's done."

She was cute when she got all teary. Her nose was red and her bottom lip stuck out, quivering until John had to fight the urge to kiss it. "How do you propose we do it, then?"

"We need to slow down. This is all too sudden."

John looked at his watch. "How much time do you need?"

"Dinner will be ready in ten minutes," said her father. "That enough?"

"Dad," she said, raising her voice. "You need to butt out of this."

There was a joyful lilt in her father's voice. "I hear the fishing up there's really good."

"Yes, sir," said John. "We've got some whoppers in

our lake. My cabin sits right on it, too. Best fishing this side of the Canadian border."

"Put the man out of his misery, girl."

"What about you?" she asked her father. "Who will take care of you?"

"I'm fine and you know it. The cancer's gone. I feel like my old self. If you want to take care of someone, have your own kids. I quit." He grabbed his keys off a hook and said, "I'm going out to meet my girlfriend. Don't wait up for me."

The door to the garage closed. A car started and drove away. Meghan still hadn't said a word.

"So, what about it?" asked John.

"I have two weeks of vacation coming," she said. "I guess I could spend it with you. See where things go."

A smile of victory pulled at his mouth. "We could spend one week here and one at my place. You could even bring your dad if you want. I don't mind."

She touched her stomach again and the wistful look on her face told him more than words ever could. "By then we should know if I'm pregnant."

"It won't change my mind. Either way, I want you in my life."

"You say that now," she said, as if it were a warning.

"And I'll be saying it twenty years from now, too. Just you watch."

"One step at a time, John. We have to slow this down."

He didn't need that, but if she did, that was what he'd give her. "Anything you want."

Chapter 22

Every available Theronai and a handful of Sanguinar were in vehicles, caravanning southeast. Madoc led the way, searching the landscape for anything that looked familiar.

Tori's memories kept flickering through his head despite the fact that he didn't need to see them again to remember them.

They'd been driving for hours and sunset was closing in—a little less than two hours away. Drake, Helen, and Gilda were in the middle seat, with Tynan, Nicholas, and Angus in the rear.

"Do you recognize anything?" asked Nika from the passenger's seat of the van. She'd asked that same question every few minutes since they'd left, but Madoc refused to lose his patience with her.

"No. Any luck on your end?"

"Not really. Every once in a while I think I'm getting close, like she's weakening, but then it's gone and I can't sense her anymore."

Madoc had been keeping tabs on the clock each time he felt Nika's excitement flutter through their link. After watching the interval between them decrease slowly, he was convinced that Tori's mental defenses went down every time she had a contraction. They were about six minutes apart now, by his calculation.

He shot a look into the back of the van, where Tynan hid from the sun. He met the Sanguinar's icy gaze. "Do you have a plan for when we find her?"

"None of us know what to expect," said Tynan, "but this certainly won't be the first pregnant woman I've tended. I'll do what I must to keep her alive."

There was no mention of the offspring, and Madoc guessed it was intentional.

"There she is again," said Nika, her voice high with excitement. "I can almost—"

Her words cut off with a cry of pain. She bent forward in the seat so fast the seat belt caught and held her.

Madoc looked at the clock. Only five minutes had passed. They were running out of time.

He laid a comforting hand on Nika's shoulder and stepped on the gas. He hated seeing her suffer like this, but there was only one acceptable way to end it now: find Tori.

Nika panted through the pain and he felt an increase in the flow of power between them. Their connection had strengthened at an amazing rate over the past few hours, as though Nika knew just how to make it happen. Of course, the fact that the colors in the luceria had settled to a bright, snowy white might have had something to do with that.

They were stuck with each other now—at least for as long as Madoc lived. The only way he would be able to let her go to a man more deserving of her now was through his death.

"Not going to happen," said Nika through clenched teeth. "I'm keeping *you*. Just you."

As much as he liked hearing that, he wasn't sure how she'd feel if he failed to save Tori. Anger and resentment were ugly things and could grow faster than cancer. He'd seen it happen before.

"Just drive. We'll fight about this later," she told him.

Madoc smiled at that. He liked it that she automatically assumed they'd have later. She wasn't pushing him away yet.

Maybe she never would. The thought was enough to make him daydream like a little girl, but there wasn't time for that now. He had a sister to rescue.

"Any word from Paul or Andra?" he asked loudly enough for Nicholas to hear him in the back.

"Not yet. I've left them ten thousand messages, so I'm sure they'll call when they're back in cell phone range. I did get a report from Briant, though. He interrogated Ricky and found signs of Synestryn taint in the boy's mind. The kid has no idea where Tori is. All he knew was that he was ordered to take Nika to a shopping center, where someone would pick her up."

Madoc glanced into the rearview mirror to say something to Nicholas, but the words fell out of his head. Behind him, the lay of the land, the slope of the hillside they'd just climbed, matched perfectly with one of Tori's memories.

He slowed the van, careful to not cause a wreck with the other vehicles behind him. The road here was undivided and relatively empty.

"You see something, don't you?" asked Nika.

"Yeah. Hold on." He maneuvered the van, making a U-turn. Behind him, the rest of the caravan followed.

He drove back the way they'd come, turning off onto a gravel drive leading into private land. The drive was bumpy, but he was able to keep sight of the land he recognized and follow it.

The gravel path ended near a barn so old it was falling down, and there was no way this vehicle would make it over the rocky ground.

"Nicholas, let everyone know we're close, but we're going to have to go in on foot."

They parked and piled out of their vehicles. Gearing up was quick and efficient. Madoc helped Nika slide on an armored leather trench coat and face shield, just in case. He wasn't planning to let her get close enough to combat to need either, but he wasn't taking any chances.

Her blue eyes flared a moment before she doubled over in pain. Madoc caught her against him and held her while the spasm passed.

"She's close," said Nika, breathing hard. Sweat had beaded up along her forehead and all color bled from her skin. "She knows we're here."

That meant the bad guys might, too. "Time to move,"

he shouted. He took a strong hold on Nika's waist and helped her over the rocky ground.

As they got farther, he got more matches between the terrain and Tori's memories. It had been dark when they'd brought her here, but there were enough similarities that Madoc had no trouble spotting the way she'd come. A few hundred yards later, the vegetation began to show patterns of wear where lots of feet had trampled it down. Those thin trails began to converge until they dropped off over the edge of a rocky outcropping.

Madoc had to jump down about six feet, but as soon as he did, he saw the mouth of the cave. It looked unchanged from the image Tori had given him, and accompanying that image was a primal burst of fear. She hadn't wanted to be taken in there. Even as a child, she'd known to fear that darkness.

"Here," he called up to the rest of the group.

He reached up for Nika, easing her down beside him. He waited until the whole group was ready, their swords drawn, before he stepped inside.

Darkness engulfed him, along with the strong smell of animal and decay. This was definitely the kind of place Synestryn loved to hide.

Madoc pulled enough power from the air around him to fuel his night vision, silently showing Nika how to do the same through their connection. He felt the subtle tug of power leave him and knew she'd caught on without trouble.

He loved that mind of hers and the lightning speed at which it moved. Every time her presence was inside him, he felt smarter and more aware of his surroundings. This time was no different. She was right there inside him, a part of him.

He didn't think he'd ever again feel whole without her.

He moved slowly down the tunnel, searching for traps or anything else that might give away their presence. Maybe the Synestryn already knew they were here, but he wasn't going to fill them in if they didn't.

The tunnel narrowed, curving to the right. It emptied

into a small opening, showing two alternate paths they could take. One was natural; the other had been gouged out by tools and claws.

He turned to Nika. "Any idea which way?"

She closed her eyes and a pulse of power flowed out of him. "No. Sorry."

Madoc checked his watch. "We'll wait a minute. You might get another chance."

Her mouth opened in shock and a faint line of pain formed between her brows. "Those pains I feel. Those are labor pains, aren't they?"

"That's what I was thinking. They're getting closer together."

"How close?" asked Tynan.

"Four, four and a half minutes now."

Nika's hand clenched on his arm, but that was the only sign she gave of the pain he knew she felt. She didn't make a sound.

When she spoke, she was out of breath. "Right. She's to our right."

Madoc nodded. "We'll go when you're ready."

She swallowed and straightened her stance. "I'm ready now."

Madoc didn't fight her. As much as he hated this, it was the only way.

He led them into the carved tunnel. It was a tight squeeze in several places, but they all fit through. There were more than a dozen men and women trailing behind him, ready and eager to have this rescue finished.

The tunnel angled down; then ahead, he saw it open up. He stopped and turned to Drake, who was immediately behind Nika. "I'll go check it out," he whispered. To Nika, he said, "Stay put a sec. I'll be right back."

To her credit, she didn't argue. He could sense her agitation and fear, along with the sure knowledge that the pain would be back again all too soon.

Madoc moved forward as silently as he could, hugging one wall. He peered into the room, powering up his vision so he could see more clearly.

It was a sleeping chamber. Dozens of Synestryn

lay huddled in piles like puppies. He didn't recognize them. He was used to seeing fur and scales, but these things—whatever they were—had mostly bare skin instead. They were vaguely humanoid, though larger than most men, maybe seven feet if they stood up on their hind legs. Their hands and feet were huge, and their wide heads bristled with stiff tufts of hair. Beside each pile of creatures, several swords were propped against debris or the cave wall.

The swords were battered, rusty, and pitted with use, but the fact that they were there at all was disturbing. Since when did monsters start using weapons instead of teeth and claws?

There was no sign of Tori, but across the cavern, there was a tunnel leading off to the right.

Madoc went back to the group. "There's a cavern up ahead full of sleeping somethings. We're going to have to go through them."

"How many?" asked Drake.

"Thirty or forty."

"Any friendlies in there?" asked Helen.

"No."

"How big is the room?" asked Drake.

"Maybe twenty by thirty or so."

Helen smiled. "I got this. Hang back."

She and Drake moved ahead. A few seconds later, there was a burst of orange light, a whoosh of heat, and the sound of animalistic screams. Smoke drifted down the tunnel, but Gilda lifted a hand and it flowed over their heads toward the exit.

Nika hissed in pain and grabbed hold of Madoc's arm hard. "There's some kind of commotion around Tori. I think they know we're here."

Drake and Helen came back a minute later. "Room's clear. I wouldn't breathe the smoke, though."

"I'll blow the smoke away from us," said Gilda. "Let's just get this over with. If we don't retrieve her before sunset, they could move her where we'll never find her."

"We can't let that happen," said Nika, panting.

"Can you walk?" asked Madoc. He sensed she wasn't fighting the pain, but letting it in—it was the only link she had to Tori, but it was nearly incapacitating.

She nodded, so Madoc helped support her weight, following Drake and Helen into the chamber.

Burned corpses lay in charred heaps, as if they hadn't even had time to move before they died. Clearly, Helen's ability had grown since she'd partnered with Drake nearly a year ago. Madoc would hate to be on the receiving end of the power she wielded.

They moved into the next tunnel and had gone a few feet when Nicholas said, "We've got movement behind us."

"Nicholas, you, Liam, and the other single men guard our escape," ordered Angus. "We have to keep moving."

Nika was leaning on him harder now, and he could feel pain tightening her body more with every step. "We're getting closer," she whispered. "I can feel her."

Behind them, the sound of combat began. The snarl of Synestryn and the thud of steel on bone grew louder as their only known exit was compromised. Ahead of them, a high, feminine scream of pain echoed off the rock walls.

Tori had tried to stay strong. She'd tried not to call out for Nika, but she'd failed. The pain had been too much to stand, and with each wrenching spasm of her body, she'd grown weaker and less able to block Nika out.

Zillah had her strapped down on a metal table, unable to move. Her knees were pinned against her chest to make room for the thing to come out. Around her Synestryn demons crouched in eagerness, as if waiting for a meal. Maybe that was what she'd become if this birth killed her. She had no idea.

We're here. Hold on. Nika's voice came through like cool, clear water flowing over her.

"She's here," said Maura. "Finally. And once I have Nika, I'm sure Andra won't be far behind. Lovely."

Panic skittered through Tori, clawing at her. *Run*, she

tried to shout in her mind, but she wasn't sure whether Nika could hear her. She couldn't focus with so much pain wringing her out. She was sure that the thing inside her was going to twist her in two.

"Guards," ordered Zillah in an almost metallic hiss of breath. "Kill the men. Without them, the women will be ours for the taking."

Tori couldn't see how many guards there were, but at least twenty were in her line of sight and she could hear more of them moving around. There were too many. There was no way Nika was going to be able to get through.

Run. Please, she shouted again, praying Nika would listen.

Maura frowned for a moment, tilting her blond head to the side as if listening. "Kill Angus first or Gilda will finish us all."

"No sentimentality for your own father?" asked Zillah.

Maura's face went hard, cold. "None. Kill him."

Another spasm of pain gripped Tori's body, wringing a scream from her. It stole the breath from her chest and locked up her lungs. Something clenched hard deep inside her and everything else disappeared in the face of so much pain. All her defenses went down. Nika appeared in her mind, strong and reassuring.

Tori gripped onto that feeling like a lifeline. She knew her time was up. The thing was coming. Nika hadn't been able to save her, but at least she was here now. At least Tori didn't have to die alone.

Nika stumbled as the connection she had with Tori flared to life, stronger than it had ever been before. Pain was her sister's whole world, but Nika focused on shutting that out so she could concentrate enough to figure out how to save her.

Madoc helped her steady herself on her feet. "Do you need to stop?"

"No. She's ahead. Close."

Nika urged Tori's eyes open, ordered her sister's muscles to move so she would look around and show Nika where she was and how to get her out. What she saw was far from comforting.

"Zillah's with her. So is Maura."

From behind her, Nika heard Gilda suck in a harsh breath.

"There are"—she counted fast—"at least thirty Synestryn in there. They know we're coming; they're on either side of the opening."

Nika sent the information to Madoc with a thought, so he could see what she did.

"Drake, take the right side. I've got the left," said Madoc.

The two men hurried ahead, swords drawn. Helen was right behind them, and Nika did her best to keep up. She could feel the heat of Angus's hand at her elbow. He didn't touch her, but he was ready to catch her if she fell.

Nika sent what reassurance she could to her sister, watching through her eyes as Drake and Madoc cleared the tunnel and attacked the guards waiting for them.

Another contraction hit Tori and a portion of Nika's consciousness went blind as her sister closed her eyes. She stumbled into the wall and felt the burn of Angus's touch as he steadied her.

She needed to sever the connection with Tori if she was going to have any chance of concentrating enough to save her.

We're coming. Love you, she said to Tori; then she let the connection fade until she could feel Tori, but could no longer hear her thoughts or see through her eyes.

By the time Nika was able to move, Helen was already in the cavern opening, fighting. A column of flame as thick as Helen's arm shot from her hand. Nika stepped up behind her just in time to see that flame set a group of three Synestryn on fire. They burned hot and fast, dropping to the ground before their screams had finished echoing off the walls.

As well as fire seemed to work, Nika wasn't going to chance it again. She sent her mind searching for sgath or any other creature here who might have ingested her blood—one she could control.

A kind of resonance shimmered around one of them, telling her it was her target. It wasn't a sgath. It was tall, stood on two legs, and gripped a bent sword in its hand, which was tipped with long, black fingernails. She'd never seen anything like it, but that hardly mattered. What mattered was that her blood flowed inside its veins and that made its mind hers.

Nika stepped back into the tunnel so she wouldn't be in the way, shed her body, and hurled herself inside the thing's head.

Its mind was a hot, alien place. The hunger for blood consumed its thoughts, but its fear of Zillah held it in place. Only when he ordered it to move would it dare set out for the food that had walked in.

Nika wasn't going to wait for an order like that. She took control of the thing's body, shoving herself between thoughts and actions. The monster roared in defiance, but the only sound it made was inside its own mind.

She propelled the thing forward, moving its odd, spindly body clumsily toward Zillah.

She was going to kill him with his own minion—cut him down before he had time to even figure out what had happened.

Zillah was bent over Tori, unfastening the restraints they'd used to hold her down. He didn't see her coming inside the borrowed body of the Synestryn. She lifted the crooked sword, preparing to plunge it into his back.

From a few feet away, Maura cried out a warning.

Zillah jerked to the side just as Nika struck. The sword hit the metal table, sliding along the edge. The movement knocked the monster Nika was inhabiting off balance, and she didn't have enough practice moving its body to recover from it. The monster fell to the ground in an awkward heap.

Nika pushed it back to its feet, but by the time she turned to strike out at Zillah again, he'd already drawn his own blade. With one powerful swing, he lopped off the monster's head.

Nika shoved herself out of its mind before the head hit the ground. She couldn't see, couldn't feel. Energy floated around her, warm and sparking against her wherever it touched.

The disorientation lasted a while before she realized she hadn't gone back into her own body. Jumping out of the monster so suddenly had left her reeling and without an anchor.

And then she felt him. Madoc. His power radiated out, glowing like a beacon. She followed that power until she could reach him.

His mind was a familiar place. Comforting. Even in the midst of battle, when his body was working hard and his thoughts were on the tactics of killing, he still eased her soul. She wanted to stay inside him, huddled in his warmth, but there was something she was supposed to do.

Tori. Tori was here and she was in trouble. Nika had to get back into her body so she could save her baby sister.

Using the luceria's link as a frame of reference, Nika followed the pathway between her and Madoc, found her body, and eased back where she belonged. It took her a moment to acclimate to her own skin and take in her surroundings again. The ground beneath her was cold and hard. The battle waged on. Smoke billowed along the rough, high ceiling of the chamber, proof of Helen's work. Bleeding Synestryn bodies cluttered the floor near the tunnel. Angus, Drake, and Madoc were slashing at demons, dropping them one by one.

Tynan was working his way toward Tori. His sole job tonight was making sure she lived through the birth, and if anything happened to him, Tori's chances for survival would plummet.

Nika struggled to stand. Dizziness plagued her, making her sweat and her stomach roll with a sickening twist.

She leaned against the rock wall, letting it hold her up. She'd been in Andra's mind enough times to know what she could do. Nika wasn't sure if her strengths would lie in the same area as Andra's, or if trying to create a shield would hurt as much as playing with fire had. Either way, it was worth a shot.

Nika pulled on Madoc's power, letting it fill her. She kept her eyes on Tynan and imagined a giant bubble forming around his body.

A second later, Tynan slammed into an invisible wall.

Right. Nika needed to let him move, taking the bubble with him.

A Synestryn's blade came down toward Tynan's head. It skittered off the wavering surface of the shield Nika had created, but that blow rang through her head, as if a giant bell had been struck against her ear.

The shock of the blow rattled her, and it took every bit of concentration she had to hold the barrier steady.

A few feet away, Zillah wrapped his too-long fingers around Tori's ankle. He grabbed one of his own demons and slit his chest open. Blood poured from the beast. Something shiny glinted in Zillah's fist as he shoved it into the bleeding demon's chest.

A blinding light flared inside the cavern, and a wave of stagnant air washed over Nika. When she could see again, Zillah was gone. The table where Tori had lain was empty.

"Tori!" screamed Nika, stumbling toward where her sister had been only a second ago.

Gilda's strong hand grabbed her arm, stopping her from flinging herself into combat. "He teleported away with her. They're gone."

"We have to go after them. Follow them."

Gilda's black eyes slid away, filled with shame. "I'm too weak. I'm sorry."

Nika wasn't going to let this happen. She wasn't going to get this close to having her sister back only to lose her like this.

She took Gilda's head in her hands and plowed her way into the other woman's mind. "Show me," she demanded. "Show me how to find her. I'll do it myself."

The knowledge was there inside Gilda's cluttered

mind, along with a mountain of other information. There wasn't time to linger over any of it, as tempting as the notion was. Instead, Nika went straight for the knowledge she needed and ripped it from the woman.

Gilda's eyes flew wide and a shocked gasp froze on her lips.

Nika had what she needed. The bright kernel of knowledge was pulsing inside her, ready to be used.

She needed to be closer to Madoc and Tynan so she could take them with her. She couldn't do this on her own. She sent a call to Madoc's mind, screaming at him to grab Tynan. Trusting that he'd do as she asked, she flung her mind out, searching for some sign of her baby sister.

Pain flared in her body, gripping her so hard she couldn't breathe. Another contraction. This one worse than all those before it. She felt Tori's fear, felt her despair.

Hold on, she begged her sister. *We're coming.*

Nika felt Madoc's hand slide into hers, heard his thoughts whispering to her that he was here with Tynan.

She grabbed tight onto his hand, opened the knowledge she'd stolen from Gilda, and sucked in a huge column of power.

The world twisted and shimmered and then everything went black.

Chapter 23

Blood rolled down Iain's forehead as he shoved his sword through the heart of the nearest demon.

He and the other Theronai with him had taken up a strategic position inside one of the tunnels, where they couldn't be easily flanked. He glanced behind him as often as he could, hoping that the tunnel didn't offer any more access points for Synestryn to sneak up on their backs.

Even though he'd taken a hit, he didn't feel the effects of any poison running through his system, so he was counting his blessings. The wound was already starting to close, though the blood stinging his eyes was becoming a dangerous problem.

The crowd of demons thinned, and the few remaining turned tail and ran.

He looked at Liam and the others. "You all stay here and hold the exit. I'm going to take them out."

Liam nodded.

"I'm going with you," said Nicholas.

Iain turned, refusing to waste time arguing with the man. He could do as he pleased. They hurried off after the Synestryn.

They'd just cleared a curve in the corridor when Iain heard the first cry for help. Human. Female. Scared as hell.

There had been a time when that cry would have affected him, but now all he experienced was cold calculation.

Pretend you have honor. That was what he told the men he'd brought into the Band of the Barren. It was a code he was determined to live by, himself.

A man with a soul would have been horrified by that sound, so Iain played along. "What the hell was that?"

"Let's find out," said Nicholas.

Both men had done enough tunnel fighting to know better than to run. It was too easy to set traps along these narrow paths, and a man going too fast had no time to avoid them. Instead, they moved along as fast as caution would allow.

The cry came again, only this time there was more than one voice. "Over here!" jumbled up with, "Help us." On top of that was the sobbing of what sounded like a child.

Rage surged inside Iain. He had to clench his jaw to keep from bellowing at the walls.

The tunnel widened out into a narrow room, and along one wall was a line of metal cages. Inside those cages were three women and two children.

"Please," said one of the women at the far end of the room. "Get us out of here."

Iain turned to Nicholas and barked, "Watch my back."

"Don't take long," said Nicholas. "I got a feeling company will be coming soon."

Iain went to the first cage, where a dirty woman clung to the bars. Her tangled hair fell to her waist. She wore a long, shapeless dress covered in stains. Dirt smudged her skin, making her pale gray eyes stand out in startling contrast. She wasn't crying. Her expression was flat. "There are keys on the wall behind you."

Nicholas grabbed them and tossed them to Iain. He moved to unlock her cage, but she stopped him. Her voice was quiet, but her command was unmistakable. "Free the children and the others first."

Iain didn't waste time fighting her. She was right to give the order, so he did as she asked, freeing the others before coming back to her cell.

She hadn't moved. The others were huddled together

around Nicholas, crying and clinging to one another. There wasn't a sign of a single tear or fear or relief in this woman's eyes.

He unlocked her cell and offered his hand to help her step through the small door. The second her slender hand hit his, Iain's head began to buzz. The rage constantly boiling inside him fell away, quieting the incessant screaming of his dead soul. Until now, he hadn't realized how much chaos had tormented his mind—how much of his pain had come from carrying around the dead, hollow thing inside him.

Both parts of his luceria lurched away from his skin for a moment, as if reaching for her. The sudden urge to sweep her up in his arms and run away where no one could find them pounded inside his skull. He wanted to keep her, to hide her away from the world, tucked away where only he could touch her.

She jerked her hand away, her gray eyes flaring wide. She backed up into the cage until she pressed herself against the wall. For the first time, emotion showed on her face, and that fear shimmering inside her made Iain want to rip away the bars with his bare hands.

"Stay away," she ordered him. He had no idea where she got such an air of command, but he found himself obeying before he even bothered to question why he should.

"I'm not going to hurt you," he told her.

"That's what they all say."

"Company's coming," said Nicholas over the heads of the women and children hovering near him. "Time to go."

Fighting with so many innocents nearby could get really messy, really fast. Iain wasn't going to watch these people be slaughtered just because one woman got spooked.

"Are you coming on your own, or am I making you?" he asked her.

She glanced at the group by Nicholas, straightened her thin shoulders, and moved forward. Iain offered her his hand again. She ignored it and moved past him without touching him in any way.

Iain had to fight down anger at her treatment of him. He'd saved her life and she shunned him? What kind of way was that to act? Even he knew better.

Whatever. She was out and he had a job to do. The dry sound of claws on stone combined with the wet sounds of salivating demons was getting closer by the second.

"I'll bring up the rear," said Iain.

Nicholas turned and led the group back the way they'd come. Iain held back, sword ready, waiting to kill whatever came their way.

Jackie had been cold for so long she'd almost forgotten what it was like to be warm.

She could feel heat from the man behind her hitting her back in waves. She wanted to turn around and curl into that warmth, but there was something about him that scared her. Something dark and dangerous.

The way he'd looked at her when she'd taken his hand—that look of raw hunger—was enough to make her keep her distance despite the chill in her bones. Better to deal with the other man and avoid the dangerous one altogether.

"There are more children here," she whispered loudly enough so he could hear her over their passage. "We have to find them and get them out, too."

"Where?" asked the man behind her. He was close. Too close.

Jackie refused to look at him. "I don't know. I've seen them pass, though."

"Which way?"

"Back the way we came."

The man behind her said, "Nicholas, keep moving. I'll catch up."

A sudden spike of fear for him shot through Jackie and she turned to tell him not to go. There were too many monsters. But by the time she'd glanced over her shoulder, the dark-eyed man was gone.

"He's going to get himself killed," she told the man in front.

He shook his head, and she caught a glimpse of the side of his face. A network of scars marred his skin, pulling tight as his jaw moved. "He can't leave those kids behind. Iain can handle it. Someone's got to go."

For some reason, Jackie didn't want it to be Iain.

Canaranth slipped away from combat once he saw Zillah port away with Tori. Their numbers were far superior to the Sentinels', so he didn't think he'd be missed in the midst of so much chaos.

He hurried through the corridors, avoiding the groups of reinforcements coming to aid in the fight.

With a key he kept hidden inside his clothing, he unlocked the door to the chamber. Ella stood there, a chair gripped in her hands, ready to bash him over the head with it.

"It's me," he told her as he slipped inside and shut the door behind him. "I've got to get you out of here."

"What's happening?" she asked. Her skin had paled over the past few months, making the freckles sprinkled across her nose stand out.

When she'd first come here, her skin had had a healthy glow about it. Now it was a sickly white. Her hair had dulled, as had her eyes.

She needed the sun on her face; she couldn't live in the darkness the way he had to. Neither could the child she was carrying. His child.

He'd done as he'd been ordered. He'd taken Ella as he had other women, seducing her until she submitted. It had always been a carefully calculated plan on his part. He couldn't stomach rape, and yet if these women didn't conceive, Zillah would have fed them to his troops. Seduction seemed the only course of action.

Canaranth hadn't planned on falling in love with her. He hadn't imagined he would care so much for their child that he would risk his life to free them.

But he did. Ella held his heart, such as it was, and he knew that if he didn't let her go, the rest of her life would be spent in torment, watching Zillah twist their child into a weapon.

"There's not much time," he told her. "We have to hurry."

Ella dropped the chair and went into his arms without hesitation. "Where are we going?"

He took her hand and led her through a series of tunnels that were rarely used. Only a few even knew they existed. "There's an exit not far from here."

They reached the crevice that hid a narrow entrance to a tunnel leading almost straight up. Canaranth took her face in his hands, memorizing it. He was going to miss her—more than he'd ever imagined.

"Go through here. Follow it to the surface. You'll have to push through some brush. It's thick, but you can make it through. From there, you need to head toward the sunset. That's where the Sentinels would have come in."

"What about you?"

"I can't go."

"I can't leave you behind."

"You must. Our child can't be born into Zillah's hands."

Ella swallowed and her dark brown eyes welled with tears. "I don't want to go without you."

Canaranth had never really thought he had a heart until now. He could feel it breaking, tearing apart with the knowledge that he'd never see her again. "It's the only way. You have to do this. Please."

"Where will I go? What will I do?"

"Go to the Sentinels. They'll be nearby. They'll take you in and care for you."

"And the baby?" she asked. He'd told her stories about them and she knew they were sworn to kill his kind.

"Lie. Tell them you were already pregnant by a human man when we took you."

"Will you come for me?" she asked.

"Yes," he lied, just to ensure her compliance. "Stay with them so I'll know where to find you."

Ella pulled him down and kissed him. The taste of her was so pure and light, he felt like he was flying whenever she touched him.

He had no idea how he was going to go on without her, but he had to find a way. As long as he was Zillah's second-in-command, he could control their armies and ensure her safety and that of his child.

"Go," he said against her mouth. The urge to tell her he loved her burned inside him, but he couldn't do that to her. When he failed to come, she'd think he was dead or he had betrayed her. Eventually, she'd find another man who would love her the way he did—one who would help her raise their child to be better than the creature who had fathered him.

Before he could say the words that would spoil her chances for any semblance of a normal future, he pushed her away, cracked one of the small chemical glow lights he'd brought for her, and helped her step through the narrow opening.

She moved down the tunnel. Canaranth watched until the pale green light disappeared, feeling like his heart had just been ripped from his body.

Chapter 24

Torr was sweating by the time he made it to the suite. The door was open and he could hear a low, frantic voice coming from inside.

Torr leaned on his sword, hobbling across the living room toward the bedrooms. One of the Gerai came out, nearly running into him. He was a human who had grown up here, and now his aged face was white with panic.

He saw Torr and said, "Stay with her while I get help. Tynan is gone, so I'm going to go find one of the Sanguinar."

Sanguinar? Grace must need healing, which made Torr's chest squeeze tight in fear. "What happened? Is she hurt?"

"I . . . I don't know." And then he was gone.

Torr was shaking so badly he could barely stand, but he forced himself to cross the distance and go into the room the human had just left.

Grace was there, lying on a mattress on the floor. She was unmoving. Her eyes were open, staring at the ceiling.

Panic slammed into Torr, knocking him to his knees. He crawled over to her, reaching out with a trembling hand to feel for a pulse.

A faint fluttering beneath his fingertips told him she was still alive, but something was definitely wrong. She wasn't even blinking.

Torr shut her eyelids so her eyes wouldn't dry out and hurt. Her skin was so soft and delicate, so warm.

He gave her a small shake and patted her cheek. Maybe she was just asleep.

"Grace," he said, hearing his voice break. "Wake up, honey."

She didn't respond.

Frantic to find the reason for her state, Torr looked around the room. What the hell had she been doing in here alone?

A case of bottled water and an unopened box of meal-replacement bars sat by her on the floor, as if she'd planned to stay here for a while. There were no books, no magazines, no TV to help her pass the time.

And she was shirtless, with only a sheet to cover her full breasts.

Torr looked over her body, searching for signs of injury. She still had on shoes and jeans, but there was no sign of blood.

He speared his fingers through her hair, feeling for any bumps or cuts. Maybe she'd fallen and hit her head. That could explain her bizarre behavior—why she'd slink off like an animal knowing it was going to die.

That image did not sit well with Torr, making him shiver at the thought of losing her. She'd been his life-line. His whole world. She was the reason he still drew breath.

And he loved her so much.

"Don't you dare leave me," he told her. "You can't leave me now—not when we can have a life together. Did you see I can move again? I'm healed. I need you to help me get strong—torture me with those massages of yours."

She didn't flutter an eyelash.

Torr's heart broke, splitting into jagged little pieces that made him bleed inside.

"You can't leave me. I love you, Grace."

A fat tear slid out from the corner of her eye. She'd heard him. Somewhere inside her she was still in there.

Torr gently raised her eyelids, moving so he was right in front of her line of sight. "You can hear me, can't you?"

He held his breath, waiting for some kind of sign, but none came.

"I know you can hear me. I need you to hold on. Help is on the way."

He closed her eyes again and pulled her into his arms. Her limp weight was difficult for him to handle in his weakened state, but he didn't care. He needed to hold her, feel her heat and the rise and fall of her chest as she breathed.

Torr slid his hands over her back, trying to comfort her. That was when he felt the hard bump on her back.

He rolled her over just as Logan came into the room. An intricately carved metal disk lay against her spine. A faint hum of vibration was coming off of it.

Torr didn't know what it was, but he knew it didn't belong there. He grabbed it, intending to pull it away, when Logan stopped him.

"Don't," he said. "Don't move it."

"Why not?" asked Torr, scowling at Logan for hesitating.

"Do you know what that is?"

"No. Do you?"

Logan nodded. His pale eyes gleamed with interest. "It's a transference device."

"Transferring what to where?" he demanded.

"Take off your shirt."

"What?"

"Do it," demanded Logan.

Fine. Whatever got the bloodsucker moving to fix her.

Torr stripped it off, feeling it drag against something on his back—a scar, maybe.

Logan pulled in a long breath. "I've heard of these devices, but never seen one. It worked so well. I had no idea."

Torr grabbed Logan's arm, pulling him down toward Grace. "Do you know how to fix her or not?"

"I'm sorry," said Logan. "She made her choice."

"What choice? Make some fucking sense, will you?" Grace's life was at stake and he was talking in riddles. If he hadn't been the only help around, Torr would have pounded him in that pretty face of his.

"This disk matches the one on your back."

One on his . . . ?

Torr reached around awkwardly. Sure enough, there was something hard and warm sticking out of his spine in the same spot as Grace's.

"I don't know where she got them, but someone must have shown her what to do."

A slow, insidious understanding began to rise up in Torr. "What has she done?" he asked, barely able to get the question out. He wasn't sure he wanted to know the answer.

"She's given you her health. She's transferred your affliction onto herself, healing you."

No. This could not be happening. His sweet Grace could not be paralyzed. "You're wrong. If she'd done that, she'd be able to talk. I was."

"She's not a Theronai. Her human body isn't as strong as yours. The poison will be harder on her than it was on you."

"Fix it," demanded Torr. "Make it go back the way it was."

"I can't. It's not the way they work. I'm sorry."

Torr was crying now. Big, fat, sloppy tears he couldn't seem to stop. Rage and denial clashed inside him, twisting his guts. "Heal her. Take it back. I don't want it. You can have all my blood. Just make her better."

Logan gripped his arm hard, pulled him to his feet, and marched him out of the room. He closed the door behind him, hissing in a low voice, "Pull yourself together. She can hear every word you say. Do you really want her to suffer more?"

Torr closed his eyes and pulled in a deep breath, trying to calm himself. The idea that he'd do anything to make this worse on her drove him crazy.

In a calm voice that belied all he felt inside, he asked Logan, "Can you do anything for her?"

"No more than I could do for you."

Which had been jack shit.

"I'm sorry." His words were final, tinged with the feel of condolence.

Torr wasn't giving up. "I'll go find another one of the things that bit me. I'll bring it back so you can study it."

Logan's face was grim. "I suggest you hurry, then."

"What's that supposed to mean?"

"It means that she's human. The paralysis is worse in her. It's only a matter of time before she can't breathe on her own or her heart stops beating."

"How long?"

Logan shrugged. "There's no way to know. Days. Hours."

Hours? Even years wouldn't be enough. He didn't want to let her go. Not now, not when he once again felt like he had a life he could share with her.

A life she'd given him.

She'd said she loved him. Those had been the last words she'd spoken to him—maybe to anyone. Until now, he'd made himself believe she'd given him the words out of pity. Until now, he'd had no idea just how much she'd meant those words.

She loved him enough to trade her life for his, and he couldn't think of a single way to make sense out of that.

"Take it off," said Torr. "I want this thing off of me."

"Try to remove it and you risk killing both of you."

Frustration and grief grated inside Torr. "And just what the hell am I supposed to do in the meantime, while it's sucking the life out of her?"

Logan's pale gaze was steady. "I suggest you find a way to say good-bye."

Nika hit the ground hard as the portal she'd opened snapped shut behind her. Her vision was blurry and spinning. Her stomach gave a hard heave and she had no choice but to lean to the side and throw up.

"It'll pass in a second," she heard Madoc say.

"If we live that long," said Tynan. His words were hard to hear over the noise coming from below where they were.

Nika's eyes watered, but she forced herself to look

up from the ground. Her teleportation had worked. She hadn't killed them and this was definitely the right place, but it hardly mattered.

They were in another cave, only this one had a huge cavern that sloped down like a bowl. In the center of that bowl was Tori. Zillah stood over her, and surrounding him were dozens of Synestryn. Maybe a hundred. From this distance, she could have easily mistaken some of them for human. Their skin was a little too gray and shiny to be human, and their faces were distorted, but the resemblance was too close to be a coincidence. They were stomping their feet and letting out snarling that sounded disturbingly like cheers.

They hadn't noticed them yet, but that wouldn't last long.

"We're going to die," said Tynan.

"Fuck that," said Madoc, stepping in front of her and Tynan. "No one's dying but the snarlies. Pull yourself together."

Nika took that advice herself and pushed up to her feet. She was shaky, but managed to stay standing.

"Back up into that dip in the wall," said Madoc. "I'll keep them off of you."

"You really think you can kill all of them?" asked Nika.

"I was kinda hoping you could lend a hand, love."

"What do I do?"

"Whatever makes you happy. Just make it deadly and figure it out quick before they see us."

Tynan pulled a sword out of nowhere the way Madoc did.

"I didn't know you could fight," said Nika.

Tynan didn't bother to look her way. He was too busy staring out at the throng of demons below. "There are a lot of things you don't know about me, and that's the way I like it."

Nika was sure there was no way they could kill all of these things. "Maybe I can teleport us again, next to Tori. You can hold them off while we grab her and I teleport everyone away again."

"I felt how much power it took you to do that the first time. You may be able to get us over there, but I don't think you'll be able to get us back out. And there's no way I can fight them off if I'm surrounded."

"Just take me," said Tynan. "If there are fewer of us, it'll be easier."

"You'll have to be quick," said Madoc. "They'll tear into you in seconds. You puke, you die."

"Right. No more puking."

"All right. Tell me when you're going and I'll draw them over here."

Nika gathered Madoc's power into her and said, "On three. One . . . two . . ."

Chapter 25

Gilda, Angus, Drake, and Helen had been driven back to where the single Theronai guarded their exit.

Exhaustion bore down at Gilda. She kept trying to pull more power into herself, but it was like trying to breathe through a narrow straw. She couldn't get enough flow to catch her breath, much less slay Synestryn.

She felt Angus's frustration pounding at her, but there was nothing she could do about it. He was right. She'd been foolish in pushing him away and now they were left weaker because of her lies and pride. Because he could not come to terms with her betrayal. Not that she could blame him.

Another pillar of fire gushed out of Helen, but she was sagging with effort. She turned to Gilda, panting. Twin tears of flame slid from her bloodshot eyes. "I'm almost out of juice. We've got to get out of here."

Normally, Gilda would have stepped up and taken over, but there was no point in that. Even as tired as Helen was, she was still stronger than Gilda right now.

From behind her, she heard a commotion and turned in time to see Nicholas herding half a dozen dirty humans into the safety of the corridor.

"There are more kids in here. Iain went to find them. I need to go help."

"Retreat," bellowed Angus. "Get the humans out. We'll protect your backs."

Liam led the way, but he came to a quick, sudden halt and drew his sword. "Too late. They must have come in from another passage or outside. The way out's blocked."

Gilda sagged against the wall in regret. They were dead. Unless Andra suddenly showed up, they were out of firepower and out of options. She was going to have to watch more of her family die.

Angus's spark of anger and determination flared through their connection. "Drake, Helen, you two blast us a way out. Gilda, you and I are going to hold this tunnel and give them time to get free."

"How?" she asked him. "I have no strength."

He looked into her eyes, and for the first time in years, she saw something truly frightening in his expression. He backed her against the stone wall, towering over her. "Then I suggest you find some. I'm not letting these innocents die because of the mistakes we've made."

"It's not as if I can simply will them away."

"Maybe you should give that a try and see if it works, because you and I are doing this. Now." He grabbed her arm and stepped up behind Helen. She had set a fire along the pathway, but right on the other side of those flames were dozens of hungry Synestryn.

"Go," Angus bellowed. "Get them out."

"What about you?" asked Helen.

"Gilda will teleport us out. Don't wait for us."

Gilda wasn't sure if Angus was being optimistic about her strength or if he just said that to get the others moving, but whatever his reason, it worked. Drake and Helen left, disappearing down the tunnel with the rest of the group.

The flames filled the space, wavering with unnatural heat. One of the demons poked a paw through and it screamed in pain.

"You know I'm too weak to teleport," she told her husband.

"I know."

"So you're content to die down here?"

"No. I simply know that you're at your best when the stakes are highest. I thought the situation might motivate you to pull your head out of your ass."

Shock rattled her, but she didn't let it show. Angus never spoke to her like that.

"Maybe I should have," he said. "Maybe if I hadn't coddled you all these years, we wouldn't be where we are now."

"I didn't plan any of this."

"I sure as hell hope not."

"How do we undo years of damage in the time it takes for those flames to wink out?"

Angus shook his head, staring down at her. The sadness in his blue eyes was enough to make her cry. He was too good a man to be suffering like this, too kind.

She didn't deserve him, but she loved him. So much. She would do anything for him—anything to make up for the harm she'd caused.

Time to show it. Time to let go of what she wanted and give him what he wanted for a change. She owed him at least that much.

She grabbed his face and pulled him down for a kiss. He was stiff at first, but it didn't take long for that to change. Heat flared between them and his tongue swept in to taste her, as if he'd been dying to do it for way too long.

A rough groan of need rose out of his chest and she felt a faint tickling at her throat. She was too busy enjoying his mouth to worry about it. They had only a few seconds before they had to get back to work. It might be the last few seconds they ever spent together.

Angus pulled away, breathing hard. He pressed his forehead to hers, and the firelight shadowed the deep lines in his face.

"I love you, woman."

"I love you, too. Always. I won't deny you anymore. We'll find a way to get back to where we belong."

"Damn right we will."

"No more secrets. No more lies."

"I'm going to be too close to you for you to have the chance."

"I'll earn your trust again. I swear it."

Angus smiled down at her and the cold spaces in

her heart seemed to warm. "You already have. All is forgiven."

As the words left his mouth, the weight she'd been carrying around for so long lifted. She felt free. Light. Young.

"Well, isn't this touching," came a high-pitched voice.

Gilda turned to see the mass of Synestryn part, allowing Maura to step up to the wall of fire.

A mother's grief tore through Gilda as she saw her baby girl. She was dressed all in black, showing far too much skin beneath the tattered lace. Black crystal glittered around her throat and dripped from her ears. Anger twisted her dainty features as Maura bared her teeth.

"I'm surprised you're still alive," said Maura. "Where are the others?"

Angus's hand tightened on Gilda's arm in warning. "Dead. We're the last left."

Maura's laugh was hollow with disbelief. "My pets are gone. You've taken them, haven't you?"

"Pets?" asked Angus.

The wall of flame began to shrink. It no longer reached the rock ceiling.

"The humans," said Maura. "I want them back. I hate being lonely."

"Then come with us," urged Gilda. "You'll never be lonely again."

"You know I can't. Dabyr is a place for people with souls. Thanks to you, dear Mother, I have none."

"That's not true."

"It is. You ripped it from me the day you cut Sibyl and me in half."

"You're wrong. I've seen the good in you. This path you've chosen is just that—a choice."

Maura smiled. "And so is this." She pointed to the floor where the flames were rooted. A hulking Synestryn to her right flung himself forward onto the fire.

It screamed and writhed, but fell silent in a few seconds. Maura stepped up onto the thing's back, using it as a bridge to cross over the fire.

Angus lifted his sword. Gilda refused to panic. She gathered power into her, readying it for use at a moment's notice.

Angus's power flowed into her more easily—not like normal, but better than before.

Maura came to stand in front of them. Not a single Synestryn had moved to attack.

Hope surged in Gilda's soul. Maybe her baby had decided to come back after all.

Gilda reached out a trembling hand toward her daughter.

Maura looked at her hand with an almost wistful expression, as if she wanted something she could never have. "Everyone I touch dies."

Gilda ached for her baby and all the mistakes they'd both made. She should have been a better example. She should have spent more time reassuring Maura that she was loved and needed. But like so many other things Gilda had done, it was too late for anything but regret.

"It wasn't always that way," she reminded Maura. "It doesn't have to be that way now. Come with us. Come home. We love you."

"You can't love someone who has no soul. I'm a thing. Plastic and hollow. A weapon. You can't love a weapon."

"You're our daughter," said Angus. "You're our flesh and blood, part of us."

Tears welled in Maura's eyes before she blinked them away a second later. "I don't belong with you. My place is here. Killing. Destroying. That is what people with no souls do."

Gilda saw the change in her daughter the second it began. Whatever cracks of doubt she and Angus may have caused healed up. Maura squared her shoulders and that evil glint came back to her eyes. The softness in her expression vanished and standing before them was no longer their daughter. It was their enemy.

"Daddy," said Maura, reaching for Angus as if to hug him.

Everyone I touch dies.

Gilda couldn't let that happen to Angus.

She used the power she'd gathered to propel herself forward toward Maura. She tackled her, bearing her down to the ground. The feel of her daughter's body against hers brought back countless memories of the times she'd held Maura or rocked her to sleep.

Each memory broke Gilda's heart all over again.

Maura fought, but she had a child's strength and Gilda subdued her easily. By the time she'd pinned Maura against her body, preventing her from moving, the wall of flames had died down enough that the Synestryn on the far side could leap over it.

Angus had placed himself in the way of their advance, but there were too many for him to fight alone.

"Stop!" shouted Gilda, imbuing her words with the power of command.

Everyone froze, including Angus.

Gilda dragged Maura up, still restraining her. She wrapped a hand around her daughter's throat and said, "I'll choke her if you come closer. Get back."

The Synestryn slithered back a few feet, but that was all.

Maura's body began to shake with laughter. "I've already won. You touched me, so you're dead. Which means Father is, too. My troops don't have to do a thing."

A throb of panic bloomed inside her, but Gilda controlled it. "Your magic won't work on me."

"No?" asked Maura.

As she spoke, Gilda felt the first stab of pain go through her. It started at her feet, sharp and intense, like someone had cut off her toes. She sucked in a startled breath, unable to hide her pain.

"See. No one can touch me and live. Not even you."

". . . three."

Nika found a spot near Tori that wasn't completely infested by Synestryn and aimed for that. She held on to Tynan and sent them through space.

She landed just as hard, only this time, it didn't make her feel nearly as sick. Whether it was because it was a shorter distance or because her stomach was already empty she wasn't sure.

Tynan wasted no time. Before the Synestryn could figure out they were right there next to Tori, Tynan scooped her up and shouted, "Now!"

Nika was still out of breath, but she ripped as much power from Madoc as she could, gripped Tynan's arm, and aimed for the spot behind Madoc.

Before she'd finished channeling the power, her body flew back through the air, hitting a rock wall. Her head exploded with pain and her vision began to fade. The last thing she saw was Zillah wrapping his too-long fingers around Tynan's neck and Tori falling from his arms onto the floor.

Chapter 26

Something powerful and wrong was happening to Gilda. She could feel the slow, insidious creep of evil Maura had inflicted upon her. She'd never felt or seen anything like it before. Pain inched up her body, setting her spine on fire, and yet she refused to let go of her daughter.

She had never been more afraid in her life. She and Angus had been through some tight spots. They'd both been injured and nearly died many times over the centuries, but never before had she felt despair like this. If she didn't find a way to stop the spread of this evil, she would die, taking Angus with her.

"Let her go, love," he said to Gilda. "We need to find Tynan."

"It's too late for that," said Maura. "He can't heal what I've done to her."

"Maura, undo this," he ordered their daughter.

Maura's black eyes met his. "There is no undoing it. She's dead. If she's lucky, it will happen fast."

No. Gilda refused to die. She and Angus had just reconnected. She wasn't going to let go and give up her chance to make amends for all she'd done.

Gilda funneled some of Angus's power into her body, converting it to a healing light. Her skin began to glow from within as that light streaked through her body down to her legs, where the pain was worst.

"You're killing both of us," said Angus.

Maura's body seemed to sag. "I know. I've known for a long time how it would end."

What must it have been like for Maura to see the future, to see herself kill her own parents?

Gilda's body screamed in pain, but she forced herself to move, to turn Maura around so she could look her daughter in the eye. "Is that why you think you have no soul?" asked Gilda. "Because you saw this moment?"

Maura looked away in guilt. "I knew what I'd become. Why fight it?"

"Because your future is not written in stone. You of all people should know that."

"Apparently, you're wrong. Things happened just as I foresaw."

There was a hard throb in Gilda's legs; then she felt the warmth of the healing light go out and the pain moved higher, up to her knees.

Gilda sucked in a breath and reached for more power. The connection between her and Angus had widened further, allowing her to bring more into herself.

She sent more light to combat Maura's infection, but the effort left her shaking.

"You don't have to do this," said Angus. "We can fix this."

"I can't. I've tried. It always ends the same way."

Angus stepped forward. Grief deepened the lines on his face, twisting Gilda's heart. "No. I don't accept that. You have to at least *try*. You don't want to kill your own mother."

Maura bowed her head. "It doesn't matter what I want or don't want. We all are as we were created to be. I was created to kill."

"No," said Gilda, barely able to hold on to Maura's arms. "You were created to love—to love a man the way I love your father, to be loved in return, to fight evil as all the generations before you have done."

Maura's dainty mouth twisted in contempt. "That will never happen now, will it? You made sure of that when you made me promise to never grow up."

Angus must have felt her siphoning off more and more power, because he came to stand by her side, cupping the back of her neck so the parts of the luceria—ring and necklace—locked into place. The contact eased the flow of energy into her, and with a sudden, hard push of will, she drove the last of Maura's infection out of her body.

The effort left her panting, but there was no time to rest now. She had to show Maura there was still hope. She wasn't a lost cause. "It was a mistake made in grief. I'm so sorry."

"Sorry changes nothing."

"It can. If you're willing to forgive, the way I'm willing to forgive you."

Maura wrenched her little body away, backing up out of reach. "There is no forgiveness for what I've done, what I'm going to do."

"You haven't killed me," said Gilda. "I cured whatever you did to me with your touch."

"Liar! You're just saying that to trick me."

"Into doing what?"

"Coming with you. You want to take the little sliver of soul I managed to cling to in the womb and give it to your favorite daughter. If you do that, maybe she'll grow up."

"You're wrong," said Angus. "Sibyl is not our favorite."

"She always did the right thing. She was always perfect."

"No one is perfect. We love you anyway."

Maura's eyes darted around, like she was uncertain about something. "You can't love someone who does the things I do."

"Then stop. Come with us. Turn your back on this evil and rejoin your rightful family."

"The Synestryn are my family now."

"Do they love you?" asked Angus.

"They fear me. That's enough."

"No, it's not, and you know it. You deserve to be loved."

Maura covered her ears. "Go. Leave before I order your death."

Gilda stepped toward Maura. "I'm not afraid of you. And there's not enough fear on this planet to make me stop loving you."

"Liar! Lies. All lies." Maura whirled around to where the Synestryn waited for the order to move. She lifted her small hand, pointed at Gilda, and said, "Kill them."

Tori crawled out from under the man's flailing feet. Zillah had some guy by the neck and was shaking him like a dog did a toy. She squatted against the cave wall, using it to support her weight.

She was so tired. Hours of pain had drained her strength, but at least it was almost over.

Another pain gripped her, and she could no longer keep from giving in to her body's demands. She had to push this thing out of her.

Hungry monsters closed in on her, eyeing Zillah to see if he was watching. If anything happened to him, she knew she'd be one more meal.

Part of her wished they'd just get it over with and put her out of her misery.

Despite the chill of the cave, sweat poured down her face, stinging her eyes.

Another wave of pain hit her and raw instincts took control of her body. Tori didn't want to be here for this. She didn't want to see whatever it was that came out of her.

She tried to pretend she was somewhere else, like she used to do, but the pain was too intense. It wouldn't let her go.

She felt enormous pressure building inside her, then a searing, ripping pain. Seconds later, it happened again, and this time, something slimy slid against her thighs onto the ground between her ankles.

Tori didn't look at it. She couldn't bear to see what it was that had been growing inside her for so long. It was gone now, and that was all that mattered.

The relief from the pain made her dizzy. She started to fall over and didn't bother to stop herself. She was out of strength and simply couldn't find enough energy to care what happened to her anymore.

Angus moved fast, thrusting himself in front of Gilda.

His heart bled anguish for his daughter. Even as his

blade moved, he wondered what he could have done differently that would have proved his love to her.

He'd failed her as a father. Completely. Utterly. His sweet baby girl didn't even believe he loved her. How could he have been so blind to her needs?

Tears threatened to blur his vision. He blinked them away madly, using every bit of grief and remorse he felt to fuel his strength.

Power flowed out of him, but he couldn't tell what Gilda was doing with it. Seconds later, he saw Maura floating through the air, fighting and spitting and clawing at a nearly invisible fist of air around her middle.

Gilda wasn't letting their baby go—not after she'd nearly gotten Maura to listen.

He couldn't agree more.

As soon as Maura passed overhead he felt the ground tremble and shards of rock burst from below, blocking off the seemingly unending mass of Synestryn.

He finished off the last three beasts on this side of the barrier, turning toward his girls before the last creature to die had even finished twitching.

Gilda grabbed Maura by one ankle and pulled her to the ground. "You're coming home and that's final."

Maura screamed in outrage, stomping her dainty foot.

Behind them came the loud crash of metal on stone. The demons were battling their way through the spikes.

"Time to go," he said, urging Gilda along.

They hurried down the hall toward the cavern they passed on their way in. Angus kept a careful lookout behind them, making sure none of those things broke through. With any luck, the other Sentinels would have left one of the vehicles behind for them to use. If not, they'd have to call for a pickup. With all the magic Gilda had been slinging around, he didn't think she'd be up to any kind of portals, even with the restrengthening of their bond.

He'd have to make sure Maura was restrained enough to keep her from touching anyone on the way home. Gilda may have been able to combat whatever it was she'd done, but he wasn't convinced someone else would have the skill and power to do so.

He owed it to Maura to make sure she didn't kill any-one else and add to the guilt his little girl already carried around. She'd made so many bad decisions. It was going to take her a long time to forgive herself as it was, as-suming she ever could.

They'd find a way to help her. He wasn't sure how, but he'd give his last breath if it meant Maura would see how much she was loved, how valuable and precious she was to him.

Gilda was dragging Maura along. Angus wanted to help, but he was afraid it would complicate things if he touched her, so he left it to Gilda to control their daughter.

She'd just walked into the cavern when she came to a dead stop. A heavy wave of fear crashed out of her through their link, driving the breath from Angus's body.

He came up behind her, searching for the threat, fol-lowing her gaze.

At least fifty of those too-human-looking, furless, sword-wielding Synestryn stood in formation, blocking the exit.

There was another tunnel on the far side of the cham-ber, but it, too, was blocked by at least another twenty guards.

Behind them, the pounding against rock stopped, and Angus heard the sound of hungry Synestryn growing louder. They'd broken through Gilda's stone barrier.

His family was surrounded, cut off from escape.

Only years of experience with hopeless situations al-lowed him not to panic. They'd find a way to get out of this somehow.

"There's no way out," said Maura. "Proof that no matter what you do, the future remains the same. To-night you die."

Chapter 27

Madoc saw Nika hit the wall and nearly lost it.

He bellowed in rage, speeding his attacks, cutting his way through Synestryn to get to her. As his body moved, his mind screamed at her to wake up. Get up.

He pushed power through their link, trying to give her what she needed to get back on her feet and protect herself.

One of the hairless things swung a blade at Madoc's head and he felt a sting burn along his scalp. The thing had scored a hit, and now Madoc had blood running into his eyes.

He couldn't take the time to wipe it away. Instead, he funneled his rage at the thing and lopped off the hand holding the sword.

The thing fell back, spewing blood, and a pile of furry, clawed demons fell on it, devouring it in seconds.

There was no time to celebrate. There were more things attacking him, trying to maneuver him away from the wall so they could get to his back.

Not going to happen. Madoc had to take the long way around to get to Nika or he wasn't going to get to her at all.

In fact, from the looks of things, Madoc wasn't sure any of them were going to make it out of this alive.

Gilda had no idea how they were going to find a way out. Maybe if they offered to trade Maura for their lives, they would be allowed to leave, but Gilda wasn't willing to use her daughter as currency. She was too precious for that.

Before the Synestryn could close in, Gilda surrounded the three of them with a ring of flame, giving her time to think.

They needed to go up. It was the only way not blocked. It was also incredibly difficult to break through the ceiling of a cave without killing them all in the process. Gilda wasn't sure she had enough strength left to do it, but she wasn't seeing any other options.

"Hold on," she said, then packed a solid disk of air under them and lifted them toward the ceiling of the cave.

The acrid smell of smoke still hovered up here, but there was no help for that now. She needed every bit of strength to bash through the ceiling of the cave and get them out.

Gilda found what she hoped was a weak spot about ten feet to the left and battered it with a blast of energy.

Rocks spilled down. A crack formed along the ceiling. Gilda aimed for that crack and punched at it again.

The crack opened and huge chunks of rocks rained down on them. She pulled more power from Angus, hearing him groan at the strain, but she couldn't be gentle right now. She had to shield them from the cascade of stone.

Tons of rock battered the shield she'd thrown up, weakening her. Angus's warm hand cradled her neck, aiding her efforts. She felt him trying to help her—pushing as much energy into her as he could.

It wasn't enough. She couldn't keep them afloat. The weight drove them down onto the pile of rock that had already formed beneath them.

Synestryn that weren't crushed began to scurry up the sides of the mound to get to them.

Gilda reinforced the shield over them and bashed again at the ceiling, frantic to punch her way through so they could get out.

They'd been deeper than she thought. There was too much earth overhead. Weight bore down on her shield, growing by the second. Rocks covered them, roaring as they tumbled down. She didn't have enough strength to spare to fuel her eyesight, so blackness closed in on her.

The rumble stopped and the weight on top of them no longer increased, but Gilda was weakening. "I'm not going to be able to hold this for long," she rasped out.

"Try to push us free."

Gilda sucked in more power, but it did no good. She couldn't lift so much weight.

She'd trapped them. Killed them.

"No," said Angus. "We were dead inside this cave. You had to try something."

"I wasn't dead," said Maura. There was no venom in her tone, only acceptance. "At least I'm not going to die alone. I'd always wondered about that."

She wasn't going to die at all. Gilda refused to be the cause of her baby girl's death.

Angus slid inside her mind, his strong, solid presence giving her strength. He knew what she was going to do. "You must," he whispered. "She deserves a chance to do the right thing, to redeem herself."

She felt his breath on her cheek. His lips brushed hers in a soft kiss.

"We love you, Maura," said Gilda. "You're a good girl. You're going to grow into a good woman."

"Right," said Maura, scoffing, but her voice cut off and she sucked in a startled breath.

Gilda found the vow her baby had given her so many years ago tucked in her memories. She pulled it up, playing it in her mind as she had so often. She could see the tears of grief staining her dress, the way her daughters' chubby arms clung to her, trying desperately to give comfort. She heard herself demand their promise never to grow up, cursing herself again at her selfishness.

No more. She was through with selfishness.

"My death will release you from your vow," said Gilda as she channeled power into that memory, highlighting it.

She hadn't been sure whether this would work, but she felt something shift—change—inside her. She wasn't exactly sure what would happen now, but she knew she wouldn't be around to see it.

She felt a trickle of blood leaking from her nose. Her eyes burned as if they'd been set on fire.

She'd used a lot of power. Angus was gathering more into his body through the stones, but it wasn't fast enough to replenish what she'd taken.

There was just enough left to teleport one of them out. Maura.

I love you, she whispered to Angus's mind.

And I love you, she heard him reply, so deeply a part of her she knew they'd never again be separated. He kissed her cheek, letting her feel how proud he was of her, how honored and blessed he felt to have been her husband. How lucky he felt that she'd been his wife.

Gilda found his hand and squeezed it. She drew on her husband's power for the very last time, opened a rift in space, and shoved Maura through, out of harm's way.

The shield holding the weight of the rocks no longer had enough magic to fuel it. It failed and tons of stone came crashing down on top of them.

The last thing she felt was her husband's love and the vow her babies had given her shatter into oblivion.

Nika felt a sense of futility coming from Madoc, along with a pounding rage and desperation to reach her side. That was what got her back onto her feet. If he didn't see she was okay, he was going to get himself killed.

She loved him too much to let him die before they had a chance to build a life together.

She let that love flow into him, reassuring him she was okay.

It was only partly a lie. Her head was throbbing and her vision was still a bit wonky, but at least she was still alive.

Tynan, on the other hand, didn't look nearly as good.

Zillah stopped shaking him and tossed him aside. Tynan didn't move.

Nika had thought to go to him and see if she could revive him when she saw Zillah lean down over Tori.

Nika blinked several times, trying to clear her vision. She channeled some power to her eyes, hoping it would help, and everything came into instant focus.

Tori was slumped on her side, but breathing. Zillah bent down and lifted something small in his hands.

A baby. Tori had given birth.

The cord was still attached. The baby boy looked normal, but he wasn't crying. He wasn't moving. His chest didn't vibrate with his pulse or rise with his breath.

A cry of rage and anguish roared out of Zillah and he jerked Tori upright, shaking her. Tori's eyes fluttered open and she tried to shrink back away from him.

"You," he snarled. "This was your fault. You wanted him to die. You killed him." Zillah lifted his hand to strike Tori.

Fear gripped Nika hard, and she did the only thing she could think to do. She shed her body and shoved her consciousness inside his, taking control of Zillah's striking fist.

The writhing, fetid evil of his mind choked Nika, sucking all that was good and pure from her. She fought it, trying to remember who she was and what she stood for, but being here, surrounded by evil, she found it so easy to forget there was good in the world.

She wanted to rip things apart, to pound them into piles of blood and bone. She wanted to scream in rage and lash out at anything that dared to move while in her presence.

Nika couldn't fight this much evil, so she stopped trying. She gave in to the need to kill and forced Zillah's body to obey. She turned him toward his troops and gave him the order to kill.

A cold, sharp pain gripped her mind, fighting for control. Zillah wasn't going to let her win so easily.

She felt him struggle just to move his eyes; then a moment later, Madoc was in his sights.

If she was going to make him kill, Madoc was going to be the target.

Nika tried to regain control. She tried to refocus him back on his demons, but he was too strong.

She called out a warning to Madoc, but Zillah caught it before it could get free and crushed the thought with a small, token effort.

It was then that Nika realized her mistake. This was what Zillah had wanted all along. He had none of her blood inside him, giving her control.

He was in charge now, taking her along for the ride.

Zillah smiled in victory, and Nika felt that smile wiggle through her like some kind of parasite. He was going to kill Madoc, and not only was she going to watch—he was going to make her help.

Chapter 28

Maura landed under a leafless tree. Her parents were dead. She'd known for years that this day would come, but she hadn't known until now just how much it would hurt.

She shouldn't have cared. She hadn't needed them for years. They hated what she'd become.

That hate had always allowed Maura to hold herself at a distance. Why should she care what they thought? Why should she bother to be something she wasn't? It wasn't her fault she had no soul of her own. Gilda had done that to her. Angus had allowed it. They deserved what they got.

And yet, there was this odd hollow space inside Maura she couldn't explain, as if an important part of her had been ripped out.

They'd said they loved her. Their words had seemed genuine, like she remembered from when she was young and foolish. How could they love her when there was no soul inside her to love? How could they have given up their lives for her if they didn't love her? They certainly hadn't feared her.

Maura had no answers. She didn't even know where she was or how far away Gilda had flung her. She needed to get moving. It was too cold to lie here and stare up at the sky, searching for answers that would never come.

She needed to see what she should do, where she should go, so she opened up that part of her that could see the future. It was, after all, her turn. Sibyl had used their power last.

But when Maura reached for her power, it was gone—only an empty, gaping spot remained where it should have been. It was as if she'd never even had the power.

Panic set in hard and fast. Without her power, she was nothing—just a child no one would listen to. No one would fear.

Maybe it was temporary—some kind of trauma Gilda had caused tonight. Maybe her power would return. She didn't need to panic.

At least not yet.

But she couldn't go back to Zillah now. He'd kill her as soon as he knew the truth. She was of no use to him.

She was of no use to anyone.

The Sentinels would kill her if they found her. Her parents had shown mercy, but she knew better than to think anyone else would.

She was on her own. Alone.

Instincts had her reaching for Sibyl before she could stop herself, but all that greeted her was blackness. Silent, yawning blackness.

Was Sibyl dead, too?

Maura began to panic. She'd never been alone before. She didn't know where to go or what to do. She couldn't be around people. What if one of them touched her? She didn't want to see anyone else die tonight.

A light came on through the trees, and now that it did, Maura could see there was a farmhouse there. She heard a muffled slam of a screen door shutting, and then saw movement.

Someone was coming toward her—probably some hapless human who saw light spilling from the portal.

Whoever he was, she didn't deserve his help, and she couldn't risk his touching her. She had to run. Get away.

Maura turned in the opposite direction and ran.

Jackie held her breath as she watched the mouth of the cave for the dark-eyed man who'd gone after the children.

There were several people here, milling about, check-

ing on those prisoners they'd helped free. A pretty
woman with braids held one of the children in her
arms, rocking him. Beside her, a watchful man stood,
the blade of his sword gleaming at his side. There were
other armed men, too—enough of them that Jackie felt
like she could draw in a full breath for the first time in a
long, long time.

The man with the scarred face walked up to her. He
gave her a reassuring smile that puckered his skin. His
eyes were a brilliant, laser blue as he looked down at
her. "I'm Nicholas," he said.

"Jackie Patton." Years of boardroom meetings had
her thrusting her hand out to shake his. Her skin was
dirty; her too-long, broken fingernails were caked with
filth. She pulled her hand back, but not fast enough.
Nicholas took it in a gentle grip.

Her skin began to warm and a slight buzzing sensation slid up her arm. Nicholas's eyes widened and a
hopeful, reverent sort of look crossed his scarred face.

"You're *that* Jackie," he whispered. "The one we've
been looking for."

Jackie pulled her hand away, scared as hell by the way
he was staring at her. She'd seen that same look of hunger on the faces of too many not-quite-human monsters
right before they bit her to ever want to see it again.

She backed away and bumped into the door of a car.
"Please. Stay back."

A hand went to her neck, where she could feel the
ridges of countless bite marks. Covering her throat was
an unconscious gesture, and until she'd done it, she
hadn't realized she'd given away her fear.

"I'm not going to bite you."

She couldn't pull any of her boardroom calm around
her now. She was too shaken. First the man with the dark
eyes had made her feel odd, and now this man.

Another man with light brown skin and matching
eyes hurried across the cold ground. "What's going on
here, Nicholas? Did you spook the girl?"

"More like the other way around. Watch." Nicholas

reached for her. Jackie flinched away, bumping into the newcomer.

Instantly, her skin began to buzz where her bare arm brushed his. He held out his hand. The odd, iridescent ring he wore swirled in a mass of colors so bright she could see them even in the dim light.

The new man grinned, smiling at her like she was the answer to a puzzle he'd been unable to solve. "Well, love. Looks like we should get to know each other. I'm Morgan."

"She's compatible with both of us," said Nicholas, clearly stunned.

"Guess we'll just have to let her pick. May the best man win," said Morgan.

"Stop," said Jackie before this . . . whatever it was could get out of hand. "Both of you stay back." She slid away from them.

There were a lot of big men here, and it was hard to avoid them. She could feel both Nicholas and Morgan watching her, so she veered away, keeping the group in sight. She'd rather deal with both of them than be dragged back into that cave by something lurking behind a tree.

Behind her, she heard a noise coming from the winter-dead brush. She froze in place as fear locked down her muscles. She tried to scream for help, but her throat was closed tight.

She couldn't go back into that cave. She couldn't let those things feed from her any longer. She wasn't sure how she'd survived it for as long as she had. If it weren't for the children looking to her for strength, she didn't think she would have made it.

And now it was all going to happen again and she couldn't even call for help from any of the sword-wielding men nearby.

A rough hand grabbed her arm and she was shoved behind a broad back. Heat poured off of him, and it was all she could do not to snuggle against that warmth.

"Do you see anything, Iain?" asked Nicholas from behind her.

The man in front of her said, "No. But she clearly did."

"I heard something," she told him in a voice so weak with fear it was embarrassing.

"I'll take care of it," said Iain. "You go tend the kids I brought out."

Iain was the dark-eyed man—the one who'd pulled her from her cage. If he wanted her to check on the kids and leave whatever was out there lurking about to the big man with the shiny sword, she could do that. No problem.

Jackie left and went to see what she could do to help. Three more children sat huddled under blankets or spare coats, shivering. She'd already given her blanket to the woman in the cage next to hers—a woman who was much worse off than Jackie. In the weeks or months or however long it had been since the night she'd been taken, that woman had not uttered a single word.

Jackie wrapped her arms around a skinny, blank-eyed girl and held her tight. She whispered words of comfort to the child, doubting it would do any good. Still, she had to try.

A few minutes later, Iain crossed the space with a very pregnant woman clinging to his arm for support over the rough ground. His dark eyes were on Jackie as they walked, and the look on his face was not a friendly one.

A chill ran down her spine that had nothing to do with the cold. Someone draped a heavy coat over Jackie's shoulders, still warm with body heat.

She looked up, saw Nicholas had sacrificed his warmth for hers, and said, "Thank you."

He nodded, staring at her with that same needful look the other men she'd met wore.

She had no idea what she'd done to draw their attention, but as soon as she figured it out, she'd stop doing it. Once she was safely out of this hell, she was going into hiding, where none of the bizarre things she'd seen— man or beast—could ever find her again.

*   *   *

"Stop!" bellowed Zillah.

Every Synestryn in front of Madoc came to a rocking halt.

He didn't waste time questioning his good fortune, simply mowed them down as fast as he could. Hot blood splattered his face. The screams of dying Synestryn rang in his ears.

"Stop or I'll kill Nika," warned Zillah.

Madoc stopped his killing spree long enough to glance up. On the far side of the bowl-shaped room, Zillah held Nika's limp body in his arms. Blood stained his hands and his black eyes promised violence.

Madoc froze.

Zillah grinned. "She's in my head and I'm not letting her go. She's nice to have around, as I'm sure you know."

Madoc reached out for Nika through their link and felt nothing but emptiness. Whatever Zillah was doing to her, it was keeping them apart.

Fury screamed through him. His blood pumped hot and hard through his limbs, and his grip tightened on the hilt of his sword.

Madoc was going to kill him, but first he had to reach him. He shoved his way through the group, making a beeline for Nika.

Behind Zillah, he saw Tynan creeping toward where Tori lay.

"Give her to me," demanded Madoc.

"Why would I do that?"

"Because it's the only way you get out of this alive."

"Hardly. You've lost. You're completely outnumbered. I have your woman. And her sister. One of them will give me a living child."

Fuck, no. There was no way in hell Madoc was going to let this fucker touch Nika like that.

"You can have me," he offered. "Let her and Tori go, and you can have me."

"I already do have you. And them. That's the part you fail to realize."

"You really should let her go. I've seen what she can do inside the mind of your kind. She'll kill you, too."

Zillah appeared unconcerned. "You've seen her kill my minions. She's never met anyone as powerful as me, I assure you. Now lay down your sword."

"Why? You just told me I have nothing to lose. You're going to trap her mind and rape her body. What reason could I possibly have not to slice you down where you stand?"

"I'll let you live. You'll be my prisoner, but I'll let you see her. Use her. Once I'm done with her, of course. Attack me and I'll have my troops kill you where you stand."

Nika! yelled Madoc in his head, forcing his voice through their link. *Get the fuck out of him. Now.*

He heard no reply, felt no spark of awareness.

Madoc was closer now, only a few feet away. Fury turned his vision red around the edges, but he did his best to hide it from this asshole. Better to let him think he was interested in his offer.

"Are you offering me a job?" Madoc forced himself to ask.

"I'm not stupid enough to trust you that much. But you might come in handy. Your blood will feed my pets. I've found that keeping you Sentinels alive and caged for your blood is much more advantageous than killing you. Though that does have its perks, too."

For one brief second, Madoc wondered if some of his brothers were held captive by this fucker, or if it was just a lie—one meant to distract him.

He wasn't going to let it. He shoved the thought away and tried again to reach Nika.

You can't leave me like this, he told her. *I need you. I love you.*

It was true. He did love her. He wasn't sure how he'd come from being a man with a dead soul to a man so full of love for a woman he'd do anything for her, but he had. Nika had healed him—brought him back to life. He owed her everything and he was damn well going to save her so she lived long enough for him to prove how much she meant to him.

Please, Nika. Come back to me.

The smallest ripple of awareness fluttered inside him. He'd know that intelligence and gentleness anywhere. It was his Nika. She was fighting to come back.

Madoc was damn well going to help her.

He stepped up to Zillah and smiled. "Guess what, asshole? You lose."

He shoved his sword into Zillah's thigh. Instantly, a dozen Synestryn blades slashed at Madoc at once and pain consumed him.

Chapter 29

Madoc woke up in a small chamber fitted with metal bars embedded into the stone itself. He was sprawled on the floor, throbbing with pain. Only years of experience carrying around a shitload of agony kept him from groaning. He pushed himself up, seeing the far wall of the chamber.

Names were gouged into the stone. The letters were different sizes; some had dates by them going back decades. Some of them were illegible, and some so faint they'd been there for a long, long time.

A lot of people had been in this cage before, long enough to carve their names on the wall.

Madoc refused to join that list.

He went to the bars, shaking them to see if he could find a way out. The cuts he'd sustained hadn't had much time to close, and the movement caused several of them to rip open and bleed more.

"I think you'll find that the magic holding those in is still in working order," said Zillah. He was outside the cage, flanked by armed guards. Nika sat slumped against the far wall. Tori was crouched next to her, naked and shivering, staring off, her expression dull and lifeless, as if she'd already given up.

Madoc was going to get both women out of here. He wasn't sure how, but he'd find a way.

Nika? Are you there?

His question echoed in the stillness between them.

He knew she was there. He'd felt her before. He tried

to push power through the luceria, urging her to wake up.

Tynan had been tossed in an adjoining cage and stood unmoving, watching Zillah with hatred glowing in his ice blue eyes.

"How long have I been out?" Madoc asked him.

"Two minutes."

Long enough to trap them all.

Zillah grabbed Tori by the arm and wrenched her to her feet. She was in bad shape. She flopped around weakly, not bothering to fight what was being done to her. She was naked, dirty, shivering. Blood seeped down her thigh.

"Heal her," demanded Zillah, thrusting her toward Tynan.

"I'm too weak," said Tynan.

"I don't care if it kills you. Heal her or I'll let you starve to death in there."

Tynan swallowed, anger twisting his perfect features. "Why do you care if she lives?"

"Because she owes me a son and I'm going to get it from her."

Tynan's voice hissed out in anger. "She can't give you a living child. Your species is too different from hers."

"You're wrong. I've done it before. Now do as I ask or you'll wish you had."

Tynan shook his head. "I can't let you do that to her."

"Are you willing to die slowly for your morals?"

"Yes."

"Fine, then I'll use Nika instead."

Madoc roared in rage, pounding the metal bars. *Nika, wake up!* He slammed the command through their link, but he couldn't tell if he'd gotten through.

"No," whispered Tori. "I'll do it." She lifted her eyes to Tynan. "He can't hurt me any more than he already has."

"See?" said Zillah, a metallic ring of satisfaction in his tone. "She wants it. Now heal her."

"Are you sure?" asked Tynan.

Tori nodded.

Tynan took her dirty wrist and lifted it to his mouth. Madoc watched her eyes flutter closed. Her body shrank; her belly flattened; her breasts tightened.

Tynan pulled away and angry blisters fattened his lips. He turned away, vomiting something thick and black onto the ground.

"I guess she didn't agree with you," said Zillah. "Too bad. I have a feeling the two of you will be seeing a lot of each other."

Nika heard Madoc's cry of rage in her mind, felt his frantic need for her to wake up. But she wasn't asleep. She wasn't dreaming. Zillah had trapped her inside his head and he had no intention of letting her free.

Nika slammed around inside Zillah's thoughts, flailing about inside the rotten depths of evil moving sluggishly through his mind. She'd never been trapped like this before and she had no idea how to get out.

A single, silvery strand connected her to Madoc, but she was losing sight of it as she weakened. Soon, she'd be too weak to fight and she'd be trapped here, forever.

Like hell.

Brute force was doing no good, so Nika stopped fighting and focused on the strand connecting her to Madoc. She shrank herself down until she was a pinpoint of light and slid along that strand slowly, steadily.

She kept her thoughts shallow, remembering little things like the feel of air against her skin or the sun on her face—anything to distract her from thinking about what she was trying to do.

The closer she got to Madoc, the stronger she became. He was urging her on, fueling her with his power. It pulsed into her, driving away the clinging tendrils of filth that snagged her, trying to hold her in.

She was almost out. She could almost feel the warmth of Madoc's mind when those tendrils thickened and barred her path.

Nika panicked. They were pulling her back in. She

couldn't fight them. They were tugging her under, driving her down into uncontrolled evil.

Fight, she heard Madoc scream. *He's going to rape Tori.*

Nika couldn't let that happen. Not again. Never again.

Fear was all around her, weighing her down. Desperate, she resorted back to the one thing that had worked to drive the sgath away: cold.

Nika took the cold in her body and shoved it into Zillah. She let the stones beneath her suck the heat out of her until she was shivering. She forced herself to remember every aching, frigid moment she'd ever felt, and used Madoc's power to amplify those memories.

Zillah's mind rebelled, and despite his intentions to keep her locked away, she managed to pull free. He screamed in pain and outrage.

Nika opened her eyes, curling in on herself in case he attacked. She felt like she'd been swimming through sewer sludge. Every part of her mind felt infected by Zillah's filth. She could almost taste it on her tongue. She was never going to be clean again.

Not that it mattered. From the fear and despair leaking out of Madoc, they were at the end of the line.

Nika pushed herself up to her feet and looked around. Madoc and Tynan were locked in cages. Madoc was bleeding, battered, and pissed. Tynan looked like he'd been hit in the mouth with a hot iron. Both of them gripped the bars of their cages, trying to break free and get to Tori.

Zillah shoved Tori to the ground and kicked her ankles apart.

"No!" screamed Nika. "Get away from her." She hurled herself at Zillah, but thick Synestryn arms caught her before she could reach him.

"Hold her," ordered Zillah. "Make her watch."

One of the demon guards put a sword to her throat, keeping her in check while two more held her arms.

Pain and anger boiled inside her, making her shake.

The cold was gone now, and left in its place was a fiery rage. This was not going to happen. She was not going to let nearly nine long years of staying by Tori's side come to this. She was not going to let her sister suffer another moment of pain or fear. She was not going to allow her to be raped. She was going to get them all out of this, even if it cost her her life.

Madoc's voice was raspy from yelling, but she felt a wave of sympathy sliding into her. "Close your eyes, Nika."

Screw that.

She tried worming her way back into Zillah's mind to stop him, but he was too strong. She couldn't get in. She pounded at his mental barriers, but all she managed to do was give herself a headache. He hadn't consumed her blood. She couldn't control him.

But maybe there was another way. None of these Synestryn had taken her blood, but that didn't mean she couldn't convince them to. They were always hungry. All she had to do was bleed. Surely one of them would take the bait and enough blood to allow her to control it. She'd use it to kill Zillah before enough of them got her blood and tore her mind apart.

"No," said Madoc, clearly having heard her thoughts. "You can't do that." His jaw was tight with anger, but the look of fear in his green eyes gave Nika pause.

She didn't want to do it—she didn't want to go back to that living nightmare where the Synestryn held her mind captive and blood and hunger and death were her whole world. But there was no other way. She couldn't let Tori suffer. She'd already suffered so much. They were so close to saving her. She deserved a chance to live free of this evil and find some speck of happiness for herself.

Nika had so many things she wanted to tell Tori, but there wasn't time. She settled for, "I love you," saying it loud enough to be heard across the chamber. She sent that same love to Madoc, letting him feel how much he meant to her, how glad she was to have been with him, even for the short time they'd had together. She loved him more than she'd ever thought possible.

Madoc was screaming at her to stop, but she ignored him. She didn't think the Synestryn would kill her. They liked having her in their heads too much. She'd live through this. Maybe she'd be splintered and crazy, but she'd live, which meant Madoc would live, too. He'd get Tori out alive. Then maybe he'd find a way to save her again.

"No!" roared Madoc, pounding at the bars.

Nika looked away from him, unable to bear the sight of his pain.

All it took was a slight shift of Nika's weight. The blade at her neck sliced through her skin and blood flowed down her chest. It hadn't even hurt.

The Synestryn on her right realized what had happened and dropped its sword. A growl of hunger rumbled out of the thing and it bent to lick at her neck, unable to resist food offered so easily.

The first swipe of its vile tongue made Nika gag. She steeled herself against the next one, watching as the demon on her left realized what had happened and joined the first.

Zillah had lowered himself over Tori.

Nika closed her eyes and searched for the connection she now had to the demons holding her. She found it vibrating between them and shoved her will upon them, forcing them to let her go and attack their master.

Her body fell back. A sea of twisted faces stared down at her, baring their teeth in hunger. One of them leaned forward to feed on her blood and another one ripped it away.

Nika tried to focus on fighting for control of the first two. She saw one of them go down under the attack of another. It ripped its fellow demon apart, tearing its throat out with its teeth.

The smell of food drove them into a feeding frenzy and they began to attack one another.

Nika forced the first Synestryn who'd fed from her to pick up its sword and attack Zillah, but Zillah was too fast. He rolled to the side, narrowly missing the blow.

"Halt," he bellowed, but it was too late. His troops were ravenous, mindless beasts. He'd lost control.

She opened her mouth to shout at Tori to run while there was at least a partial distraction, but before the word came out of her mouth she felt the first tug on her mind. Then the next and the next, until her thoughts began to crack and her mind began to splinter.

Nika pulled on Madoc's power, trying to shield herself from the mental attack, but she was too late. These things were too strong, too fast. They devoured her mind, ripping away little parts of it to hold for their own.

She saw through dozens of eyes, felt through dozens of bodies. Hatred pounded at her, making her snarl with the force of her need to kill. She wanted blood. Gallons of it. She was starved for raw flesh and the warmth of a fresh kill.

Some of the eyes turned to Madoc and all Nika saw was food. They were going to kill him and she was going to enjoy letting them.

Chapter 30

Madoc knew the moment Nika was lost. Her mind was gone—splintered into too many pieces to count.

Fight, he ordered her as he tried to feed her the power she needed to do so. *Don't you dare give up on me.*

But there was no Nika left, only the hollow echoing where her essence had once been.

Grief swelled up in him so thick, he couldn't breathe. She was gone. His sweet Nika was alive, but torn to pieces.

Zillah had fled down a dark corridor, two of his guards on his heels. Madoc was going to find him and kill him slowly, stripping his flesh from his body one inch at a time before he staked him out in the sun to fry.

But first he had to get out of this fucking cage.

He pounded at the bars again, feeling them vibrate, but not give an inch. They were solid. It was going to take him weeks to bust out of here, assuming he lived that long.

Nika wouldn't. He could still feel that she was alive, but how long would that last? How long would it be before she bled out or one of the demons decided blood wasn't enough and went for her flesh, too?

Then, like a dirty, timid angel, Tori appeared in front of him, a ring of keys jingling in her trembling fingers. She was naked and shaking with cold, shock, or both, but she hadn't given up.

Madoc stripped out of his shirt, ripping open wounds

that had begun to close, passing it to her. "Here, put this on. Give me the keys."

She did as he said, then stood there, watching the demons feeding from Nika.

"Can you find me a sword?" he asked, more to distract her than anything else. He'd kill with his bare hands if he had to, but he didn't want this memory adding to the other horrible ones he knew Tori had gathered.

One of the Synestryn grabbed Nika's limp body and scurried out with her. All the others followed, growling in hunger, racing after it.

He couldn't let them get away with her. He couldn't lose track of her.

He cursed the fucking keys, shoving another one into the lock. Tynan had reached through the bars and pressed a hand against Madoc's back.

Pain flared under his skin, sinking into his wounds as Tynan used his magic to knit them shut. "It's not much, but it's all I can do."

Madoc almost thanked him, but a key finally turned and he blasted out of his cell. He tossed the keys through the bars to Tynan, took a battered sword from Tori's hands, and rushed after the pile of Synestryn that had Nika.

He found them in the chamber they'd first entered, and came to a dead stop. There were more of them. He had no idea where they'd all come from, but he knew for a fact that he'd never seen this many Synestryn together in one place at the same time ever before.

They were so dead.

Still, there was no way he was giving up on her. He'd free her or die trying.

Tynan appeared at his side, sword in hand. He was breathing hard and the tip of the sword vibrated in his hand. He was either really weak or really scared. Either way, he wasn't going to be of much use.

"Get Tori out if you can," bellowed Madoc as he hacked off the head of another demon. "I'm going after Nika."

"There's too many of them. You'll kill yourself."

"I'm dead without her, anyway. Now go."

Madoc didn't wait to see whether Tynan did as he'd asked. He waded into the group that had descended into a feeding frenzy. They were turning on themselves, ripping one another apart for a drop of Nika's blood.

He cut his way through, slashing at them like wheat, not bothering to see whether they got back up or not. Bodies littered the ground, and hunched over each of them were several more, ripping flesh away with their bare hands.

One of the demons lifted a sword as if preparing to cut off Nika's hand. Madoc wasn't going to let that happen.

He lunged for the thing, slipping on blood. He missed lopping off its head and instead sliced a deep cut along its chest. More blood splattered to the floor.

Madoc made a grab for Nika, caught her ankle, and pulled hard, ripping her from the demons' hold. He was sure he'd hurt her being so rough, but it was a hell of a lot better than what they were going to do to her.

He stood over her body, fending off as many of the things as he could, but there were too many. He couldn't defend his own back.

Something sliced across his ribs, making him grit his teeth in pain. He lifted his sword awkwardly, realizing something vital to movement had been severed. His right arm was useless.

He switched the sword to his left, going completely defensive. This whole clusterfuck wasn't going to last much longer. He knew a lost cause when he saw one.

They were both going to die in here, and the only solace he could find was that he'd been able to love Nika. She had made sure that he'd die with his soul intact, and without his soul, he couldn't have loved her. Loving her was one of the greatest gifts he'd ever been given.

Madoc did his best to fend off the blows of the few beasts that weren't too busy feeding to fight him. None of the demons managed to hit Nika, but he'd taken more than a few cuts. He felt his strength draining as his bleeding increased.

More blows landed on his arms, slicing his skin open. The hilt of his sword became slick and hard to hold. His heart started beating faster, fluttering in his chest as it tried in vain to pump blood to his extremities.

Love you, Nika. I'm sorry I failed you.

Madoc's love flowed into the tiny sliver of Nika that was left huddled in her mind, hiding from the things that wanted her blood.

Until now, all she'd felt coming from him was determination, pain, despair. The love spilling out of him glowed bright, searing her with its intensity. It filled her up, made her strong. Even with all the other parts of her missing, he somehow managed to make her feel whole.

Nika slid inside his mind, needing to bask in that love. Everything was so wrong and confusing right now, and the only good thing she could find was him. She needed that goodness to reassure her.

The link between them had grown, or maybe she'd shrunk. Either way, the little bit of her that was left felt tiny as she moved into him, needing to be as close to him as she could get.

Once she was there, Nika realized what was happening. He was under attack. Synestryn were hurting him, killing him. She could feel his pain and the seep of blood from his body. He struggled to find enough breath to keep moving, but he managed somehow.

Through his eyes, she saw the horde of demons. They already had her blood and now they wanted his.

Rage rose up inside her, so strong she felt her very soul shake with the force of it. Her connection with these things shimmered in the air, humming, taunting her. They pulled at her, urging her to come into them and kill. Feed on Madoc's blood.

She was going to kill every last one of them.

Nika searched out the source of Madoc's power and sped toward it. Like a huge, shimmering lake of glowing liquid, she saw it looming ahead of her. Without thinking about what might happen, she dove in, immersing herself in that power, soaking as much of it in as she could.

It writhed inside her, needing to be set free. Nika wasn't going to disappoint it.

She reached out for one of the demons tugging at her and slammed a chunk of energy straight into its head. The thing didn't even have time to scream before she felt it die. The slice of her that it had stolen came back to her, but she barely noticed such a small piece. She was too busy searching for her next target.

Madoc could no longer lift his sword. He curled his body around Nika's and let the blows hit him. This was the end, but he thrust all the pain and fear from his mind and concentrated on the feel of Nika in his arms, letting it comfort him.

He didn't think they'd kill her—at least, not once the feeding frenzy was over and they remembered their orders. All he had to do was stay alive long enough to keep her safe until then. One of his brothers would come for her and save her. Andra would come and blow them all to hell. Nika would be okay. He had to believe that.

The frenzy behind him went quiet. No more blades sliced through his skin, which surprised him. Maybe he'd gone into shock and couldn't feel anything.

But if that was the case, then how could he feel the smoothness of Nika's skin? Feel the sweep of her breath against his face?

Confused, Madoc glanced over his shoulder.

The demons were no longer fighting or feeding. One by one they clutched their heads, then simply fell over, dead. At first, it was just a few, then more and more until not a single demon was left moving.

Nika. She was doing this. She was killing them from the inside, taking control of their minds, using their hunger for her blood against them.

Brilliant, beautiful woman.

Madoc slid his hand so the halves of the luceria locked together. He tried to make power flow into her more easily—doing what little he could to help her.

He eased into her thoughts, looking for something more he could do. What he saw made him reel back in horror.

Her mind was twisting with hunger for blood and a frenzied desire to kill. Holes were gouged out of her, ripped away. He could almost see the slimy ties that connected her to the Synestryn, thick, oily, and dripping with black blood.

She was screaming. Fighting to regain those lost chunks of her mind.

Madoc had to help. He had to slay these things before they ripped her sanity away again.

He intended to set her behind him and take up his sword against the Synestryn, but his arms weren't working right. His legs buzzed with weakness and he couldn't even shift her weight, much less stand. All he could do was shield her with his body and hope she was strong enough to save herself.

Madoc stared down at her, praying it wasn't for the last time. There was so much he wanted for her. So many things she hadn't experienced, so many things he wanted to show her. She'd lost years of her life to the Synestryn. It didn't seem fair that she'd die now.

He wished like hell she'd open her eyes and let him know she was okay.

The wet thud of bodies falling to the ground went on for a long time before it finally stopped. Madoc didn't have the strength to lift his head. He tried to squeeze her tight to let her know he was there, but his arms were too weak to manage even that. He'd lost a lot of blood. He didn't see how he was going to get either of them out of here.

"I'm sorry, Nika. I failed you." That failure bore down on him, driving the breath from his lungs.

Her eyes opened. They were bloodshot, which made them look so blue, just like the skies from his childhood. So pretty.

Her delicate hand cradled his cheek and he felt a tingling sweep out over his skin. "You didn't fail me. You never will."

She said it like she thought they had a future together. Madoc had been hurt enough times to know that it wasn't looking good. He was bleeding out.

"I've called Tynan. He's coming."

"How did you . . . ?"

"He drank my blood. We're connected now."

"I'm not sure how much I like the idea of your being connected to another man."

"You'll get used to it. And once we get home, I'm going to show you exactly how you're different from any other man in my life."

"Now, that's something to live for."

She gave him a weak smile. "He's almost here. You're not going to get away from me that easy."

Footsteps came around the corner, but Madoc didn't have the strength to see who it was.

"Looks like you could use more patching up," said Tynan.

Relief made Madoc dizzy. "A little."

"Yeah. And I'm Santa Claus. Hold on; this might hurt," said Tynan. "We're in a bit of a rush."

Madoc braced himself, but whatever Tynan did felt like he'd taken a blowtorch to his back. When he laid his hands on Nika, Madoc nearly stopped him, but figured pain was preferable to bleeding to death.

She pulled in a harsh breath, but showed no other signs that Tynan had hurt her.

Tynan was shaking when he pulled his hand away. "There. That'll do for now. We need to move before it's too late."

"Where's Tori?" asked Madoc.

"Waiting outside, freezing," said Tynan. "Let's go before we can't."

Chapter 31

Tynan was so exhausted, he barely made it back to his suite. The trip home had been long and filled with silence. Gilda and Angus hadn't made it out. No one had heard from them. Tynan feared the worst.

Fatigue weighed him down, so strong he could hardly feel the hunger rumbling through him, weakening him. He'd pushed too hard tonight. It had been necessary, but it had nearly killed him.

Later he would feed more. What he'd taken from the Theronai hadn't been nearly enough to replenish his strength. Right now he needed to sleep, but it had to wait for just a few more minutes.

He went to the spare upstairs bedroom where he kept his lab and took the tiny, lifeless newborn out from under his shirt. There had been so much chaos, none of the others had noticed him hiding the baby under his coat.

And it was a baby, unlike the previous creatures they'd found. It was perfect, every tiny facet of its body an exact replica of a human, or a Sentinel.

Tynan didn't know why it hadn't lived, but he intended to find out. And then, when he had, he'd bury the boy in the graveyard with the others who had fallen. This child did not deserve to suffer for its parentage, and Tynan refused to treat it like so much garbage, leaving it lying on a dirty cave floor.

He understood why Tori couldn't face her child's death right now, but one day she'd be ready. When she was healed. When she was older. She was still a child

herself, but one day he'd be able to lead her to the un-
marked grave of her baby, giving her a place to grieve.

Tynan wrapped the infant up in a clean towel and laid
it gently in his lab's refrigerator. It seemed a dishonor to
the life that could have been, but there was no help for
it. He would do what must be done, as he always had.

Andra raced into Dabyr, ignoring all the chaos. Paul was
right on her heels. Neither one of them had slept in days,
but her fatigue seemed to evaporate the closer she got
to home.

She knew from her phone call that Nika was safe, but
Andra wasn't going to relax until she saw her sister firsthand. And when she'd done that, she had an even bigger
issue to deal with.

Nika had found Tori. Alive. After all these years.

Andra still couldn't believe it—not even after having struggled with the life-changing news for the hours
it had taken to get back home. Andra had buried what
she thought had been her sister's remains last year. How
could this have happened? How could she have been
so wrong? Was Tori's "appearance" now a trick by the
Synestryn, or was the trick played on her when she'd
carried a stranger's bones out of that cave?

If it weren't for Tynan's vow that the blood of the girl
they found was unmistakably linked to her and Nika,
Andra probably still wouldn't believe it. Maybe part of
her still didn't. She needed to see Tori with her own eyes,
hold her in her arms like she used to when Tori was a
little girl.

Andra sped through the corridors toward their suite,
praying that Nika hadn't been fooled and this wasn't all
some kind of horrible trick the Synestryn were playing.
She so desperately wanted this outcome to be real.

Andra burst through the door. Madoc jumped to his
feet and pulled his sword before he recognized her. As
soon as he did, his big body melted back onto the couch
in a pile of exhaustion. Nika left his side and went into
Andra's open arms.

Andra hugged her hard, breathing in the scent of her

little sister's pale hair. She felt delicate inside Andra's embrace, but no longer quite so fragile.

When Nika pulled away, her blue eyes were wet and she wore a bittersweet smile. "Tori's alive."

Emotions swelled inside Andra, jumbled together in an almost indecipherable pile. She felt relief and joy that her baby sister was safe, but shame that she'd written her off for dead. "I need to see her."

Nika nodded and led her down the hall to the spare bedroom.

Tori lay on the bed, sleeping. She looked pale and thin, but what was most striking was that she looked exactly like the girl Andra had seen in her mind last year. She'd been trying to find Sibyl, who'd been abducted, and instead she'd found a girl she'd thought was a younger version of Nika.

In that moment, Andra knew the truth: This young woman was the baby sister she'd lost nearly nine years ago—her sweet Tori.

Tears burned Andra's eyes and her throat ached, fighting the need to cry. All these years. She'd left Tori in the hands of those monsters, abandoning her for dead. Shame welled up inside her so thick she couldn't breathe. How could she have seen Tori and not known who she was? How could she have walked away without recognizing her own sister?

Tori opened her eyes, but there was no warm greeting in them—just a cold, distant stare from a stranger.

"I'm so sorry," she whispered, unable to find enough air to speak. Not that it mattered. Nothing she could ever say would make up for what she'd done—what she'd allowed the Synestryn to do to Tori.

Tori said nothing. Not that Andra blamed her. What was there to say? The common response of "It's all right" simply didn't apply. What Andra had done wasn't all right. Neither was Tori. Part of her was missing, as if the Synestryn had scooped out something vital and left a hollow spot behind.

Andra reached out, but Nika's subtle jerk on her hand stopped her. "It was you I saw last year, wasn't it? It was your mind I reached, thinking you were Nika."

"Yes. That was me."

"Oh, baby," breathed Andra, breaking Nika's grip. She couldn't hold herself back any longer. She had to hold her baby sister in her arms.

Tori sat straight up and held her hand out. "No. Don't touch me. I don't like to be touched."

Andra stopped as her heart broke open, pouring a river of anguish into her chest. "I'm so sorry. I didn't know you were alive."

She felt Paul's presence slide into her mind, comforting her. A moment later, his strong hands were on her shoulders, giving her silent support.

"It doesn't matter," said Tori. "What's done is done."

Andra wanted to say she'd find a way to make it up to her, but how could she? How could she do anything to make up for years of imprisonment, torture, and rape? How could anyone? All she could offer was another hollow apology. "I'm so sorry, baby."

"I'm tired," said Tori. "Please leave."

Andra found the strength to walk away, because it was all she could think to give her sister. Nika was right behind her. As soon as the bedroom door clicked shut, she let loose the tears she'd been choking back.

Paul gathered her into his embrace and held her while she cried, stroking her back.

"She's so broken," said Andra into Paul's shoulder.

"So was I," said Nika. "I got better. So will she. We just need to be patient."

Andra looked at her little sister, seeing her in a new light. She was no longer a fragile girl in need of protection. She was a grown woman with a quiet kind of power all her own. And at her side was one hell of a formidable warrior who would give his life to keep her safe.

She hadn't failed Nika. Even though things had looked hopeless less than a year ago, here Nika stood, proof that among the Sentinels, miracles could happen.

Andra was going to see to it that Tori found her own miracle.

She sniffed and straightened her spine, gearing up for a fight she knew would be more against her own nature than anything. "Then patience is what she'll have. As much of it as she needs. However long it takes."

She'd abandoned and buried her sister once. She wasn't going to do it again.

Logan left Grace's side, driven by the need to sleep. There was nothing he could do for her, just as there'd been nothing he could do for Torr. Grace had made her choice to give up her life for another. He didn't want to belittle the selfless gesture by questioning it.

He passed into the main hall, heading toward the Sanguinar wing, fatigue pulling at every heavy step he took. A large group had congregated around the biggest dining table. Joseph sat at the head of the table, speaking quietly. There were at least two dozen Theronai there—likely deciding what to do in the aftermath of last night's events. Tynan had phoned Logan earlier on the drive home and told him about the humans they'd rescued—about the child Andra's and Nika's sister had borne.

Logan hadn't had much time or energy to digest the information, but he was sure that once the sun set, Tynan would call the Sanguinar together for a meeting of their own.

He was too worn-out to stop and eavesdrop, so he passed the group by, ignoring them. It wasn't until he could see the lounging area that he came to a stop. Sitting on one of the leather sofas, staring sightlessly at some animated TV show, were three children Logan didn't recognize. They looked as if they'd been recently scrubbed clean, and half-empty plates of food and glasses of milk sat on the coffee table in front of them. Skinny, listless, and pitiful, the three children drew Logan to them.

He could only imagine the kind of hell those poor little souls had been through.

Logan ignored his fatigue and went over to where they sat. The boy was probably about seven, as was one of the girls. The other one of the girls was older, maybe nine. Each of them clutched a blanket around their skinny shoulders as they stared up at him with huge, haunted eyes.

"Mind if I sit?" he asked.

They continued to stare for a long moment until the older girl asked, "Are you an angel?"

Logan smiled at that. "Hardly."

The little boy scooted over, making room for Logan on the couch. Logan sat and felt three pairs of eyes follow his every move. He wasn't sure whether it was because of his unnatural beauty or whether they feared what he might do.

He sat very still and pretended to watch the TV. Hunger rumbled inside him, and the bone-numbing weariness of too much strain combined with daylight tried to drag him under, but he resisted the pull of sleep. The longer these children waited for care, the harder it would be to help them.

Besides, he couldn't stand the idea of letting them suffer with their nightmares for even one more day.

Logan gathered up his meager strength and let it trickle out of him. He sent out calming waves of energy to the children, hoping to rid them of any anxiety they might have. The effort left him shaking, but he kept up that subtle flow of power, slow and steady.

The little boy was the first one to react. He climbed up into Logan's lap, wrapped his skinny arms around his neck, and began to cry.

Logan slid his hand over the boy's back, hoping to offer comfort.

His tears must have triggered something in the girls, because they joined in the group hug. The younger girl was sobbing and clinging to Logan's arm, but the older girl's tears were silent and heartbreaking.

Logan had to fight his body's need to shut down. Every cell inside him was screaming out in hunger and exhaustion, but he didn't want to fail these poor little souls. He just needed to keep the flow of power up for a little longer.

Now that the children were receptive, he pushed

harder, abandoning subtlety for efficiency. He would need to take their blood to permanently cleanse their memories, but for now, he could fog them—ease the children's pain long enough for them to rest and eat and recover.

Soon, the tears slowed, then stopped as the children drifted off into a deep, healing sleep. They were still piled on top of him like puppies, seeking out the basic comfort of physical contact. Their warm little bodies held him perfectly still, and Logan's shirt was tear soaked in several places.

He never should have allowed himself to get this close to them. Having these precious, tiny people clinging to him for comfort made him wish for things he dared not even name.

Sanguinar did not allow themselves to have children. Doing so was considered the pinnacle of selfishness, as those children would be doomed to dwell in darkness and starve for the whole of their long lives.

He and his kind had to be satisfied with enjoying the children of others. Sure, most parents kept their little ones a safe distance from the predators, but right here, right now, there were no parents to keep Logan from reveling in the miracle of these precious children.

He knew he should go. Staying here was only going to be torturous to himself. It was better to never have a taste of something that could never be his, than to get a glimpse of what he was missing.

Time to get up. Time to leave and let the Sentinels take it from here.

One of his legs had gone numb and hunger was now screaming inside him. He was too weak to move, much less stand.

Nicholas was suddenly standing over him, his scarred face staring down at the scene. "Thank you. We thought we were going to have to give them drugs to help them sleep."

Logan shrugged off the uncomfortable thanks, making the little boy's head shift on his shoulder. "You're going to have to help me up so I can sleep, too."

"Will I wake them if I move them?"

"No. They're too deeply asleep."

Nicholas gently picked up each of the children, moved them, and tucked a blanket around their bodies. Logan was working to get the feeling back in his legs so he could stand when Nicholas came back to him.

He offered Logan his wrist. "Go ahead. You look like you're about to pass out."

The offer so freely given startled Logan. He was used to having to fight for every drop of blood. He didn't know what to say, so he said nothing and took the blood Nicholas had offered. It flowed into him, warm and rich with power, quieting the worst of his hunger.

Logan didn't want to prevent such an act of kindness from happening again, so he took only what he needed to make it back to his suite. Sleep would help strengthen him, and then he could go hunting once night had fallen.

Nicholas pulled him to his feet.

"Thank you," said Logan.

"No big deal. Get some rest. I'm sure Joseph will have plenty for you to do come nightfall."

Logan took one last look at the children to make sure they were all sleeping soundly, then turned and walked away. They no longer needed him. It was time to go.

The darkness of his windowless sleeping room below called to him. He wanted nothing more than to crawl in bed and find the oblivion of sleep, but he couldn't bear going to bed without washing up first.

He stripped out of his coat and clothing and headed for the bathroom. When he walked inside, he stopped dead in his tracks. The smell of fresh blood filled his nose, making his belly rumble. It wasn't just any blood, either. This blood was pure. Perfect. Undiluted by humans. The blood of an Athanasian.

On his mirror, scrawled in an awkward script, were words written in that blood. There was an address, and below that he read: "You have not been forgotten. You are not alone."

Logan stood there for a long time, staring. He had no

idea what the words meant or who could have written them, but there was one thing he did know. For the first time in decades, he felt the faintest stirring of hope.

Later that night Nika stood in the doorway of her old room—the one where Tori now slept. She was in bad shape. Whatever the Synestryn had done to her was going to take a long time to undo.

Tynan had checked her out on the drive home and he wasn't even sure it was possible. Nika had kept that news from Andra to protect her. Tori needed Andra to be strong, not wallowing in shame and regret.

Nika was still weak from battle and blood loss, but moving around felt good. For the first time in almost a decade, her mind was her own. She could still sense a connection with Synestryn, but they were no longer calling the shots. Nika was.

They cowered in their dank hidey-holes, fearing her, knowing she could destroy them with a mere thought.

Nika didn't, though. She had other plans for those creatures. She was going to use them—force them to be her eyes and ears among the enemy. All those beasts cowering in the dark were now *her* army, and she was going to use them to ensure that no other child ever suffered the way Zillah had made her sister suffer.

"Those are not restful thoughts, love," said Madoc. His strong hands slid over her shoulders, pulling her back against his broad chest. "Tynan said you needed to rest, remember?"

"I will. Once I know Tori is better."

"She'll pull through," he said. "She's strong, just like the rest of the Madison women."

"Tori will get better fast. You'll see."

"I'm sure she will," said Madoc.

"Tynan said I could try to use my mind to rid her of the Synestryn blood once I'm strong enough. He's going to do the same. At least I don't have to drink it to filter it out." She shivered at the disgusting thought.

Madoc nodded, his chin brushing her hair. "I saw the

blisters on his mouth. I can't imagine that's any kind of fun for him."

"Sunlight might help, too. Once she can tolerate it." The first accidental brush of sunlight on her skin on the way home had been horrible, leaving Tori screaming and convulsing in pain.

"We'll do whatever it takes."

"I hope Tori will, too."

"Of course she will. Why would you think otherwise?"

"She wouldn't let Tynan take her memories. He offered, but she refused."

"Did she say why?" he asked.

"No. I have no idea."

Nika grabbed his hands and wrapped them around her, savoring his warmth. "Even if her body heals, she still has a long way to go. Her mind . . ." She couldn't bring herself to think about it too long. Tori had spent years being abused. For all they knew she might never be normal. Never be happy.

"We'll be here for her. We're her family and we'll do whatever it takes to see her well again."

Nika felt a swelling of love for him burst inside her. She hadn't known love like this existed until Madoc. It was consuming, powerful—the kind of magic that melded hearts together and changed reality. It made her tremble, while at the same time filling her with strength.

With Madoc by her side, she felt like there was nothing she couldn't do—nowhere she wouldn't be safe. He was her everything, and even though Tori was so sick and hurt, with Madoc holding her, she felt hope. For the first time since the night her family was destroyed, Nika felt like she had a future.

She was going to do everything in her power to see to it that it was a bright one. For all of them.

Tori pretended to be asleep while Nika stood over her. She'd gotten really good at pretending over the years.

The idea of having all those horrible memories erased

was getting harder to resist. Tori couldn't shut her eyes without feeling like she was back in that cave, cold and alone.

But she wasn't alone now. She had a powerful group of people who felt sorry for her. Poor little Tori. Been through so much.

Their pity disgusted her. It made her feel small and weak, like a child, when the truth was she hadn't been a child for a very long time.

She had been through a lot, but she wasn't going to let it stop her from the one thing she wanted to do more than anything else in the world, and for that, she needed her memories intact.

She was going to get healthy, get strong, and kill Zillah. By the time she was done with him, he was going to wish he'd never laid eyes on her. She was going to return tenfold every hurt, every chill, every pang of hunger and sickness he'd caused over the years. She was going to make him pay for her life and the lives of all the other children he'd stolen. And then, when he'd screamed his last scream and finally filled up the yawning void inside Tori, she was going to kill him and feed him to his guards.

She had his blood in her veins, and there wasn't a place on Earth he could go where she wouldn't find him.

Read on for a sneak preview of the next novel
in the Sentinel Wars series,

BLOODHUNTING

Coming soon from Signet

W*hen death comes for you, it will not be gentle.*
Logan hadn't truly understood Sibyl's prophecy of his death until this moment. But now that he was staring into its jaws, he realized what she had meant.

A Synestryn demon crouched behind a run-down three-story building, its eyes glowing a bright, feral green. It was huge, making the Dumpster beside it look like a milk crate. Heavy muscles bulged in its limbs, quivering with anticipation of the kill. Its breath billowed from all four of its nostrils, creating pale plumes of steam in the cold night air. Bright moonlight gleamed across its skin, reflected off the viscous, poisonous fluid that leaked from its pores.

Logan had never seen anything like it before, but the human, Steve, groaning in pain on the pockmarked asphalt near the demon's feet, was testament to the power of its poison.

The man's wife, Pam, stood pressed against the cold brick, staring in horror at her husband. Her pregnant belly protruded from her slim body, promising the hope of a new generation.

Logan could not let anything happen to that child.

Steve was still moving, but if Logan didn't do something soon, he wasn't going to survive. Not that there was much Logan could do. After days without feeding, he was weak, his powers dwindled down to little more than the ability to walk upright.

Hunger churned inside him, demanding he seek out the blood he needed, but there was no time to feed. No time to gather his strength. No time to call for help.

If this couple and their child—a child he'd worked so hard to see created—were killed, many of his people would starve. Logan could not allow that to happen.

The nameless creature lunged for Logan, bounding up from the pavement in a powerful leap so fast it made the thing look like a streak of moonlight.

Logan pitched his body to the left, hoping to avoid the attack. His shoulder slammed into a brick wall. Pain lanced across his back and down his spine. He slid to the dirty ground before he could catch himself.

The demon careened into a loading dock door, busting through it like tissue paper. The metal screamed as it deformed. Corrugated strips flew into the darkness of the run-down building, leaving behind a giant, gaping hole.

A blow like that had to have stunned the demon, or even knocked it out.

Logan needed to carry Steve away from this place, knowing his wife would follow. He'd made it only a few yards when he saw the feral green glow of two large eyes within the gaping doorway.

A sickening sense of defeat churned in his empty belly. Not only was the Synestryn still on its feet; Logan now knew he was completely outclassed. If barreling through that metal door didn't slow the thing down, there was nothing Logan could do to stop it, as weak as he was.

The demon lumbered through the opening, angling itself for another attack.

Steve pushed himself to his knees. He wavered there, next to a frozen mud puddle, between a discarded mattress and a rotting wooden pallet. His skin was roughened with goose bumps. With every passing second, poison went deeper into his system.

Time to grab the couple and run. Leave the Synestryn for someone else. It wasn't his place to destroy the demon. That was best left to those who were stronger than he.

Which currently included ninety percent of the planet's occupants, no doubt.

Logan shoved himself to his feet and sprinted across the slick pavement toward Steve. The tread of his boots slipped over the remnants of dirty snow left from the last storm, but he managed to stay upright and close the distance.

Behind him, the demon snorted out a heavy breath.

Logan spun around to face the thing, putting his body squarely between it and the pregnant woman.

"Please," whispered the woman in a voice trembling with fear. "Save him."

"Go," ordered Logan. "Run. I'll protect him."

"I'm not leaving him."

"Think of your child."

"I am. He needs his father."

There was no more time to argue. The demon charged.

The woman let out a frightened whimper. The heartbeat of the baby boy inside her sped up, as if sensing the danger it could not see.

That child deserved to live. If this demon got hold of the mother, both she and the baby would die because of the blood flowing through their veins.

The injustice made outrage unfurl in Logan's body, spreading dark wings of anger. That demon was not going to take the child—not while Logan still drew breath.

Claws extended from Logan's fingertips and his fangs lengthened. His natural weapons were nothing compared to the wicked blades the Theronai carried, but he refused to go down without a fight.

In the back of his mind, a hysterical part of him giggled at the notion of defeating such a creature. At his full strength he'd have a chance, but he was far from that—so far he couldn't even remember what it felt like not to be weak and hungry and cold.

But he had anger on his side, and it fueled him now, giving strength to his wasted limbs.

With a burst of speed, Logan charged the oncoming monster. He leaped to the top of a trash can and propelled himself over the thing's shoulder. His claws dug deep into the demon's slippery flesh, making it howl. Slick, mucuslike poison collected under his fingernails.

Logan straddled the demon's back, trying to choke it with his legs. One wide paw batted at him, its talons raking across his forearm.

Pain sliced up Logan's arm. Poison entered his system.

His first instinct was to shove the last of his dwindling reserves of power into creating an antidote, but there was no time for that. He had to kill the Synestryn before the poison incapacitated him, or being poisoned would be the least of his problems. And Steve's.

The creature headed for the cavelike shelter of the building, carrying Logan along for the ride. As they shoved through the opening, jagged metal sliced his skin, tearing a cry of pain from his lungs.

Logan fished beneath his coat for the dagger he kept hidden there. He stabbed it into the top of the creature's head, hoping to skewer its brain. Its skull was too thick and the blade slid to the side.

The cut to its scalp was deep, making the beast roar in pain. It reached back, grabbed Logan by the head, and whipped him off.

Logan slammed into the concrete floor. Or maybe it was a wall. His vision was full of bright lights, so it was hard to tell. All he knew was pain and a foggy weakness that kept him pinned to the ground.

A deep vibration beneath him told him that the demon wasn't through yet. It was still on its feet and it was getting closer.

Steve was growing weaker by the second. He pushed himself to his feet, and the effort left him panting.

Pam was by his side in an instant, her precious face staring up at him in worry. "We need to get you to a hospital."

"You know that won't help," he told her. As one of the Gerai, he knew enough about the Synestryn to realize that there was nothing a human doctor could do for him. "I need Logan."

His wife's face paled as she realized what he meant to do. "You can't. You can't go in there."

"I don't have a choice. I'll die without his help. And he'll die without mine."

"No," whispered Pam. Tears flowed down her cheeks. "You can't go in there. Please."

A wave of weakness shook Steve, telling him he was running out of time. "Go. Someplace public. Well lit. I need to know you and the baby are safe."

"I won't leave you."

"There's no time to argue. You're going. But I won't be long. Promise." The vow settled over him, comforting him. He kissed her mouth, praying it wouldn't be the last time. "Go, love. For our baby. Go."

She nodded. Sniffed.

Steve pushed Pam away gently. She stared at him, her expression a mix of fear and love. "Don't you dare die."

Steve hid his weakness the best he could as he bent down and picked up a discarded section of two-by-four. It wasn't much of a weapon, but he'd find a way to make it work.

He promised to be quick, and he'd never once broken a promise to his sweet Pam.

The color of suffering was a dark, sickly yellow, and Hope Serrien knew she'd see it on a night like tonight.

A cold front had swept down over the city, slaying any hope that spring was coming soon. Power lines glistened with a layer of ice, and icicles dripped from street signs. The sidewalk under her feet was slick, but even that couldn't keep her indoors tonight. A night like this brought death to those who had no place to escape the cold.

And cold wasn't the only enemy on the streets. There were things out here. Dark, evil things. People were going missing and Hope feared they hadn't simply moved on to warmer climes.

Sister Olive was a middle-aged woman who ran the homeless shelter where Hope volunteered. She'd insisted that Hope stay indoors tonight, but the nun had never truly felt the frigid desperation of having no place to go. She'd always had a warm, safe place where she knew she belonged.

Not everyone was so lucky.

Hope shifted the canvas bag on her shoulder and walked faster. She always carried sandwiches and blankets in case she ran into those in need—those who refused to come to the shelter. With any luck, they'd all have better sense than to be stubborn on a night like this.

She scanned the street, paying close attention to the dark crevices between buildings and inside recessed doorways. That glowing yellow aura of suffering was hard to miss.

Or maybe Hope had just had a lot of practice at spotting it.

If Sister Olive knew how Hope found people in need—if she knew Hope could see auras—the nun would probably have her committed. Good thing that wasn't something that came up in normal conversation. Hope wasn't sure she could lie to a nun.

A flicker of unease made Hope pull her coat closed more tightly around her neck. She'd seen things at night—things she knew couldn't be real. Dark, monstrous things that slinked between shadows, hiding from sight. Their auras were black. Silent. She couldn't read them, which made her question whether the monsters even truly existed outside her imagination.

She probably should have brought one of the men along with her to ward off any problems. But how would she explain to her escort how she knew where to go? It was better to do this alone and keep her secrets. Fitting in among normal people was hard enough when she *didn't* draw attention to her ability.

Hope forced herself to head toward the one place she hadn't yet searched for those missing souls. She hated getting near the run-down Tyler building—it brought up too much pain and confusion, too many bad memories. She'd promised herself that tonight she'd put her ridiculous fears aside and look for her friends there.

The three-story brick structure rose up into the night sky. The lighting here hadn't been maintained, leaving deep pools of darkness to hover about the building like an aura of decay.

A heavy thud and a screech of wrenching metal rose up from behind the structure.

There was definitely someone back there. Or some-*thing*.

Images of those dark creatures flickered in her mind. Her muscles locked up in fear, and for a moment, she stood frozen to the pavement.

The real danger out here tonight was the cold, not monsters, and the longer people were left to suffer in it, the more dangerous it became.

Hope forced her legs to move. Her first steps were slow and shuffling, as if her own body was working against her. Then slowly, she picked up speed, shoving all thoughts of monsters from her mind.

As she crept down the alley that led to the back of the building, she heard more noises she couldn't quite identify. There was a grunt of pain and the rattle of wood tumbling about. Once, she almost thought she heard a woman's voice, but she couldn't be sure. The only woman she knew who was too stubborn to come in out of the cold was her friend Rory.

Hope cleared the corner, and the first thing she saw was the gaping hole where the overhead door had been ripped open and partially off its track. The metal looked like it had been punched in with a giant fist, leaving jagged shards behind.

From inside the opening, Hope saw a brief flash of color—the sickly yellow of suffering.

Rory.

Desperate fear washed over her, making her lurch forward through the ragged opening. It was too dark inside to see, so she fished inside her satchel for the flashlight she always carried.

A feral growl of rage rose up from her left. It wasn't a human sound. Not even close.

Primal fear surged through her, and she had to fight the need to curl into the smallest space possible so she could hide.

Her search for the flashlight became frantic, her gloves hindering her as she fished around in her bag.

She located the hard, heavy cylinder, only to have it slip from her grasp.

Heavy, pounding steps shook the floor. A woman cried out in fear somewhere to Hope's right.

She grasped onto the flashlight and powered it on as she ripped it from the bag. The beam of light bobbed around, catching motes of dust as it passed.

Hope aimed it toward the sound of torment. The light bounced off of something huge and shiny. Something pulsing with muscle, and moving so fast she couldn't keep the light trained on it.

Its aura was black nothingness.

Panic gripped her tight. She needed more light to ward off the thing. Something as hideous as that would hate the light. She felt it on an instinctive level, as if she'd been taught how to protect herself from the monster.

Hope swung the light around to the employee entrance next to the pulverized overhead door, hoping there would be a switch nearby. Surely, whoever came in through that door would need to have access to lights, right?

The beam of light shook in her grasp, vibrating with the trembling of her hands as she searched. It seemed to take forever, but as she neared the door, she saw a series of switches.

She sprinted over the dusty floor, praying that the power here was still on—that whoever was trying to sell this place had left the lights on for potential buyers.

Hope shoved all four switches up at once. There was a muted thunk, then an electric buzz. Light poured down over the room, and while many of the bulbs were burned out, it seemed as bright as the surface of the sun compared to a moment ago.

She blinked her eyes and turned, forcing herself to look at what her flashlight had touched.

The room was large and open. Lines that had been painted on the floor to outline separate areas were now covered in dust. A stack of wooden pallets had toppled, and the dust from their fall had not yet settled.

Across the room was a giant, hulking creature poised over someone she couldn't quite see. All she could tell was that they were surrounded by that yellow aura of hunger and suffering she'd come to know so well on the streets.

The beast's head swiveled toward her, the movement sinuous and fluid. Its green eyes fixed on her, and she swore they flared brighter for a brief moment.

An unnatural fear rose up inside Hope, screaming for her to run. She knew what this thing was. She didn't know its name or where it came from, but she knew that it wanted her blood.

A roar filled her ears as a distant memory tried to surface. Her head spun and she clutched the wall behind her to stay on her feet.

Please, God. Not now.

As much as Hope wanted to remember her past, she wouldn't survive the distraction. She fought off the memory, mourning its loss even before it passed.

The beast snorted out a heavy breath, sending four curls of steam into the cold air. Its mouth opened, revealing sharp, wicked teeth.

Hope was sure the thing wore a sinister grin.

"Run!" shouted a man.

She couldn't see him, but it was his aura that peeked out from behind the monster. It pulsed with a flare of bright blue courage, and a second later, the monster roared as if it had been struck.

Now that its attention was no longer focused on Hope, her knees unlocked and started working again. She needed to find help. Fast.

She turned to do just that, when she caught a glimpse of an aura peeking out from behind the toppled pile of pallets.

Hope rushed over and found a man lying unconscious on the floor. One side of his face had darkened with a bruise, and in his loose grip was a board covered in the same shiny stuff that coated the monster's skin.

His aura was faint, the colors flickering like the flames of a dying fire.

He wasn't going to make it if she didn't do something.

Across the room, a crash sounded as the fight wore on. Hope didn't waste time figuring out who was winning. It was going to take all her strength to get this man out of harm's way. Just in case it was the monster who won.

She shoved the pallet pinning him down off of his legs. His jeans were dark with blood.

Hope patted his face, hoping to wake him. His eyes fluttered open, but she doubted his ability to focus. His pupils were huge and a cold sweat covered his brow. "Logan. I need Logan. Poison. He can fix it."

Hope didn't know how he knew that, but she doubted he'd waste his breath lying.

Her gaze slid across the room to the fight. The man battling that beast must be Logan. She had to help him. She had no idea how to defeat the monster, but she'd seen a length of metal pipe back near the door, and she wasn't afraid to use it.

Logan looked up from the floor where he landed. The spots cleared just in time for him to see the demon's giant, slimy foot hurling toward his head.

Logan rolled aside, dodging at the last instant. Chips of concrete flew into his face, stinging as they hit. He smelled his blood a moment before he felt the hot trickle of it sliding down his cheek.

The creature's foot was raised, poised for another attack. Logan's body shook with weakness, so cold he could barely feel his limbs. Only the dull throb of pain managed to get through the growing numbness of his body.

He was running out of time. Soon, the poison would incapacitate him, making him an easy meal.

There was no way Logan was walking away from this alive. The child had to be his first priority. He just needed to buy Pam enough time to escape. If her child survived, he could one day save others of Logan's race.

The thought brought him a sliver of solace.

It was time to pull out all the stops. He gathered up a bit of power and burst from the ground, shoving his dagger deep into the demon's groin. The beast howled. Black blood spurted from the wound.

Logan shoved the blade sideways to slice open a large wound before jerking it out. He stumbled backward as the demon clutched at its wound, trying to stop the flow of blood. Not that it would do any good. That blow was fatal. It was just a question of how long it would take the demon to bleed out and whether Logan would survive until it did.

It thrashed around, spraying blood across the floor in a black arc. One giant fist lashed out at Logan, knocking him back into a wall. Pain radiated out from his spine, but at least now he was out of the way of more blows.

The demon's eyes flared bright green as they fixed on him. He saw a streak of movement, heard a battle cry. A woman ran across the floor, wielding a pipe like a sword.

Logan screamed for her to stop, but he was weak and out of breath. All he managed to get out was a growl of warning too low to reach her.

She slammed the pipe into the demon's leg. It roared in anger and turned around to face the new threat.

She hit it again and jumped back out of its reach. It took an awkward step toward her and slipped on its own blood. It toppled to the ground, nearly crushing the woman beneath it. She got out of the way just in time, backing up until she hit a large wooden crate.

Black blood pooled under the demon. Its tongue swept out to lap up its own blood in a vain attempt to heal itself. But it was too late for that. It was bleeding too fast.

Finally, with a last shuddering breath, the demon died.

There wasn't time to revel in the kill or celebrate their victory. Logan staggered away to where Steve had landed, so he could rid the man of poison. He'd just made it to Steve's side when his legs simply gave out.

The longer he waited to finish this, the more likely it was that the scent of his blood would draw other Synestryn to him.

Steve, his family, and the mystery woman needed to be long gone before that happened.

Logan closed his eyes and concentrated on manufacturing an antidote to the poison within his veins. It was slow, and every bit of energy he used had to be dragged out of the deepest recesses of his body. Each spark of power slowed his heart. His breathing became shallow, and he was so cold that his breath no longer misted in the frigid air.

By the time he was finished, he was blind, shivering uncontrollably, and could barely move. Even his own head was too heavy to support.

He couldn't draw the antidote from his veins as he normally would have done. There was no syringe and no time. Instead, he closed his mouth over Steve's and forced the antidote through his saliva glands and into the human's mouth.

Moments later, Steve moved. The movement was weak at first, then grew as the man's strength returned.

"You need blood," said Steve.

"Not yours. Poison."

"I'll find help." Like a rag doll, he moved where Steve pushed him, too weary to even speak and tell him not to bother. There wasn't time.

Cold sank into his body—a bone-deep cold he knew would never leave him. His breathing began to falter and his heart's rhythm stuttered as it slowed.

Pain and cold surrounded him as death came for him. And as Sibyl had said, it was not going to be gentle with Logan. It was going to scrape every last breath from his lungs and wring every last beat from his heart, forcing him to endure every second of pain and cold and hunger. He would find no peace in oblivion.

There was still so much work to do and now he was leaving his brothers to do it all alone. But selfishly, that was not his last thought. His last thought was how much he wished for one single moment of warmth before he died.